Bolan downshifted and braked, bringing the rig to a halt

He put the vehicle in Reverse and barreled backward along the lonely stretch of highway. The vehicle backed across all four lanes, over the shoulder and slammed into the trailer.

The Executioner jumped out and approached the vehicle, his Desert Eagle up and ready, circling to the front of the downed cab, looking for survivors. There were none.

He removed a block of C-4 and a detonator from his shoulder pack, placed it on the truck's front fender and activated the tiny radio transmitter. He repeated the procedure twice more as he moved along the length of vehicle.

Retiring to a position of safety, he retrieved the radio transmitter and pressed the button. A second later the trailer and its illicit cargo were engulfed in a white-hot inferno.

The Executioner had initiated his war against Don Cariani. One of them wasn't going to survive.

Other titles available in this series:

Stony Man Doctrine
Terminal Velocity
Resurrection Day
Dirty War
Flight 741
Dead Easy
Sudden Death
Rogue Force
Tropic Heat
Fire in the Sky
Anvil of Hell
Flash Point
Flesh and Blood
Moving Target
Tightrope
Blowout
Blood Fever
Knockdown
Assault
Backlash
Siege
Blockade
Evil Kingdom
Counterblow
Hardline
Firepower
Storm Burst
Intercept
Lethal Impact
Deadfall
Onslaught
Battle Force
Rampage
Takedown

Death's Head
Hellground
Inferno
Ambush
Blood Strike
Killpoint
Vendetta
Stalk Line
Omega Game
Shock Tactic
Showdown
Precision Kill
Jungle Law
Dead Center
Tooth and Claw
Thermal Strike
Day of the Vulture
Flames of Wrath
High Aggression
Code of Bushido
Terror Spin
Judgment in Stone

DON PENDLETON's
MACK BOLAN.®

Rage
FOR JUSTICE

A GOLD EAGLE BOOK FROM
WORLDWIDE.®

TORONTO • NEW YORK • LONDON
AMSTERDAM • PARIS • SYDNEY • HAMBURG
STOCKHOLM • ATHENS • TOKYO • MILAN
MADRID • WARSAW • BUDAPEST • AUCKLAND

First edition February 1998

ISBN 0-373-61458-6

Special thanks and acknowledgment to
Tim Somheil for his contribution to this work.

RAGE FOR JUSTICE

Printed in U.S.A.

The worst sin towards our fellow creatures is not to hate them, but to be indifferent to them: that's the essence of inhumanity.

—George Bernard Shaw,
The Devil's Disciple,
Act II

Few men who have marched down the road of inhumanity can be dragged back, even when faced with death.

—Mack Bolan

CHAPTER ONE

Urumchi, China

The tall, bulky guard couldn't help noticing the young woman in the black wool sweater as she crossed the street wearing a wide, innocent smile. He smiled in return, his posture growing more erect, and she looked as if she were about to say good morning.

Instead she reached under the sweater and withdrew a Heckler & Koch MP-5 SD-3 submachine gun. She unfolded the collapsible metal stock in the second it took for the guard to overcome his confusion, then it was too late for him to do anything except stand there and look foolish.

The woman still smiled, only now the guard noticed an icy glint in her dark eyes. He shifted his feet.

"Don't move." Her voice was cold, the smile disappearing, and he noticed a very faint American accent under her near perfect Chinese. She whistled, and a Chinese man emerged from a building on the other side of the street, approaching at an unhurried pace but with a hand in the front of his jacket, firmly gripping an out-of-sight weapon.

They spoke in English when the man was close, and

the guard found it incongruous that such obviously foreign voices should originate from two figures that would look perfectly at home on the streets of any city in the People's Republic of China.

But his attention was drawn to the muzzle of the subgun, which wavered a little. The young woman was looking up and down the empty street, as if expecting a tail. She was so small and pretty he couldn't believe she would actually fire the weapon.

And she was distracted. The guard wondered if a promotion was too much to expect for the capture of American spies. He bent quickly and snatched at the Chinese-made AK-47 propped against the brick wall, but even as he felt the cold metal come in contact with his palm there was a sound like a sudden tear in the atmosphere. Shots were erupting from the subgun, the noise muffled by the factory-installed sound suppressor. A half-dozen rounds ripped through his torso, and his last thoughts were that he had made a very serious mistake in underestimating the American woman.

"DAMMIT." The woman craned her neck up and down the street again, then squatted quickly, her hands rummaging in the big front pockets of the corpse's coat. They were empty. The unmistakable sound of a city bus, wheezing and rattling, reached them.

"Let's get inside," the man suggested.

"Yeah, just a second."

She patted the corpse's front pants pockets and dug at the contents, pulling out a small handful of change and a rusty bolt. She flopped the corpse on its stomach. The bus engine revved and seemed just yards away.

"Come on!" the man urged.

"Okay!" Jumping to her feet, she tucked the MP-5

under her arm and shouldered the door open, quickly checked for occupants in the small room and grabbed at the corpse's arms. Kim Ping took its feet, and they hoisted it over the threshold as the bus emerged into the street. The corpse crashed to the floor. Ping raised his arm to the door frame as if engaged in casual conversation with the young woman, trying to block the view of the bus occupants.

Xiaoliao "Cello" Jiahua smiled and pretended to flirt as she examined the bus over his shoulder. None of the bored-looking riders behind the muddy windows, nor the driver, gave them more than a passing glance. The bus continued down the narrow, deserted street and was gone.

Jiahua kicked the corpse out of the way of the door and allowed her companion to jump inside before slamming it shut.

"Dammit!" she exploded.

Ping ignored her and stepped to the old desk, grabbing the rickety steel chair and moving it to the middle of the room. He stepped onto it, flattening his hands on the ceiling to steady himself as the chair wobbled and threatened to collapse. He slammed his palm sharply into an old wooden ceiling panel, and it popped out of its spot.

Jiahua watched Ping without breathing.

What if the file was missing?

It had been obvious to them when they returned to their hole in the wall less than fifteen minutes earlier that their cover was blown. There was a guard at the door, waiting for them. One of the perpetrators they'd been trailing for the past two months. But how much did he know? Why had the local police posted only one man? The pair hoped it was because the cops were only vaguely suspicious. If they knew the full truth, there would have been an army waiting for them.

If the evidence was gone, they were in deep trouble. If it was there, then they just might have enough leeway to escape the situation alive.

Ping groped in the ceiling hollow and withdrew a familiar-looking leather attaché case. He unzipped it hurriedly and pulled out a sheaf of papers and photographs. His mouth twitched into what passed for a grin. Jiahua felt a great swell of relief, which instantly drew up cold when she spotted the small white box attached to the wall. The 5 mm autoiris lens glimmered darkly.

"Damn!"

Ping whirled as he hopped to the ground, and he recognized the tiny surveillance camera instantly. "Let's get out of here."

In answer Jiahua raised the MP-5 and triggered a short burst. The small white box fragmented and dangled from a cable leading into the wall.

Ping cracked the door, glanced through, then swung it open. They rushed into the street, and in that instant a black car with dark windows roared around the nearby corner on protesting tires. It homed in on the two agents, accelerating as they raced across the cracked pavement.

Jiahua slowed suddenly, jammed the MP-5's metal stock into her shoulder and aimed at the side of the vehicle as it raced in her direction. The rear window slid down, and a hand and face became visible. The Chinese gunman's expression revealed his surprise just before a volley of lead ruined his face. Jiahua jumped out of the way as the vehicle swerved at her, knowing any attempt to take out the other gunmen behind the bulletproof windows was pointless. The car scraped the brick wall with a crash and flurry of sparks then swerved into the street again.

"Come on!" Ping grabbed her sleeve and dragged her into a narrow alley. The ground was blackened with oily grease, runoff from whatever industry worked in the adjacent factories, and Jiahua ran unsteadily in the shadowy darkness, orienting on her partner's figure just a few steps ahead. She found herself wondering, just for a second, if they were going to survive.

Hazy daylight blossomed around them, and Ping looked wildly around before pointing right and running in that direction.

They heard the rush of a high-speed auto and turned to find one of the government cars roaring at them. A few pedestrians scattered to avoid being crushed. Jiahua planted her feet firmly on the road.

Ping was astonished when he realized she was no longer with him. "Cello, let's go!"

"Not this time." She brought the subgun to bear and triggered it. The government cars didn't have the benefit of bulletproof glass or armored body panels, and she knew it. She watched the rounds trail across the windshield and bloody the side of the driver's head. Jiahua didn't know if she'd killed him and redirected the rounds at the front left tire as the vehicle loomed large in her field of vision. The tire shredded, and the vehicle veered to the left, the heat of its passing blowing over her before the car crashed into a nearby storefront.

She caught up to her companion as the black armored car cut into the street before them and headed in their direction. A figure in a dark sport coat poked out of the passenger window, and Ping and Jiahua jumped into the nearest alley for cover, heavy-caliber handgun fire burning in the street behind them. Ping spotted the grease-covered window just above their heads, swung halfway open.

"This way!"

He joined his fingers into a stirrup. Jiahua stepped into them, and Ping hoisted her into the window easily. She clambered through and landed on a large metal table covered with greasy black machine parts. She groped out the window with her free hand, dragging Ping in after her. Lastly she looked out the window for signs of the armored black car. It hadn't appeared yet.

"What's going on? Who do you think you are?" A mechanic in blackened coveralls faced Ping in a threatening stance, reaching for the large wrench protruding from his belt pocket.

"Don't do it," Jiahua warned.

The mechanic saw her—and the SMG—and changed his attitude. His hands went to shoulder level as he backed away quickly.

"Don't shoot me!"

"Where's the front door?" she demanded.

The mechanic pointed slowly to a door on the far side of the room, and she and Ping headed for it. They found themselves at the front of the building in a small hallway. The armored car, visible through a wide-meshed screen window in the front door, was rolling slowly down the street, its occupants obviously wondering what happened to their prey.

"They're not going anywhere fast," Ping observed.

"How are we going to get out of here?"

"Back door."

"They've got to have the streets all covered by this time."

"Then we stay here?"

"No way." She wheeled and headed to the mechanic's room. The man was still waiting quietly, hands in the air. "I haven't moved!" he cried.

Jiahua headed to a low shelf filled with various bottles of chemicals and grabbed a couple of two-gallon plastic jugs.

"Is this gasoline?"

"Yeah."

"What do you use as lubricant?"

"That stuff." The mechanic pointed to several opened cardboard boxes. The Chinese characters indicated it was heavyweight motor oil.

"Grab it." Jiahua and Ping bent to the task, lifting the entire box and heading to the front of the building.

The car with the darkened windows was driving slowly down the street. Jiahua quickly started to unscrew the lids on the canisters of gasoline.

"Got a light?" she asked.

Ping fished the tiny plastic lighter out of his pocket.

"Good. Let's go." She yanked the door open and started to toss the bottles into the street. The contents gurgled out, forming a tiny lake that quickly spread from one side of the cracked pavement to the other.

"They see us," Ping said with a sense of urgency. Jiahua saw the car executing a hasty three-point turn.

"Let's go!" She bolted out the door, firing at the car until the MP-5 cycled dry. She rushed into an alley, Ping hard on her heels.

"Lighter!" she demanded. Ping slapped it into her hand and she fired the instrument, waited as the auto gained speed, waited until she was sure that it wouldn't have time to brake.

"Get down! Get the gas tank!"

Ping fell to the ground as if shot, his Beretta 92-F

appearing in his hands, aiming at the empty street before him. "Okay!" Jiahua breathed.

She touched the flame into the liquid on the street and felt the sudden heat when it wafted to life. The clean flame from the burning gasoline melded with the smoky, greasy oil fire. The darkened car braked and skidded, then entered the periphery of the oily spill and lost all stopping power.

"Now, Kim," she grated. He fired low, under the fender, hoping the men who armed the car hadn't counted on a shooter going for the gas tank from underneath.

They hadn't. The fourth round punctured the tank, and a rush of fluid spurted from the underside as the car skidded sideways, wreathed in flame. With the auto fuel added to the mixture, the conflagration erupted and the back end of the car turned to a ball of fire.

Jiahua yanked Ping off the pavement and they ran, feeling the hot thundercloud burst when the bulk of the car's fuel exploded.

THE HOTEL WAS an American franchise, and some attempt had been made to match the lifeless sterility of a midpriced U.S. hotel. Somehow it made Jiahua feel a little more secure as she walked away from the front desk. But she made an effort to kill that line of reasoning. There was nothing making this hotel any safer than standing on a street corner in her low-rent neighborhood. She was, after all, still in Urumchi.

She crossed the lobby, carpeted in a hunter green with an oversize paisley design, and headed to the hallway. Off to her left she spied a figure moving along the wall in her direction. She shifted her gaze just enough to ascertain it was Ping. He followed her at a safe distance, pretending to be looking for a room number. For all she could tell, they were alone in the hall, but there might have been security cameras she hadn't yet noticed.

She let herself into her room, assured herself quickly that it was empty, then opened the door again the instant she heard Ping's quiet knock. She bolted the door and slipped on the chain.

She and Ping looked at each other, saying nothing, but both considering the fact that the chain and the door would be useless if the Chief found out where they were and sent an armed force to get them.

She sat on the narrow bed in the tiny room and picked up the phone. With the help of the local operator she dialed a number in Beijing.

A man greeted her in Mandarin at the other end. "Yes?"

"Ling Ye?" she asked.

"What?"

"I am trying to reach Ling Ye."

"You must have the wrong number."

"I am sure this is the right number. Are you sure Ling Ye is not there?"

"Yes, of course I am sure!"

"I apologize."

Jiahua hung up and looked at Ping.

"Now what?" he asked.

"Now we wait," she said. "I'm taking a nap."

"There's only one bed," Ping observed.

"Don't get any ideas," she retorted, and tossed him a pillow.

PING WENT TO SLEEP at once, but Jiahua stayed awake for twenty minutes, then started to drift. She never knew what it was that suddenly brought her wide awake. A sixth sense warning her of danger, maybe. An errant noise she couldn't later identify. She lay there in the dark, staring at the ceiling, expectant. Then the door imploded, actually sailing across the room and collapsing against the far wall.

Ping jumped up from the floor as three men entered, their Type 56 Chinese military AK-47 replicas homing in on him. He jumped toward them, taking them off guard. Two of the men fell back. One man triggered his weapon, and Ping curled like a bug as the rounds ate into his chest and stomach.

Jiahua had snatched her Colt All American 2000 DA pistol from the tiny bedside table and triggered a round into the gunner, knowing it was far too late to be of help to Ping, then turned the 9 mm handgun on the other two hardmen. The second victim absorbed several rounds and looked at the woman in surprise before flopping into the wall. The last man had gathered his wits and was leveling his assault rifle. His comrade collapsed into him, and his aim was thrown off. A burst of rounds chopped into the wall to Jiahua's right, inches from her arm, and she triggered the pistol again. The first shot went wild, but the second shot found the gunner's pectoral and the rifle fell from his grip. The third and fourth shots finished him.

Jumping to her fallen friend's side, she yanked at his clothing. There was no tenderness for the dead, not in her business. More important was her need for what Ping had been carrying.

It wasn't on him. She knew he had it with him when they went to sleep.

She grabbed his pillow. The leather attaché was lying underneath it, and she snatched it up. Without this,

Ping's death was a waste. In her other hand she groped for the MP-5, undisturbed where she had propped it against the wall, and raced to the door.

She glanced into the hall. People were shouting on the floor above, and someone was moving at the end of the corridor in the lobby. Probably just innocent people alarmed by the gunfire. Well, she was going to make sure they stayed too alarmed to get in her way. She triggered the MP-5 in their general direction, making certain the rounds buried themselves in the floor. Then she raced down the corridor, away from the lobby, to the nearest exit.

The door ahead opened suddenly, and a man stepped inside, dropping into a shooter's crouch. Jiahua fired as he raised his weapon, and he probably didn't even hear the suppressed sound of the gunfire before it tore into his arms and stomach.

Her luck ran out a second later. A hotel-room door swung open suddenly, and a massive figure flew out of it, crashing into her before she dodged. They traveled across the narrow corridor together, colliding with the wall so hard it caved in, and Jiahua found arms groping her like heavy steel cable. Her hands were pinned to her sides and she was pushed against the floor with amazing strength. The impact was blinding, and the breath rushed out of her body as flashes of pain ran like surges of lightning into her limbs.

The man towering above her was a couple of heads taller than she was and probably outweighed her twice. His hands, big enough to cover her face, fisted and crashed into the side of her head. She felt her hold on consciousness slipping and she willed herself to concentrate on something tangible.

She couldn't breathe. It was simply an impossibility.

Then she realized she still felt the cold presence of the MP-5 in her right hand.

Her attacker grabbed at the attaché in her left hand and yanked it away effortlessly.

Jiahua gritted her teeth and raised the MP-5 toward the faceless, shadowy form.

There was a sound of surprise and she put all her effort into triggering the weapon. There was a burst of three or four rounds, then the meaty hand slammed into the gun barrel and the remaining rounds fired into the wall.

And the shadow disappeared.

Jiahua gasped for breath, struggled for better awareness. The ceiling focused and she pushed for more control, flipping onto her stomach and finally managing to breathe. The air heaved in and out of her, and she looked up.

The giant was staggering away from her. She'd shot him after all. The carpet was puddling with his blood, and he didn't have long.

But he did have her attaché.

The woman lunged to her feet and, not much more gracefully, staggered after the dying giant. Then the door at the end of the hall swung open again. Two more men stepped over the dead gunner and raised their machine guns.

"Get down!" one of the men ordered the giant.

Jiahua raised her weapon before the giant had the chance to get out of the line of fire, and she opened up with the remaining rounds in the MP-5. The man's back opened up with fresh crimson, and he toppled like an old tree while the gunmen retreated behind the wall. Jiahua stepped forward and saw that the attaché was under the giant. The Heckler & Koch was empty. The gunman at the far end of the corridor began to fire.

She ran, feeling the impacts of the rounds in the wall beside her and knowing she was a fish in a barrel. She swerved into the nearest closed hotel-room door, mustering the strength to pop the security chain. A Chinese businessman was sitting in the tiny bed, obviously awakened by the gunfire, and was regarding Jiahua with amazement as she ran through his room and to the window. She shoved it open and scrambled through the narrow opening, her hips almost preventing her from getting through the aluminum frame.

Then she tumbled to the earth. The night was dark and still, and there were few lights about the hotel parking lot. She crept alongside the building to the front, where she slunk into a large, dense shrub.

She watched for signs of more attackers, but none was obvious. But anyone might be hiding in the darkened vehicles in the nearby lot. She had to take a chance and make a run for it now, before reinforcements arrived.

The thought that she had lost the attaché almost made her want to cry. But Cello Jiahua wasn't the type of woman who cried, not when there was still hope.

Obviously she couldn't count on her Chinese contacts for help. Her CIA link was compromised—it was the only way the locals could have tracked her down so quickly. And one couldn't just go phoning up Langley when in need of help. Anyone might overhear the conversation, and the government of the People's Republic of China wouldn't be terribly pleased to learn that the U.S. Central Intelligence Agency had operatives at work on its soil, whatever the intent of those operatives.

Jiahua had another agency in mind, although she

didn't know what it was called. She wasn't even sure if it was a legal U.S. entity. And she certainly wasn't positive that she could get in contact with it.

But it was the only ace left up her sleeve.

Stony Man Farm, Virginia

THE CHIEF of communications sounded abashed even over the small intercom speaker.

"I'm sorry. I didn't know what else to do. It sounds like an emergency, but it is coming through one of our old lines. It's not secure and to be honest, I wouldn't have guessed somebody could still get in on it."

"Do we have any idea who this person is?" Barbara Price asked.

"No."

She sighed. "Patch it through. And record it."

Barbara Price ran her fingers through her honey-blond hair and blinked the sleep out of her eyes. Grabbing the phone, the mission controller said, "Who is this?"

"Dammit, I want to talk to Belasko! Where the hell is he?"

"You're not talking to anybody until I find out who you are and how you got this number."

The connection was less than crisp and delayed by a fraction of a second. It could be coming from any Third World nation on the planet, but Price still heard the exasperated sigh.

"My name is Cello. And that's all you get from me. I worked with Belasko a while ago in Malaysia. I happened to be watching him when he dialed in to you one time...."

"You mean you spied."

"It's what I do. Now I'm in trouble. I can't get through to my local people, and I can't exactly go phoning all the way home for help. I need Belasko's help. Now, where is he?"

"He's not here."

"Dammit!" There was a tinge of desperation in the stranger's voice.

"Where are you?" Price asked.

"Urumchi. Can you get him?"

Barbara Price was considering.

"Listen, lady, I'm in deep shit here. I need help and I'm not getting it from anywhere else."

Price heard the fear in the young woman's voice. "I'll promise nothing," she began.

"Shit! I've got to go!"

Price found herself holding a telephone and listening to the sound of gunfire from halfway around the world.

TWENTY MINUTES LATER she was listening to the gun-shots again, this time sitting in the communications center at Stony Man Farm with Hal Brognola and Aaron Kurtzman. The chief of communications switched off the tape after the line became disconnected.

"How is it that we've left a communications link lying around for months without dismantling it?" Brognola demanded.

"The link is unused, sir," the communications officer replied.

"But it was once active and secure?"

"Yes, sir. But as you know, the security codes are changed cyclically."

"In other words, we didn't experience a compromise of our security?" Kurtzman suggested helpfully, noticing beads of sweat on the com officer's forehead.

"No, sir! There is no evidence Farm security was compromised. And as far as we can tell, that line has remained secure, as well. Otherwise we would never have accepted incoming communications. The system notified us immediately when we got the call that it was on an outdated line. I would have terminated the call immediately except—"

The communications officer looked at Brognola. The big Fed's expression offered him no further encouragement.

"Well, the caller did use the name Belasko and did say she was with the CIA. I performed a procedure that electronically verified that the possibility of a trace on the incoming line was very low."

"What I want to know is why the line wasn't wiped out and made unusable the instant we decided we didn't need it anymore," Brognola said, looking expectantly at the com chief.

"I think our priority ought to be determining how to react," Price interrupted.

Brognola's gaze turned to her and softened so slightly only those who knew him very well could have detected it. Price and Kurtzman did.

"Let's start with the ID of our caller," Kurtzman said.

Price nodded. "Akira?"

Akira Tokaido, a young man of Japanese heritage, sat at a nearby computer terminal, snapping his gum as his fingers danced across the keyboard.

"Right. Cello's legit. Here she comes." With a few more taps the computer screens throughout the room flared to life with an identical image. It was a photograph of a very attractive and impossibly young looking Chinese woman.

"Xiaoliao Jiahua, nickname 'Cello,'" Kurtzman said. "Born in Chicago. Parents were first-generation Chinese immigrants. Doesn't say how they got out of the PRC. Cello is CIA, and our files from a debriefing of one of Striker's missions indicate they worked together in Malaysia several months ago."

"That information isn't currently available," Kurtzman said. "To my team, anyway."

Brognola took the hint. "Right. Maybe I can do better." He drummed his pen on the table for a few seconds, staring into space. Then he grabbed a phone and dialed. He apologized to whomever he woke up at the other end, then said, "I need to call in a favor, Sam."

AN HOUR LATER the meeting resumed.

"Kim Ping and Cello Jiahua," Kurtzman read from a newly accessed CIA computer file, "have been in China for twenty-two days trying to locate the source of massive amounts of electronics merchandise coming in to the U.S. through an operation in Texas. A Mafia Family in Houston is running the U.S. end of the operation. The Carianis are small but aggressive. They don't have the connections or the muscle to carve out a territory for distributing drugs, so they're making their profits with less potentially explosive merchandise. They're bringing in Chinese-made electronics at prices that can't be legitimate. At the Chinese end the preliminary reports from our CIA friends indicated that the goods were being assembled in slave-labor factories staged in and around the city of Urumchi. And now it seems they got too close."

"Did you talk to the Man? What's his opinion on the situation? And what's the CIA's explanation for leaving its agents high and dry?" Price demanded.

"Same old story—Langley bit off more than it can chew. Now it can't risk the international repercussions if it was to send in a force substantial enough to find and free Ms. Jiahua. If she's still alive. Obviously the Man doesn't want the mission abandoned. He doesn't want slavery used to supply goods to the U.S. He had originally wanted to put a halt to the operation through diplomatic channels."

"I assume the U.S. already requested an investigation if we suspected the situation existed," Kurtzman said.

"Yes, but the report we got was less than sincere. No real investigation was actually performed. It's a case in which the provincial leader is making a success out of a backward city of the PRC that has seen little industrial improvement in decades. So the government in Beijing isn't going to argue with his methods. At least, they aren't going to look as closely at those methods as they might otherwise."

"Slavery in any form is reprehensible," Price stated, staring at the tabletop. "Surely the President doesn't want to leave this lie?"

"Of course not. But use of further CIA personnel is out of the question. If there's dirty work to be done, it can't be attributable to the U.S."

"That means us," Price said.

"Right. I assume you've already got a fix on Striker?"

"Sydney. And he's willing to lend a hand."

"You've spoken to him?"

"Forty minutes ago. He's ready to travel."

"Good. The logistics?"

Kurtzman nodded. "Not a challenge. If we have executive authority we can arrange a USAF flight from Sydney to Hong Kong, leaving as soon as Striker arrives. From there he'll need to take commercial flights into Beijing and then to Urumchi.''

"Is that the quickest way to get him there?" Price asked.

"I'm afraid so. We can't send an Air Force jet into Urumchi. Sorry."

Kurtzman's eyes met hers for a moment. He and Brognola both detected her special interest in this mission. Maybe they didn't understand it. Maybe they thought she was somehow irrationally emotionally involved. She didn't care.

Maybe her interest *was* emotional, because she had identified with the strange, desperate woman calling to her in the middle of the night from the other side of the world. She heard Jiahua for what she was—a warrior in need, strong, motivated and capable, but in a situation that was dire enough to test the steel and resolve of any agent in any agency. Afraid, as nearly all warriors were sometimes afraid. The woman had made a call for help, and as far as Price was concerned, Stony Man Farm was being too slow in responding.

"We don't have anything we can fly in over China undetected?" she queried.

"Not that we have access to or would gain us more than an hour in the long run," Kurtzman replied.

"We've got to assume that Kim Ping is dead," Brognola stated.

"I think it's pretty safe to assume the same of Cello Jiahua," Kurtzman added.

"She might have made it," Price said, "and every minute she's on her own brings her closer to execution if she is in the hands of her enemies."

Kurtzman placed his hands on the wheels of his chair.

"Taking Striker in through Hong Kong is the best way."

"Good," Brognola stated. "What about hardware?"

"Striker won't be landing with any, but he can more or less pick and choose whatever he wants and we'll have it driven in from Xi'an. We've got plenty of pull there and can come up with whatever he needs. It will get to Urumchi in time to meet him when he arrives."

Price nodded. It sounded as if everything were under control, as much as it could be.

CHAPTER TWO

The wheels had been greased in China. Mack Bolan didn't know who Stony Man Farm's Xi'an contact was; he only hoped that contact was going to deliver the goods, because at the moment he was armed with nothing more than his wits.

Going anywhere unarmed made Bolan feel naked. Landing without hardware in a hostile city in China, where the trouble was in progress and accelerating, wasn't his idea of a good situation.

The Air China 747 taxied to a halt on the Urumchi airport tarmac, and airfield personnel hurried toward the aircraft with a rolling stairway.

Bolan deplaned and walked across the tarmac with his carry-on, a black sports bag containing a few changes of clothing that had been intended for an excursion into the Australian outback. But the clothing was just as well suited for the brief, hot summer months of Urumchi.

Barbara Price had contacted him just hours earlier, telling him about a panicky phone call she had received in the middle of the night, from the far northwestern Chinese city of Urumchi.

"She said her name was Cello Jiahua," Price told him during her initial contact with him in Sydney. "She said she got the number when she spied on you making a call when you were working together in Malaysia. That name ring any bells?''

"She's CIA. Why's she contacting the Farm?"

Price gave him the full run-down during her next call, less than an hour later. A massive amount of electronics products was coming into the U.S. through a Houston-based Mafia Family called Cariani, and it was sourced out of China. Jiahua and another CIA agent, Kim Ping, went in to get the proof necessary to force the PRC to shut it down. Now it sounded like Ping was dead and the woman was on the run.

Bolan remembered Cello Jiahua, and she didn't scare easily. She had to be in real trouble.

The soldier had gotten the first available flight out of Sydney.

Now he crossed the tarmac and stepped inside the small terminal.

The plan was for his hardware to be delivered by rental car from the city of Xi'an. The contact was to have left Xi'an at the same time Bolan was leaving Sydney in order for the delivery to coincide with the Executioner's arrival. A key to the car was in his pants pocket.

The terminal was small, and he felt himself spotted as he exited the gate into the open public area, a cavern of a room with a small restaurant, a bar and a car-rental agency. The spotters leaned against a counter at a currency-exchange booth and homed in on Bolan. They were wearing police uniforms without insignia, and the Executioner knew he had to be prepared for action when they approached.

"One moment, sir."

The glass doors to the street were still fifty paces

away. The officers had .38-caliber handguns holstered at their waists, unsnapped for instant access. More importantly one gripped a Chinese-made version of an AK-47, his finger inches from the trigger.

"Passport and visa please, sir."

"Certainly." He handed them over.

"No luggage, sir?"

"No. I'm here for one night and then back to Hong Kong."

"Mmm."

Bolan took a casual stance even as he glimpsed two more uniforms appear at the entrance to the terminal. He pretended not to notice, but saw they also had assault rifles slung over their shoulders. They were watching the encounter.

"I'm afraid your papers are not in order."

Bolan's eyebrows rose, unconcerned. "Oh?"

"Yes. The date of travel indicated is not correct."

"Oh, I can explain that." He pointed at the visa in the officer's hand, then slammed his palm into the officer's nose, crushing the cartilage and slamming the bone fragments into the brain, launching the suddenly limp guard into his companion. Bolan stepped into the collapsing bodies and snatched the AK-47 from the second guard.

He tucked the weapon into his body and turned it toward the distant doors, triggering a burst when he saw them bringing their AK-47s to bear. They hadn't reacted quickly enough to the sudden acceleration in the pacing of events. Bolan's AK-47 rattled in his hands, and the 7.62 mm rounds sliced through the glass doors and the guards, sending a shower of shattered glass and ruined, bloody flesh to the floor. He then turned his attention back to the nearby guards.

The AK's previous owner was scrambling for the .38 at his waist and was trying to bringing it to play while rolling out from under his partner. He should have concentrated on one task at a time because he couldn't match Bolan's reflexes.

The Executioner triggered the assault rifle, and the guard stopped moving.

As Bolan sprinted for the front entrance, the path was well cleared. Pedestrians were crouched against walls and behind any object that might provide protection. Many were screaming.

Another officer stepped from behind a squared column and leveled his automatic rifle, his shots going wild but cutting the air in Bolan's direction. The Executioner returned fire, the first round hitting the gunner's weapon before the follow-up rounds slammed into his body. The gunner collapsed next to his clattering gun.

The AK in Bolan's grip cycled dry, and he poked among the glass shards as he reached the shattered front doors, coming up with a weapon that belonged to one of the fallen guards. Another Chinese uniform moved from behind the square column, and Bolan leaped over the dead men and fired as he landed in the glass. The maneuver might have saved his life. The surviving officer was already firing, the round slamming into the twisted steel frame of the door. But four of the soldier's rounds slammed into his chest, puncturing his rib cage and damaging his heart and lungs, bringing him to a sudden stop and dropping him like a sack of bricks.

Bolan exited the building to find another officer racing toward him, lured by the gunfire. The Executioner leveled the AK at the newcomer, who regarded the weapon with unblinking eyes. His uniform was somewhat different, and it was possible that he was legiti-

mate airport security. Maybe he was an Urumchi cop.
Bolan didn't have time to determine, and there was no
way he would shoot this man without knowing who he
was.

On the other hand, he couldn't afford to allow this
cop to plug him between the shoulder blades as he tried
to get away. He held out his free hand.

"Your gun."

Bolan knew many Chinese spoke English. This one
did or had a sharp intuitive sense. He brought out his
handgun and offered it to the Executioner butt first.

He took it and bolted.

The parking lot in front of the Urumchi airport was
small and half-empty. Bolan jogged through it, searching for the blue Daihatsu while watching for pursuit.

The car was parked in the northeast corner. He
jammed his key into the trunk's lock and opened it. A
quick glance confirmed that most of what he had asked
for was there. He had been concerned that the welcom-
ing committee he'd met had located the car or appropriated its cargo.

He picked up the Beretta 93-R and the mini-Uzi,
along with two extra magazines and a packet of incen-
diaries.

A screech of tires drew his attention back to the terminal. A BMW with darkened windows screeched
around a tight turn, bringing it into the lot. It cruised in
Bolan's direction.

The Executioner slammed the trunk and jumped into
the driver's seat, knowing he was seriously outmuscled
in the Daihatsu in terms of horsepower. He did have a
slight advantage in terms of maneuverability. As the
BMW approached, Bolan backed into its path as quickly
as he could. The driver was already braking but was

forced to swerve to avoid impact, bringing the car to a halt in the lane. Bolan cranked the wheel with one hand and stepped on the gas. The Daihatsu zipped in a tight turn, bringing the BMW into clear view. The darkened side windows were rolling down, and Bolan found use for the mini-Uzi. Two faces appeared in the windows of the BMW, and as the hardmen brought handguns into firing position Bolan triggered the mini-Uzi. The rear face became a mess of blood just before it flopped out of view. The front gunman managed to squeeze off a round, and Bolan heard the bullet impact the metal roof of his car, inches from his head. Before the gunner got a second shot off, three 9 mm rounds punctured his chin, nose bridge and eye, before exploding out the back of his skull.

Bolan stomped on the gas and wheeled in the direction of the exit. The lot was enclosed by a steel guardrail, and he considered trying to make it through, but envisioned the underpowered Korean car getting hung up on the rail. He aimed for the exit, where a guard was watching the activity in front of his small shack and zebra-striped gate.

In the rearview mirror Bolan saw the driver of the BMW was attempting to clean the gore-covered windshield with a piece of cloth.

The guard at the gate had no illusions as to Bolan's intentions as the Daihatsu reached redline revs and he shifted into fourth. The guy raised a rifle hesitantly to his shoulder, and Bolan steered the car in his direction. The guard's courage transformed to horror, and he fled to the rear of the shack. Bolan homed in, steered into the gate and crouched below the dashboard. The front end of the small car slid easily under the striped wooden gate. In the next fraction of a second the windshield and gate destroyed each other.

Bolan sat up again and used the mini-Uzi to punch a small hole through the windshield. He spotted another darkened car, this time a Toyota, and cranked the Daihatsu in the other direction, the lightweight back end fishtailing wildly. Bolan steered into it and managed to exert enough control on the vehicle to force it on the two-lane highway that would take him into Urumchi proper.

In the rearview mirror Bolan spotted a figure emerge halfway from the passenger-side window of the Toyota and aim a shotgun at the Daihatsu. He triggered and the rear window of the Korean-made vehicle blew out in a shower of glass. The gunman almost lost the weapon to the recoil but managed to cling to it and aim again.

Bolan pushed his luck. He yanked the wheel to the right, and the Daihatsu left the pavement, spun through the dust and lurched into the air over the narrow ditch alongside the highway. It slammed onto all four tires again in the dirt parking lot. He fought the steering wheel, regained some control that kept him from plowing into a parked dump truck and steered around it.

The Toyota was on his rear bumper, and Bolan hit the brakes hard, making the front end shudder, and pulled the car as tightly around the truck's front end as he was able without rolling his vehicle. The Toyota didn't make the turn and went into a spin that raised a cloud of dust.

Bolan grabbed the satchel in the passenger seat and withdrew a fragmentation grenade, keeping an eye on the Toyota. He waited for it to start after him, then trod on the gas, raising his own billow of dust. He dropped the grenade out the window, hiding it in the dust, and drove back in the direction of the highway as if he were headed for escape.

As the Toyota followed, Bolan counted mentally down. His timing had been an educated guess at best, contingent on the response time of the Toyota's driver. It couldn't have been more accurate. The grenade detonated, blasting hundreds of pieces of shrapnel into the Toyota, the passenger-side tires and the side of the car. The gunner in the window grabbed at his face and screamed, flopping to the ground while blood poured over his fingers. The Toyota lurched to a halt.

Bolan stepped out of the Daihatsu, the Beretta 93-R in hand. He had the fire-selector switch set to 3-round-burst mode. From the marginal protection the Daihatsu offered he sighted and fired on the Toyota as the driver's door opened. The driver stepped into the three rounds, which slammed him into the car as if he'd taken a tire iron to the face, and he dropped to the ground.

Bolan sighted on the open door and fired twice, and the two unscathed occupants were motivated to vacate. They hastily jumped out on the far side to use the car as a shield, firing heavy-caliber handguns over the top of the Toyota.

The Executioner targeted his prey with unmatchable accuracy. The first gunner caught a burst in the forehead and slumped to the earth. The second gunman shouted and moved away from his freshly killed comrade. The move bought him two extra seconds of living as the 9 mm rounds sailed through the open air where he had been standing. But his movement had been careless, and Bolan spotted an exposed shoulder. He adjusted his aim. The first three 9 mm rounds drilled into the shoulder, shattering the bones. The man staggered into view, and the next triburst took him in the forehead and punched him to the ground.

The shotgunner clutched his face and writhed on the ground, dull metal pieces protruding from his flesh. The shrapnel that had done the most damage had buried itself and was unseen. Amazingly the man wasn't totally blinded and he staggered to his feet when he saw Bolan coming for him.

The black handgun was targeted on him, and death claimed him so fast he didn't even hear the sound or feel his body fall.

Bolan groped in the jacket and pants pockets of the corpses, finding nothing but a money clip full of currency—more than most PRC citizens made in a year.

A squeal of brakes on the highway got his attention. The driver of the BMW had solved his dirty-windshield problem by shooting the windshield out from the inside. He veered off the highway and came at Bolan head-on. The Executioner had no choice but to face down the car, at the last minute leveling the Beretta 93-R at the vehicle. He fired twice into the passenger as he brought a handgun into play, taking him down. Bolan achieved a new target on the driver, adjusted to the man's attempt to steer out of the line of fire and triggered quickly.

The driver slumped, and the BMW slowed and drifted across the lot.

A rear door opened, and a figure with a .44-caliber handgun tumbled out while the vehicle continued to move, landing flat on his stomach in the dirt as the dead BMW drifted away and came to a halt.

Bolan approached unhurriedly as the survivor dragged himself to his feet, searching for his lost .44. Bolan straddled the piece, which lay several feet away. The survivor looked at the handgun almost hungrily.

"Who's your boss?" Bolan asked.

The survivor replied briefly in Chinese.

Bolan took a step toward the survivor and raised the 93-R to eye level. "You'd better learn English in the next two seconds."

"They'll kill me if I talk."

"Look around you," the soldier said. "What do you think I'll do to you if you don't?"

He moved the muzzle of the 93-R a quarter inch closer to the man.

"Yan Whan," the survivor said.

"Who's Yan Whan?"

"My boss."

"How did you know I'd be flying into Urumchi today?"

"We didn't know."

"I hate liars."

"It's not a lie. We knew the woman got through to someone before we got her. We've been watching all ways into the city for the past twenty-four hours—airport, trains, highways, everything, watching for Americans who might be her reinforcements."

"When you say you got the woman, what do you mean, exactly?"

"We took her."

"Alive?"

The man hesitated. "Well, when we caught her she was alive. I don't know what happened to her since then."

There was plenty to read between those lines. Jiahua might have been tortured or killed since she was brought in, but there was also a chance, a small chance, that she was alive still.

"Where is she?"

"I don't know."

The 93-R moved close enough for the man to kiss.

"I don't know, I swear!"

The pressure was too much for him; the man snapped. He tried to push the gun aside, then launched himself directly at Bolan with a shout. The Executioner sidestepped the wild attack and fired the 93-R. The force of the 9 mm rounds exerted on a human body from a distance of less than a foot was incredible. A portion of the attacker's torso splashed into the hard, dusty ground.

Bolan raced to the Daihatsu. The little Korean car was a write-off. Good riddance. He hastily transferred its cargo of arms into the BMW and cleared the German car of the corpses. He left the scene forty-five seconds before the first Urumchi police car arrived.

THE PEOPLE'S REPUBLIC of China would have denied the existence of widespread prostitution within its great realm, but it was certainly there.

Mack Bolan recognized the establishment for what it was the moment he walked inside. He found it somewhat amusing that Cello had called the place a "boardinghouse" in the report she'd filed with Langley.

"Hey, Joe, how you doing?" asked a plump Chinese woman in a bright red silk blouse. She had graying, tightly curled hair, and bright green eyes that were busily checking out Bolan from head to toe.

"The name's Mike," he corrected her, "and I wonder if I might have a few minutes of your time."

"You're a flatterer, Joe, but I don't do that any more. I run the place now. I am Lo. My name is on door. But not to worry. I will have something that you will like."

"I want conversation only, but I'll be glad to pay for

your time," Bolan said, pulling out the money clip full of cash.

"Okay, you have got a deal," Lo said, and led him into a small, garishly decorated parlor off the main entrance.

Bolan placed half the cash on a small table and held it down with one hand. "This buys information. Then you forget I was here."

"You got it." Lo's eyes were glassy as she stared at the pile of cash. Bolan removed his hand and she jumped at the cash.

"This is about Cello Jiahua," Bolan stated.

The woman froze. "Who are you?"

"I'm a friend of hers."

"She never mentioned you."

"I'm guessing she didn't talk about her past much."

"She's not here. Gone now."

"I need to know more than that."

"That's all I know. Sorry."

Bolan had the other half of the wad of bills between his fingers.

"What more you want to know?"

"I want to find her. I'm not part of whatever it was that took her. I'm a friend of hers from the United States." His voice dropped lower. "Cello tried to reach me in the U.S. on the night she was caught."

"I see. You should go talk to her boyfriend."

"Kim Ping is dead."

The name and the news got Lo's attention in a hurry. "I see."

"We know Cello was staying with you sometimes. That's why I came here."

The madam nodded. "We heard the cops got her."

"She was arrested? What for?"

"Not the regular cops," Lo hissed. "The Chief's cops. Big difference. His private army. They got her. That means Yan Whan has got her."

"Just who is Yan Whan?"

Lo's voice was a whisper. "Yan Whan is the man in this town. He runs things. The Chief works for him, and the Chief's private army of special police works for him."

"I see. I suppose he gets a slice of your pie, too?"

The woman glared at him. "Bad joke, Joe! Yeah, he takes his cut and I don't get cut, understand?"

"Yeah."

"Cello rented a room from me, but didn't do work for me, understand? Just stayed here. I don't know why she didn't live with her boyfriend."

Bolan wasn't about to explain that they lived in separate domiciles so simultaneous assassination or capture was less likely.

"How did you hear that the Chief's men got her?"

"I asked around. She was gone. I wondered where. One of my girls found out from one of her regulars who works for the Chief. She told me."

"Did this man say if Cello was alive or dead?"

Lo might have struck Bolan dead with the look she gave him. "Didn't say," she hissed. "Who the hell are you, anyway?"

"I'm Cello's friend. If she is alive, I'm going to find her."

"You going up against the Chief and his men? He'll have you for breakfast."

"Maybe. But I'll give it my best shot."

Lo nodded and plucked the rest of the bills from Bolan's fingers. "I wish you luck, Joe. You'll need it. You heard none of this from me."

"Of course. One more favor."

She gave him another harsh look.

"You know anybody who'd be interested in buying a BMW, cheap?"

THE EXCHANGE REQUIRED just minutes, then Bolan took to the streets of Urumchi again, now in a small Sazuki automobile. He had made an even trade for the BMW, which would fetch three or four times as much as the Sazuki was worth on the black market—after its windows were replaced and the interior shampooed. He felt less obvious, less like a moving target in the more common, less ostentatious car.

He headed downtown to the central police station, which was where Lo said the city jail was located and where Cello Jiahua would have been taken—if she was still alive, and if she hadn't already been sentenced to the provincial prison, located outside the city.

One of the last things Lo had said, almost to herself, was, "If she is in that prison, she might as well be dead."

Bolan wanted to question her about that, but time was growing short. Almost a full day had passed since the call had been made to Stony Man Farm. If Cello was in jail, and if she was being interrogated, how long would she last? If she wasn't being interrogated, how long before she was transferred to the prison, where she might as well be dead?

The sun was disappearing behind the buildings in the central areas of the city, and the shadows covered the streets even while the upper floors of the taller structures still basked in dusky sunlight. The central police station was a five-story structure on a street feeding into the main thoroughfares. It was a large, bleak, utilitarian building. Police motorcycles and cars came and went from a large, fenced-in lot clinging to the building's flank.

The infiltration wasn't going to be easy. Bolan had a rule about never drawing on a lawman, no matter how dirty, which limited his options to subterfuge or covert activity. He cruised past the building for the third time and tried to come up with a workable strategy.

Shifts changed as night closed in. Bolan waited it out as vehicles and policemen on foot streamed in at approximately ten-minute intervals and replacement forces departed. Soon the relieved officers were leaving again, mostly on bicycles, in civilian clothing. The soldier parked down the street and waited for activity to cease, then he stepped out of his vehicle.

He slipped on a cheap sport coat, purchased at a clothier's two streets over. Buttoned over his abdomen, it hid his hardware adequately. He strolled to the police station and entered.

There was a man at an entrance desk who sized him up curiously. He wore the light blue uniform shirt and the white armband with its insignia identifying him as city police. He started saying something in Chinese, then stopped. "Yes?"

"I'm the attorney for Xiaoliao Jiahua, from the U.S. consulate in Beijing. I want to see my client."

"Xiaoliao Jiahua?"

"She was arrested early this morning in Urumchi. I assume she is here?"

"I have not heard of her."

"Does that mean she is not here?"

The man looked nervous. "I will get someone else to help you."

He retreated through an office door, and Bolan could

hear a conversation proceeding rapidly in Chinese, followed by what seemed to be a conversation taking place over the phone. The policeman reappeared.

"Our captain will be down in one minute to help you."

It was less than a minute, in fact, before a figure descended the stairway at the rear of the open hall and approached Bolan. "We were not told of a visit by an attorney," he said immediately.

Bolan went on the offensive at once. "Are you the man in charge? Captain, are you aware that Xiaoliao Jiahua has a diplomatic visa extended by the government of the People's Republic? Do you know that international and Chinese law requires you to notify the U.S. consulate in Beijing within one hour after the arrest of a diplomat within China?"

"I do not know this Xiaoliao Jiahua. I think you are mistaken."

"We were told that this office had arrested Ms. Jiahua. We called here this afternoon and confirmed this information."

"Yes?"

"Captain, are you trying to deliberately stall the release of a diplomatic prisoner? Do you know that by doing so you are breaking the law and are subject to imprisonment?"

"I will check to see if we have a Xiaoliao Jiahua in holding. Please wait for one minute." The captain stalked into the nearby office.

The desk officer watched the door close behind the captain, then grabbed a pen and wrote an address painstakingly in English on a scrap of paper. He handed it to Bolan quickly. "Put this away!" he said softly.

The Executioner barely glanced at it before stuffing it in his jacket pocket.

"There's more than one police jail in Urumchi just as there is more than one police force," the man whispered. "I will say no more and I have told you nothing!"

Bolan barely nodded. The captain reappeared.

"I think there is a mistake. No Xiaoliao Jiahua here." He gestured with a clipboard.

"Fine, Captain. I'll be in touch."

He stalked out suddenly, leaving the captain looking after him in slight dismay.

THE ADDRESS WAS in an industrial section on the north end of the city. The nearest inhabited neighborhood started seven blocks to the southeast so that, in the night, with the factory workers gone home and the engines of industry idle, the district was dark and deserted. Lack of lights left the spaces between the wide buildings black and oily, clouded with the smell of old grease and ripening garbage.

The address on the scrap paper was easy to find. It was the only lighted building for blocks. Bolan halted the Sazuki blocks away, regarded the low building from a distance and turned a corner when he saw a police vehicle pull away with a sudden flashing of blue lights. He parked the car quickly at a curb and killed the lights. The flashing police car zoomed past the intersection without noticing him.

Bolan shrugged off the sport jacket. He wasn't going to be bluffing his way inside this station. He wore a blacksuit instead, uniform for a different type of infiltration. The tools were different, as well. The Ka-bar fighting knife was snug against one hip, the eight-inch blade anodized a flat black. An armpit rig held the Beretta 93-R. The handgun was one of his favorite tools—with its custom-made sound suppressor firing subsonic rounds, the weapon was whisper-quiet, while its select-fire capability gave him the option of firing 3-round bursts or single shots. In the combat webbing at his free hip Bolan strung nonlethal grenades: smoke and flash-bang. In case the police he ran into were truly officers of law, the Executioner didn't want to defend himself with lethal force.

But just in case the men in that strange, secondary police station were criminals and killers in the uniform of lawmen, he would be ready for them, too. Three extra clips for the Beretta went into the webbing.

As he moved wraithlike into the blackness, he heard a scream of agony.

LEE MIN HAD LIVED through the horrors of the Communist state for as long as he could remember, enduring decades of communal living in which food was scarce, privacy nonexistent and hope—for a better life for oneself or for one's children—was a fantasy. The rambling and meaningless diatribes of the government only served to reinforce the realization that it had no true understanding of how to manage a nation of a billion-plus people. But most importantly Lee Min had seen no substantive improvement in the quality of his life in the past five decades, and no improvement of the lives of the people in his village, a rural community five miles outside Urumchi. That was evidence enough to him that the system was unworkable, that it should be disposed of. He didn't have the enthusiasm for fighting, as did the young people he saw around him today. They would change China. They would make of it a new, viable nation. And if it wasn't through revolution, it would be through gradual adoption of the capitalist mechanisms of the rest of the world.

But now he was old, and he didn't have the patience for the intolerance and the corruption that was the government in the district. He found it impossible to keep his opinions to himself. When the police had arrested a young man in the streets of his village the previous day for what they called "plotting against the people of China," Min had been arrested, as well.

They had taken the young man to the new provincial prison, but an old man like Min was of no use there. So they took him to their local jail where he might provide entertainment.

He had borne their petty torture during the night. He was an old man, he said to them, so they could do to him as they pleased. He knew that if his response was mild, they would get bored of him soon enough and either kill him or let him go.

What he hadn't counted on was the breadth of their cruelty. When he hadn't given them sufficient pleasure, they had returned to his village and taken his grandson out of the field and brought him to their jail.

"What do you think of us now, old man?" asked the captain of the "police" squad.

The captain had ordered the grandson, just a boy of eleven years, tied up by his wrists and ankles. He dragged him across the room and slammed the boy into the jail-cell bars. The boy collapsed to the concrete floor.

"Stop, please!" Min had begged. "I will do or say whatever you want. Let the boy go free."

"Too late now. You should have thought of that earlier," the captain said. "You should have shown a little respect."

Min swallowed his pride. "I didn't realize the kind of men I was dealing with. I didn't realize you were men of strength, determination and power."

He never would have said those words to slime like the captain and his "police" if it had been only his own life on the line. But there was nothing he loved more than his grandchildren. He would die a hundred times for each one of them.

"Nice words, but you'll have to do better than that."

The captain stepped to the dazed, prone boy and landed a foot in his stomach. It wasn't a hard kick, but the boy was small and he curled into a ball, making a horrible sound, gagging and gasping for breath.

"Please!" Min begged, reaching his wrinkled arm through the bars of his cell as if he might tug on the captain's shirt. "Don't hurt him! Don't hurt the boy any more."

"I am not the one who is hurting him, old man. You are the one. You and your poor attitude. If you would have treated me with some respect, the boy wouldn't even be here, would he?"

"Yes, of course, it is my fault! And I am sorry! You are a strong, benevolent man—you will let the boy go! Take out your anger on me instead!"

The captain's mouth twisted into a sneer. "Good words. But too little and too late."

Two guards were lounging on chairs at the far side of the room. They ignored the old man when he turned his gaze to them. They had seen the captain play games before and knew where it was going. It might last for a few more hours yet. One of them leaned back against the concrete wall and yawned.

The captain took a large knife from the leather sheath at his belt and bent down with it suddenly. Min's eyes went wide as he watched. The captain grabbed one of the boy's fingers and sliced it off at the base. The boy, still breathless, heaved in pain.

That was when Min screamed in agony, so loud the voice carried into the darkness of the night and echoed among the abandoned buildings of the industrial district.

FIXING IN HIS MIND the direction of the scream, Bolan stole quickly through the blackness until he found a window in the police station. Inside was a pair of men on steel chairs watching a black-and-white television, a bottle of vodka sitting half-empty between them. Their AK-47s stood against the wall within easy reach. One of them was looking in the direction of a rear door with an annoyed expression.

Another window showed him the rear room, which contained two more guards. One leering man held a slim, dripping object in his hand and a bloody knife in the other. The old man in the jail cell was the screamer. Tears were rolling down his face. His hand was grasping between the bars at the small, wounded figure lying on the floor.

Bolan circled around to the front door, drawing the Beretta as he entered the building. Only one of the TV watchers heard him, and clawed at his side arm. Before he could draw the weapon, three 9 mm rounds drilled into his neck, shoulder and jaw. The chair slid out from under him and collapsed loudly.

The second man turned just in time to see his dead friend descend on him with only bloody ruin where his face had been. He tried to push the corpse away and succeeded in upsetting himself onto the floor, his own

chair scraping on the concrete. Rolling from under the
corpse, he reached for the nearer AK-47. He felt a flurry
of pain and realized his forearm had just been crushed,
chewed almost off his body. Then everything went
black as a second burst from the 93-R took him out of
the play.

Bolan flattened against a wall and waited for reaction
from the next room. It came quickly. A hardman with
an AK-47 stepped through the door, then his eyes fell
on the carnage and he glimpsed the moving shadow out
of the corner of his eye. He wheeled on Bolan, but his
hand never had the time to close on the trigger of the
AK.

The Executioner squeezed off a burst, and three
rounds rocketed into the gunman, crashing into his ribs
and piercing his lungs. He slammed into the wall, relaxing his grip on the Kalashnikov and falling to the
floor.

Bolan stepped through the doorway, where the second guard was heading in his direction. The gunman
triggered his weapon blindly, impulsively, and the soldier withdrew quickly. A dozen 7.62 mm rounds peppered the concrete wall and the open doorway. As the
firing paused, Bolan stepped into the open again, the
Beretta leading the way, and stroked the trigger. The
guard didn't react quickly enough the second time.
Three 9 mm parabellum rounds knocked him to the
floor, his abdomen, chest and face leaking blood.

The room was silent now, except for the gasping of
the wounded boy. The old man in the cage was staring
at Bolan wide-eyed, then he pointed through the rear
door. The torturer had left that way.

The big American took only enough time to snatch
the keys off the corpse's belt and toss them to the old

man, then he paced through the rear of the room. He came to a small hallway with four doors, one of which was drifting quietly to a close. Bolan stepped to it and kicked it open. The guard was leaning into his sawed-off 12-gauge shotgun, and the soldier directed his first three rounds into the guy's shoulder, spinning him sideways. The 12-gauge's blast filled the room a split second later and peppered the wall, showering Bolan with concrete crumbs.

He leveled the 93-R and fired a burst into the shotgunner's skull, and the man collapsed to the floor in an untidy heap.

Bolan dropped the magazine from the weapon and inserted another, giving him twenty more rounds, then proceeded down the hall. Three doors remained. He burst through the first, finding an empty office. He retreated and kicked open the next door. The room was large and contained another jail cell. Its occupant was standing, fists gripping the bars, watching expectantly, and she smiled when she saw him.

Bolan didn't have time for a greeting. There was a rattle of an assault rifle, and the hallway filled with 7.62 mm rounds coming from beyond the untried door. The tattered portal was flung open, and the child-torturing captain burst into the hallway, then whirled to the open door at his side. Bolan was facing him and stroked the trigger of the 93-R. The triburst ripped into his abdomen and rib cage, generating hundreds of flesh-shredding splinters. The captain tried to scream but only managed to gurgle through the blood pouring into his throat, and then he was collapsing senselessly into the floor.

"Nice shooting," Cello Jiahua commented.

"Thanks."

Bolan found keys on the captain's belt loop. He opened the tiny cell and Jiahua burst out, grabbing him around the neck quickly and planting a kiss on his neck.

"God, it's good to see you!" she cried.

"Yeah, but let's do this later," Bolan said, freeing himself from her embrace.

"I think you tagged them all."

He raised his chin, listening. "Only for the time being. Arm yourself."

Jiahua nodded, following Bolan as he made his way to the front of the building, dragging the AK-47 out of the captain's grip.

The old man had let himself out of his cell and was bending over the raggedly breathing boy, struggling as if trying to lift him. Jiahua gasped when she saw the wounded child.

Bolan heard the slam of a car door, followed by another, and positioned himself with a clear shot at the front door.

The first uniform entered the building and stopped cold at the sight of two dead guards before the muttering television. He clawed at the Makarov pistol hanging at his belt and twisted when the three 9 mm rounds cut into his side. He stumbled outside, taking his unseen companion with him. There were shouts in Chinese. Bolan raced after him and found the wounded man had staggered into the middle of the street before his fatal wounds dragged him to the ground. A second uniform yanked at the door of their car. The Executioner steadied the Beretta and fired with two hands, dead-on target. The second uniform crumpled against the car and slid to the ground.

The industrial district of Urumchi was quieter and darker than it had been in a long time.

CHAPTER THREE

Before she would leave, Cello Jiahua smashed the lock on a tall metal cabinet standing in one of the offices. It contained her Heckler & Koch MP-5 SD-3 submachine gun. She also found her Colt side arm. They both went into a denim gym bag.

"Let's go," Bolan said.

"We can't." She rummaged through the contents of the cabinet. "You've got to help me search, Belasko. That captain took the evidence Kim and I put together."

"You sure it's still here?"

"No."

She described the small black leather attaché with a brass zipper. They quickly ransacked desks and closets, finding nothing.

"Dammit," she said, standing in the midst of the carnage. "We need to get that attaché back!"

"Well, it's not here," Bolan said. "Let's go."

The old man had tied a strip of cloth around the bloody stump where the boy's finger had been. He was cradling him on his lap now, weeping softly. He looked up when Jiahua and Bolan reappeared, not knowing what to expect of them. Then, when Bolan lifted the semiconscious boy and carried him away, the old man followed as rapidly as he could.

Jiahua spoke to the old man quickly in Chinese as they climbed into the car.

"He doesn't want to go to the doctor's. He wants to be taken home," she said. "He said his daughter can care for the boy better than a doctor. He's probably right."

After driving several miles they reached the old man's village. Bolan carried the boy into the tiny living area of a hut and deposited him on a small pallet. The boy's mother cried out and ran to the side of her wounded child. Bolan handed over a package of antibiotics from his first-aid kit and, with Jiahua interpreting, instructed the woman in how to use them. The old man had thanked them again and again, and the two Westerners left. Then it was just the two of them in the car, alone in the night.

"Geez, Belasko," she said, slumping down in the seat beside him and grinning, "I've never been happier to see anybody than you when you came through that door tonight."

Bolan glanced at her in the darkness. Jiahua was a small Chinese American woman, with distinctly mild, youthful features—short black hair, a soft, small mouth and green eyes that glinted in the darkness. But she was also CIA, a well-trained agent and an experienced warrior, as the Executioner knew from personal experience.

"All right, Cello, you've got some explaining to do. Starting with how you came to acquire a top-secret telecommunications access code that I know for a fact I never revealed to you. At least on purpose."

"You can't make me sorry I swiped that number from you, Belasko. Turned out it was the smartest thing I ever did. In fact it saved my life. But I got the feeling that the woman on the other end wasn't very happy when I called."

"No, she wasn't. Quite a number of people weren't very happy when you called."

"On the other hand here you are. So I guess they believed I was who I said I was."

"They checked you out, and they checked out your story. And they realized there was no way the CIA was going to be able to bail you out of the situation it had gotten you into."

"Well, you've got me. Now what? You didn't come to take me back to Langley, did you?"

"I came to help you clean up this mess."

"Good."

"But first I need to know everything you know about it. I'm not even sure of the scope of this organization, what its purpose is, who the players are. I assume you can get me up to speed."

"Kim Ping and I have been living it for the past three weeks. And now Kim Ping isn't living anything anymore. They gunned him down."

"Start at the beginning," Bolan said.

LANGLEY DIDN'T REVEAL where it had come by the initial intelligence pointing to a slave-labor organization near Urumchi. The goods were mostly consumer electronics coming into the United States bearing well-known brand-names. The stuff entered the U.S. through Texas, where it was getting attached to falsified import paperwork and sold at below-market prices. Somebody was making huge profits off gullible U.S. consumers and the misery of oppressed Chinese.

Agents Ping and Jiahua were sent undercover into Urumchi to find out the truth and bring back evidence.

U.S. importation of goods produced by prisoners was illegal. If Jiahua and Ping could get evidence of the manufacturing of electronics in the Urumchi prisons, the U.S. would have what it needed to stage raids on the American end of the operation, bring its paperwork falsification out into the open and close down the Texas import end of the business. Without that demand there would be no need for supply, at least until another market for the goods could be developed. In the meantime, if the American authorities had evidence, pressure could be applied to have the People's Republic close down the operation. And the PRC, desperate to put on a good human-rights front, wouldn't risk such evidence reaching the world public.

It would have all been worked out diplomatically, making full use of the bureaucracy in each nation. Eventually maybe it would have accomplished its goal.

But when Jiahua and Ping tracked down the operation at Urumchi, they found an organization that was far more sophisticated and far-reaching than they had anticipated.

"The guy at the top of the organization is Yan Whan," Jiahua said. "He's kind of a mystery man. Nobody knows where he was born, though he grew up largely in Malaysia and Hong Kong. He came to China just a few years ago and set up shop by buying his way into the province, purchasing some factories, lining the pockets of the provincial directors. But instead of just paying off the heads of the province of Urumchi, he gives them percentages of his new business. Now they have as much stake in his success as he does. They'll go to great lengths to maintain their profit margins."

The wages and working conditions of the average Chinese factory worker amounted to little more than slave labor to begin with. But Yan Whan quickly began to squeeze more and more profit out of his factories by employing laborers who didn't have to be paid at all.

"With the cooperation of the provincial government, he began busing inmates of a provincial prison to his factory. He didn't have to pay them one thin yuan. After the local dignitaries saw how their income levels soared with the use of free labor, they were more than happy to expand this new inmate-employment program. That was fine and dandy. But then Yan Whan ran into a little impasse—the demand for his goods exceeded the prison-labor capacity of the province. He bought a new factory. His distributors across the Pacific increased the size of their orders. More labor was needed. So he talked over the problem with some of the provincial government heads. They decided it was time they started instituting longer sentences. Essentially everybody who is supposed to be up for parole is suddenly no longer eligible. Everybody's jail term is lengthened indefinitely.

"Still Yan Whan is running short on labor when he buys another local factory. That's when the arrests begin."

"I get the picture," Bolan said.

"Maybe not the whole picture, though. Yan Whan's been responsible for hundreds of extra arrests in Urumchi. At first he was at least going to the effort of pinning on trumped-up charges. Theft, acts of violence, anything mundane. No national-security charges because he didn't want to bring in any extra attention from the national government. I assume it costs him a pretty penny as it is to keep the national government's eyes averted.

"But as it stands now, he more or less takes whoever he wants off the streets. He's gradually been replacing the local police force with the type of ethically motivated peacekeeper you met this evening. Bet you can't guess where the good cops go when they're replaced."

Bolan nodded as he drove. The portrait Jiahua was painting was indeed expansive and intricate. "So what kind of numbers are we talking about?"

"Yan Whan's street forces? I'd have to guess sixty or seventy. That doesn't count the staff he's got on hand at each of his factories. The staff at the local prison is under his command, too. They're well armed and well trained. The word I heard is that he brought in talent from his U.S. partners. They funded the operation's start-up costs, for all I know. He now trains his personnel at his house, outside town. That place is a fortress. He likes having all that firepower close at hand, I guess."

Bolan remained silent, and Jiahua looked at him in the darkness of the car's interior.

"What do you think?"

"How're you feeling?" Bolan asked.

"Energized."

"Good. Let's go see what damage we can inflict."

THERE WAS LITTLE TRAFFIC in the north end of Urumchi in the middle of the night. Bolan cruised past the city hall, glancing over the building, then ducking out of sight into an alley a block away.

The police chief of the city had an office in the city center, just five blocks away. But that was the metropolitan district, with foreign hotels where wealthy Hong Kong businessmen came to visit and conduct business. There the Western amenities were provided for the visitors from non-Communist nations: hidden casinos, glitzy sex parlors, neon-fronted restaurants that got first choice of supplies coming into the district. That wasn't the place for the clandestine activities of a police force gone bad.

So now the base of operations was in a darker location, away from the watching eyes of the foreign visitors, away from the bright lights that illuminated the night.

Bolan and Jiahua watched the street from the alley entrance, eventually convinced that they were unnoticed. There were undoubtedly some of the Chief's men on duty in the building. It was possible they hadn't even received news yet about the debacle at the lock-up.

But they would be there.

A police car pulled to a stop in front of the building, and the two men that emerged had AK-47s slung over their shoulders. They didn't even bother to wear uniforms, although Bolan was quick to notice the black armbands with a distinctive red Chinese character. Some of the torturers at the jail had been wearing them, too. The men conversed loudly as they entered the building through a side door. Above them were five floors, the top two dark.

"Chief Li's office is on the top floor, the nearest front corner." Jiahua pointed. "If he's kept the evidence Kim and I collected, that's where I think he would have it. He can't think that it would be vulnerable there."

"Is it?" Bolan asked.

"I guess that depends on the number of crooked cops he keeps on hand overnight. And the answer is, I don't know. I never had a reason for making that determination."

"Then let's go count them."

They walked down the street in the darkness, ducking in a doorway when a car rolled past. It was a taxi with no fare in the back seat, maybe a driver on his way home after a long shift. He continued down the road without noticing them.

They chose the side door for their entrance. As they walked down the dank hallway, lit by a bare bulb, one of the crooked cops emerged from a door at the end, zipping his pants. He looked up and said something sharply, reaching for the weapon holstered under his arm. Bolan unleathered the Beretta 93-R and fired three 9 mm parabellum shockers. The guard never got to his handgun and he dropped onto the floor.

Jiahua stood watch as Bolan grabbed the corpse by the collar and dragged it into the men's room. He dropped it heavily onto the white tiled floor.

The distinctive throaty voice of the suppressed Heckler & Koch MP-5 drew the Executioner's attention and he stepped quickly into the hallway, just in time to watch the death tremors of another gunman. He had emerged from the end of the hall and into the firing range of Jiahua's subgun.

They stepped over the corpse and checked out the remaining room, which was empty.

The sounds of a radio drifted from the floor above. They ascended the stairs, reloading as they did, and found a wide-open area. The lights were on from one end to the other, and a half-dozen cops wearing armbands were on duty. None had heard the racket below, probably due to the music blasting from the boom box resting on one of the desks.

But one man happened to glance at the stairs when Bolan reached the top. He snatched at the Makarov on the desk as the Executioner triggered the 93-R. One of the three rounds went through the hand just as it touched the Makarov, and the guard screamed, jumping to his feet, sending the wooden chair clattering behind him. He stared at his ruined hand, then his eyes were drawn to his abdomen, where ragged entrance wounds would have allowed him to insert a finger into his liver. His screams drowned out the second burst, and the 9 mm parabellum rounds bowled him to the floor, dead before he hit.

Bolan was already determining the next man most likely to bring his weapon into target acquisition and he targeted the newspaper reader, who was dragging a pistol from his armpit holster. The Executioner's next three rounds drilled his chest and stopped his heart instantly.

Jiahua stepped to his side with the MP-5 leveled, the metal stock braced against her shoulder. The weapon pumped out a half-dozen rounds and cut down the two men trying to put down their bowls of noodles and get their weapons.

There was a blast of gunfire from behind one of the desks. Bolan fired a volley of rounds into the desk, forcing the shooter to stay low, then quickly angled at the last visible player, who had taken the time to grab his AK-47 from where it leaned against the wall. He triggered the weapon as he was angling it from the floor, and the Executioner cut him off with three rounds to the belly before he could finish the movement. He tipped forward and crashed treelike into the desk, the AK fire splintering the tile floor until it cycled empty.

Bolan had already turned his attention back to the gunman behind the desk, who was reaching out to get off a quick shot. The Executioner fired at the emerging weapon, scoring with at least one of his rounds. The handgun dropped to the floor—in the open. The gunman cried out and made the foolish choice of diving for it.

The soldier fired a round at his skull just as Jiahua

unleashed a flurry of rounds from the MP-5, cutting through the diver's spine. He fell on top of the handgun and didn't move again.

Bolan fired a burst at the boom box. The sound stopped after an electric flash, and in the sudden silence they heard a thump almost directly above their heads.

Jiahua spun toward the stairwell and triggered her weapon, the 9 mm rounds clattering into the ceiling, which would give pause to any gunman about to make the descent. Bolan took just seconds to release the empty magazine and install a fresh one, then he led the way up the stairs, the 93-R above his head like a periscope.

He moved more slowly as he came to eye level with the third floor, which housed another sprawling office. The lights were on, but no one was in sight. Desks, wooden partitions and steel file cabinets offered a wide range of hiding places.

Bolan snatched one of the grenades from his combat webbing, yanked the pin and tossed the bomb to the far side of the room. From their hiding places the gunmen saw it, recognized it for what it was. They screamed and fled into the open.

And in that instant the grenade exploded. Following a heavy thump, the room clouded with black, oily smoke, the billowing clouds not quite reaching the stairway. The gunmen fired blindly, running for open space in confusion and terror—into the waiting guns. Bolan fired at the figures as they emerged from the blackness. Three, then four of them swirled out of the oily cloud, rubbing their eyes, still clinging to their weapons. The Beretta triggered, singly now, taking out the hardmen.

Within half a minute the black smoke was dissipating

through the open windows and the room was quiet again.

But silence guaranteed nothing. They stepped up the next flight of stairs quickly and carefully, prepared for the sudden onslaught of more gunmen. It never came, and they didn't have the luxury of time to hunt down others who might be hiding. They reached the top floor and flipped on the lights. Two locked offices faced the south end of the building. Bolan kicked open the first one and found it contained a rumpled cot and a coat rack full of clothes. Somebody lived here on a regular basis, probably Chief Li himself. But he wasn't around now. The next office contained more files, a safe, a large desk and a small bar stocked with Russian vodka and Japanese rice wine. A large window looked over the roof of the building next door, with a clear view into South Xinhua Road. The street appeared quiet. Reinforcements hadn't yet arrived.

Bolan wasn't about to assume their arrival wasn't imminent.

"Let's search this place and get out quick."

Jiahua headed to the desk and began to empty drawers on the floor, finding a handgun, some newspapers and files, but not much in the way of paperwork. Bolan made quick work of the file cabinet. Most of the files inside were years old, and there was no evidence of the CIA attaché case.

"Can you open that?" Jiahua asked, nodding at the safe.

Bolan examined it. It was far from bank quality. "Yeah," he said, drawing his 93-R. The 9 mm bullet crashed into the lacquered combination knob, transforming it and the locking mechanism to scrap. Bolan yanked at the door, and it opened with a ping of broken metal. There was money inside, both yuan and U.S. dollars, but no attaché case.

Jiahua kicked the wall and tore open the cabinet under the bar, the last unsearched crevice of the room, finding nothing. She grabbed the vodka bottle by the neck and flung it into the wall.

"Dammit!"

Bolan grabbed several wads of yuan and stuffed them in his pocket.

"What do you want with that?" Jiahua demanded.

"Funds for the coming battles."

"What battles?"

"We haven't found your evidence. That means there's no government that will stop Yan Whan and his slave labor operations. We'll have to do it ourselves. This will help. More importantly it's an extra slap in the face to the Chief," Bolan said. "Help us get his attention."

Jiahua grinned. "Yeah."

She started to help him scoop up the cash.

CHIEF QUAN LI WALKED from the car to the front door and stood on the threshold. The blackness of the city behind him disappeared at the door. The interior of the building was garishly illuminated, and every drop of spilled blood was visible.

The angry conversations died to murmurs when he entered. He stepped to the first body, then to the second, then spotted the third.

"How many were killed?" he asked.

His lieutenant answered. "We are not sure yet, Chief. Let's see, there were three here, four in the next room. There was the lieutenant in the next room—"

Li raised his hand, shaking his head. "Wait. How many survived?"

The lieutenant looked slightly startled. "I thought you'd heard, Chief. None survived."

Li had to consider that possibility. "None?"

"Not one man."

The Chief nodded. "This and the mess at the airport proved the American woman did get through to somebody before we snatched her," he said. "There must be a whole team in the city. An army, by the look of it."

The lieutenant nodded, then was called to the telephone. Li stood among the ruin feeling useless, yet calm. Now was not the time for anger. Now was the time for cautious actions.

The lieutenant returned, his face white.

"Give me good news, Lieutenant. Tell me the men who accomplished this act have already been caught. Or that you have evidence of them fleeing this city."

"I'm afraid the news is not good at all, Chief."

Li pushed one of his underlings out of the way and walked among the ruin of his main city station with a cavern of fear yawning open in his chest. His men had been killed, yet not a single one of the attackers had been taken down. Or if they had been, their comrades had hauled off the bodies when they departed, leaving no evidence.

He began to nod when he reached his office and saw the mess, the papers strewed about, the safe burst open.

"They were searching for the evidence the American woman collected," he said aloud, but as if to himself.

"Was it here?" Lieutenant Lin asked.

"No. I turned it over to Yan Whan."

"Well, let's hope that is that, then."

Li looked at him. "What do you mean?"

"Well, they came to get the woman and the evidence. They got half of what they wanted. Now they'll leave. Their only options are to stay and keep attacking us until they uncover the evidence. That won't happen— the Americans wouldn't wage a terrorist war. They'll be happy with what they got and leave the scene. I'll bet they are gone now. At the most, they'll leave another spy."

"At the most?" Li looked at him oddly. "You're very optimistic."

Lin shrugged. "What are they going to do if they stay here? Go after Yan Whan? I'd like to see the look on their faces when they try getting at him."

"I wish I shared your cavalier attitude," Li said icily. Lin was about to protest, but the Chief raised a hand for silence.

Li was thinking that he had to consider the possibilities resulting from the ruthless attacks. He was hoping Lin's evaluation of the American's behavior was correct. He was genuinely fearful that the man was wrong.

There was something about the merciless aspect of these killing fields. The slaughter was too complete, and was unlike the CIA. But if not CIA, then who?

"Now is not the time for rash action," Li said carefully, measuring his words like ingredients in a complicated formula. "But it is time for swift action. I want all of my men called onto the streets. Do you understand? One hundred percent of them. I want everyone searching the city. Let's keep a watch on all our stations and maintain communications links at all times. Let's look for new people on the streets. Check all hotels for newcomers.

"I want this city saturated and watched from every corner, do you understand, Lin?"

"Yes, sir."

"Now is not the time for hasty action. It is time for careful planning. It is time for spreading a meticulous net. If we are careful, we can round up this American group and dispose of it quietly. I want this trouble to fade away as quickly as it has come upon us. Understand, Lin?"

"Yes, sir."

The Chief dismissed Lin with a look, and the lieutenant began to bark orders. Li's subordinate was a good man, but always in a hurry, stormy and dramatic.

Perhaps Lin didn't see the need for this large-scale mobilization of their forces in Urumchi. He obviously thought the attackers had gotten part of what they came for—the female spy—and would call it quits at that.

Li stared at the mess in his office, sincerely hoping that Lin was right and he was wrong.

But feeling very sure that the lieutenant was wrong.

CHAPTER FOUR

The summer sun possessed a searing quality that turned the roof of the apartment building into an oven before 9:30 a.m. Bolan sweated it out, sipping from a canteen to avoid dehydration, and sat with his back against the roof-mounted heat exchanger for the furnace.

At 9:45 a.m. he crawled across the searing rooftop to the brick wall where he looked out over Urumchi. The city was wide-awake and its people were busily going about their daily routine. He was more interested in the activity across the street, where a crew of officers had been collecting papers and righting the furniture in the office of Chief Li. The Chief entered as the cleanup crew was leaving. Standing at the door, he effectively blocked their way out, unspeaking, arms folded, scanning the room from corner to corner. Their work had to have passed muster; he allowed the men to exit.

Li sat at his desk, back to the window, providing Bolan a clean head shot if he wanted it. He didn't. Not yet. Li was a knight in this particular game, maybe a rook. Certainly he was no more powerful than that. Bolan knew he had to reach the king in order to shut down the game.

Removing some of the lower-level players in the

game, though, was a sure way to weaken the king's defenses.

Bolan saw two possible ways of removing the lower players. He preferred the first method—frighten them into defection. The defection of the Chief from the ranks of Yan Whan might very well remove all Yan Whan's police muscle. It would be a serious blow, but an unlikely eventuality. Li didn't rise to the ranks of Chief in the Urumchi police by backing down to anyone, and it was doubtful Bolan could convince him to back down now.

Not that he wasn't going to be very persuasive.

At the Executioner's specific request a sniper weapon had been among the substantial supply of arms tucked into the Daihatsu when it was delivered to him. His weapon of choice was a Ruger Model 77 Magnum Mark II, a rugged powerhouse that would stand up to the abuse of a long-term operation. The scope was a 12-power Leupold, which, fitted to his eye, brought the back of Li's head clearly into view.

Bolan was tempted, but the gains coming from killing Li now were outweighed by the potential gains of simply scaring him away.

All that was required was the proper motivation.

Three rounds of motivation were nestled in the Ruger's magazine.

Bolan knelt in a comfortable, sturdy posture—he would need it to ride out the rifle's recoil—then twice depressed the button on the walkie-talkie hanging on his belt.

CELLO JIAHUA SAT in the apartment two floors directly below Bolan, watching Li's office. The current occupants of the dingy flat were probably at work. Bolan had worked some tricky business on the lock with a stiletto he pulled out of a sheath on his calf in order to get them in. All they needed was a telephone, which the flat provided, with the bonus of a line of sight to the office. It was too low to serve as the attack stage, but Jiahua would have a good view of the action when it came down. She had been watching the cleanup crew, then saw Li arrive. She knew the signal would come soon.

The walkie-talkie buzzed, once long and once short, meaningless static to anybody in the vicinity monitoring the channels. She picked up the phone, then dialed.

"Chief Li is being attacked in his office!" she cried in Chinese. "Get somebody up there right away!"

She hung up, knowing the fun was about to begin.

LI SAT STRAIGHT AND TALL at the desk and pondered the possibilities of the previous night's strike from a more optimistic point of view.

The woman had been American, which meant CIA. If the CIA had come and taken her, they would have then come to his office for the evidence she had collected. Of course, they hadn't found it.

Empty-handed, how would the Americans proceed from that point? They would surely be intent on closing the operation. On the other hand would they risk the exposure of an operation on Chinese soil? Just to close down an illegal smuggling operation?

That was unlikely. There was no risk to national security, and there was risk to U.S.-Chinese relations.

In addition, cognizant of their exposed position, and vastly outmanned even if they had a ten-member team on-site in Urumchi—which Li doubted—they would know the likelihood of their success was slim.

The U.S., Li judged, wasn't the type of nation to engage in a no-win clandestine operation.

He nodded to himself slightly, looking at the safe on the other side of the office. Yes, his logic was sound. The Americans wouldn't remain in Urumchi after the failure of the previous night's attack. In fact he wouldn't be at all surprised if they had already beaten a retreat. They were probably on that morning's flight to Beijing.

He breathed a long sigh of satisfaction.

The door burst open and crashed into the wall, causing Li to spring to his feet, and a tall, broad officer ran into the room with his Tokarev automatic pistol sweeping the room. Three more men followed close behind him, handguns drawn.

"What is going on here?" Li demanded.

The officer pulled his gun to his chest and looked confused, the others forming a half circle behind him.

"You are alone?" the man asked.

"Can't you see I'm alone? What were you thinking?"

"We received a phone call—"

They were the policeman's last words. He made a gurgling noise in his throat at the same time the crash of broken glass filled the air. Chaos erupted.

BOLAN RODE OUT the recoil and sighted again. The big man had gone down, and the other occupants of the office were quickly realizing he'd been shot. The face of the man in the middle turned to the broken window, and the Executioner targeted him and fired. The recoil felt like a small pickup truck slamming into his body. It was the caress of a lover to the Executioner.

He sighted again. Chief Li had dropped out of sight, as had one of the two surviving officers. The third was scrambling out the door. Bolan targeted direct center of the door frame and fired the Ruger a third time. He lowered the weapon and saw that the plate-glass window had finally collapsed.

Through the waterfall of crystal the fleeing man had been spun in a circle. The .458 Winchester Magnum round had punched him in the chest and flung him into the doorjamb. He was propped up by it, eyes open, the glimmer of life dimming fast.

Bolan grabbed three more cartridges from his pocket and made quick work of reloading the Ruger. When he looked up again, the dying man had slid to the ground.

"WHERE THE HELL is it coming from?" Li shouted.

The survivor was on the floor in the corner, hands protecting his head. "Across the street—he's on one of the rooftops!"

Two more officers appeared in the doorway, saw the three dead men and disappeared instantly.

Li yanked the phone off the desk by its cord and dialed a two-number extension.

"Get ten men into the apartment building across the street, now! Get the rest up here. I want this guy picked off or trapped inside. One way or another he is not to get away!"

Li slammed the phone into place. "You! In the hallway! Are you going to do something or just stand there with your head up your ass!"

One of the gunmen entered with a handgun, a powerful .44, crabwalking quickly among the bodies and the glass to the wall at Li's side. He flattened under the window, sucking a fresh cut in his thumb and staring wildly into space.

There had been no shots for one full minute.

"Think he's gone?" the officer asked.

Li listened. "Maybe…"

The guy nodded quickly and jumped to his knees, resting the barrel of the .44 against his forearm and firing.

"You see him?" Li demanded.

There was another shot from across the street, like distant thunder. The officer keeled over on Li's lap, gore sluicing from a massive wound in his skull. Li cried wordlessly and kicked the corpse away.

BOLAN HEARD an attention sound from the walkie-talkie on his belt and spotted the figures poking out from the front doorway of the building. They were talking among themselves, then a line of men bolted into the street.

The Executioner stood quickly and shifted his aim to the forerunner. He fired one time and saw the runner sprawl. As the group screeched to a halt, he sighted on a second figure and squeezed off the last round in his current load, hoping it would be enough. Another man toppled, and the group behind him fled the way it had come. Bolan rummaged for more rounds in his pocket and reloaded the Ruger as he left the roof.

THE PHONE RANG and Li grabbed it.

"What the hell is going on down there?"

"Chief Li, this is your conscience calling." The caller spoke English.

"Who is this?"

"Call me Abe. I'm your new neighbor across the street."

"You bastard! You know you just bought yourself more trouble than you can handle!"

"I don't know what you're talking about, Li. I fire

six bullets, and six of your men are dead. No trouble whatsoever.''

Li sputtered.

"But it doesn't have to be this way, Li. My real reason for calling is to make a deal.''

"What? You want to make a deal?''

"Yeah. You see, you really aren't all that important in the scheme of things. It's Yan Whan I want. Yan Whan is causing all the trouble.''

"I don't work for Yan Whan!''

The voice on the other end changed from sardonic to ice cold.

"Don't play games with me, Li. You back off. You disassociate yourself and your men with Yan Whan. And as a symbol of your new, cooperative attitude, you hand over the attaché of evidence my friend collected on Yan Whan.''

"You can't tell me what to do!'' English failed him, and he sputtered in abusive Chinese.

Bolan cut him off. "You do what I say Li—you bow out now—and I won't have to mess up your office again.''

JIAHUA GAVE Bolan an I-told-you-so look as he hung up the phone.

"Does he sound cooperative?''

"No, but I'll give him time to mull it over.''

She glanced out the window. Two dead cops lay in the middle of the street. The group hovering in the doorway hadn't yet gathered the courage to try another sprint across the open space. The sound of sirens reached them.

"Okay, Belasko, now how do we get out of here?''

Bolan stepped to the window and raised the Ruger,

aiming at the corner where he predicted the car would appear. A small vehicle skidded around the corner, the single blue revolving light on its roof flickering. Bolan pulled the trigger, and the copper-jacketed round crashed through the windshield. The car failed to straighten out of the turn and swerved into a building with a crunch of metal that killed the siren and turned off the light like the flick of a switch.

He turned the Ruger on the group in the doorway. He could see only glimpses of body parts around the corner and under the overhang. He fired into the overhang itself, and the round plowed up concrete, spraying the street with it. The last round he placed in the street inches from the feet of the gunmen.

That would convince them to stay put for a few seconds longer.

"Let's go," Bolan said.

"SEE THAT ONE? That's a regular Urumchi city cop. The insignia means PAPF—People's Armed Police Force." Jiahua pointed out the window of the tiny café near the Youhao Market where they were drinking bottles of soda. The man she indicated was in the typical Chinese police uniform.

"Even they don't know the extent of Yan Whan's control in this area," she was explaining to him. "They know there is corruption. They know that the city allows what is essentially an illegal auxiliary police force to operate here. But they don't understand the extent of the operation."

"Why don't they report what they know?" Bolan asked.

"Report what? Corruption among the city officials? Get real. This is China. Every city official is corrupt, every bureaucracy operates on corruption. It's standard operating procedure in socialist states. But there's a difference between corruption and atrocity. There are your perpetrators of atrocity.''

She indicated a man in a dark coat and slacks, wearing a heavy wool jacket. He was crossing the street to a small shop selling used rugs.

''See the armband? That's the designation for the Xinjiang Uygur Autonomous Region Special Enforcement Agency.''

Bolan already knew the armband. All the agents at Chief Li's building had been wearing them. The gunmen at the station where Jiahua had been imprisoned had been wearing them. Li himself had one on when Bolan had spotted him through the scope this morning.

''The only problem is that the Xinjiang SEA doesn't exist. Not officially. It is an official-looking front developed by Yan Whan in cooperation with city officials. They allow the XSEAs to operate. They get a cut. Yan Whan staffs XSEA with all his own men. The people don't complain because in China you just don't complain—especially about a government law-enforcement agency. Those who do complain get nabbed by XSEA. If their complaints do reach someone at a high level of authority—someone at the national level—Yan Whan purchases their silence.''

Bolan got the picture.

''So you see why it will be difficult for Li to stop working for Yan Whan. He'll essentially be putting himself out of a job.''

''Unemployment is better than death,'' Bolan said.

''You think Li or the XSEA staff realize precisely what their choices are?''

''We'll make it clear as crystal.''

They stepped into the busy afternoon foot-and-bicycle traffic, Bolan in a wide-brimmed hat that hid his features to all but the closest passersby, who were generally not interested. He waved at a passing taxi, and the car pulled to the side.

"Tell him to wait here a minute and he'll get a good tip," Bolan said.

Jiahua spoke quickly to the driver and handed him a bill. The driver nodded and slumped into his seat, closing his eyes.

They proceeded to the shop, and the voices they heard coming through the open window were angry.

Jiahua nodded and said under her breath, "He's shaking down the owner."

The voice rose angrily. A second man was obviously pleading.

"He says he has sold nothing. The XSEA guy is telling him he has to pay whether he sells or not."

Bolan had heard enough. He stepped through the door quickly, and two heads turned to look at him. The man he had seen from the street had a hand in his coat.

"I was wondering what the price is on this rug?" he said, holding up a small, tattered rug. It had seen much use and had an inch-wide hole near the edge.

"Uh, price is forty yuan," the shop owner stammered.

"That seems unreasonable," Bolan said, dropping the rug and revealing the Beretta 93-R. The muzzle of the gun was trained on the man in the wool jacket. His hand jerked, quickly withdrawing a Chinese army handgun. He was lightning fast, but that wasn't fast enough. The Beretta spoke once, and the man rolled his eyes up to the sudden crimson hole in his forehead. His collapse onto a stack of carpets raised a cloud of dust.

The owner stepped back with his hands in the air, crying out.

"He says you can have the carpet free of charge," Jiahua said from the door, where she was keeping watch.

"Tell him I'll take this big one instead," Bolan answered. He found a wad of bills in the dead man's inside jacket pocket. He flipped it across the counter to the shopkeeper and quickly began to roll the corpse in the rug on which he lay, then hoisted the wrapped corpse onto his shoulder.

"We're not taking him home with us, are we?" Jiahua quipped.

"No. He's a gift but not for you."

Bolan jerked open the rear door of the taxi and wedged the roll of carpet inside. He handed the driver a massive sum of money.

"Tell him this gift is to be delivered to Chief Li of the Xinjiang Uygur SEA, courtesy of Abe."

The driver took the stack of bills, grinning and nodding, leaving in a puff of dust.

"There'll be others in the area," Jiahua suggested. "They work in groups, spreading out to do their dirty work, then getting back together throughout the day to pool their resources."

"Then let's find them," Bolan said.

The delivery of the small-time hood in the carpet roll would serve as an insult to Li. Bolan now was searching for a more substantial follow-up—add some injury to that insult.

THEY SPOTTED their next XSEA thug within minutes and followed him as his rounds took him to shop after shop, mostly one-person operations bringing in scant sustenance for the operator, a few extra yuan a month to add to the family pot. And much of it went to make Li, and Yan Whan, wealthier.

The faces of his victims bore the stamp of resignation, of swallowed pride. This was nothing new to them. Who knew how long the Chief Li–Yan Whan organization had been stealing from them? Those who had the will to fight had stated their opposition a long time ago. They had acquiesced eventually, or they were no longer around to state their opposition.

That was how it worked.

Bolan had to make an effort to restrain himself when the hood entered a small dry-goods stall. The girl behind the counter was in her early teens, dressed in frumpy olive-and-gray clothing, but was beautiful, a fact the hood had not failed to notice. He wore a leering smile when he approached the stall and said something short and crude. The girl shrank to the back wall and regarded him with quiet fear.

Her father emerged from behind a curtain in the back wall. He began to speak quickly, taking money from a pocket and thrusting it at the hood, urging him to take it.

The hood was bargaining. Bolan didn't need to hear the words to know what he wanted. The father spoke again shortly, shaking his head and withdrawing more cash from his pocket. The hood snarled and grabbed the cash, stalking out of the stall. The girl began to sob and ran to her father.

As Bolan turned, he saw a single tear forming in Jiahua's eye. She glanced at him and wiped it viciously away. Bolan said nothing.

"She's just a little girl. She shouldn't have to live in fear of that bastard."

Bolan nodded. "I agree."

"And she'll never have to again."

The Executioner knew that was true, as well, but said nothing, asking no questions. He was reminded once again that he wasn't the only warrior haunted by ghosts from the past.

The hood, dressed in a dark blue shirt and blue cotton trousers, checked his watch and stalked down the street to an eating establishment. The open front area contained several narrow tables. The lunchtime crowd was getting heavy, buying bowls of cold rice and steaming vegetables and noodles. They were jamming together at the tables and standing on the street outside to eat. The hood worked his way through the crowd without effort. The crowd was made up of regular customers, who knew him and knew the armband, and they weren't about to mess with either. He disappeared around the corner.

"You take the front," Bolan directed. "Wait for my signal."

Jiahua didn't ask what signal. She shoved her way through the crowds and bought a bowl of plain rice, then leaned against the wall outside the entrance to the back room eating it, as close as she dared without appearing out of place—locals would know enough not to go back there.

The lunchtime rush became heavier. The din of ordering and chatting filled the room. Jiahua hoped her partner wasn't about to get some civilians killed.

She put her hand in her jacket and touched her pistol. She was ready when Belasko was.

She didn't have to wait long.

BOLAN MOVED around the building into a grassy alley overflowing with garbage. The wall was brick, but a wide rear window tarpaulin had been rolled up to allow the air to circulate. The back door also stood wide open, stopped with a brick, so the air could flow through. The stench of the garbage and the steaming smell of the food made a nauseating combination. Bolan didn't bother to contemplate how the diners could stand it. He was too busy scoping out the clientele.

One table of seven men sat in the rear of the establishment. Every one of them wore an armband, and the hood they had been following was facing the door. He was the first to notice Bolan's approach.

"Hey, American, what do you want here?"

"Sorry to bother you, but I think I'm lost. Could you help?"

"Yeah, but it will cost you plenty."

Bolan brought the Beretta 93-R to bear in an instant, leveling it over the table at the hood. "How much do you have in mind?"

The hood froze, but several of his cohorts reached for their weapons. Bolan spun to his left and stepped back, bringing a short, black-bearded man into target acquisition and triggering once, then again, shredding vital organs with both shots. He spun at another gunner, who was bringing up a small pistol. The Beretta spoke once again, the shot crashing through the gunman's rib cage, ripping at his heart with jagged metal and bone fragments. Just a slight movement targeted a third man, who had grabbed a knife from his belt and was starting to rise. The Beretta flashed in his face, coring his skull with two rounds and dropping him like a rock.

More gunfire erupted from the other side of the room, and Bolan whirled, spotted Jiahua making her entrance with her Colt blasting, taking out a fourth gunman. She sought out the hood they had been trailing all afternoon, then stalked to him with a look of grim purpose on her face. The man had a handgun drooping from his fingers. As he stared down the muzzle of her 9 mm pistol he never even tried to use it. Bolan thought the words he uttered might be pleas for mercy.

Jiahua ignored what he said. She was seeing the scared little girl in the market, thinking about another little Chinese girl facing unspeakable terror and humiliation at the hands of a despicable man, and she fired repeatedly. The ruined face fell to the dirt floor.

Bolan had turned on the two survivors, firing at the first flash of gunmetal he saw, ripping the hand to pieces and sending the gunman to the ground writhing and screaming. The second gunner leveled his autopistol at the same instant the Executioner sent two parabellum manglers into his gut and groin. They curled him over, bringing him to his knees. Firing the autopistol out of reflex, unprepared for the recoil, he allowed the gun to jump out of his hand. He collapsed on his side and lay still.

The Executioner stood over the screaming survivor and aimed the muzzle of the Beretta at his forehead.

"Do you want to live?"

The wounded man appeared to think it over. "Yes."

"I want you to deliver a message to Chief Li."

"Yes!"

"Tell him Abe says hello."

The man stared at him, his amazement momentarily overcoming his fear and pain.

"Repeat it."

The man nodded. "Abe says hello?"

Bolan nodded, leaving the wounded man lying where he had fallen.

"Hey, Belasko, what's with this 'Abe'?"

"First thing that popped into my head—you know, Abe Lincoln."

"Oh, I get it. Freeing the slaves and all that."

He nodded.

"Hysterical," she said.

"You didn't contact me for my sense of humor."

"So what's on the agenda next, Honest Abe?"

"We wait a little while for news of recent events to spread, then we phone a friend."

Jiahua had rented a tiny flat above a vegetable store a mile south of the Youhao Market. Bolan had stayed out of sight while she did the negotiating. Urumchi wasn't a big tourist city, and Americans were an unusual sight. He would need to keep a low profile.

Using Li's money, they were able to get a flat with a refrigerator and hot water—luxuries.

"If we have time to kill, I'm going to take a shower," Jiahua declared.

Bolan opened one of the Chinese-brewed beers they had purchased and sat at the tiny, low kitchen table. He willed himself to relax, savoring a rare moment of inactivity. The shower was running in the bathroom. He knew he had turned up the heat on the Yan Whan organization. If things proceeded the way he had planned, these stolen moments of calm might be the last for him and Jiahua for some time to come.

CHAPTER FIVE

Bolan dialed the Chief's number only to find that it was no longer operating. He didn't see that as a serious problem. He was sure Li would take his call. He called the XSEA headquarters and asked to speak to the Chief. "Tell him it's Abe calling."

There was a minute of silence.

"Listen, you son of a bitch, I'm going to scour this city and I'm going to find you. And I'm going to waste you good. I'll string you up like a pig and bleed you—"

"I take it you aren't ready to make a deal."

"I wouldn't bargain with you to save my mother's life!"

"You should be worried about someone even more important, Li—yourself. Because I'm going to take care of you eventually. And if I don't, I'll make you look so bad your boss will do it for me."

"Who do you think you are you—"

Bolan hung up.

No deals with Li, no evidence for Jiahua. It was time this war of attrition got serious.

JIAHUA'S HEAD WAS bursting with ideas for strikes. She had, after all, been staking out Chief Li, XSEA and Yan Whan properties for three weeks prior to Bolan's arrival. Her memory was nearly photographic when it came to the sites she had reconned with Kim Ping.

During their discussions, Bolan came to a new appreciation for her abilities. Her cognitive ability was natural and adept, and it was easy to see how she had become a strong field agent for Langley.

The list of operations could have been applied to virtually any organized-crime boss in any city in the world. Yan Whan smuggled drugs, ran gambling dens and sold stolen cars. Being in an isolated section of the world gave him a major advantage: the citizens of the town and the surrounding area had no nearby cities they could visit as an alternate source for these illegal goods and services. Yan Whan was the only player in town.

Bolan listened to the myriad possibilities and chose a target. The window of opportunity for this specific target was small. If they were going to strike, they had to do it that afternoon or wait a week. And it would demonstrate their versatility to Chief Li.

Because they were striking outside the city itself, they could risk using the Sazuki one last time.

They began the long drive southeast through the dry grasslands.

XIE SHAO WAS AFRAID, and he had every reason to be. Chun Shi had threatened to kill him, and a man as crazy as Shi might make good on such a threat.

Shao was old and tired. He had seen much trouble in his long life. Most of it, however, had been distant. The coming of the Communists when he was young, the rebellions and ethnic troubles, the strife between the Chinese and the Russians—events had unfolded around him but didn't involve him personally. He was just a locomotive engineer. How could he get tied up in such troubles?

Now trouble had come to him.

Shi had been assigned to be an assistant engineer on the run a year ago, and brought discord with him. Within a week he had suggested an opportunity for Shao and the other engineers who worked the run to make some extra money, a substantial sum of extra money.

Shao was an old man. He wouldn't be working the run much longer. Then he would stay at his home and live out his days. What did he need with all that extra money? He had never had it before.

But the others had quickly accepted Shi's offer. When Shao had protested, they threatened him, so he had gone along with the others to keep the peace.

But he had to swallow his pride to do it. What they were doing was wrong, and they could all be found out and severely punished.

Shao was too old for jail. Living in jail would kill him. He really had no choice but to go along with the others. If he didn't, they would band together and have him removed from the job.

The task was simple enough. Their weekly run started at Lanzhou. They would take the train out about two hundred miles until they were due north of Xining. There they made an unscheduled stop at an old intersection, installed when the line was built with the intention of some day adding an extension down to Xining. The extension was never put in, and the rusty intersection simply stopped after one hundred yards. Here an automobile-carrying train car, full of shiny cars, source unknown, would be quickly linked up to the train. The train would start up again and be on its way. It was a simple operation that took ten minutes.

Five hundred miles later, just outside Urumchi, the train made another extra stop. This time the intersection in the track was brand-new. Whoever had organized the operation had arranged for the intersection to be put in, and the extra track traveled around a bend, behind an outcropping. There the extra auto carrier was removed from the train, and the train then proceeded into Urum-chi.

On the return trip they picked up the then empty auto carrier, which they left at the original pickup point.

Both the unscheduled stops occurred in the middle of nowhere, in places where few people dwelt and fewer would care about the stopping and starting of a passing train.

They told Shao no one would ever know, and they probably were right.

But what if someone did find out? What would the consequences be? Obviously the activity was illegal. The cars in the auto carrier had to be stolen, or they would have been shipped in a less clandestine manner.

Shao didn't want any part of it, but he had no choice.

He was old, and his arthritis was getting the better of him. He had told the other engineers that this would be his last run, that he was retiring to live with his daughter. The little money the government provided, and his share of the payment received for their dirty work, would help pay her for the food he ate and the space he took up in her already crowded house.

Shi stepped up close to him when their shift together began, grabbing him by the collar and spinning him. The old man's bones cried out in pain.

"Are you going to call the authorities, old man?" Shi demanded.

"No. Why would I do that now? I've been going along with the scheme for almost a year."

"You've never gone along with it. You just stopped fighting it. Now I think you are leaving this job and you don't care what happens to us anymore so you'll try to cause trouble for us."

"I won't cause trouble for you because I don't want trouble for myself!"

Shi reached behind his back and withdrew a shiny black handgun, and the feel of the cold metal pressed under his chin made Shao close his eyes and tremble.

"If we do have trouble, I'll know where it came from. If we do have trouble, then this is what you'll get!" The gun muzzle pushed so hard into his neck that it closed his windpipe. "You'll get it, and your daughter will get it and her husband and all your grandchildren will get it. Do you understand?"

Shao tried to nod but couldn't move his head.

Shi let go of him, and Shao slumped against the wall, pain racking his bones and his lungs, gasping for breath and unable to stop trembling.

"Slow the train, old man," Shi ordered. "It's almost time to make our stop."

In the hours since then, Shi had been regarding him with such enmity that Shao had been unable to eat. He had hoped there would be no trouble, that this trip would go as smoothly as all the others before it. Then, when he got back to Lanzhou, he would get off the train and never board it again. He would hole up in his daughter's house and shut out the world.

If he only made it through this last trip.

Jiahua pulled off the road eighty minutes outside the city limits of Urumchi. There was a wide gravel area alongside the highway and a rise in the land. Only when they drove into the grass at the end of the gravel did Bolan see the trail left by the passage of vehicles.

"Watch for them."

"What are the chances their pickup crew is on the scene already?" Bolan asked.

"Slim. The train usually gets into Urumchi at the same time every week, which means, I assume, that they arrive at the pickup point at more or less the same time each week. Kim Ping and I only actually followed them out here during one of their pickups. When we were sure it was just stolen cars they were dealing with, we lost interest."

The trail from the highway meandered a quarter mile through the tall desert grass and down an incline, coming into a clearing alongside a rocky hillock. The tracks traveled around the hill to the main line.

The pickup crew had not, in fact, arrived. The site was empty.

"They hide the car behind the hill, where it can't be seen from the rails or from the highway," Jiahua said, pointing to the end of the line, where a small track-mounted engine, designed for manipulating train cars, sat silent.

They drove farther behind the hill and left the car parked close to the rock where the likelihood of discovery was low.

Yan Whan's pickup staff could arrive at any time.

A reception was already planned.

Bolan crouched in the grass. The breeze was gentle, the sky blue and clear. The sun was bright, but Bolan couldn't feel it on his skin. It was a calm, warm day in the broad, empty grasslands of Xinjiang, but it would be getting considerably hotter in a very short time.

The rumble of the train could be felt in the tracks, and there had been a whistle in the distance. He and Jiahua had been watching Yan Whan's pickup staff for almost half an hour.

The Executioner caught his first glimpse of the train, still a mile off and slowing, and checked his hardware. For this action he had chosen a Steyr AUG assault rifle. The unit featured a grenade launcher, and Bolan wore a shoulder pack full of 40 mm MECAR rifle grenades.

The 30-round mag, plus the extras on his belt, meant Bolan was prepared to inflict some serious damage.

The train came between him and the outcropping, where Yan Whan's staff was waiting. Since arriving, they had been lounging there in their three vehicles, unaware of the Americans observing them.

The train slowed to just a couple of miles per hour, with the rear car, the auto carrier, finally moving past Bolan. The train halted a dozen feet later, and Yan Whan's men got to work.

Several moved to the front of the car to disconnect it from the train. Two of the engineers hopped from the engine and started back to the rear.

The small train-car mover emerged from behind the cliff with a puttering of its heavy-duty diesel engine, its front latch open to connect with the auto carrier and drag it behind the cliff, where the truck waited to load them up.

The plan was to strike when the train was on its way again. Bolan didn't know how thoroughly the engineers were involved in the plot. He wouldn't chance attacking them along with Yan Whan's men.

But his plans changed within minutes.

One of the engineers shouted and shoved one of the others, who Bolan saw now was an old man. He fell heavily and lay on the ground for a long moment before he got to his feet again, his face covered in dirt.

The other engineer had a handgun pointed at the old man's head.

Yan Whan's men crossed the tracks and met the engineers. The young engineer was gesticulating, pointing at the old man.

Bolan wished he knew what they were saying. Maybe the old man wasn't going along with the program and was threatening to tell the authorities. It was possible he didn't even know what was going on and had been asking too many questions.

Whatever it was, the young engineer was explaining it loudly to Yan Whan's men. One of them shrugged, said something short and to the point.

Bolan's entire body was tense, his finger tight on the Steyr's trigger.

The young engineer grinned maliciously and leveled the handgun at the old man's head.

The Executioner fired a burst. The shots went wild, but from his distance he couldn't hope to hit the gunman without risking hitting the old man, too. The 5.56 mm rounds rattled against the railcar and the autos.

The engineer wheeled on Bolan and fired once, the shot zipping through the air above his left shoulder, and the old man fell to the ground with his hands over his head, as Bolan had hoped. He targeted the gunman and triggered, rattling off five rounds in half a second, cutting into the gunman with at least two of them, sending him into the grass. He turned the weapon on Yan Whan's men, who were unholstering their weapons too slowly. The assault rifle rattled for one solid second, and most of the rounds ripped into them, killing them where they stood.

The plan had to be abandoned. The plastique Bolan had planted in the front end of the railcar mover was designed to take out the mover and the railcar itself, along with all the stolen vehicles. But the railcar-mover operator was scrambling out of the machine. It would never reach the railcar now. Bolan grabbed the tiny transmitter from his belt, activated it and depressed the red button.

The railcar mover shattered in a blast of white-and-yellow fire, lifting the operator as he jumped to the ground and propelling him through the air like a flaming comet.

Bolan launched himself toward the explosion, spotting another of Yan Whan's gunmen picking himself up shakily. The Steyr stuttered in his hands, cutting into the gunman.

The old man raised his eyes cautiously from the dirt.

"Get that train to Urumchi. You never saw a thing."

The old man stared at him, probably unable to comprehend a word. The older generations, unlike the younger, hadn't grown up with English-language instruction as a common school subject. Bolan gestured with the Steyr, and that did the trick. The old man hobbled to his feet and lumbered off toward the front of the train.

Submachine-gun fire reached Bolan from the far side of the auto carrier. That would be Jiahua, or someone firing at her. He shielded his face from a sudden flare as the diesel tank of the car mover was reached by the fire and ran across the tracks.

Jiahua had attacked from the rear, and as he watched

she propelled herself to her feet, the MP-5 rattling in her hands. A scream answered from Bolan's left. He spotted one man slumping forward on a car hood, sliding to the ground, but there was at least one more gunman taking shelter there. The Executioner fired a high-explosive grenade toward his quarry. It impacted and exploded behind the car, sending two stunned gunmen running panic-stricken toward him. Bolan stood his ground and emptied the magazine into them. They never stood a chance.

He grabbed a fresh mag and jammed it into the Steyr, his eyes scanning the area for more of Yan Whan's men.

A truck revved to life far behind Jiahua's position. She stood up and laid on the MP-5, blasting into the semitrailer's windshield, tearing it out. The driver had ducked and was barreling toward her. The CIA agent sprang out of its path, tossing the subgun into the dirt and tearing at the Colt pistol holstered under her left arm. She fired round after round into the tires of the semi and its empty automobile rack as it barreled past her, taking out two tires—not enough to even slow the vehicle down.

But Bolan had now set his sights on the semi. Triggering the Steyr at the driver's-side window, he obliterated it, then launched another high-explosive round, timed to land in the path of the semi. The HE hit the dirt within two feet of the semi's front end and exploded a moment later, directly under the cab. Almost instantly the fuel tanks blew. The semi jackknifed, the trailer skidding suddenly at Bolan like a giant hand coming to sweep him off the game board. He spun in the other direction and ran, hearing the crash and tear of wrenching metal behind him, feeling the flying dirt and rock pounding on his back.

He jumped over a small rise in the earth and landed in a clump of tall grass.

A few feet in front of him, he saw the train wheels begin to turn, slowly, as if with tremendous effort.

He turned back to the battleground, staying in a crouch, and scanned the open area for signs of the living.

The fire burned steadily in the overturned semi cab, and the train-car mover was burning itself out already, although black smoke seeped from the engine. The clouds of dust were drifting away across the grass and settling again.

"Belasko?"

Jiahua stood up out of her own grassy knoll across the open ground.

Bolan waved and stepped into the open, the Steyr AUG planted firmly against his side.

"Relax. We got them. Let's get out of here."

Bolan didn't relax, but he guessed she was correct.

They'd gotten them.

"Let's go. We'll leave the car," he said.

"Then how do we get back to town?"

Bolan nodded at the train, gaining speed almost painfully. "But first..."

The big American finished the job at hand. Three HE grenades, one after another, sailed into the abandoned automobile carrier. They exploded underneath it, sending it rolling slowly backward. The bottom level of stolen cars, bound for Urumchi, twisted and crackled, sending up more black clouds of smoke.

By the time Bolan and Jiahua were stepping onto the rear of the train, the flames had reached the upper level of cars. One of them had to have had a full tank of gas. Broken metal and shards of glass flew in all directions.

"You didn't leave a messenger," Jiahua argued.

"The Chief will know who was here. He can tell Yan Whan all about it."

THEIR AGENDA for the evening was the Barracks.

"That's what Kim and I called them," Jiahua explained as they crouched on the train, chugging back to Urumchi. "We found two different buildings in the city where Li housed his XSEAs. They're satellites of Yan Whan's central housing complex, which is on his property, and he runs them like resorts. Real life of luxury. Part of the incentive for enlisting in the Yan Whan organization is a quality of life that's unachievable to the average Chinese. They have satellite television, booze, good food, pool tables, you name it. They even keep a bevy of prostitutes on staff. I think they rotate them among the facilities so the men don't get bored."

They headed for Barracks One.

GUI XIANGDONG LOUNGED in the stiff steel chair at the front entrance of the house feeling at once sorry for himself and self-satisfied.

He was on his way up. There was no doubt about it.

So what was he doing at the front door for five hours playing guard duty?

The idea was repulsive. Guard duty was a job given to a lackey, a peon, and Xiangdong certainly considered himself above it.

He'd been born a Kazak. Most of his people were still out in the Junggar Basin living the lives of nomads. They were backwater savages as far as Xiangdong was concerned.

His father had felt the burning desire for civilization and dragged his reluctant wife to the big city of Urumchi. She had fled back to her people when Xiangdong was a newborn and had tried to take him with her. Xiangdong was forever thankful that his father had prevented the abduction, rescuing him from that life, and had given him a Chinese name. Urumchi life was hard and monotonous, but the life of a desert nomad—no thanks.

Xiangdong grew up knowing that, in terms of discrimination, Urumchi, as bad as it was, was far better than most of China. Urumchi was something of a melting pot: Kazaks, Hui, Sibo, Tajiks, Uzbeks, Russians, Mongols and a dozen other races mixing in a kind of Far Eastern melting pot. Most of China was Han Chinese.

Gui Xiangdong had struggled to overcome discrimination through assimilation, and he failed. No matter how he tried, his features were too swarthy for him to pass muster.

He had then rebelled against the society that wouldn't accept him. He turned to thievery, robbing simple market stalls, then a larger restaurant. When he tried to rob a Han Chinese businessman, he overstepped the bounds of the local crime organizations. They hunted him down and almost killed him.

But at his lowest point Xiangdong was offered the chance of a lifetime.

Almost a year later it was hard to believe his luck. He lived like a king, far better than he had ever dreamed, as well as the Western visitors in their fine hotels on North Xinhua Road, with food, women and booze that was just as good. This house was a huge dwelling for just these twenty men. He was waited on; he was pampered.

Just as important as the life-style, he had discovered, was the fact that he liked the work. He was good at shaking down people for money, at enforcing the laws of his new boss, at taking control of the situations that needed controlling. He had even learned to work within the guidelines of the organization, which catered to aggressive, ambitious, gutsy men such as himself. As a result he had been promoted twice in his first year and then, out of the blue, a third time, just that morning. He knew it was because his predecessor had been killed in the recent troubles.

He had heard about the trouble downtown. The rumors said there were Americans on the loose in Urumchi, threatening Yan Whan and the Chief. Gui Xiangdong wasn't worried. He would deal with them like he had dealt with all the other obstacles that had come in his way. He would strike them down.

Let them come; he was ready. He was a man on his way up.

Not, however, that you could tell at the moment. There was an extra need for guard duty, he had been told, the need to watch for the strange enemies that had struck the Chief's headquarters that morning.

As if they would come here, into the midst of Yan Whan's forces, Gui Xiangdong thought. No American would have the nerve to pull a stunt like that.

THEY SPOTTED THE GUARD sitting in a steel foldable chair outside the front door of the house. A Chinese-made AK-47 leaned against the wall behind him, within easy reach.

"There's never been a guard there before," Jiahua

said quietly. "Our activities must have them on the alert."

"I think we should also assume everybody inside will be extra-attentive," Bolan said. "That means extra care with every step."

"Count on it. But what do we do about the guard with the rifle?"

Bolan was already withdrawing the Beretta 93-R. The gun was fitted with its custom-engineered sound suppressor and was switched to autofire. Bolan leaned his shotgun against the fence.

"Geez, that's got to be a pretty tough shot."

Bolan had to agree. They were in the fenced-in front yard of what had to be one of the wealthiest residences of Urumchi. The clean, neatly paved street was four lanes wide. Add the distance of the lawn, and it totaled almost fifty yards.

The added challenge was taking out the guard without alerting anyone inside. Estimating that as many as half the twenty inhabitants could be at home at that moment, Bolan wanted to eliminate as many targets as possible in silence.

Surprise was their only advantage.

He aimed carefully, steadying the muzzle of the weapon on the wooden fence. He aimed high and outside to compensate for the distance and a light, steady breeze. When he fired, he needed to be ready to compensate instantly for a miscalculation and trigger again. Otherwise the alarm would be raised.

He squeezed the trigger, and the Beretta spit three times, the noise barely carrying the distance to the house.

The scene remained unchanged, except that the guard slumping in the steel chair looked more relaxed than ever, and his face was a welling mass of shattered bone and blood.

"We're in," Bolan said.

BOLAN WORE his wide-brimmed hat when he crossed the street, then jammed it over the face of the corpse to cover its ruin. The pose didn't look natural for someone taking a nap, but with the face covered no one would be immediately alarmed.

The front door was unlocked. Why lock the door when you've got an armed guard outside? Bolan pushed it open and stepped inside an empty vestibule. To the right was a living room, and they heard raucous canned laughter from a French sitcom on the television. Bolan looked through the door and found a single occupant with his back to the door watching the show, unaware that his death loomed up behind him like a dark, sentient shadow.

Bolan withdrew into the vestibule. He and Jiahua silently stepped up the stairs.

The plan was to take care of those in the bedrooms first. They were isolated and could be silently removed from the equation before the real battle erupted.

They came to the first of several private bedrooms on the second floor. Bolan knocked.

A voice said something inside in Chinese. There were footsteps, and the door opened. The Chinese man looked at the strangers for a second before focusing on the Beretta 93-R. Bolan triggered the weapon, and the round shattered the man's Adam's apple and severed his trachea. He tried to scream as the second round pummeled him in the stomach and bent him over. Blood seeped from his mouth onto the carpet. Bolan grabbed the hardman's collar and lowered him to the floor, waited for the weak struggling to cease, then checked the room quickly. There were no other occupants and no other way out. He locked the door and closed it from the outside.

They knocked on another door and received no answer. Stepping inside, they found it empty. But they heard voices next door. A television was playing a soccer match, and two men were arguing over the performance of the teams.

"Your play," Bolan said.

"No problem."

While Bolan waited in the empty room, she stepped into the hall and knocked on the door. The argument halted, and one of the men invited her in.

Jiahua opened the door and found herself in a wide bedroom. The furnishings were plain but not cheap. The room had a king-size bed, a kitchenette and a sitting area. The two men were on the couch drinking beers and facing a twenty-five-inch Japanese television.

"Hi. I'm Xiaoliao Jiahua, the new girl."

The men perked up at once.

"I was told to come over and meet the man in the room next door, but there is nobody there."

"Well, that would be me, young miss," said one of the men, a corpulent figure who stood up at once, yanking his shirt down over his stomach.

Jiahua smiled. "I'm compliments of Chief Li."

"Aren't you going to finish watching the game?" the other man demanded.

"Are you joking?"

"Yeah," Jiahua said playfully, "are you joking?"

She took the fat man by the hand and into the darkened room next door.

"Chief Li is an okay guy," were the fat man's last words.

Bolan stepped up behind him and rapped the 93-R hard against his skull. He let the body fall onto the bed with a bounce.

This time it was Bolan who entered the room next door. The surviving beer drinker looked up with alarm, his hand inching toward his side arm.

"Who are you?" he asked.

"I'm the new guy," Bolan replied, leveling the 93-R and peppering him with 9 mm rounds. He drained his last beer on the carpet, watching the ceiling and spasming.

Bolan shut the door behind him.

So far so good.

They moved on to the next room.

The Executioner's instincts didn't warn him that all hell was about to break loose.

Jiahua knocked on another door. There was a call from inside, and she tried the door but found it locked.

Then the door across the hall opened suddenly. A Chinese man spotted her, barked a single syllable and slammed the door behind him. Bolan fired through the door several times, fully aware he was probably wasting rounds.

"He recognized me—he was there when I was arrested!" Jiahua said.

The first door opened, and a sleepy-eyed man failed to react quickly enough. Bolan drilled him once in the skull with the 93-R and didn't wait for him to fall. Instead he jumped across the hallway and shouldered the door, instantly dropping to the floor inside.

The quick-thinking man was already on the phone, shouting into it and scrambling with a handgun. Bolan fired from the floor, hitting him in the chest and shoulder, sending the phone flying. He collapsed on the phone table.

"He alerted somebody!" Jiahua warned.

Bolan got up, holstering the side arm. The time for stealth was past, and he wanted something that did serious, widespread damage. His big gun for the hard probe was a Beretta M-3 P police shotgun, a 12-gauge, selective-action weapon. Bolan brought it to bear as footsteps approached from the stairway, triggering as the first gunman rounded the corner. The boom was like a thunderclap in the close confines, and the gunman was hurled back down the stairs.

His companion followed so close behind him he had to have leaped over the falling body. Bolan fired the instant the large Chinese handgun poked its nose into view. The blast was largely wasted on the ceiling, but the Chinese tumbled onto the carpet and its owner retreated, screaming.

Bolan spun, alerted by a cry from Jiahua when one of the four unexplored doors at the rear of the hallway edged open. She triggered the MP-5, its suppressed noise not much louder than the ripping of the wooden door frames and wallboard. The door slammed shut.

"I missed him!"

The Executioner ran to the door and triggered a blast from inches away, shredding the door and lock and punching it open. Someone responded with a heavy-caliber round. Bolan triggered again instantly, without aiming. The shot caught the occupant off guard, and he screamed, clutching at his face, dropping his handgun.

Three rooms remained unexplored.

"No time," Bolan said. "Let's move."

Jiahua answered by triggering the MP-5 at the stairs,

missing the fleeting shadow of a head that appeared and quickly retreated.

"We'll have to make a run for it."

"I'm up for it," the woman told him. "I hope you're leaving something behind!"

Bolan finished replacing the magazine in the M-3 P and snatched a small cylinder from his belt.

"What is it?" Jiahua asked, her eyes flickering in every direction.

"Phosphorous."

"Shit, man, I hope we make it out of here!"

"If we don't, we're dead, end of story."

Jiahua glanced at him. Her eyes said she could think of better ways to die than eaten alive by a phosphorous charge.

"Let's go!" she shouted.

They jumped forward together, bounding to the stairs, Jiahua triggering and sweeping the SMG across their path like a garden hose. The gunman who had been trying to get up to them tried to get away from the sweep and failed, shuddering as the 9 mm rounds chopped into his legs. Bolan fired once, the 12-gauge blast plowing the man end over end down the stairs. The Executioner freed one hand from the shotgun long enough to drag the pin out of the grenade and lob the bomb behind him.

"It's hot," he said.

"Let's get out of here!"

They plummeted down the stairs. Jiahua aimed at the open door to the living area, where some sort of shadow moved. Her subgun shook in her hands and stopped short, its 30-round mag spent. They landed at the bottom of the stairs, Bolan triggering at the opening to the living room, shotgun pellets splattering the walls. Out of the corner of his eye he glimpsed two men emerging from the bedrooms he and Jiahua had missed.

Then he and his companion were out the door and fleeing across the lawn, ducking behind a parked car for cover.

The phosphorous made a fiery blast. The two men on the second floor were as good as cooked, and anybody who stayed inside wouldn't live long.

A Chinese man staggered from the flaming building, screeching in agony, as the phosphorous burned into his body, worming through bone and tissue mercilessly. It would eat straight through him if it didn't consume itself first. Bolan drew the 93-R and stepped into the open long enough to deliver a single, close-range mercy shot. The burning man dropped, silent, his agony ended.

Another man appeared in the doorway, burning alive, arms whacking at his face and body. Blinded by fire, he didn't know he was standing in front of the door he was seeking—not that getting himself outside would have done him any good at that stage. Bolan fired quickly at the figure, but it fled too fast into the flames that were quickly becoming a conflagration, and his screams continued another twenty seconds.

A car cruised down the street, slowing, the driver staring at the flames. He stopped the car and stepped out, wearing the armband that designated him a member of Chief Li's XSEA forces.

The man walked slowly toward the fire, then saw the smoking ruin of the corpse on the scrubby grass.

When he looked up again, Bolan was just paces away with the 93-R aimed at him, held in a tight two-handed grip. "You want to live?" the Executioner asked in a graveyard voice.

The man nodded, tongue-tied.

"I've got a message I want you to deliver to Chief Li. Tell him Abe was here."

The man nodded again.

"Say it."

"Abe was here."

"Good."

Bolan grabbed the handgun from the man's belt holster and tossed it several yards away. He and Jiahua then ran to the policeman's car, got in and sped away.

CHAPTER SIX

XSEA officers swarmed the building like termites over a mud hill, burning nervous energy.

The sun had descended over the hills, and now it was evening. The Chief had instructed his men to be on the alert. No sleeping tonight. As if any of them could sleep, when so many of their number had been obliterated.

Nag Tsai thought it was utter nonsense and said so.

"What do you mean by that?"

"It's bullshit, somebody's lie."

Tou Seiwei shook his head, smirking humorlessly. "I don't know what you're getting at."

"It's a conspiracy, a scheme. Somebody is getting at us from the inside."

Seiwei didn't understand.

Tsai sucked hard on the cigarette, making his cheeks draw tight against his skull, enhancing the gaunt aspect of his profile. He hissed long and low, like a leaking tire, the smoke sieving through his teeth, while he stabbed the cigarette against the brick wall.

"I mean, friend, that we've been working together, hand in hand, with Yan Whan and his men. And Yan Whan has been getting stronger and stronger for all these months. Now things are reaching a head. Yan

Whan thinks he has the manpower to go it alone. He doesn't need us anymore. He's decided to get rid of us."

Seiwei looked alarmed. "They say there is an American attacking us."

"And you believe it?"

"One guy saw the American. He even said he had an American accent."

"Maybe that's who he saw. But there's no way that place was busted up by one guy. Who's to say the American isn't just one of the hired hit men?"

Seiwei shrugged. "What about the woman? She was Chinese once, maybe, but she's definitely American now. They say she's CIA or something."

Tsai rested his hip against the brick wall and repositioned his foot slightly to bring it in contact with the AK-47, which leaned against the wall, assuring himself out of habit that it was still with him. "You're not thinking this through. Consider this—at the start Yan Whan teams up with an American crime Family and hires protection in Urumchi. Now it's a year later and he needs to trim some of the fat. So he brings in some anonymous help from overseas. The fat gets trimmed—that means us. And we're none the wiser because the Americans are pretending to be CIA. How would we know the difference?"

Seiwei considered that. He looked up and down the empty street as if he expected the object of their discussion to appear at any second. But the street was empty. The only movement was a wisp of smoke from the far side of the building where another pair on the doubled guard duty stood at their post smoking Turkish cheroots. From inside the luxury living quarters of Li's men, Seiwei heard shouts and movement as the occupants strove to deal with the news that suddenly, inexplicably, they were being hunted down and exterminated on their own turf.

"You don't believe me," Tsai stated.

Seiwei shrugged. "I don't know. It makes sense, I suppose...."

Tsai looked purposefully into the distance.

"Whoever it is, you think they'll be after us here, too?"

Tsai nodded almost imperceptibly. Seiwei stepped close to the low wall and craned his neck to see up and down the street, ready for whatever might be coming for them.

BOLAN ASSESSED the second barracks from his lookout point across the street and tucked in the coarse leafy cover of a wild bush. A blacksuit and liberal use of combat cosmetics made him a living shadow in the evening, and the guards, two at each front corner of the building, were unaware he was scrutinizing them.

The barracks was a large, single-story structure. It housed, Bolan guessed, another twenty of Li's special troops, but there was no way to get an accurate head count at the moment: some would be on duty and refugees from the still-burning first barracks might have taken up residence there.

Taking out the building wouldn't be a problem, but effective elimination of all the current occupants was going to present a challenge. The Executioner had no intention of leaving survivors.

He was eyeing the front door when he heard a faint noise behind him, then Jiahua appeared at his side with a hand on his arm.

"What's the deal?"

Bolan indicated the front entrance. "I'm going to play shepherd. I'll try to get everybody running in one direction—out the front door."

"And me?"

"You get to be the she-wolf."

"Meaning I nab them as they exit."

"Yeah. It'll be dirty work." With a look he asked her if she was up for it.

"Oh, I can handle it. What I don't like is that I'll be sitting here with my thumb up my H&K while you get active duty."

"It might not be that easy on this end."

"And I don't have a choice," she added.

"Correct. You brought me into this war. Now we fight my way. This may very well turn out to be a suicide probe. I'm not going to ask you to do it."

"I volunteer."

"Forget it."

Bolan left her crouched against the bushes and crept away, backtracking down the incline then cutting across the street out of sight of the barracks. He approached the building from the side, cutting across open stretches of weedy land, hiding in stands of grass. The approach took fifteen long minutes.

And when the fifteen minutes was done, he had arrived at a point almost directly across the street from where Jiahua crouched. She still waited against the shrubbery, a dim outline even he might not have spotted had he not known her location. She didn't see him at all.

Neither did the two guards. They waited at a low decorative wall that separated the barracks from the surrounding undeveloped land. Its isolation made the work easier for Bolan. Less chance of innocent people getting hurt. He could strike with impunity, execute without regard.

And the first executions of the evening were about to occur.

He wedged the barrel of the Beretta 93-R in a crook of the bush for extra support and sighted carefully on the two men, standing at the wall, heads and shoulders visible.

It was required that he take the guards out silently. If the alert was sounded before he infiltrated, the probe would fail.

A COUGH SOUNDED in the night. Tou Seiwei had no idea what the strange sound was and peered into the darkness, Tsai tumbling into him. At the same instant there was another quick cough, and he was kicked to the ground, knocking over the leaning autorifles.

"Tsai, what's the hell is the matter with you?"

Seiwei pushed at his partner, who was deadweight. Was he sick? Had he passed out? And what were those strange sounds? He felt crumbs of stone falling onto his face and arms, then he spotted the glistening mass that had been the side of Tsai's head.

Seiwei realized his comrade was dead and moaned, shoving the corpse away and scrambling to his feet in a panic.

Then it occurred to him what those coughing sounds had been, and he realized what had caused the brick to shatter where he had been standing. But realization came too slowly. He collapsed to the ground next to Nag Tsai when a silenced round punctured his brain.

BOLAN CROSSED A DOZEN PACES of open space and hurled himself over the low wall, rolling across the grass next to the bodies and jumping to his feet again, landing with his back against the wall of the building. When there was no sign of alarm, he stepped into the open long enough to drag the corpses into the shadows against the building.

Then he stepped into the open in the front of the barracks and waved widely with one hand, whistling once loudly, getting the attention of the two guards stationed at the opposite corner.

Bolan shouted the phrase Jiahua had taught him in Chinese. "Come here! I see something!"

He stepped behind the building and waited, listening to the guards approach in an urgent trot. When they rounded the corner, they had their AK-47s in hand, but weren't prepared to defend themselves instantly. Three suppressed rounds slammed into the torso of the first guard. The second had time only to gasp and stop abruptly. Bolan fired again. Three rounds drilled into the guard's gut as he raised his hands in a vain attempt to protect himself.

Bolan moved on, crouching under windows and stepping to the front door. He pulled the pack from his back and removed one of the HE grenades. He stepped at the front door, primed the piece and pulled the door open.

Two guards were conversing animatedly as they headed to the door, maybe on their way to relieve one of the pairs of guards Bolan had neutralized. They looked up, alarm appearing on their faces.

"Good evening," Bolan said, and lobbed the HE grenade in their direction.

The guards wheeled, their AKs tangling briefly, and sped away from the bouncing metal sphere. They reached the door at the far end of the long vestibule and yanked it open. A thunderclap of fire erupted, the concussion slamming them into each other and shoving them through the doorway. They were broken rag dolls when they hit the ground.

Bolan was already on his way to the north end of the barracks. He didn't duck into a crawl when he came to the next window, but lobbed another HE grenade at the glass. The small pane shattered, and the grenade was gone. As the Executioner circled the north end of the building, the bomb erupted.

Four large windows looked out from the north side of the building. Light shone from two of them, and in the light Bolan made out frantic movement. By now the entire building would be on the alert.

Bolan's goal was to transmute that sense of alert to animal panic.

He had a pack full of the appropriate tools for the job.

He grabbed one, determined by feel alone that it was an explosive, primed the bomb and tossed it through the first lighted window. The timer in his head went from two to three as he chose another grenade—this time an incendiary—and from three to four as he jogged past the second lighted window. The incendiary grenade made an almost musical sound as it tinkled through the glass. The count reached five in that instant, and the tinkling changed to a powerful sound of the building structure cracking. Bolan rode out the tremor and rounded the south end of the building.

He approached the back door, watching as several men raced outside. Another incendiary sailed in their direction, and one of the men spotted it. He started to shout a warning, clawing at the others, trying to retreat into the building. The incendiary grenade fired to life, and the fleeing man and his companions were engulfed in flame.

Bolan heard a crash and rounded the corner to spot a steel chair flying into the lawn in a shower of glass. He snatched the Beretta from its armpit holster and targeted the leg that appeared through the broken window. He fired once and saw a chunk of flesh explode off the shin. The night filled with a scream, and the escapee lost his balance, falling forward onto the shards of glass still wedged in the window. Bolan stepped directly in front of him. The screaming man spotted him and pleaded in Chinese.

Bolan delivered a mercy round, then fired an HE round through the window.

He raced swiftly to the southeast corner of the building, back where he'd started. He paused with his back to the building long enough to feel the impact of the latest explosive, and the last intact window disintegrated. Bolan stepped to it and found two men recovering from the blast. They'd been heading to the window, and now it was a wide-open avenue of escape.

But it was an escape from life itself.

Bolan triggered the police shotgun at the nearer target. The blast turned his chest and stomach to red as if he had been the recipient of an oversize paintball blast, and internal parts glistened in the starlight for a moment before he flew onto his back.

The shotgun was empty. Bolan raised the 93-R and triggered a single shot, and the second enemy gunner dropped.

The Executioner used the shotgun barrel to scrape the glass from the bottom of the windowsill, then climbed into the building and checked the door. There were shouts of confusion and rolling thunderheads of smoke pouring from two directions.

He reloaded both weapons during the lull, then took one of his remaining explosives from the pack, activated it and dropped it between the corpses.

He stepped into the hall, kicked at a wide set of double doors and found himself in a social room. At one end were pool tables and table-tennis tables, at another a set of chairs and couches around a sixty-inch television screen.

There was a cry of anger, and Bolan wheeled in time to see a small, red-faced man slamming into him with a pool cue. Bolan turned deftly and allowed the cue to break against his back, while he fired under his shoulder at the attacker. The 9 mm round burned through his enemy's flesh and shattered his hip before exiting again, sending him to the floor.

Bolan spotted movement on the far side of the room, where one of Li's gunmen was using a couch as a bunker, peering over the back with his AK-47. Bolan dived to the ground as a flurry of 7.62 mm rounds cut through the air above him for almost a full second.

Bolan rose to his knees and searched for the gunman with the AK-47. An inch of muzzle appeared over the back of the couch. The Executioner sighted a good foot and a half below it and fired. The 9 mm round was slowed somewhat by the couch, but Bolan heard a yelp of pain.

The guy had learned that upholstery wasn't bulletproof.

The door burst open behind Bolan and two XSEAs, intent only on escape, stormed through the door. The big American twisted onto his back, firing up at them as they realized their predicament. One grunted and collapsed, but the second pulled back too fast and the 9 mm round slammed into the doorjamb where he had been standing.

Great. Now he had situations to the front and to the rear. If that guy came back through the door with a weapon drawn, Bolan would be helplessly exposed. He walked on his elbows and knees and pushed open the door. Bolan fired as the XSEA policeman spotted him and triggered his weapon. The 9 mm round slammed into him a millisecond sooner and spoiled his aim, sending his round into the wall a foot above Bolan's prone position.

Bolan fired again at the tumbling gunman, cutting into his chest at a sharp angle just before he hit the floor.

He switched the 93-R to autofire and propelled himself to his feet, leveling it at the couch-sitter's location and firing before he had the location accurately pegged. Three rounds pierced the couch, then three more, all within six inches of one another. Bolan heard a clatter that he knew was the AK hitting the floor. He ran toward it and found the gunner moving slowly, bleeding from several distinct wounds and fumbling for his weapon. But his vision was blurring fast, and Bolan kicked the assault rifle away. He watched a large blood bubble form from the wounded man's mouth, then it stopped. There was no more breath to further inflate it.

Bolan moved to a side door, yanked it open and stepped into another hallway. No movement in either direction. He headed to the rear of the building, twisting into another doorway, into what proved to be a large dining area. Ceiling rubble littered the single huge table. A voice addressed him rapidly in Chinese.

The big American sank to his knees, leveling the

shotgun. The gunmen hiding under the table realized then he wasn't one of their own. Two of them raised their hands to ward off the shotgun blasts that followed. A useless gesture, as they discovered. The third man had scrambled away from the warrior and received a load of shot in his rear. It was a crippling blast that knocked him on his face. Bolan circled the table, giving the enemy gunner the opportunity to crawl painfully to his feet. When he spotted the shotgun aimed at him for a killing shot, he sobbed once and squeezed his eyes shut. The blast flung him off his feet.

Another dining-room entrance door swung open under a barrage of AK fire, and Bolan dropped to the floor. On his knees he fired the M-3 P, sending the door flying in the other direction, but spotted nothing visible in the smoke and flashes of flame outside the door. But as the door swung shut, he heard a shout from behind it.

"Fuck you, American!"

A barrage of AK fire cut the air at chest level. Bolan scrambled in his pack, withdrawing his final grenade. He sent it bouncing across the floor and through the door before the stream of 7.62 mm rounds halted and the door swung shut. There was a pause, and Bolan curled into a ball, protecting his face. The door shredded in a blaze of orange-and-yellow light. Stinging high-velocity splinters cracked against his body and embedded in his hands and scalp.

He didn't wait for the dust to settle before he was on his feet again.

JIAHUA USED an extremely potent Mandarin vulgarity as another explosion rocked the barracks and she watched her companion riding it out at the side of the building. A moment later he was firing into the window.

Whatever he was firing at had to have died because he climbed into the window after it and was gone. Several seconds later another blast destroyed his point of entrance.

"Shit!"

The woman was scared. She spent a lot of her time with Belasko being scared. But that was because the situations he tended to be attracted to were the most dangerous situations imaginable.

On the other hand it was impossible to conceive of another human being more capable of wading through such danger without getting them both annihilated.

She clearly heard a blast from the shotgun Belasko was dragging around with him. She swallowed hard, dry-mouthed. He had more or less just walked into hell, into a chaos of his own creation. Would he walk out again?

He'd better. She didn't make the most dangerous phone call of her life to have him come over here and get himself killed.

She just wished he had left her with something to do. There was nothing worse than just standing here watching—

Movement. Two men were crawling through the shattered, smoking ruin of the front entrance of the building, trying to get free from the seemingly perpetual explosions and escape.

Jiahua checked the road in both directions. She ran across the open street, now lit by several flickering fires, though in their struggle to get free of the burning building the two men didn't spot the small woman coming at them until she was within twenty paces.

"Hey!" one of the men shouted, bringing his AK to bear. Jiahua triggered the MP-5. Several rounds chopped into him, and he collapsed in the rubble. His buddy grabbed at the fallen AK and swung it at his attacker, but the MP-5 was already firing and the two rounds he managed to trigger went into the rubble. Then he fell into it himself.

Jiahua turned to the street, where headlights had appeared a hundred yards away. They changed to high beams, and the car raced in her direction. She ran into the street and stood her ground long enough to trigger a volley of rounds at the approaching vehicle, then dived back into the bushes that had served as her cover.

The station wagon screeched to a halt in the street, and Jiahua laid on the MP-5, sweeping it back and forth across the side of the car, shattering windows and puncturing body panels before the weapon emptied. She fell to her knees, retreating backward in the bush into a small depression, then grabbed a spare mag from her belt and slapped it into the MP-5. She flattened on her stomach as the station wagon gunners finally returned fire with a couple of AKs and at least one large-caliber handgun. Her bush didn't stand a chance. If she had still been in its vicinity, pieces of her would have been flying around the field, as well.

"Turn your lights on the field."

"Can you see her?"

"No. She's dead. We'll go get her later."

"She might still be out there."

"She's dead!" There was a rattle of more AK fire from within the building. "Come on! Sang, you stay!"

"Sang, you're mine," Jiahua muttered. She rose cautiously to her knees and began to creep to the road again. Sang was a gaunt, tall man. He was pacing in a slow circle, keeping one eye on the field and one on his companions as they waded into the rubble of the burn-ing building.

The others disappeared, and he turned his attention fully on the field. Sang, for one, wasn't totally con-vinced that she was dead. Smart man. What Jiahua needed now was a distraction so she could move in close enough to reward the man for his caution.

There was another explosion from the barracks. Jia-hua grimaced and mentally thanked Belasko for his clairvoyance. Sang spun toward the building and watched the ball of fire that burst from the roof of the building.

Jiahua ran through the weeds, the rolling thunder of the blast covering the sound of her footsteps. She hit the pavement before Sang heard her. He wheeled, but the MP-5 was already speaking. He got off a few rounds, Jiahua diving to the left to avoid the 7.62 mm rounds that cut into the street. She hit the pavement, executing a judo roll. The guard was deflating on the pavement when the woman returned to her feet and trig-gered a few extra rounds in his skull. He slumped dead. She kicked him in the ribs once, then rifled his pockets, withdrawing a ring of keys.

The CIA agent faced the building. The various small fires and the newest explosion of flame were spreading rapidly. Soon the entire building would be ablaze. Be-lasko was in there alone, and another three gunman had just gone in after him, cutting off his only exit.

She checked the mag in the MP-5 nervously. A gas line or something overheated and blew, and a fresh plume of yellow-and-blue flame jetted toward the sky. There was the sound of gunfire.

"Damn you, Belasko!" Jiahua whispered fiercely, then ran into the conflagration.

BEYOND THE DINING ROOM was a kind of board-room—or it had been before Bolan's last HE grenade transformed it to rubble. The ruined chairs had been covered with rich leather, and the shards of the table looked like highly polished cherry wood. A bar against the wall was dripping, the air heavily laden with the smell of rum. A whoosh of sound greeted Bolan just as he entered the room, and the distilled spirits ignited, making a sudden bonfire of the wall.

A hint of movement beyond the next door drew Bolan's attention, and he threaded quickly through the rubble to stand behind the door when it was shoved open.

The first man to enter saw the remains of one of his comrades and made a long, low exclamation. He stepped to the edge of the mess, followed by another man. The second man glanced away from the human ruin and scanned the room, finally spotting the big American.

Bolan stalked in their direction, and the shotgun blasted in his grip. The first man flopped to the floor. The second twisted his neck toward his attacker, and never had the opportunity to use the gun in his hands. The shotgun roared again, and he was flung onto his face.

Gunfire erupted in the next room, and Bolan headed quickly for cover. None of the rounds was making it into his room, and he heard machine-gun fire, noticeably different from the AK fire. The living inferno was creeping at him like it knew he was there. It was time to depart.

He watched a figure backing into the corner of the next hallway, his AK rattling into the wreckage that had once been the front door. It was impossible to see who the newcomer was, but Bolan knew. He drew the 93-R and fired three rounds, stepping into the hall after them. The enemy gunner looked at him with surprise, not registering his fresh wounds, and for a moment Bolan thought he was going to ask him where he had come from. Then he simply died.

"Cello!"

"Belasko! You okay?" She didn't give him time to answer—he saw her rise from a toppled section of wall and retreat to where the front door had been.

"Reinforcements arriving!" she shouted.

Picking his way through the rubble, he reached her side as she was slamming another mag into the subgun and checking her Colt. A single dark automobile was slowing outside.

"That's one of Chief Li's armored cars," Bolan noted.

"Yeah."

"Wait until they are away from it to attack."

"Okay."

The car rolled to a halt in the street, as far away from the building as possible, and the occupants sat inside for fifteen seconds.

"Belasko, it's getting hot in here," Jiahua warned.

Bolan nodded. He could already feel the searing fire crawling toward them.

The rear car door opened, and a single man stepped onto the asphalt with a Browning Hi-Power gripped at chest level. He didn't close the door behind him, and Bolan saw no other occupant in the rear seat.

He also noted the aura of yellow flame around them. His back was burning hot.

The gunman stepped cautiously around the abandoned car, spotting Sang's corpse. He nudged the body with his foot, then faced the building again and shouted.

"He asked if there is anybody here," Jiahua commented.

Bolan nodded. "I'll take care of him. On my signal you go for the car. Try to stop it."

She nodded, panting. Her face was red and drenched in sweat. Bolan knew how she felt. The temperature in the space had risen about forty degrees in the past minute, and he could almost feel the fire licking his back.

The gunman peered into the wreckage, unable yet to make out the human shapes crouched inside. He took another step, and Bolan glimpsed sudden alarm in his eyes.

"Now!" he said loudly, standing up all at once and leveling the 93-R. Three 9 mm rounds chugged into the surprised gunman, hammering his collarbone and forehead. Jiahua launched lithely into the open, laying on the MP-5's trigger, going for the tires as the car screeched to life, filling the night with the white smoke of stressed rubber. Then the rear tire popped, deflating instantly. The car continued to pull away, the rear door swinging shut, chunks of ruined rubber flying.

Bolan and Jiahua extricated themselves from the burning building.

"They've got drivable rims," Bolan said. "Too bad."

Jiahua grinned and held up a ring of keys. "Look what I've got. Too bad for them."

Bolan nodded and grinned. "I'll drive."

CHAPTER SEVEN

It took less than two minutes for Bolan to bring the station wagon up on the rear of the fleeing car.

"Now what?" Jiahua asked.

"Take out more tires," Bolan said.

"What good will that do? The bastard's running fine on a rim."

"Do it!"

The woman rolled down her window. Bolan accelerated suddenly, coming alongside the armored car, and Jiahua triggered the MP-5 into the front tire. It popped and deflated.

"That ought to do it," Bolan told her, drifting behind the armored car again.

"Do what?" she demanded.

"He's riding on rims on the left side."

"Those rims are good up to fifty miles per hour!"

"But they loose maneuverability quickly at faster speeds," Bolan explained, and floored the battered station wagon. The vehicle slammed into the rear of the armored car and kept accelerating. Bolan pumped the speed up to fifty-five before the other driver started to apply his brakes.

They began to descend a small hill, and Bolan made the most of it, pushing the two cars to faster speeds, feeling the shuddering of the armored vehicle as the brakes tried to fight him. They reached the bottom of the hill at sixty-five miles per hour.

A curve loomed a few hundred yards ahead of them.

The armored car was shuddering desperately, and the smell of the burning brakes was pungent. Bolan felt a lurch and knew that the brakes on at least one of the wheels were gone. His foot was to the floor, and he pumped it, trying to gain more power from the engine of the station wagon.

The cars shook and rumbled, and Bolan felt another lurch as something else on the armored car failed. He revved the engine one last time, feeding the armored car one small extra push. The two vehicles were traveling together at seventy-three miles per hour.

Then he applied his own brakes.

The armored car shot ahead, brakes smoking, wheels twisting as the driver vainly attempted to navigate the curve, the rims on the right side pulling the vehicle to the left. The armored car flopped off the pavement and bounced through the empty land, slamming into a depression with a crash and bouncing out again, the rear end flying several feet into the air, hovering there for a fraction of a second. The nose of the vehicle hit the ground first, crunching, and the rest of it came to a rest with the subtlety of a collapsing skyscraper.

Bolan pulled to a halt at the shoulder of the road and made his way to the wreckage. He yanked at the driver's door and aimed at the interior with the 93-R.

A single man flopped at his feet, his forehead possessing a curious concave shape. His skull was completely coated with blood, his hair matted and dripping. In the dim light of night the figure's eyeballs rolled up to Bolan with a curious white glow.

"Think he'll live?" Jiahua asked, approaching with her Colt gripped in both hands. The eyes rolled to her as she spoke.

"Probably. At least for a while," Bolan said. "Which means he's useful."

CHIEF QUAN LI ARRIVED at his new temporary offices at 2:12 a.m. At 2:13 a.m. he lifted Wau Niax by the throat and slammed him into the wall. His hands were instantly covered with Niax's blood. The man's eyes fluttered open, curiously white against the bright red aspect of his head. If he recognized Li, he didn't react.

"I want to know who did this," Li said as evenly as he could. "I want to know their names and their tactics and every word they told you."

Niax slid down the wall, streaking it with blood, until he rested in a half-recline on the cot that had been hastily prepared for him. The crater at the front of his skull seemed to inflate and deflate like an air bladder.

"An American man and...the same Chinese woman."

"Who else?"

"No one."

"That's a lie."

"I saw no one else," Niax protested weakly.

Li paced the length of the small office. Lieutenant Lin and Lieutenant Hai sat in their chairs against the wall. Both knew when silence was the best tactic.

"All right. What did they say to you?"

"He said to tell you his name was Abe."

"I know that! Don't you think I know that? What else did he say?"

"Only that I was supposed to tell you to be at your

office with your two top lieutenants at 2:25 a.m. That he would call you here and present his demands.''

"His demands! Demands! Who does this bastard think he is?''

Niax hadn't the strength to reply.

The plain truth was Chief Quan Li was scared. Not of the American—his new office was windowless. He no longer traveled anywhere without the two bodyguards waiting just outside the door. The American could never get at him now.

It was Yan Whan. Whan had already received word of the attacks. He knew Li's men were getting killed off and had summoned Li for a meeting with him at noon—ten hours away. Who knew what Whan would do when he found out the extent of the compromise of Li's forces? More than fifty percent had been obliterated. Not to mention the attack on the stolen-car transport. Whan would consider that an attack against him personally—but an attack that Li's men should have been able to fend off.

And Li had no idea what he was going to say in defense of himself.

The phone rang.

"This is Li," he said in Mandarin.

"Speak English."

"This is Li," he repeated in English. "Who is this?"

"This is Abe. I'm ready to make a deal if you are, Chief."

"To hell with you! You hear me? No deals!"

"I'm going to get that book of evidence, Li. What's it going to take to convince you to give it up?"

"You better get out of my town because when I find you I'm going to rip your throat out! And I'm going to shoot—"

The line went dead.

Li stared at the phone, and Lieutenant Lin could almost see the rage seeping out through his eyes like compressed steam whistling through the leaks in a boiler seal. Then the phone was flying across the room and hit the bloody spot on the wall where Niax had been resting. It fell on the cot with Niax, who lay with his eyes open, staring at nothing, mocking the Chief from death.

Li realized he had let his rage get the better of him. He had the man on the phone. He should have been able to put together some sort of plan to draw him out, make him show himself. He gazed at the dead gunman on the cot and forced himself to regain control.

Rage accomplished nothing.

"Let's go."

With his entourage of two lieutenants and two bodyguards, he marched down the two flights of stairs, considering his alternatives.

Maybe he could have figured some way to grab the American by the following morning. It would have been infinitely better if he could have gone to Yan Whan with the perpetrator of all his problems in captivity.

Forget it. It was too late to undo it now. He had to concentrate on protecting what was left of his forces in Urumchi.

The evidence he had taken from the woman illustrated her in-depth knowledge of Yan Whan's operations. She and her partner had done an expert job of mapping out the Li–Yan Whan organization, the members, where the various operations were located and what they did. It was obvious the American was making good use of this information.

Well, at least Li could minimize future damage.

"Lin, we are going to move all the men. Now."

"Tonight?"

"Now. I want all our current barracks and offices abandoned. If our American friend targets one of them, I want him to come up empty, understand?"

"Yes. I'll get right on it."

"Hai, I want a new barracks identified by tomorrow afternoon. Someplace that can be better defended and with an unbreachable security system. Starting tomorrow night we'll have everybody in one locale. We will make it a fortress that's impossible to penetrate."

"Yes. Good plan."

They stepped into the street. Hai locked the door behind them. Urumchi was dark, cool, silent, and it was hard to believe the city was out of his control when it seemed so peaceful.

"Damn car's got a flat," one of the bodyguards said. Then his head exploded from his shoulders.

THE NIGHT-VISION SCOPE on the Ruger sniper rifle brought Li's men up close and personal. Bolan watched them exit the building, waiting for the door to shut behind them and carefully getting a fix on the location of each man. There were four targets. He chose the driver first, a burly man who said something to the others— probably noticing the tire Bolan had knifed.

The .458 Winchester Magnum cartridge was a hammerhead that exploded the driver's skull like a slab of concrete dropped on a chicken egg. Bolan searched quickly, found the second bodyguard and directed the next Magnum round into his chest. He sighted on one of the lieutenants and fired a third time, but the darkness and Hai's reaction time conspired against Bolan. The round crashed into the concrete where the lieutenant had been standing.

Bolan inserted three fresh rounds into the magazine while surveying the situation. From his vantage point across the street and five stories up, the only hiding place was behind the car. None of them had figured out where the attack was originating.

Hai was running in one direction down the street, while Lin and Li were heading down the other. Bolan sighted on Hai, rode out the blast of the round and was satisfied to see him collapsing on the street. He swept the Ruger to the left, sighted on Lin and triggered again. The man fell. Li pulled up short and gazed at the body. He looked wildly for an avenue of escape, but none presented itself. He ran forward, blindly, for the nearest alley, a good twenty-five paces away. The concrete exploded under his feet, and he flopped to the ground, the pavement scraping his palms.

"Ready to deal now, Li?" Bolan shouted when the booms of the gunshots had faded and the night was quiet and still. Li realized that he was suddenly alone.

"Think fast, Li."

The Chief raised his bloody hands. "All right! Don't shoot! What do you want?"

"You know what I want, Li. The attaché. The evidence. All of it, intact."

"I'll get it for you! I don't have it now!"

"I've been watching you, Li. I know where you stay. I know where you sleep. I know where you eat." It was an exaggeration, but Li didn't know that. "If I don't get that attaché tomorrow, I'm going to come after you. I'll hunt you down as easily as I hunted you down tonight. Understand?"

"Yes!"

"I want you to bring it to the village of Rong. Be in

the main square of the village tomorrow at 9:00 a.m., with the attaché, alone.''

''All right!''

''Repeat it.''

''Rong, town square, 9:00 a.m., alone!''

Li sat in the street waiting for more instructions.

''What do I do now?'' he asked finally.

There was no answer.

''You still there?''

Li waited another twenty seconds, then got slowly to his feet. He walked to the sprawled forms of his lieutenants and bodyguards. None lived.

The Chief allowed himself to vent a screech of impractical, unproductive rage into the night.

RONG VILLAGE WAS a dismal farm collective ten miles northeast of the city of Urumchi. Ramshackle wooden hovels housed large, crowded families that would have known better living conditions living naked in huts in the jungle. Situated on the very southern edge of what would be considered arable land in the Urumchi area, the villagers fought to force the land to produce dryland crops—sorghum and millet, mostly—to meet government-mandated economic incentives that, when achieved, meant adequate food. When not achieved, winters were long and lean.

Jiahua knew the village well enough, knew that at 9:00 a.m. it would be largely empty. Grandmothers too old for field work would be in the homes cooking lunch. The children would be in the fields or in the school at the south end of the town.

She served as a lookout, planted in a small flat looking out into the square. Her walkie-talkie hissed at 8:30 a.m.

"You should see what's rolling into town—he must have fifteen vehicles," Bolan told her. "Now they are splitting up and circling. They're trying to surround the town."

"What're we going to do about them?"

"Ignore them."

"You don't really think the Chief's going to come through with my attaché?"

"It's possible."

Twenty minutes later a single car rolled into the small town square. The Chief stopped it in the street and left the engine running. The square was empty. Li looked around, then spotted the radio Bolan left standing on a crude decorative brick monument. He headed toward it, picked it up, spoke into it.

"I'm here. Where are you?"

"Leave the attaché. Leave town. Take your troops with you."

Li scanned the square, but saw no movement.

"Not good enough," he said into the radio.

"I spared your life. Are you not a man of honor, Chief Li?"

"I'm not a man who bows to cheap intimidation."

"I cost you dozens of men and two pieces of real estate. There's nothing cheap about it."

Li didn't answer. He went to his car.

Jiahua quickly snapped to the frequency the Chief used. She beeped Bolan three times, indicating he should switch to their alternate frequency. "He's ordered a search."

"I already see them coming. Keep me up-to-date."

Bolan clicked off.

Two gunmen started on the end of the small street, kicking open the door to one of the homes. They stomped inside, looked around quickly and reappeared. There weren't many places to hide in the meager homes of the Rong people.

And not too many homes to hide in. The village had less than fifty dwellings, buildings left over from China's enthusiastic collective-farming days.

Bolan watched them enter the next house. They would reach him in five minutes tops if he waited for them.

He had no intention of doing so.

He stepped into the street. An old woman across the patch of dry earth saw him emerge. She knew at once the Westerner shouldn't have been lurking in her neighbor's house. He withdrew the Beretta 93-R from his shoulder holster, and she chose not to interfere.

Bolan had expected this battle. There had been only the dimmest hope that the Chief would come through with the attaché and save himself a lot of trouble. Few men who had marched that far down the road of inhumanity can be dragged back, even when faced with death.

Now the Chief was in a desperate situation. He had only two choices: kill Bolan, or be killed by him.

Bolan stepped quietly through the dusty space between the buildings and waited for the two hardmen to emerge.

The two officers were shouting angrily inside the house, and a woman's voice, sobbing and pleading, answered them. Bolan couldn't understand the words, but the meaning was clear enough. He hugged the wall of the building.

They stepped out of the house.

"Hey."

They turned in unison, and the Beretta coughed

twice, drilling each of them in the skull from just a yard away. They crumpled to the dirt.

There was a gasp, and Bolan turned the 93-R instantly on the doorway of the house. Another old woman was standing there, hand to her mouth, regarding him with teary-eyed terror. She squeezed her eyes tightly shut in the face of the autopistol.

She opened them a moment later and saw that the gun was no longer aimed at her. The Westerner who held it raised a single finger to his lips.

Quiet, he was saying to her.

Quiet she could be. She closed the door and burrowed into a storage nook behind a bag of rice.

Bolan bent and relieved one of the corpses of its assault rifle, then grabbed the magazine from the other dead man's weapon.

He listened and heard shouts from a hundred yards off. Bolan stalked them to their source. Another two XSEA officers were searching a house. Their technique was more intelligent. One stood guard outside while the other covered the dwelling. They alternated tasks at the next house.

Bolan waited behind a wall as they shouldered open a door. As one man entered, the Executioner approached the guard. Before the man could heft his weapon, he leveled the 93-R and triggered a round. His intention had been to maintain the silence, but the dying guard didn't cooperate. He crashed to the ground, screaming, and managed to trigger his Kalashnikov.

The rattle of autofire was a summons that traveled from one end of the tiny village to the other.

Bolan stepped to the wall, waiting until he heard movement in the window above him. The second guard had opened the window just enough to find out what was happening and saw his companion lying in an expanding pool of blood.

Bolan stepped into the open and aimed at the window with the 93-R set on burst mode. Three 9 mm manglers ripped into the second guard mercilessly. Bolan heard his screams and would have to assume the man was out of commission. He couldn't afford to hang around one second longer.

He bolted toward the center of the village, grabbing the walkie-talkie from his belt.

"Cello?"

"Jesus, where've you been? They heard shots! They're going crazy!"

"Describe what's happening."

Movement to his left brought the soldier up short, and he fell back behind a wall. The open ground between the buildings became dusty with autofire ripping into the dirt where he had been running.

Bolan probed blindly around the corner with the stolen AK and triggered a dozen rounds, then backtracked, circling the small building in seconds, coming upon his two attackers staged behind a kitty-corner building. One was yelling into a radio. Bolan bolted in their direction, firing the AK on the run, and their heads jerked up. The rounds cut across their chests, shattered the radio and the hand that held it, and they slumped to the ground.

The Executioner navigated the bodies, spotted movement to the right and triggered the AK, the line of 7.62 mm rounds stitched a path up the hardman's leg, into his groin, stomach and chest.

Bolan reloaded the Kalashnikov and set off toward the center of town.

He had a promise to keep to the corrupt chief of police of Urumchi.

Li FORCED HIMSELF to speak calmly into the radio.

"Where's it coming from?"

"Northeast of your position."

"Tell me you've got men moving that way."

"Yes, sir. We are redeploying the search parties from the south part of the village with vehicles."

"I want all other personnel in the village moving in a sweep in that direction. We'll make a sandwich out of him."

"Got it."

JIAHUA TURNED from her radio monitor to her walkie-talkie. She was risking being overheard if Chief Li had somebody scanning the frequencies. Not likely, she judged. She explained Li's orders to Bolan.

"Where's Li?" he asked.

"I'm watching him now. He's stationed himself in the square."

"I'm coming in."

"You're going to have to be damn clever to get past them."

She heard nothing more, again forced to stand and wait. Why couldn't she go out and get Li herself?

But she'd promised Belasko to stay there and monitor the situation. The information she fed him was worth more than her fighting skills at the moment, and Belasko would join her. She had every confidence. He was pretty damned clever, when it came down to it. The most skilled warrior, in fact, that she had ever known.

But there were twenty or thirty less-skilled hardmen marching through the town at that very moment, Belasko their one and only target. She watched a group on the far side of the square pass through. They waved briefly to Li.

At some point strength in numbers would inevitably overcome skill.

Had Belasko reached that point?

THE RUMBLE OF AN ENGINE signaled a four-wheel-drive vehicle careening around the corner, and Bolan slid behind a wooden refuse box in time to remain unseen. Two men stood in the open back, scanning for any sign of him.

He saw one of the men wave briefly as he headed toward the center of the village. More men were coming, maybe planning an ambush. Bolan cut across a stretch of open ground and checked quickly for other patrols.

Rong was a streetless town. The wooden structures had been erected in what was essentially a haphazard fashion. The open stretches of bare dirt between the structures served as yard and as street, although there were probably few motorized vehicles in town. The unstructured configuration confounded search patterns. At the same time, it made it harder for Bolan to judge where searchers would be likely to appear.

He found the men he was looking for, a three-man team this time. He contemplated skipping over them; neutralizing three men silently would be next to impossible.

But they took their search in his direction. Ignoring them was no longer an option unless he could locate a hiding place in a hurry.

Two had their AKs at the ready. Another stood at the door of a small house, peering inside. Bolan contemplated his strike—how could he get the two of them before they returned fire?

The walkie-talkie squawked at the belt of one of the

gunmen. He lowered his autorifle and raised the communicator, speaking into it briefly. A string of orders came from the tiny speaker. The radioman nodded and returned the device to his belt at the same instant the lead man was turning away from the open door. That was the instant Bolan chose to strike.

He stepped into the open and fired three rounds from the 93-R into the gunman, who snatched at his chest and gagged on blood. As he was dropping, the soldier turned the handgun on the radioman. He wasn't fast enough to get his Kalashnikov operative and was driven to the ground by three manglers.

The lead man shouted wordlessly and snatched at the pistol in his belt. He was fast. The pistol was out and discharged faster than Bolan would have judged the man was capable, but his precision didn't match his speed. The rounds zipped a few feet to Bolan's left.

The Executioner's precision, however, was good—the three rounds nearly cut the hand holding the pistol off the body and the man fell to the ground, triggering the weapon into the air.

The shouts and the gunplay would bring Li's men running. Bolan shot off through the village. Speed would have to carry him now, speed and luck.

A gunman with an AK ran into the open before him, gaping in surprise at the big American, who swerved and plowed him to the ground. He retained his grip on his AK and waved it wildly, trying to get a fix on Bolan. A carefully placed kick landed against the gunman's skull, and he was effectively taken out of play.

Bolan's earpiece buzzed. "Where are you?" Jiahua demanded. "They think they've got you fixed!"

The Executioner grabbed his own walkie-talkie. "Get to the car!"

"Where are you?"

"I'll be in the square in two minutes. Meet me there."

"Li's there!"

"Alone?"

"At the moment."

"Pick me up there. Be ready to move!"

BOLAN SAW THE SQUARE ahead and at the same instant detected footsteps behind him. He bolted to the right suddenly, twisted so that he was running backward, and got a fix on the pursuit. A gunman was trying to slow from a run and acquire a target. Bolan backed into the square and triggered five rounds from the AK, only one making contact with the gunman, who grabbed the side of his head and yelped.

The Executioner faced the square and spotted Chief Li running at the garage as Jiahua was extracting their car. Li wheeled at the sound of the nearby gunfire, revealing a machine pistol in his right hand. Bolan triggered the 93-R and Li screamed, rolling to the ground, dropping the machine pistol but at once grabbing for it with his good hand. Bolan stepped into him and kicked the weapon away.

"Who the hell are you, anyway?" he demanded.

Without waiting for a reply, Li made a desperate move, going for his hideout weapon in an ankle sheath.

Bolan triggered the 93-R, and a burst of 9 mm rounds ripped through Chief's Li's torso, destroying his heart, splintering his ribs, flooding his lungs with blood before nailing into the ground beneath him.

CHAPTER EIGHT

The sun set late over the Junggar Basin. The mountains were impossibly distant, and the land was impossibly wide, growing virtually nothing except for scraggly tufts of grass. The wall that rose suddenly out of the grassland resembled nothing so much as some mythical lost wasteland city in an *Arabian Nights* tale.

Sun Hwang had been trained in the Yan Whan complex but never failed to be impressed by the almost medieval grandeur of the wall standing in the flat grassland. He had never dreamed he would be ushered inside it as an honored guest.

In fact, when he woke up that morning he wouldn't have thought it possible that by the end of the day he would be thrust into the leadership position of Yan Whan's Urumchi-based XSEA forces.

Fate was a funny thing. Just when he was feeling like his years of struggle were getting him nowhere, it all paid off spectacularly.

A person took opportunities when they presented themselves.

The opportunity Hwang sought had come just thirteen hours earlier, when he had been running around the small village of Rong, northeast of Urumchi, chasing the man who had been gunning down XSEA troops with uncanny success in the past few days. He had been on search-and-destroy detail with his longtime friend Cheng. Cheng was his immediate superior among Chief Li's ranks, by virtue of his three weeks of seniority. That position had never resulted in Cheng actually issuing orders to Sun Hwang. They were more like partners.

Then the killing had started. Impossible that there was a single man involved. They found several dead throughout the village before they heard the news over their radio that Chief Li was dead and the perpetrator and his female Chinese accomplice had escaped.

Hwang and Cheng headed back to the village square. All the men would be gathering there. No one seemed to be in charge anymore. Apparently Li's new lieutenant, appointed just a few hours before, was among the dead.

Hwang thought about that situation quickly. All of a sudden Cheng had risen to the top of the survivors list, and Hwang was right behind Cheng.

He ran for one of the buildings, calling for his friend.

"Another American!" he cried. "I saw him go inside this building!"

Cheng and Hwang burst into the home. There was no one on the lower level. The family members were in the field. Silently, wide-eyed, Hwang pointed upstairs.

Cheng nodded and led the way up. Hwang was right behind him, drawing his stiletto, chopping at Cheng's Achilles tendon and yanking him backward down the steps.

The look on Cheng's face was one of shock, then the pain set in and the realization that his best friend had done the deed.

"Why?"

Hwang said nothing. Cheng tried to fight off the stiletto. He couldn't, not lying on his back and with one arm broken. The blade cut his throat ear to ear.

The killer wiped the blade on the corpse's shirt and stalked quickly to the village square. He jumped onto the only bench in the square.

"XSEAs!" he called out. "I'm in charge now. Anybody have a problem with that?"

Fate was a funny thing.

The gate opened to the Yan Whan compound. Four guards waited inside. Security cameras watched him from the inside of the wall and from the top of the small guard cabin. The guards looked at him and made a phone call.

Sun Hwang had always been uneasy around Yan Whan's men. They weren't ex-cops or street recruits like his men. Very few of them even came from this district. They had presumably come with Yan Whan when he started up his Urumchi operations. They were an effective fighting force, and he knew they managed Yan Whan's manufacturing operations in a highly efficient manner.

The guard hung up the phone and waved the car toward the house.

"I THINK WE'RE GOING to have to resign ourselves to the loss of your evidence."

Jiahua stalked to the window. This time she had rented a tiny flat in the Red Hill district on the east bank of the Urumchi River. In this quieter, more residential section of the city, they were less likely to be noticed. They came and went through a walled, junk-filled rear entrance, which allowed them to come and go from their vehicle with some measure of privacy.

She looked out into the dusty street, where a woman with a hand-drawn wagon was struggling up the incline. She said under her breath, "Kim Ping died for that evidence!"

"No. He sacrificed himself to free the people Yan Whan subjugated."

"Regardless. That sacrifice hasn't meant much to them, has it?"

"Not yet."

"What do you mean by that?" Jiahua turned to face him.

"If we walk away now, then his death will have meant nothing, no legal moves in China or in the U.S. to stop the slave labor or the smuggling of the goods. Everything proceeds as normal."

"Are you saying you want to try to put it down ourselves?"

"I'm game."

"No, you're insane, Belasko. Taking on the XSEAs was dangerous enough. Yan Whan's got twice the men. They're more skilled, and they're very well equipped."

"You've scoped them out. You know the location of all the slave-labor operations, the manufacturing facilities, the prisons, the housing for his hardmen. You told me yourself you've got in-depth intel on all aspects of the operation—everything except Yan Whan's home compound."

"Yeah, and that intel and a little common sense lead me quickly to the conclusion that going up against Yan Whan is sure suicide." Jiahua looked out on the street again. The woman with the cart had stopped to rest. Life was an uphill struggle.

The quiet grew uncomfortable. "You're staying," she said into the hanging silence.

"As incongruous as it sounds, I've embarked on suicide missions before."

"Yeah, I bet."

"You don't have to stay. I'll debrief you and arrange for you to get transported out of Urumchi. You can go back to Langley for some recuperation time."

"I don't want to go back to Langley!" She stomped to the table and flopped into the seat across from him. "All right, we'll commit suicide together! I'm staying."

THE DOOR OPENED into an office that was the size of the house Sun Hwang had grown up in. The carpeting made him feel like he was walking on cushions.

"Sit down. Would you like a drink?"

The woman who emerged from the side door was statuesque and corn-silk blond, a distinct oddity in the northwest corner of the People's Republic. She spoke English with an accent that Hwang thought might be German.

"Yes, thank you," he said.

She poured him something from a black-labeled bottle. Only then did Hwang realize he should have specified what precisely he wanted to drink. He sniffed the glass she brought him. Whatever it was, it grabbed his throat when it went down.

The blond woman smiled and leaned against the desk. "Yan Whan will be with you shortly."

Hwang nodded and sipped the drink again. He smiled at the warmth already filling his insides.

The woman laughed and touched his shoulder when she walked by. Hwang watched her leave the room. She was dressed in the kind of tight, high-slit, low-cut dress he had seen in European dinner parties in the movies.

"Impressive, isn't she?"

Yan Whan entered the room, and Hwang jumped to his feet.

"Sit down," Whan said impatiently. He laid a small stack of folders and papers on the desk before him, separated them into nine different stacks and arranged them in a neat grid on the desk. Then he sat down himself and, one at a time, transferred the documents from their position to the empty blotter directly in front of him. He studied each and every document in turn until Hwang began to wonder if Whan remembered he was there.

"Born in 1968 in Urumchi to Muslim parents and attended Urumchi University," Whan said suddenly, and Hwang was shocked to realize the document was about him. "Initially studied agriculture and industrial mechanics. Later added course work in management and law enforcement. Graduated 1989. Joined the Urumchi police force in 1990. Became an initiated member of the XSEA three years ago."

Hwang didn't know how to react to this information. "Yes, sir."

"You've risen fast under Chief Li."

"Yes, sir."

"And now you are in line to take command of the XSEAs."

Hwang didn't know what to say to that so he said nothing.

Whan leaned back. His chair was a highly polished leather that seemed to match his slate gray suit. The suit was expertly tailored for Whan's lean frame, and it cost more than most Chinese families made in two years. Whan was a thin, neat man in his early fifties, with clear dark eyes and tanned skin that was just beginning to sag at the jowls and under the chin. He took off gold wire-frame glasses and tapped Sun Hwang's file on his desk as he regarded the man.

"Chief Li failed me, Sun Hwang."

The statement hung in the air.

"He did his job well enough for many years. But when the crisis emerged, he was unable to function adequately."

Hwang considered his response to this. He nodded slightly. "Yes, sir."

"Can you say anything else, Sun Hwang?"

"I don't wish to speak badly of my predecessor. He died only this morning."

"He died because he acted impulsively. There is no reason not to speak badly of him.

"I don't know who you are, Sun Hwang. Normally I would have followed the career of potential XSEA officers. I would have watched your progress, received reports from your superiors, observed your rise through the ranks. But not this time. Due to out-of-control circumstances, I'm putting you in charge and I haven't the faintest idea who you are. You can see why this would be worrisome."

Hwang nodded.

"You're going to have to earn my confidence. You're going to have to demonstrate your ability to lead the XSEAs—such as they are. If you demonstrate competence, you'll retain that position."

"I will. You'll see. I'm ambitious and I'm a skilled leader."

"So was Chief Li. You'll have to do better than that. You're taking control at a dangerous time. You know that well enough." Whan put on his glasses again, then picked up the file. "The XSEAs are mostly Uygur. Do you think you will have any problems convincing them to follow a Muslim?''

''I won't let that become an issue.''

''Good. Then there's the problem of the American.''

Hwang nodded. He wished he hadn't taken the damn drink. He couldn't figure out what to do with the glass.

''What are your thoughts on this problem?''

''I think that Chief Li's plan to draw him out was good, but he failed to follow through with it. He acted rashly, failing to keep his operation organized.''

''And you think you can organize and execute a better plan?''

''I know I can.''

''Good. Because—make no mistake, Sun Hwang—finding and neutralizing the American and his accomplice is your one and only responsibility. Until he's found and exterminated, normal operations cannot continue. Once he's out of the picture, you can take over where Chief Li left off. Do you understand?''

''Yes.''

''Chief Li became a very rich man working for me. You know that, don't you?''

''Yes, sir.''

''You could be wealthier than he was before you turn thirty-five. You can be one of the wealthiest men in the city of Urumchi.''

Hwang nodded and smiled.

''And wealth very definitely has its advantages. Whan touched a button on his phone, and almost instantly the door opened and the blond European woman entered.

''Yes, sir?'' the woman asked.

''Birgitte, fix Mr. Hwang another drink.''

THE NEW TOYOTA HAD BEEN rented at one of the American chain hotels on Xinhua Road. Bolan cruised the industrial districts all morning, waiting for Jiahua to identify their target. They were about to make their first strike directly against Whan.

It had been twenty-four hours since the attack at Rong. Things were entirely too peaceful for Bolan's tastes.

Just before 11:00 a.m. Jiahua said, "Now we're cookin'." She indicated a large stretch limousine pulling to a stop in front of a concrete slab of a building—a building they had patrolled three times already that morning.

Four men stepped out, buttoning their full-cut jackets in the fashion of gun-toting hoods and law enforcers worldwide. They were followed by a small, crew-cut old man with a wrinkled brow and a suit that looked threadbare and faded.

"What've we got?" Bolan asked.

"We've got Ivan the Russian. He works for Yan Whan as a shakedown man. Those goons are Ivan's personal staff," Jiahua explained.

"And who are they shaking down?"

"Little Swan Ceramics is the name of the place. It's a small business making replicas of ancient Chinese dynasty vases. Maybe fifty employees, marginally skilled."

"What does Yan Whan want with Little Swan?"

"He wants the business itself, mostly because it's a successful business in his territory and he wants to control all of them. Little Swan is making some money because it sells to two U.S. department-store chains. Whan's goal is to take over the business and make a few changes. If he can install his own staff of what is essentially free labor, he'll increase his profit margins.''

"Where does Ivan fit into this scheme?"

"Protection. The oldest game in the book. Since it's a manufacturing business, Whan retains the protection rights to it. The XSEAs won't mess with it. In fact, they'll come running if Ivan decides he needs a little extra muscle. But he won't today. The guy who runs Little Swan is an old man who's too afraid to resist. He'll pay what Ivan wants. Eventually the cost will be too high and the old man won't be able to pay. Maybe that will be today.''

The four men had walked to the front of the building and let themselves in. Bolan reached into the back seat for his pack.

"No. It won't be today.''

THERE WERE ENOUGH Russians in the northwestern corner of China, but so few in Yan Whan's ranks that Ivan Szenko was considered a novelty. Thus the nickname. He didn't mind it. Chinese people in this corner of the world were born with a distrust and fear of Russians, and Szenko exploited that fear. He carefully cultivated a Russian accent he had never had. He learned and used Russian words in his everyday speech, especially when he was angry.

He'd turned himself into one of the most intimidating enforcers Yan Whan had ever employed, and intimidation was the single most important character trait for his line of work.

Szenko opened the door to Mr. Chui's office. The old man looked up from his desk and made quick work of finishing his phone conversation. Szenko watched his face age a few extra years when he saw the muscle entering the office with him.

"Yes, yes, I've got the money," Chui said, grabbing a canvas sack from the bottom drawer of his desk and dropping it in front of Szenko, who was making himself as comfortable as possible in the single steel folding chair Chui kept for visitors.

Szenko looked at the canvas sack, then at Chui, disdain on his face. He knew what he would find in the sack, his expression said, and knew it would be inadequate, and he was irritated that Chui even expected him to pick it up and make the count.

But he did it, withdrawing the two stacks of yuan, rifling through them in less than a minute.

He returned them to the canvas sack and threw the sack at Chui, hitting him in the chest, making the old man flinch.

"Not enough."

"It's more than I can afford. Take it and be happy with it."

"It is not enough. You were informed last week that the cost was increasing."

"I tell you it is all I can afford! Take it!" Chui placed the canvas sack in front of Szenko again.

"We've been through this before, Chui. Each time you anger me more."

"I tell you I can't afford your extortion! I had to lay people off just to come up with enough money to cover this! You're driving me out of business with your business tax or whatever you call it."

"I tell you what I call it, Chui," Szenko said, leaning over the desk, making the old man draw back. "I call it ransom. Because it keeps you from getting killed."

"Where are you going to be when you run me out

of business? You won't have any more income from me if this place stops selling anything!''

"That won't happen, Chui. You know it won't. This place will keep going, with or without you."

"You couldn't run this place. There is some skill involved in ceramics, you know—you can't just flop some clay in front of somebody and tell them to start making vases!''

"I'm really growing weary of arguing with you, Chui. We agreed on a sum of cash one week ago. I want that sum now."

"We never agreed on that sum! I told you then that I couldn't possibly afford it, and I'm telling you now!''

Szenko reached across the desk again, this time so quickly it took the old man off guard, and slammed his palm into the old man's eye. Chui bounced out of his chair and slammed into the wall. He clung to it for a moment, gasping, then fell back into his chair, his eye already starting to swell shut. He heard the click of metal and found himself staring into the two-inch barrel of a Smith & Wesson Model 640 Centennial pistol.

"You have mere seconds to live, comrade," Szenko said. "Give me my money."

Chui shook his head slightly. "You will have to kill me, then. I tell you, I have no more money to give!''

Szenko nodded. "So be it."

Chui closed his good eye. He didn't want to look upon the human filth of Szenko and his goons as he died. He wanted to pray. Divine intervention was all that could save him now.

BOLAN AND JIAHUA CROSSED the street quickly, ignored by pedestrians and workers. A cop in a regular Urumchi police uniform was rounding the corner and didn't give them more than a passing glance. The side doors of Little Swan Ceramics were wedged open to allow in the breeze.

They found themselves in a low-ceilinged factory. Even with the doors open, the airflow was barely noticeable and the atmosphere was stifling, radiating from a blazing kiln at the back wall.

A woman at a nearby wheel glanced at them. When Bolan removed his hat, she stared, watching as Bolan and Jiahua headed for the office.

When she saw Bolan draw the Beretta 93-R from under his windbreaker and peer through the slatted window into the office, she got to her feet and silently fled.

The soldier couldn't see more than the back of two of the goons' heads. Jiahua was listening through the slats next to him.

"The old man doesn't have enough," she whispered. "Ivan's threatening him, telling him he better come up with the cash."

Bolan heard a smack, the undeniable sound of flesh impacting flesh. He pictured the old Chinese man crumpling under the fist of Ivan the Russian, and the image angered him.

"Let's go in," he said.

"Yeah, we'd better," she replied, fisting her Colt All American pistol.

Bolan put his hand on the doorknob and nodded to his companion. He yanked it open quickly and fired the instant he spotted one of Ivan's goons. The 93-R slammed him in the head and tipped him into the wall.

Jiahua stepped into the office, sighted the Colt and triggered it.

The conditions had already been crowded with six men in the small room. Now chaos erupted. Bolan fired a round at another enforcer who tried to get at the handgun under his arm, punching him to the floor.

The Colt blasted again, and as another goon fell to his knees, Ivan the Russian took aim at Jiahua's head with a .38 Special. Bolan didn't waste words on a warning. She would never have been able to react quickly enough anyway. He concentrated his efforts on taking out Ivan before the man took out her. He fired the 93-R once before achieving his target, hoping to distract the Russian.

Ivan glanced at Bolan, but fired his gun at Jiahua. A second round from the 93-R took Ivan in the face, slamming him backward onto the desktop.

Bolan stepped to the last standing enforcer, only to have the man collapse in front of him. One of Jiahua's 9 mm rounds had killed him on his feet; it had taken him a moment to realize his condition.

Bolan surveyed the room quickly. Everyone was down except for the old man.

"Oh, my God!" Jiahua stood shakily, patting a black spot on her shoulder where the round had burned her clothing. She surveyed the room full of death and grinned weakly.

At a slight sound Bolan twisted and leveled the 93-R at the doorway. There stood the Urumchi cop they had seen on the street. His own handgun was leveled before him in a two-handed grip.

He regarded the Beretta without alarm, looking around the room, breaking into a grin. He holstered his weapon, speaking in rapid-fire Chinese.

"He says the XSEAs are on their way and we'd better get out of here," Jiahua reported.

"Good advice," Bolan said, putting away the 93-R. The cop spoke again.

"He says he'll tell them we escaped before he got here."

"Tell him thanks," Bolan said.

"You welcome," the cop returned.

"Tell them we took this with us," Bolan added, grabbing the canvas sack. He dumped out the cash and shoved it at Chui, and they exited through the now silent factory. Bolan dropped the canvas sack in the street, and they strode quickly to the rental car.

CHAPTER NINE

It was time to do some serious damage to Yan Whan's profit margins.

Their first target of the afternoon would be the Friendship Electronics Factory. The acres-large facility was on the north end of the city, in an industrial district largely owned by Yan Whan.

The front entrance was redbrick and decorated with a white-and-red banner fading in the sun.

"The mayor presented the factory with an award for its spectacular productivity gains and its contributions to the welfare of the district," Jiahua explained.

"Was it a ruse? Or is the mayor just blind?"

"The mayor is an ignorant man—he also believes that the XSEAs are a major benefit to the peacekeeping efforts of the Urumchi police."

Bolan had known officials such as the mayor, men so gullible and blinded by their own rationale they'd believe anything if it seemed to benefit their aims. Such ignorance was almost criminal.

Five cars were parked in front of the factory. All were expensive vehicles, far beyond what any factory worker could afford. On either side of the small main entrance stood a twelve-foot chain-link fence. Its bottom was buried in concrete, and it was topped with a twisted coil of barbed wire.

They entered the factory front and were greeted with a blast of mechanically cooled, comfortably dry air. A young, professionally attired woman smiled and stood from behind a neat desk covered with little more than an appointment book. She spoke pleasantly.

"Do you speak English?" Bolan asked before Jiahua could answer in Chinese.

"Yes, a little."

"I suggest you leave the premises at once."

The receptionist looked confused. Maybe her limited English vocabulary didn't yet include words like *premises*. Perhaps the request was so odd she thought she had misunderstood.

Jiahua dropped the cheap piece of cloth that made the bundle around the MP-5 and the Beretta police shotgun. The receptionist looked to Bolan for explanation, saw him withdraw an evil-looking handgun. He looked at her meaningfully, and she left the building in a run.

They made their way to the offices, a series of open and closed doors stretching along the wall behind the receptionist's desk. A voice called out from one of them. There was a pause and the man spoke again, loud enough that it seemed he was speaking to the receptionist. He stepped to the door of his office a few seconds later. By that time Bolan was five feet from the door and already training the 93-R on the spot he would emerge.

The Chinese man snarled when he saw Bolan, started to raise his hands as if in surrender, then flung himself back into the office, sounding an alert. Bolan jumped to the door of the office and saw the man emerging from a crouch behind his desk with a pistol. The 93-R spoke before the man had the chance to fire, a single round ripping through his face and shoving him to the floor.

"Belasko!" Jiahua called. Another gunman had run through the door of his office, saw them and pulled back inside just in time to save himself from the spray of 9 mm rounds from the MP-5.

"Cover me!" Bolan said.

"What're you going to do?"

"Go down the line," he said, nodding at the office doors. He dropped to the floor and crawled on his elbows to the next office door. A man was peeking around the corner, a pistol at chest level, ready to fire. Bolan twisted onto his back just as the gunman spotted him and aimed the handgun. The difference in their timing wasn't measurable on a stopwatch, but the soldier had the advantage of skill. The 93-R chugged out three rounds that cut into the victim's chest just under his rib cage, tearing through his lungs at a steep angle. Bolan crawled into the office, finding it empty. Two offices remained.

A man came to the door with a surprised look on his face, wearing a suit jacket but no tie around the collar of his faded white shirt. The man looked at him with an almost saddened face. Bolan immediately had the impression of a timid older man, maybe living under the oppressive yoke of gangsters who had assumed control of his business.

That impression was wrong.

The tieless man suddenly whipped out a stainless-steel P-91 Ruger, firing a .40-caliber S&W round.

Bolan had relaxed his guard slightly and only momentarily, but it was enough. When he saw the Ruger flash, he didn't have time to return fire. He rolled fast toward the enemy gunner, and the round sliced into his shoulder instead of his chest.

A second later the Executioner was in a prone position. The 93-R was clear again, and he fired from the floor into the gunman's groin just as the Ruger thundered a third time. The 9 mm manglers crashed into him and spoiled his aim, chopping through his rib cage like a butcher's saw, bringing him down on top of Bolan.

The soldier caught the falling body on his upraised hands and launched it over himself, into the other side of the wall, where it crashed to the ground. A screaming pain tore at his shoulder. Bolan sprang to his feet, mentally berating himself for allowing his guard to slip if only momentarily.

The final office was empty.

"So much for the white-collar staff," Jiahua said. She came close and gently pulled at the material of Bolan's shirt where the blood was flowing.

"How is it?"

"I've had worse," Bolan replied.

Jiahua looked in his eyes, seeing the self-reproach. "I'll bet you have."

"Come on."

THE LOCKED REAR DOOR WAS four feet wide and composed of reinforced steel, and a red alarm was mounted in the wall next to it. Hong Hui knew the door intimately because he spent forty-eight hours a week standing guard at it.

He stood at the door and stared at the workers going about their endlessly repetitive duties, bored out of his skull.

The interior of the factory was stifling hot that time

of the year; barely any fresh air seeped through the high windows. Instead what Hui felt was the tantalizing traces of machine-cooled air that seeped around the edges of the door from the office. The office was comfortable and bright and mercifully quiet next to the constant grind and roar of the factory. He received brief glimpses of the office when the door opened, which was seldom enough. Yan Whan's managers left the hour-by-hour operation of the factory to their foremen, and they left the security to the guards. Who could blame them for never wanting to leave the comfort of the office?

Every once in a great while a break in the routine occurred; a fight among the prisoners, an escape attempt, even an argument among the other guards—though they weren't within speaking distance and Hui wasn't allowed to leave his post. And Yan Whan punished slackers severely.

All in all, Hui felt no better off in many respects than the miserable wretches who did the labor in the factory, although his shifts were eight hours instead of twelve and he was paid. And had a nice home to return to when the shift was over.

Still, he would kill for any interesting distraction.

The door buzzer rang, startling him. He couldn't remember it ever ringing before. The office workers used their keys when they wanted to get into the factory. He realized one of them had to have lost the key.

It never even crossed his mind that someone would try to break *in* to the factory.

THE DOOR CLANKED and Jiahua smiled at the guard. The expression on the man's face told her instantly he regarded her an unexpected pleasure. She grabbed him by the collar and dragged him into the doorway.

Bolan shouldered the heavy steel door hard, and it crushed the guard's shoulders, knocked him sideways and smashed his upper torso. His AK clattered to the floor, and Jiahua snatched it as Bolan took the guard by the shirt and pulled him inside the office. The guard lay gasping for breath on the carpet until Bolan rapped the butt of the 93-R against his temple and he was still.

"Belasko," Jiahua called.

She stood in the doorway looking into the factory. He came to her side and saw what she saw.

One hundred fifty men and women, and children as young as ten, were on the daytime shift at the Friendship Electronics Factory. They were linked together by rusty iron chains. The prisoners were covered in grease and dirt so that they blended with the oily darkness of the factory, but their wasted condition couldn't be hidden. Universally they displayed the bulging eyes, sunken cheeks and skeletal aspect of those who were starving to death.

The plant was a blast furnace of heat, and Bolan felt the sweat seep onto his skin within seconds. The air had the wet thickness of the hottest air he had known in the jungles of his early war; but at least the air of the jungle wasn't sullied with the stench of chemicals and cooking plastic.

They walked through a sort of entranceway formed out of several layers of chain-link fence and black-painted plywood sheets, and at the end of it much of the expanse of the factory spread out before them. Four long lines of prisoners were hunched over crawling conveyor belts, fumbling with plastic parts, unspeaking. The wall of noise that assaulted them came from the huge belt motors, a wheezing compressor powering a plastic-trimming machine and a plastic-thermoforming unit spitting out plastic components.

Through it all, Bolan heard the subtle clank of the iron shackles.

The potent stench of urine mixed with the plastic odor. The prisoners weren't allowed to move from their stations during their shift.

Bolan had crossed paths with all kinds of human monsters during his war everlasting, but he'd seen few sights to equal this exhibition of starvation, slavery and suffering.

A guard appeared from nowhere with a large plastic jug and several small tin cups. The line workers snatched at the cups and held them out greedily, making animal noises, licking their lips. The guard stepped back and poured the water running onto the floor as the line workers jostled to get their cups under the stream. A tiny form was pushed to the floor. He stood up, as quick as he was able, but the guard had stopped pouring and his tiny cup was empty.

He was a boy, maybe twelve years old. A child. There was no child on the planet that deserved such suffering.

The other line workers had sucked at the meager cups of water before noticing the boy's plight. They brought their cups together and emptied them over the boy's cup. Together they were still able to come up with no more than a trickle of water.

The boy watched it fall drop by drop into his cup, then he sucked it into his mouth with closed eyes, as if he were a connoisseur tasting the finest wine.

Mack Bolan had had just about enough. He didn't see Jiahua next to him with tears in her eyes; he simply withdrew the police shotgun from her hands and strode into the open factory floor. There were guards all around him. He holstered the 93-R with a thrust and stepped up behind the water bearer.

The line workers put down their empty tin cups and were staring at him with amazement.

"Hey."

The water bearer turned and, eyes wide with surprise, dropped the jug and fumbled for his side arm.

Bolan slammed the barrel of the police shotgun into the guard's abdomen and yanked on the trigger. The 12-gauge shot blasted through him, spraying the floor with blood and gore, which the water bearer collapsed into.

The plastic jug rolled on the floor and Bolan kicked it in the direction of the boy.

Two guards ran for cover behind the plastic machine. Bolan triggered the shotgun again, spreading shot behind them but missing. He gestured to Jiahua to follow them, then he bolted around the huge machine in the other direction.

He jumped onto the conveyor belt and down again, the prisoners stretching on their chains to get out of his path. As he hit the ground, he saw an AK barrel poke around the corner of the machine and he hit it skyward with the barrel of the shotgun, then snatched the collar of the gunman with his free hand, pulling him bodily into one of the steel girders that supported the machine like a giant insect leg. The man's head collided with the metal, and another gunner appeared from behind the machine with a yell.

Bolan achieved one-handed target acquisition and fired, nearly losing the shotgun to the recoil. But the shot slammed the gunman to the floor, screaming and bleeding massively from countless small wounds.

Bolan had managed to keep hold on the other gunman, who was dazed to the point of semiconsciousness. The Executioner walked him behind the thermoplastic machine, waited for five seconds, then thrust him bodily between the massive heated pieces of the steel mold as they slammed together. He didn't wait to see what happened to the body when the mold halves separated again, and the machine started to buzz in alarm. Instead he looked for the power conduit and shot it out. The machine quieted.

"Belasko!" Jiahua called, flattening against a standing control podium.

Two guards were running at them. They spotted Bolan and dropped behind one of the conveyors.

Prisoners were shackled to either side of them, just a couple of feet away despite their best efforts to move as far as the chains would allow.

They were looking at Bolan with the blank dread of concentration-camp inhabitants.

Bolan withdrew the 93-R. The shotgun was obviously out—the guards too far off and the prisoners too close—but even using the handgun was risky. The Executioner was a great marksman, but the risk of spilling innocent blood...

The guards appeared in unison and targeted their AKs. Bolan crouched behind the podium with Jiahua and rode out the first barrage of 7.62 mm rounds that rattled against the concrete floor and the steel control unit.

He found the grenade he wanted and activated it with a simple movement of his thumb.

"What're you going to do?" Jiahua demanded.

"Don't look." He reached behind the podium and sidearmed the grenade across the floor in the direction of the gunners, then quickly buried his eyes in his forearm, hunching his shoulders over his ears as best he could.

The flash filled the factory with white light and an insane screeching noise that lasted seconds, cutting like a white-hot knife into his head. Jiahua screamed and pressed her face into the ground, squeezing her eyes shut and putting her fingers in her ears.

Bolan thrust himself to his feet as the brilliance faded suddenly. He found the two guards, as well as the nearby prisoners, on the ground, writhing in agony from the pain of the light and noise. The prisoners would recover. Bolan was determined that the guards wouldn't.

Running to the conveyor, he jumped up, straddling the moving belt by standing on the steel rims. He pointed the Beretta at the two guards, who were clawing at their eyes and moaning. They'd taken the blast without preparedness and were blinded.

"Hey!"

The guards tried to look at him. One scrambled for his AK, which he swung toward the sound of the voice.

Bolan triggered the Beretta from just seven feet away, the barrage of rounds nearly cutting the guards in two.

Two guards raced through the door, late arrivals bursting in to see what was happening. The first thing they saw was Bolan standing on the belt and drifting in their direction. The Executioner loosed a burst, and the rounds slammed into one of the new arrivals while his companion dived for cover outside the door. Bolan launched himself over the huddling forms of the prisoners, covering the distance to the door in four great leaps, then stopped just inside the door, listening.

JIAHUA WATCHED her partner get conveyed through the factory and out of sight like some intensely dangerous mannequin on the production line.

She heard steps in the other direction and crept low to the wall, where she huddled next to two cardboard barrels. A single guard appeared from the back, peeking behind a steel girder and disappearing again. Jiahua didn't let herself get distracted by the gunfire, coming from Belasko's direction, and the voices arguing in Chinese. They were aware of the deaths in the past few moments. They knew they were up against the people who had killed several of the XSEAs in the past few days. Several wanted to wait for the arrival of reinforcements.

Others knew they had to go in now or risk the escape of the enemy.

Jiahua counted four voices, maybe five.

More gunfire erupted at the other end of the factory. Belasko was tied up at the moment. Could she neutralize this squad? Outgunned five to one, armed no better than they were?

Such odds she didn't need to consider. There was a way. Odds were for surmounting. Experience with Belasko had taught her that, if nothing else.

Five feet away from her stood the hopper for the plastic-molding machine, filled with plastic pebbles ready to be melted down and molded into cases for cheap stereos.

The men outside had decided to make a combined attack.

Jiahua crept across the space, watching the point where they would enter, and stepped into the bin of resin pellets. It was about five feet square, and three-quarters full. The CIA agent sank into them, finding them lightweight, almost like foam peanuts. She waded through them, into the corner, and scooped them around her, leaving only the top of her head and her eyes exposed. Chameleonlike, her black hair and her dark eyes were camouflaged against the shiny black pellets.

And the black barrel of the MP-5 was invisible.

ZENG LONG WAS a young man. He had been lured into the employ of Yan Whan by a naturally vicious nature—he could kill for a living without feeling the strains of an overactive conscience—and by his lust for the money and the life-style Yan Whan promised. He didn't know how strongly his own foolishness figured into the equation.

Now it was finally dawning on him.

He was the lowest-ranking gunman in the squad of four that had been guarding the rear entrance to the factory and had been summoned in by the gunfire. Now the leader of the group, Shyy Kangjung, had told him to lead the way in.

Long had always been suspicious of Kangjung. Now he knew how the man had gotten ahead. He had let others do the dirty work, then probably he took the credit when the time came.

He had sent Long in first, into this deadly situation, knowing that Long would take the brunt of the gunfire should it come their way.

Long stepped over the huddled forms of the prisoners, some sobbing, some simply still, as if resigned to their fate. Long wasn't resigned. He poked the AK around a corner to find an empty alcove behind a piece of machinery. He wouldn't stand for being volunteered for hazardous duty. He would take care of Kangjung.

He walked along the row of shackled prisoners and

stepped quietly around the huge thermoplastic injection-molding press, seeing the remains of one of his comrades.

He heard gunfire, far across the facility, and walked in that direction a few more steps, trying to see what was going on. Instead he spotted unexpected movement out of the corner of his eye.

Long turned on it quickly, but the strange movement had already turned to gunfire. He felt the crunches of the impacts in his body and he found himself propelled backward, into the wall, where he landed with a heavy thud. Then he stood there for a moment, ready for the killing pain that would engulf him.

Now he saw his killer, in her ingenious hiding place.

"Zeng Long!" It was Kangjung, calling out for him as if full of concern.

Long managed to speak normally, although he could feel the great rush of blood running through his body in a strange way. "I got him! I shot him dead! You've got to see this!"

The others rushed across the darkened, torrid factory floor, and when Kangjung came around the machine he saw Long on his knees, covered in blood, smiling and collapsing.

Then there was movement to the side, and the woman appeared, standing up out of the bin of plastic pellets. They were flowing off her like water, and the submachine gun in her hand was firing.

Kangjung turned the AK on her as he watched his other two men seem to melt into the floor under the barrage from her sputtering, efficient fire, and he knew he was too slow. He triggered his weapon before he achieved his target, turning the firing machine on her as he felt the shattering of his arms and his ribs. The gun flew out of his hands. The darkness and heat of the factory seemed to suddenly swell and consume him.

Jiahua stood in the bin, eyes peeled for more movement, more danger, as she swapped out the mag in the MP-5. There was no noise except the far-off blast of the Beretta shotgun.

THE ESCAPED GUARD might have been just on the other side of the corrugated-steel wall, an inch away from Bolan. The Executioner brought the police shotgun to bear, so that it would fire at the first thing that walked through the door. He didn't breathe, and tried to hear the breath of the man who had jumped to safety from Bolan's AK fire just seconds before. If it was there, it was masked in the heaving and groaning of the factory.

He couldn't hear breathing, but the stealthy footsteps of an approaching gunman were another matter. The man was coming through the factory, behind the stacks of wooden pallets, very close.

Bolan drew the 93-R with his free hand and watched for a sign of the approaching gunman. He glimpsed a movement in the shadow, a shift behind one of the piles of pallets, and the image came to him of one of the prisoners, scared witless, somehow out of his chains and trying make a desperate run for freedom.

The Executioner wouldn't spill innocent blood. He would wait to see what emerged from behind the piles of pallets. If it meant he lost the advantage in the fight, then so be it.

A figure came to the edge of the pallets, pausing as if he were convinced the enemy hadn't detected him. Then he came around the corner just enough to level the barrel of his own sawed-off 12-gauge shotgun.

Bolan cut loose the 93-R, the three 9 mm rounds

blasting into the gunman low, in the crotch, shattering one hip. As he doubled over as if from a fist to the gut, the 12-gauge thundered, the fire holing the thin steel wall. There was a yelp of pain from beyond it.

That hadn't come from the shotgunner, who was dead on the floor. Bolan jumped out the door, into the hot sun, and found the gunman he had been waiting for, now making a painful run for safety. His ankle was bleeding as he limped away from the door.

He looked over his shoulder and saw Bolan watching him run.

The gunner turned, lifting the AK he had been using as an imperfect crutch, making his last, desperate stand. He never had time to even find the machine gun's trigger. The 93-R chugged out three rounds that sent him sprawling in the dry dirt.

Bolan snatched a bloody ring of keys from the corpse's belt and heard his partner shouting from the depths of the factory.

"I'm here," he said from the doorway.

Jiahua appeared a moment later, her MP-5 still scanning everywhere for Yan Whan's personnel.

But she grinned. "I think we cleaned up."

"We did. And now we set everyone free."

CHAPTER TEN

Jiahua found her partner staring at the factory ceiling. She could have sworn he was counting.

"The prisoners are gone. All of them," she reported.

"You're sure of that?"

"Yeah."

"We're leaving, too. Soon."

"It's already been half an hour. How much longer are we going to wait?"

Bolan pointed to the window, a rectangle, a foot and a half tall by two feet wide, about eight feet off the ground.

"What about it?"

"There are seven of them. They're all open to let the hot air out. There's very little else in the form of ventilation."

"So it wouldn't pass a health-department inspection—so what?"

"So I think gas would build up very quickly up there if those windows were closed," Bolan said.

She followed his pointing finger to a large gas main in the ceiling. It descended into a huge furnace unit at the far side of the factory, meant to give the room some semblance of warmth when the temperature outside dipped well below freezing in the long winter months.

"So boost me up."

Bolan laced his fingers, and Jiahua stepped into them. He easily lifted her lithe form to a window. It was covered in grease and filth, and it groaned loudly when she tried to budge it. Then she put her weight on it, and it shut with a slam.

That was one.

It took them less than ten more minutes to close the others.

Bolan climbed on top of the furnace box, half of which protruded through the wall, and loosened the six-inch-wide pipe from the box with three powerful kicks. He spun the hand wheel as far as it would go. The gas flowed from the pipe with a hush, and immediately the odor became overpowering.

He held his breath, grabbing a small ignition device from his pocket and arming it with a click of a button. The red light glowed. He placed it on top of the box where it would be out of sight of the floor.

"Let's go!" Bolan said, jumping the seven feet to the floor.

They ran for the exit, across the parking lot, and were heading for cover when the rolling forces of Yan Whan appeared on the street like an army of Nazis marching through a small, helpless town.

Bolan came to halt against a pile of scrap rubber a full quarter mile away. The Friendship Electronics Factory sat like a giant, dark splotch of misery on the scarred, lifeless industrial landscape.

The Steadyscope GS 982 binoculars brought the factory and the attacking army up close. Gunners encircled the building, facing it like a police force facing a hostage situation. Their cries for surrender went unanswered. Bolan watched a man in navy blue coveralls shouting for an attack, and twenty men obeyed him, charging through the open gates and inside.

Where they would find nothing but their own dead—and their own deaths.

SUN HWANG FOLLOWED his men, feeling the oil-soaked ground squelching under his feet, experiencing growing alarm caused by the pregnant silence. The sounds of working machinery should have been audible.

One of the doors to the factory hung open, and a dead man was facedown in the oily dirt some twenty-five paces away. His assault rifle lay near him. It was one of Yan Whan's men.

Hwang knew that many men were stationed here. Surely the American couldn't have pegged them all. Surely, the American's luck would finally have run out.

As bad as he imagined it would be, Hwang wasn't prepared for the reality of the situation.

The man at the door pulled back sharply and ran to Hwang.

"There's nobody inside. We saw a couple of bodies. That's all."

"The prisoners?"

"No prisoners. None at all."

It took several long seconds for Hwang to grasp what the messenger was saying. "No prisoners?" he almost whispered.

"No. The shackles are opened. They've been freed."

The concept moved through Hwang like a pot of thick liquid coming to a sudden, violent boil.

"Search the factory! Every inch! I want a report of who's dead and who's alive, and if you see anybody who isn't one of our men or who isn't in chains, shoot him dead on the spot!"

As Hwang entered the factory himself, he found his men spreading out, their air of readiness giving way to a more relaxed searching behavior. Their alarm was gone. They were finding nothing but bodies.

Hwang approached a corpse. It was gutted, the machine-gun signature plainly discernible. Another dead man was an arm's length away. Both were Yan Whan's guards.

"Is there even one prisoner left in this building?" Hwang demanded.

"We haven't found any yet," one of his men answered.

"Survivors?"

"None."

Hwang didn't want to contemplate Yan Whan's reaction when he learned an entire factory full of prisoners had escaped.

Hwang had been in charge for just a day, but he knew who would get the blame for this fiasco.

"What is that smell?"

One of his men was several feet away and was looking at the floor, as if expecting one of the corpses to exhibit signs of rotting, even though it had been dead less than an hour. Then he lifted his head, sniffing, raising himself on his toes.

The man couldn't see what was making the odor, but Hwang was far enough away that he could see the broken end of the pipe over the furnace. He saw the Flammable sign.

"Gas!" he shouted, breaking into a run. "Get out of here now!"

BOLAN'S THUMB caressed the button on the tiny transmitter. Through the binoculars he spotted the first man burst out of the factory, a sign that they had smelled his trap. He depressed the button.

The detonator on the top of the furnace exploded, a small and insignificant burst of flame.

A fraction of a second later the cloud of gas ignited and filled the factory with fire.

The orange fireball that had been the Friendship Electronics Factory filled the lenses of the Steadyscope, so bright Bolan almost felt it burn his eyeballs.

THE PRISON WAS more like a fortress. Its concrete walls were forty feet high, and a jungle of barbed wire nestled against the base of the wall. Floodlights illuminated the grounds for one hundred yards in every direction. The walls were manned by innumerable troops.

Bolan stood in the shadow a mile away and observed the structure through his binoculars.

He wasn't getting in there, not by himself.

Not yet.

The physical barriers were far too tough. The entire place was too well lit, too heavily staffed.

He glanced at his watch. It was almost time for the midnight shift change.

WHEN YAN WHAN'S recruitment force found evidence of Bi Luo-Yi's anti-Communist leanings, they checked up on him. When they found out he was a young, strong man, they snatched him off the street.

Two months earlier, if you had asked him for his opinion, Luo-Yi would have told you that life in Communist China was unnecessarily difficult, burdened by the government. Progress was stifled. People suffered as a result, unable to live comfortably, let alone prosper.

Luo-Yi knew from bitter experience that, when he

had spoken of suffering, he had no real frame of reference, not back in those days when he was a young and vibrant man.

Now suffering, true mind-and-body misery, was a companion to him. He lived in hell on earth, a hell that might never end until death claimed him.

Death just might come soon, for Luo-Yi's temper was quick to ignite against his oppressor, who placed no value on his life, only on his ability to work. They would shoot him dead without too much forethought and certainly without regret if he gave them reason.

He lay in the cot, watching the sky. The moon was in the barred window overhead. Soon the siren would sound, and it would be time to work. Twelve long hours in a stinking, smelly factory. Twelve hours of mind-numbing monotony. That was almost worse than death.

The flies buzzed and landed on his face. He had learned to ignore them. He had ceased to flail at them all night long, keeping himself awake, draining his energy.

He didn't meet the eyes of the other men and boys around him. They wouldn't speak to him any longer. They knew he was a troublemaker; they were sure that he was going to get shot dead very soon, and they didn't want to be in any way associated with him when that time came.

The bowls of watery rice and boiled beef parts were ladled out, and Luo-Yi slurped his down at once.

There were no second helpings.

It was time to get on the bus.

They were marched across the grounds in single file. The grounds were brightly lit, almost like daytime. The guards, armed with AK-47s and long-range rifles, watched them from their posts on the walls and from the gates. Luo-Yi had seen four men try to escape. He had watched all four dance the bullet dance and fall dead on the ground.

Maybe one day soon Luo-Yi would make that same break for freedom. The shouts and the firing would commence immediately. In seconds the nightmare would be over.

But what happened then?

That was the question that kept him from making the drastic move so far. But it wouldn't hold him back much longer. The question was too philosophical. The reality was too real.

But the concept of eternal nothingness was frightening enough to keep him in check for now. He walked to the bus without causing his guards trouble. He boarded it and slid into the plastic seat without speaking or even looking at anyone.

Luo-Yi, like all his fellow prisoners, had found that loneliness was the worst part about being a prisoner.

He heard the giant steel door roll open, and the bus lurched out of the prison walls into the night.

BOLAN SAW the bus coming, and he was ready for it.

The plastique was planted in the road. The detonator was armed. The same radio transmitter he had used just hours ago would be utilized again.

He half slid, half walked down the steep, dusty hillside and crouched in the tall grass on the side of the road. He was now several miles from the prison, too far for the jailers to hear any ruckus he might raise. The hill would help block the noise. The bus would never know what hit it.

It was a good plan, as far as it went. The plastique was detonated, the bus stopped.

From that point he would improvise.

With a whine of its laboring engine the school bus swung around the hill, downshifted, then headed Bolan's way. He waited until its nose just reached the tiny gray brick in the middle of the road, then pressed the detonator button.

The front end of the bus flashed orange and bounced into the air while inertia drove the vehicle forward. When the front end landed, the wheels disintegrated and it plowed into the asphalt, skidded sideways on sparking, twisted metal, and abruptly halted with the front end wedged in the grassy shoulder.

Bolan was already in motion. He yanked at the door. The driver was picking himself up and pulling shards of glass out of his hands. He spotted the intruder and reached for the handgun on his hip.

The Executioner triggered the 93-R and sent the driver sprawling again.

Another guard was seated just behind the driver's seat and was making quick work of bringing his AK to bear. Three more parabellum rounds from the 93-R nailed him to his bench.

The rattle of AK fire filled the tight confines of the bus from the rear, and only then did Bolan see how packed with prisoners the vehicle was, their wrists manacled on short chains, pushing and shoving one another to get down, out of the line of fire. Bolan crouched in the entrance steps as the 7.62 mm rounds slammed into the metal bus frame and into the clinging triangles that remained in the windshield frame.

He raised his head slowly, looking for the gunman. They sighted each other simultaneously. The AK rattled again, controlled and brief but enough to send Bolan back into his crouch. Twisting, he crawled to the ground and crabbed along the side of the wreck, beneath the windows, and only stood again when he was at the rear, looking in through the bars covering the window of the bolted emergency door.

The gunman was stalking toward the front of the bus, the AK held as high in his hands as he could raise it and still fire a controlled shot. He was waiting for Bolan to stick his head out again so he could blow it off.

Poking the nose of the 93-R through the bars, Bolan said, "Hey."

The gunman twisted, but the 93-R was already chugging its three deadly missiles in rapid succession to drop . him down in the aisle among the terrified prisoners.

Bolan heard another vehicle approaching from the prison. He returned to the front of the bus and grabbed the keys and the handgun from the belt of the dead driver.

"Who here speaks English?" he shouted.

"I do!" said a small, shriveled prisoner.

Bolan tossed him the keys and the gun. "Find out who can fire that weapon and free him and whoever knows how to use that AK. We're going to have to defend ourselves, and the odds might not be in our favor."

The shriveled man caught both items in his tiny hands and deftly undid his manacles. He was already yelling in Chinese as he stood on his seat and shouted to the rest of the bus. He threw the keys to a man near the rear of the vehicle while others passed back the AK from the dead man in the aisle.

"He fired a gun like that before. I will handle this beauty myself with pleasure," the old man said with a grin.

Bolan saw one of the blacked-out vehicles rounding

the corner. He didn't know why they had come. Maybe somebody in the bus managed to get out a radio alert when the attack began, or perhaps they were just following the bus by chance. It really didn't matter why. They were here.

Now they had to go.

The Executioner yanked at the weapon peeking over his shoulder, and the straps freed his Steyr AUG assault rifle. More importantly it sported a grenade launcher, and Bolan's shoulder pack held a supply of 40 mm MECAR rifle grenades.

The vehicle spun into a tight, braking turn and came to a screeching halt two hundred feet from the bus. Bolan stepped into the open long enough to level the Steyr and launch a grenade. The bomb had an effective range of one hundred yards, and the car was a sitting duck.

Two men were jumping from the vehicle on the protected side and leveling their handguns over the roof. The spiraling grenade hit the pavement on the near side and exploded. The two men disappeared momentarily in the blast.

LUO-YI WATCHED with mounting excitement as his neighbor struggled with the locks on his manacles. Then they fell away, and Luo-Yi was a free man. He grabbed the AK-47 and stood, punching out the window glass with the barrel of the weapon. Two men were getting out of the car, both with handguns.

Luo-Yi spotted their American savior come out of the front end of the bus just long enough to fire something from his own automatic weapon, then the car burst into fire and flame. Luo-Yi grinned. The American had a grenade launcher!

This was going to be a much better way to die.

NO RISK, NO OBLIGATION TO BUY...NOW OR EVER!

GUARANTEED

PLAY "ROLL A DOUBLE" AND YOU GET FREE GIFTS! HERE'S HOW TO PLAY:

1. Peel off label from front cover. Place it in space provided at right. With a coin, carefully scratch off the silver dice. Then check the claim chart to see what we have for you – FOUR FREE BOOKS and a mystery gift – ALL YOURS! ALL FREE!

2. Send back this card and you'll receive hot-off-the-press Gold Eagle books, never before published. These books have a total cover price $18.50, but they are yours to keep absolutely free.

3. There's no catch. You're under no obligation to buy anything. We charge nothing – ZERO – for your first shipment. And you don't have to make any minimum number of purchases – not even one!

4. The fact is thousands of readers enjoy receiving books by mail from the Gold Eagle Reader Service™. They like the convenience of home delivery; they like getting the best new novels BEFORE they're available in stores...and they think our discount prices are dynamite!

5. We hope that after receiving your free books you'll want to remain a subscriber. But the choice is yours – to continue or cancel, any time at all! So why not take us up on our invitation, with no risk of any kind. You'll be glad you did!

YOURS FREE!

SURPRISE MYSTERY GIFT
COULD BE YOURS FREE
WHEN YOU PLAY "ROLL A DOUBLE"

"ROLL A DOUBLE!"

Place label here

SCRATCH HERE

SEE CLAIM CHART BELOW

164 CIM CE5U
(U-M-B-01/98)

YES! I have placed my label from the front cover into the space provided above and scratched off the silver dice. Please send me all the gifts for which I qualify. I understand that I am under no obligation to purchase any books, as explained on the opposite page.

NAME _____

ADDRESS _____ APT. _____

CITY _____ STATE _____ ZIP _____

CLAIM CHART

4 FREE BOOKS PLUS SURPRISE MYSTERY GIFT

3 FREE BOOKS PLUS BONUS GIFT

2 FREE BOOKS

CLAIM NO.37-829

THE GOLD EAGLE READER SERVICE™ — HERE'S HOW IT WORKS

Accepting free books puts you under no obligation to buy anything. You may keep the books and gift and return the shipping statement, marked "cancel." If you do not cancel, about a month later we will send you 4 additional novels and bill you just $15.80 — that's a saving of 15% off the cover price of all four books! And there's no extra charge for shipping! You may cancel at any time, but if you choose to continue, every other month we'll send you 4 more books, which you may either purchase at the discount price...or return to us and cancel your subscription.

*Terms and prices subject to change without notice. Sales tax applicable in N.Y.

If offer card is missing, write to: The Gold Eagle Reader Service, 3010 Walden Ave., P.O. Box 1867, Buffalo NY 14240-1867

BUSINESS REPLY MAIL
FIRST-CLASS MAIL   PERMIT NO. 717   BUFFALO, NY

POSTAGE WILL BE PAID BY ADDRESSEE

GOLD EAGLE READER SERVICE
3010 WALDEN AVE
PO BOX 1867
BUFFALO NY 14240-9952

NO POSTAGE
NECESSARY
IF MAILED
IN THE
UNITED STATES

Unless it was over already. There was no sign of life from behind the burning car. Then both men staggered out of the flame and smoke, to Luo-Yi's right. He aimed and fired, feeling the trembling power of the AK in his hands. The rounds chomped into the street at the feet of the men. Luo-Yi adjusted his aim quickly as the men dived for cover in the weeds and grass on the side of the road.

Another pair of headlights appeared from around the bend. Reinforcements. More fighting. More opportunity to kill the men who had imprisoned him.

BOLAN WATCHED the survivors flee the AK fire and saw the approach of new arrivals and knew they would be better prepared to meet his assault. The car swerved around the first vehicle and headed directly at the bus, men poking out of the windows on either side.

The Executioner triggered the Steyr AUG, sweeping it left to right across the front of the car, watching the gunman in the passenger window shake under the impact of the rounds. Before his trail of hot fire reached the driver's-side window, the gunner on that side had pulled in under a barrage of AK fire from the bus. But the crash of the windshield had already informed Bolan that the car wasn't one of the armored vehicles. The car missed the bus by a yard, disappearing around it.

Bolan stepped out of the bus doors into the open. Three shots rang out behind him, and he heard the impact of one of their handgun rounds in the bus hood inches from his shoulder. Then he ducked around the front of the vehicle and put it between himself and the footmen.

LUO-YI HEARD the handgun rounds, far to his right, and realized the footmen from the burning car were still alive and kicking. He turned the AK to the far side of the road, looking for them. The flickering of the burning car revealed one in the shadows of the grass, on his hands and knees, handgun held in front of him. If that man had killed the prisoners' American friend...

Luo-Yi aimed as carefully as he was able and squeezed the trigger, the rounds ripping across the street into the patch of weeds and grass. The figure crouching there reached out, as if beseechingly, then fell on his face and didn't move again.

But the AK had dried up. Luo-Yi swore vehemently and spotted movement to the far right—the second footman ran across the road and came alongside the bus, creeping toward the front, sneaking up on the American.

Luo-Yi didn't have time to get the magazine from the other AK. He dropped the weapon and grabbed at his discarded manacles. The heavy chain was about a foot and a half long—long enough to work with. His nemesis approached.

The man was a huge Kazak with a Makarov, who inched along the bus, back to the prisoners. Luo-Yi didn't know what the American was up to at the moment, but he would be damned if he would let this soldier of Yan Whan bring him down.

He waited patiently, but with a glowing lust for vengeance.

The Kazak stepped directly beneath the window, and Luo-Yi reached out quietly and swiftly, slipping the heavy chain around the man's neck and crossing it behind his head. Then he dragged the big Kazak into the air.

The man immediately began kicking and flailing, twisting his head back and forth and trying to pound the Soviet gun against his enemy's hands. Luo-Yi's muscles screamed in his arms, and the chain was ripping into his fingers. He felt the metal slip under his flesh.

"Help me!" he demanded.

Several others had by now freed themselves, and two men crammed themselves into the seat beside Luo-Yi and grabbed for the chain. Luo-Yi felt the Kazak lifted higher into the air, and his kicking became the desperate thrashing of a rabbit caught in a tightening trap.

BOLAN WATCHED the vehicle brake and spin. The driver trod heavily on the pedal, tires smoking on the pavement as it accelerated toward the bus again, turning in his direction. Bolan stepped into the open and faced it down, launching a grenade directly into it. The driver anticipated the move and swerved. The 40 mm bomb plopped into the street and detonated, wasted on asphalt, and the car slid sideways to a halt.

The bus rocked for a moment, and Bolan ran to the car, triggering the Steyr AUG. Its tires squealed as it tried to make an escape, but for one long half second it failed to move. A figure appeared in the rear passenger window, tracking Bolan with a big handgun, but the Steyr perforated his forearm, slammed into his shoulder and crashed into his chest. The Executioner hurried to the front passenger window and leveled the assault rifle at the driver, who took his foot off the pedal and grabbed at the AK-47 in the hands of the corpse next to him.

A short burst from the Steyr ended the play.

THE RINGING OF THE PHONE was obscenely loud.

Yan Whan didn't even act surprised as he rolled away from his companion and got out of bed.

"Yes? All right, give me a full report. What were our losses?" he said. "And how many prisoners?" He paused. "That's a substantial number. Were there any survivors among our men?" A moment later he added, "This is very serious."

He hung up the phone.

Sitting in an upholstered chair next to a small bedside table, he looked out into the night through wide patio doors. He lit a cigarette and inhaled deeply.

"The American attacked one of our buses," he said finally. "He killed the driver and the guard, as well as seven more of our men. The prisoners escaped on foot—the entire busload."

"That'll cut into production."

"Substantially."

"This guy is causing havoc," Birgitte said. She reached out her hand in the darkness, and he handed her the cigarette. "He's got to be stopped."

"I've been attempting to stop him since he first appeared in Urumchi," Yan Whan reminded her. "He is very skilled."

"Your Urumchi men are not up to the task of finding him and stopping him."

"You're correct," he said. "We need more highly trained staff to take him out."

"Who do you have in mind?"

"I have in mind involving our American partners. It is their business at stake, as well as ours. Their country sent over this menace. They can supply a cleanup team to eradicate him."

Birgitte fell back on the pillow, considering the implications of this latest attack. Yan Whan couldn't handle it himself. What did that mean? Was he weaker than she thought? If so, how much longer would he be able to sustain his power base?

Even if he did wipe out this particular American menace, would the U.S. government rest before they buried Yan Whan's operation?

Birgitte considered that it might be time to look for another position. She had no desire to be on hand if and when this whole thing fell apart.

She hadn't been in Frankfurt in years. Maybe she should make her way back there.

Yan Whan was speaking evenly and briefly into the phone. He was a man of few words. Those who listened closely to everything he said, and treated every utterance as vitally important, went far in his organization.

He hung up the phone. "We'll have company tomorrow. A chartered jet will be leaving Houston, Texas, within an hour."

"It will still take them a day to get here," Birgitte argued.

"Yes. In the meantime I don't have the resources to guard the factories. I'm concentrating them all in the Happy Family plant. That's our most important product line in terms of profit. The rest will have to cease operations until the crisis is passed."

"You think even stationing all your guards in a single operation will be sufficient?"

Yan Whan shook his head slightly. "I do not know. It is a calculated risk I must take."

CHAPTER ELEVEN

By the time the jet set down in the city of Urumchi, Jethro Parl was bored to death. Never mind that it was a spacious, well-appointed jet fit for a millionaire. He'd been cooped up inside of it for almost a full day, with only short stops for refueling in Honolulu and Beijing.

He deplaned, then sniffed the air with disgust. Other than a couple of evening pleasure excursions into Matamoros, Mexico, he'd never been out of the United States. He didn't like foreigners. Even the old-country types in the Family rubbed him the wrong way, with their exaggerated emotional outbursts and their accents.

Being surrounded by Orientals wasn't something Parl felt comfortable with, either. He got the impression they silently regarded him as foolish, as if they were laughing at him behind their stoic expressions.

All in all, going to a backwater city like Urumchi wasn't his idea of a good time.

But Don Cariani had ordered it, and that was reason enough. The business the Family did out of China was spectacular, and was only getting better. There'd been plenty of cash in recent months as a direct result of the success that was being seen out of this operation.

Parl had once thought the idea was a bad one. Sell

electronics? Had the Cariani Family suddenly become Sears or something?

But the goods started coming in, and the Family started to reap profits. The numbers started to add up, and Parl had decided it was a good idea after all. The Family was making money while the U.S. government concentrated its manpower behind stopping the smugglers bringing in heroin and cocaine.

There had even been some talk about moving the business slowly into legitimacy in the years to come, which would have put Parl out of a job. What he did for the Cariani Family had nothing to do with legitimate business, and there was no way a man like him could be shoehorned into a corporate structure.

But he wasn't worried.

Parl wasn't a well-educated man, but he had a certain sense of philosophy. He knew human nature didn't change rapidly or substantially. What a man was when he was twenty was pretty much what he was when he was sixty. The same with a Mafia Family. It grew and expanded its scope and altered its organizational structure, but it didn't grow into something new, something legitimate.

That just didn't happen.

The Cariani Family was young, as the U.S. Families were judged, and Don Cariani was only fifty-two. But he was aggressive, bloodthirsty, manipulative and greedy, Parl's kind of boss.

Jethro Parl wasn't worried about his job security. He just hoped he didn't get any more foreign jobs like this one.

Twenty-three men had filed off the chartered jet and stood waiting for his instructions.

"Let's kill this asshole quick and get back home," Parl said.

He knew that the Chinese leader of the operation, Yan Whan, had established a special relationship with a group of customs officials at Urumchi. Nevertheless, getting twenty-four American men and a substantial amount of luggage into the country unchecked had to have taken some major wheel-greasing.

Had the luggage been checked by any other airport customs staff, Parl and his men would have been arrested immediately. They were packing arms sufficient to outfit a front-line platoon. Yan Whan had told Don Cariani that he would be glad to provide his men with whatever they needed. He had a substantial supply and source of arms and took pride in his ability to procure what was needed. But Parl had opted to bring his own. He wanted the hardware he knew and trusted and had flown into Urumchi with a jet full of it.

Overkill, he was thinking. That much hardware, this many men, all to take out two CIA agents, one a female?

But the report Yan Whan had been feeding them told them the American man wasn't ordinary CIA, maybe not CIA at all, since Yan Whan's CIA links had failed to find a trace of him. This agent had stormed through Whan's defenses, wiping out large numbers of personnel, numbers so large they had to be exaggerations.

Didn't matter. This man might score against Yan Whan and his Oriental soldiers. But just wait until he got a taste of what a U.S. Family could dish out.

YAN WHAN DIDN'T LIKE the looks of Jethro Parl. He was dressed in black jeans, cowboy boots, a denim shirt and a cowboy hat.

"This isn't a Western motion-picture matinee," was his greeting to the chief Cariani Family enforcer.

"Long way from it," Parl snorted derisively, noting Whan was in a business suit with a starched white shirt and a yellow silk power tie, like he was some businessman in downtown Houston. Like there was anyone in the entire province who might see him all dressed up and be impressed.

"You've been briefed on my problem here?"

"Brief is the word for it, yeah," Parl replied. "From what I hear, you kill an American CIA agent and catch his babe. Next thing you know she gets broken out of jail by another American who starts killing every one of your guys he runs into. That about right?"

"More or less. He has attacked several of my compounds, probably based on information the woman is giving him."

"I think he was probably here all along. You just never saw him before he broke the girl out of jail."

Whan shook his head and leaned back in his chair with his hands on the rests, regarding the enforcer Don Cariani had delivered to him. The man looked the perfect fool in his cowboy costume—he even wore a ponytail! "I don't think so, Mr. Parl. This man appeared suddenly, with the intention of making himself known, and to shut down my Urumchi businesses. I have to say he has made some significant progress in that direction. I want him terminated before he makes any more."

"I heard we had company."

Birgitte entered the room, and Parl got to his feet instantly.

"Morning, ma'am," he said.

Birgitte smiled like some idiot teenager. "It's late afternoon, actually. Birgitte Werner."

Parl smiled and took her small hand in his. "Jethro Parl," he said. Their eyes were locked on each other. Whan sat forward suddenly, disgusted.

"All right, Mr. Parl, what is your intention?"

Parl dragged his eyes away from Birgitte and took just a second to recover his train of thought.

"We'll stake out your operations and flash some cash. Somebody will know something. Once we hit the right price point, the information will become available. Even the prisoners will be willing to offer information for the right incentive."

"My men have already performed several rounds of questioning, Mr. Parl."

"I think we can do it better, Mr. Whan."

"And if you cannot?"

"We'll wait until your friend shows up. From what you're saying, he's overdue for another strike anyway. We'll take him out then."

"Simple as that?"

"As simple as that."

Whan lit a Turkish cigarette without offering one to his guest. "I don't think you have the slightest clue what you are up against. If this man was stupid, he would have been annihilated days ago. He's avoided my gunmen repeatedly."

"Your gunmen don't rate with mine, to be frank, Mr. Whan—isn't that why you had us fly in?"

"I called you in because I'm tired of sacrificing my own men. For a little while, at least, I'd rather let someone else's staff become fodder for this...executioner."

"I think we'll do better than you expect." Parl looked back at Birgitte. A smoldering smile touched her lips.

Whan waved his cigarette in disgust. "Then get out of here and start doing it!"

Parl left without another word. Birgitte gave Whan a cold look and returned to their living suite.

Whan sat at his desk and found himself half hoping that Jethro Parl found himself at the wrong end of their nemesis's gun.

THE BEAUTIFUL SUN FACTORY had only recently come under Yan Whan's control. The people who worked there were free. They went home at the end of the day, and they even received a wage—enough to live on, if one didn't mind eating old vegetables and rice.

Then the Americans came. They stormed into the factory at the beginning of the evening shift, dressed in expensive clothes, carrying big, shining weapons.

They flashed around a small fortune.

Wang had never possessed so much money in all his life. He looked at the stack of bills in the hands of the Americans and almost drooled. It was more than he made in two years at the factory. It was more than his father had made in his entire life.

"With that much money you could get passage to Beijing," Yanrong observed. Yanrong had been his assembly table partner for the past four months. During the long hours of working at the table, they had discussed their ambitions, passing away the interminable hours, and Wang had told Yanrong of his dream of moving to Beijing. There he could get a real job, make a decent living, learn English, live as a civilized, cosmopolitan Chinese man of the late twentieth century should live, leave the misery of backward Urumchi forever.

But Beijing was a 1,600-mile train journey from

Urumchi, and was impossibly expensive to a man like Wang, who barely made enough to feed himself.

The Americans began to bring small groups of workers into the office, and when they left the room the workers looked thoughtful. But the Americans didn't seem to be finding the person they deemed worthy of giving the big stack of cash they were waving around.

Wang became increasingly excited when Yanrong went into the office with the next group. He assembled motor parts absentmindedly, trying to imagine what the Americans could possibly want, would possibly be willing to pay for.

YANRONG RETURNED to the worktable slowly, deeply thoughtful, and he looked hard at Wang as his work partner went to join the next group in the office with the Americans.

The Americans had made a strange request: they were looking for another American, a big, dark man with blue eyes and hard features. He might be in the company of a Chinese American girl.

They didn't say why they wanted this man and his companion, but they did say they would give the stack of cash to whoever could tell them where to find him.

The problem was, Yanrong knew where an American man was staying. He had seen him just the day before entering a small flat, as he was walking home from work with Wang. They had cut through an alley behind the flat, and Yanrong remembered wondering why an American was staying in such a place and why he chose to enter through the back door. He knew Wang had seen the American man, too.

Yanrong suspected this was tied to the trouble going on about the city. There had been deaths, shootings, somehow linked to the rumors of atrocity and slavery that had been spreading for the past several months.

One thing Yanrong was convinced of was that these Americans wanted to find this blue-eyed American and his Chinese girlfriend for no good purpose. In fact, he thought, they probably meant to kill them.

One thing more he knew—if Wang did remember seeing the American he would jump at the chance to collect the money.

The office door opened, and the workers filled out. All except Wang. The door shut again. Wang was still inside, talking to the Americans.

Yanrong headed for the rear exit.

EARLY EVENING SHADOWS grew cool and dark in the city. An oily rag lay on the small table. Bolan had just finished fieldstripping the Beretta 93-R and he reassembled it carefully, glancing across the small apartment to the narrow bed. Jiahua was sleeping, and in the afternoon heat she had thrown off the covers. She looked young and vulnerable as she lay there.

He stood up and paced around the small open space, restless and expectant. The dark couldn't come fast enough. He was more than ready to continue his campaign of harassment against the local slave lord.

Something moved outside.

He froze, as stiff as a cat about to pounce, knowing that the prey would make itself known if he was patient. He waited, and was rewarded with more movement.

Behind the flat was a narrow set of rickety steps that descended into a junkyard of sorts, property of their landlord, who ran the tiny tavern on the first floor. Most of the litter and refuse was so worthless it wasn't even worth stealing. Now a lanky Chinese man in his mid-twenties was stepping quickly from behind a threadbare tractor tire and coming toward the steps in a hurry, looking over his shoulder repeatedly. He ascended the stairs on his toes, wincing with every tiny creak. As he was about to knock on the door, Bolan yanked it open, grabbed the young man's wrist and dragged him inside. The muzzle of the 93-R buried in the soft underside of the young man's chin, and he became wide-eyed.

Bolan shut the door behind him. "Who are you?"

"Yanrong."

"What do you want?"

"Yanrong tell you go?"

Bolan shouted for Jiahua.

She sat up and took in the scene immediately. "Who the hell is that?"

"You find out," Bolan said, dragging the young man into the middle of the room and transferring the muzzle to the base of his brainstem.

Jiahua questioned him in Chinese. The man responded in a flood of explanation that the woman had to bring to a halt with a gesture.

"We've got to go, Belasko. This guy said there's a bunch of well-armed Americans looking for us. This guy and his buddy saw us from the street yesterday, and he thinks his buddy is going to sell our location to the Americans. They may be on their way now.

Bolan nodded and removed the gun from his prisoner's skull. "Okay, get your things and let's go. We'll get a more detailed explanation later."

He quickly patted down the young man and found him unarmed, then they assembled their belongings, most of which was hardware.

In minutes Bolan put together a surprise for the nameless Americans.

THE SMALL FLAT was above a hole-in-the-wall tavern. There was a yard full of junk out back, with a stairway leading out of the flat, then an alley. A staircase led up from the interior of the tavern. There was no side window or door.

Parl stood in the street with Wang and five of his men.

"Tony and Mike, you go around the back. If anybody tries to escape out the back door, shoot them. No ifs, ands or buts. Got it? Heavy, you stay out front. Anybody gets past us and tries to make a break for it, you shoot them. I mean it. Kill them dead on the spot. You understand?"

Heavy said he understood.

"Joey and Frank, you're coming with me, along with our friend here. We go in and we see what we can do. If we can keep them around long enough to find out something, then that's great. But if we have to do them on the spot and be done with it, well, that's fine, too. Okay?"

"Okay, Jet."

"Yeah, let's get this over with so we can get out of this freaking country," Frank growled.

Parl pulled open the door to the tiny tavern. It looked more like a greasy diner than a bar to his way of thinking. He pointed a gun at the man in the apron.

"Tell him not to make a sound," Parl said. "If anybody tries to yell or to run away, they get shot dead. Tell him that."

Wang nervously translated. The barman agreed to those terms enthusiastically.

"Now, you stay here until I get back. Tell everybody in here that I've got a guy out front with a gun. He'll shoot anybody who tries to go get the cops. Tell them that."

Wang translated, then sank onto a stool as the Americans started upstairs. He wiped his forehead with his hand. He had never intended to become a part of this operation. He just wanted to say what he knew, take the money and go. But Parl had insisted. He had to come along. He only got the money when the lead turned out to be good.

A few more minutes, Wang thought, and it would all be over. The next day he'd be on the train to Beijing and a new life.

Tony Pergo and Mike Martens circled the building and into the alley.

"Look at all this crap, would you?" Pergo said. "What do you suppose he's keeping it all for?"

"They don't have nothing good to keep, so they keep all the crap, I guess." Martens was looking at the rear window of the flat. There was no sign of movement inside, although he made out the glow of a dim bulb.

They waited at the edge of a fence that separated the minijunkyard from the street. The sun was behind them, behind another row of two-story retail buildings. The shadows were long and cool.

By now Parl would be making his way upstairs. Things might start to happen any second.

Pergo fell forward and smacked face-first into the fence, his gun dropping to the ground. For the first few seconds Martens thought he'd tripped on something.

But Pergo stayed down, unmoving. There was flash of glistening liquid that in the dusky light looked as if it might be blood....

Martens whirled, pointing his Browning handgun into the darkness. A man was standing there, barely visible. The hardman heard a slight coughing sound, then felt a crushing pressure against his chest. The Browning dropped because he couldn't make his hands work anymore. The dusk became darkness, and Martens slumped on the ground beside his partner.

SILENCE. PARL GOT no response from the tiny apartment when he yelled for the occupants' surrender. He stepped inside and aimed his Colt Double Eagle pistol into every visible corner. The kitchen area with its tiny table, the bed, the small couchlike assemblage of cushions were all visible. Across the room was a single door.

Parl pointed at it and nodded to Frank Marchetti. The two men stepped to the door, and Marchetti leveled his MAC-10. Parl yanked the door open.

Empty.

There was a flash of blinding light and immense noise, and Joey Borland screamed. He ran across the room, roaring in pain, tearing at his eyes. They'd walked into a trap.

"Let's get out!" Parl said. He pushed Borland out of the way and shouldered open the back door, Marchetti directly behind him. "Borland, come on, man, this way!"

There was another flash of light and sound as he started down the steps.

Then he saw the man in the yard below. He was tall, with dark hair, obviously not Chinese, and had an automatic rifle aimed at them.

The gun flashed as Parl was trying to bring his Colt to bear and dive out of the way simultaneously.

BOLAN SAW the lead man plummet sideways off the stairs and knew he hadn't plugged him. He turned the Steyr AUG assault rifle on the second man, who crossed his arms in front of himself as if to ward off the onslaught of bullets. Several rounds ripped into his forearms and were wasted. The rest cut across his chest, and he crashed down the last eight or nine steps with definitive lifelessness.

Another man emerged from the apartment, screaming and clawing at his face—he'd received a close-range blast from the flash-bang grenade Bolan left for them. As he groped for the rail, the Executioner triggered the Steyr AUG and the blind man never knew what hit him. His screams died, and he slumped to his knees on the landing, then pitched down the stairs.

"Belasko! Let's get out!" It was Jiahua, pulling up in their latest automobile acquisition. "Cops are on the way!"

"Which cops?"

"Who can tell? But I heard the call on the radio. Let's move before they get here."

Bolan got in the stolen car and left the scene.

PARL LIFTED HIS HEAD, then his strength failed and it dropped to the ground again. His body was awash with pain. He managed to drag himself to his knees, then to his feet.

"Heavy" Cicotte wandered around the side of the building.

"Where the fuck have you been!" Parl snarled, and his head throbbed with fresh pain.

"You told me to stay up front no matter what, Jet. Jesus, what happened?"

"The bastard got us, that's what! Got everybody but you and me!"

"Holy shit. What do we do now?"

"We go to war," Parl replied.

CHAPTER TWELVE

Two of Parl's men picked Wang up by the armpits and walked him to the door of the foreman's office. Parl lifted Wang's chin.

"That man entering the factory right now," Parl said, "is that Yanrong?"

Wang forced his right eye open and struggled to focus it. His other eye was swollen shut from a night of beating. He nodded as best he could; it was almost imperceptible.

Parl waved him back with his good hand.

The enforcer hadn't yet reported back to his superiors in Houston. He would tell them there was phone trouble or something. And he sure the hell hadn't gone back to Yan Whan, not after his humiliating failure. He'd go back when he had that American agent's head on a pole.

"Go get him," he said.

Pescara and Forlini marched down to the floor where the morning shift was filing in. Yanrong was already at work, assembling motor parts at his workstation. Pescara and Forlini approached him from either side.

"Come with us," Pescara said.

Yanrong asked them something in Chinese. Pescara didn't have the patience for it and grabbed the man by the arm. Forlini grabbed the other, and Yanrong was firmly escorted across the factory floor and up the four steps to the foreman's office.

Another pair of workers entered through the wide side doors. One was a beautiful young woman with short black hair, her companion an old, stooped man wearing his sun hat. The young woman crossed the floor to a workstation near the foreman's office. A moment after escorting Yanrong inside, Pescara and Forlini emerged again and took up seats outside the door. Each lit a cigarette.

"I speak little English good."

The young Chinese woman waited modestly five paces away, smiling shyly, in a shabby frock and pants but obviously beautiful.

"You would like to speak English to me so I can practice?"

"Sure, we would, miss," Pescara said. "What's your name?"

"I am Xiaoliao Jiahua."

"Zay-low?"

The young woman giggled. "That is good. Are you on holiday in Urumchi city?"

"You could say that, Zay-low. Maybe you could take me on a city tour, how would that be?"

"You first need to ask my father for permission," she replied.

Pescara and Forlini turned simultaneously to find that an old man in a sun hat had come up behind them. He looked both of them straight in the eye.

Pescara jumped to his feet, dragging the handgun out of his belt. The old man, who turned out to be a much younger non-Asian, leveled a large handgun and fired it once. The round slammed into Pescara and knocked him to the ground. The next shot kicked Forlini in the gut and dropped him on his back.

Jiahua kicked at the door and fell away from it. The expected torrent of fire didn't materialize.

Yanrong appeared in the doorway. ''He took off when he heard shots!''

Bolan raced into the foreman's office and found a back window standing open. A door on a rental car was slamming shut, and the vehicle raced away from the factory.

DON CARIANI'S VOICE, even over a bad connection stretching many thousands of miles, had the cool, aloof tone he used when he was very angry. ''Yan Whan tells me you blew it big-time, Jet.''

Jethro Parl glared across the office at Yan Whan with blatant hatred. ''The man didn't give you an accurate picture of the situation before he called us over, Don. This place is entirely out of control. Yan Whan's men are useless, and this asshole American set a trap for us with local help.''

''Correct me if I'm wrong, Jet—we are talking about one American man and one Chinese American woman, correct? That's who's causing the problems?''

''Well, yeah. But like I said, he had local help.''

''I don't want to hear it. You've let me down, Jet.''

Parl was stunned. He hadn't been chastised or talked down to by the Don in years. Of course, his jobs had been pulled off with consistent success. This was his first major failure in years.

''I'm sorry, Don Cariani,'' he replied formally. ''I'll take care of this guy. You'll see.''

''You know what's on the line here, Jet?''

"Yes, sir," he answered. But he knew the Don was going to explain it to him anyway.

"Major business for the Family, Jet. Millions of dollars in business. It was a major stroke of luck us hooking up with Whan, and now that the cash is starting to roll in he's threatening to move his business. You know why, Jet?"

"No."

"Because he says we're not able to provide the backup support he counted on from us."

Whan was leaning back behind his desk, with his hands on the arms of the chair, a self-satisfied smirk on his face. Parl resisted the powerful impulse to jump across the desk and smash that expression to a paste.

"He says he's got other interested parties in Hong Kong. Says they could take over our import operations in a blink of an eye. Says they have the manpower on the Asian continent to deal with his problems efficiently, unlike the Family. We got to prove him wrong and we got to do it soon."

"Yeah," Parl said.

"This is vital, Jet, to this Family and to your career."

Parl felt cold. He had never been threatened by the Don, but what he had just heard could be construed as nothing less.

"Don't worry, Don. I'll get this guy."

"I am worried, Jet. It's up to you to prove my worries are groundless."

"Yeah."

Parl slipped the receiver onto the phone on Whan's desk.

"I hope Mr. Cariani straightened out a few things."

"He did," Parl replied. He wanted to say much more.

"So, do you have a plan this time? Or do you intend

to simply deploy your men around town again and wait to see what turns up?''

''No. I've got a strategy. I'll need command of your men. I assume that won't be a problem.''

''No. You can have all of them—except for those I keep here at the compound for my personal protection.''

''And your police in the city. I'll need them, too.''

''You can have whatever you want, Mr. Parl. I don't care what measures you take. As long as this threat is eradicated and I can get back to my business.'' He folded his hands together and leaned across the desk. ''What is your intention?''

KHOU VILLAGE LAY within the city limits of Urumchi. The small subdivision was home to approximately four thousand people. Combined, the annual income of all the residents probably wouldn't equal that of several middle-class American families.

The homes in Khou Village were ramshackle, plywood collective-housing units where the summer air stagnated and the winter temperatures plummeted to near-freezing. The residents worked in a local factory and in the nearby fields, eking out what existence they could. They were the poverty stricken under a government structure where poverty wasn't supposed to exist.

The group of young men hardly noticed the school bus squeak to a halt and continued home, worn out from a day of hard labor in a sorghum field nearby.

Then the police car coming from the other direction accelerated and turned in front of them, stopping suddenly. The young men recognized the XSEA officers that stepped out, one of them raising a handgun. He pointed it at them, and the boys stopped still, hands in the air.

Before they knew it, they were searched, manacled and marched into the school bus.

They were the first, but the bus began to fill rapidly.

JIAHUA AND BOLAN HEARD the calls as they began to come in over the police radio frequency in their stolen car. Jiahua translated, but the picture that emerged was unclear.

"They're calling about the police arresting innocent people," she told him, "in Khou Village, which is on the southern outskirts of the city, in the northwest residential corner and in the Lingzheng neighborhood. They're calling to ask that the police come and stop the other police. Oh! It's the XSEAs—they're rounding up villagers and busing them away."

Bolan nodded. "They're trying to replace the prisoners we freed. What are the regular police doing about it?"

"Hard to tell. The new chief is ordering the regular police away from the Khou Village vicinity, but it sounds like some of them are headed there anyway."

The Executioner nodded. "Let's get there and see if we can slow them down a little."

THEY RACED SOUTH through the city, arriving at Khou Village in ten minutes. It looked as if they had stumbled upon a ghost town.

"Everyone is in hiding. They know the arrests are random," Bolan commented.

They heard activity and followed it around a corner, where Bolan spotted a rattletrap bus much like the one he had attacked outside the prison. A pair of chained men was being prodded inside by an XSEA policeman with an AK-47. Two more XSEAs were shouting at a

pair of Urumchi police officers. The police were ges-
turing at the bus, plainly enraged. The XSEAs were
holding their AKs by the barrel and waving them,
clearly threatening. The police gave up the argument
and got back in their car. They screeched away from
the scene angrily.

Three more XSEAs were emerging from a side street
with a half-dozen shabbily dressed men and women
chained together in manacles.

"Free labor," Bolan muttered.

"What're we going to do about it?"

"All we can."

They pulled around the corner and found themselves
on another deserted street, where they exited their vehicle.

Bolan was fully armed. The 93-R was in its familiar
shoulder holster. In hand was the Steyr AUG assault
rifle. Extra magazines and several 40 mm grenades hung
from the combat webbing he wore over a blacksuit and
underneath his roomy black windbreaker. Within easy
reach was a selection of bladed weapons and conven-
tional grenades. He was a man ready to engage in serious battle.

Jiahua was equipped with her holstered Colt handgun
and the Heckler & Koch MP-5. She, too, was equipped
with extra magazines and had a large knife in a sheath
on her belt.

They were a deadly pair, about to face an unknown
multitude of enemies.

The odds were tough to call.

THE AVENUE WAS NARROW and fetid, the leaning buildings close on either side. The Executioner glimpsed
frightened faces peeking out of windows, but they dis-

appeared quickly. They were right to be afraid. Their community was going to become a battleground.

A door burst open, and a young woman with long dark hair was pushed into the street, hands chained together behind her back. She turned back to the doorway, her face a mask of fury. Shrieking with rage that transcended courage or foolishness, she ran back at the XSEA that emerged from her home and tried to charge him. The man raised his AK-47 to block the attack, then flung her to the street.

The XSEA spotted Bolan and the 93-R, already aimed directly at him. He manipulated his AK into firing position anyway. A single suppressed shot from the 93-R struck his chest, crashing through his ribs and heart and sending him to the ground.

Bolan stepped to the doorway of the house and swept it with the handgun, but there was no one else inside. Jiahua was already helping the young woman free herself with the corpse's keys.

The moment they were open, the woman shrugged off the manacles and stepped to the corpse. Her foot collided heavily with its skull and the lifeless head flopped sideways, but she kept kicking him, grunting and heaving, until Jiahua put her hands on the woman's shoulders. The woman stopped and stood trembling under the CIA agent's hands, tears streaming down her face.

"Go inside and hide," Jiahua told her in Chinese. "Don't answer the door and don't look outside again tonight."

She steered the woman into her house, then shut the door and followed Bolan, who was already creeping down the street in the direction of the bus.

They arrived at a corner a block south of the bus and

observed a new contingent of prisoners being marched onto the vehicle, and four XSEAs were coming in their direction in search of more recruits.

"Bring them to me. I'll be ready," Bolan said from cover.

"Right." Jiahua left the subgun leaning against a wall and walked out into the street as if she were a pedestrian. She stopped when she saw the band of four XSEAs walking toward her, made a small cry and fled the way she had come.

The men shouted and raced after her, running around the corner, too fast to spot the man waiting against the wall. Then the 93-R began to fire suppressed tribursts, chopping the men to pieces and punching them to the ground.

The loudest sound of the exchange was when the AKs clattered to the earth.

"Good work," Bolan said, watching the fallen for signs of life. There was none.

Jiahua stepped over the corpses and retrieved her MP-5.

Two XSEAs seemed to be standing guard at the bus when they spied on it again. There were at least a hundred yards of approach. It would be a difficult job to get at the guards and take them out quietly.

"How long did you want this operation to remain silent, anyway?" Jiahua asked.

"The longer our presence is unknown, the safer it is for both of us."

"Amen to that." She glanced around the corner. "How about now?"

The two guards were walking to the west, talking to someone, more XSEA arrivals with more prisoners, probably, and that meant the guards were temporarily distracted.

"As good as any," Bolan replied.

They walked into the open and started down the street in a quick trot. Bolan had the Steyr AUG primed with a grenade and ready to fire. His mind considered the bus full of prisoners and the damage a stray 40 mm round could cause.

The space between the buildings at the north end of the street was ten feet wide at the most, opening into the main thoroughfare where the bus was parked. The guards disappeared behind one of the west-side buildings and reappeared with another pair of prisoners chained together. Bolan slipped into a doorway and pulled Jiahua in after him. The prisoners were shoved onto the bus.

They'd crossed maybe two-thirds of the distance to the guards. Bolan watched them around a doorway edge and witnessed them conversing with the out-of-sight XSEAs who had delivered the prisoners. Then the talking stopped. The guards stayed in position. Bolan quickly ascertained that he and Jiahua weren't going to move a muscle without being spotted, let alone engage in a frontal approach.

The time for silence was over.

"Let's go," he said.

The CIA agent hugged the butt of the MP-5 into her stomach like a security blanket. "Amen to that."

Two AKs were held ready but pointing at the asphalt. It wouldn't take long for a man to bring that weapon into firing position, thumb the selector switch to autofire and send a stream of steel death in Bolan's direction. He stepped into the open with that reality foremost in his mind. But he was too well trained for it to be a distraction.

The 40 mm grenade flew from the Steyr AUG before the guards had even focused on him and exploded several feet in front of them. The concussion blew the guards onto their backs, and a quick rattle of AK fire was drilled uselessly skyward. Bolan raced toward the bus, triggering several rounds into the collapsed figures as they weakly tried to raise their weapons.

Another grenade was primed as he came to the end of the street and spotted the guards who had just delivered the prisoners. They had been a good hundred paces away when the first explosion caught their attention and now were trying to achieve some kind of cover. The round detonated in their midst, and the three bodies were tossed in different directions.

Jiahua examined the bodies, finding that any immediate threat had been eradicated.

"Search for keys," Bolan ordered.

He jogged to the bus and found that only one of the dead guards had a set of keys. It would take a long time in battle terms for a busload of prisoners to free themselves with only a single set of keys. He tossed them to a pair of men in the front seat.

"No more keys!" Jiahua said as she came to the slave transport. "But the reinforcements are getting their act together." She nodded to the west, where a large group of XSEAs were gathered, out of range of their weapons, watching the activity at the bus.

The collection of corpses and the sprays of blood marking their demise would be as clear as beacons at that distance. As Bolan watched, another handful separated from the buildings and joined the others, leaving their manacled prisoners forgotten at the side of the street.

"I make out ten men," Bolan said.

The first of the freed prisoners were coming to the door of the bus. Bolan waited until five men stood there. He directed Jiahua to explain the location of their first five kills. He sent two more back to their parked car to retrieve the rest of the hardware. "Tell them to arm themselves and get back here at once."

Jiahua explained rapidly, and the men ran off while Bolan gathered the two AKs from the dead guards and handed them to the next two men to emerge from the vehicle. No translation was needed. The men didn't grip them with the familiarity of soldiers, but Bolan knew that few weapons were more easily utilized by an amateur than a Kalashnikov. And it wasn't as if these men had any choice—they were fighting for their lives and freedom.

Bolan weighed his options as he stared down the gathering XSEAs several hundred yards down the street. They were watching the bus activity with their own obvious confusion, directionless—maybe one of their leaders was among the recent dead. But Bolan could do little himself. He was waiting for the chained prisoners to free themselves.

And then what?

The answer was strapped in the satchel he had draped over his shoulder. He dropped it to the ground and started fitting the Ruger together. In a minute the Model 77 Magnum Mark II sniper rifle was intact and loaded, and when he placed it to his eye the twelve-power Leupold scope brought the distant XSEAs up close and personal.

Bolan had seen more men than he could count from

just such a perspective, and most of the time those he saw had just seconds to live.

He pulled the trigger, and the Ruger slammed into his shoulder as if someone had taken a baseball bat to it. He'd discarded the shoulder pad in the interest of traveling light and regretted it. But the pain would fade. The destruction the Ruger caused on the other end was more permanent.

The first XSEA dropped to the ground. Bolan aimed again, triggering almost before he had the second man in sight, and the .458 Winchester Magnum round stabbed into the second man. The XSEAs were reacting, and Bolan knew he had seconds before his targets fled. There was just one Winchester round left in the weapon. He had to make it count. He ignored the throbbing in his shoulder and centered a running man in the cross hairs. The Ruger spoke a third time, and Bolan had the satisfaction of watching the running man get flung to the ground.

His hand automatically went to the pocket where the big rounds were stashed and reloaded the sniper's rifle with the calm speed of a practiced sniper. But when he sighted again his targets, as predicted, had fled for cover.

By this time the five locals had appropriated the weapons from the dead XSEAs and were returning.

Bolan gestured to the newly armed men and issued quick commands to Jiahua. Then he started down the street, staying close to the wall and keeping the others behind him. He knew he was leading an army of civilians. They weren't trained soldiers and couldn't be expected to behave like soldiers.

But he expected them to fight for their lives.

They arrived at the corner where the XSEAs had fled

for safety from Bolan's Ruger fire. The street to the left at the intersection was empty. The XSEAs had disappeared down it.

Bolan heard a cry from a terrified child coming from a nearby hovel.

Communicating with his hands, he instructed the Khou villagers to stay where they were and watch the front of the structure, a tiny shack composed of wood and aluminum sheets. There was a single, dark window, and nothing could be seen behind a heavy drapery. Bolan knew he might be on the wrong track. He would have to be extremely cautious about IDing his targets.

He circled and found another window, crouched outside and listened.

There was no further sound from within.

Bolan found himself wondering what had become of the crying child. He shouldered the back door and entered the room, this time with the Steyr AUG leading the way. The XSEAs were heading for the front door. A man, a villager, lay on a nearby bunk with a bloodied head, motionless. There was no sign of the child.

But Bolan heard the child cry out again in the same moment the XSEAs heard him bursting in behind them. They turned back to face him, and Bolan triggered the assault rifle, cutting down the three nearest him in seconds.

The child was there, among the four survivors, with a Makarov 9 mm pistol jammed against his skull.

The Executioner achieved target acquisition on the owner of the Makarov and fired a burst. The boy screamed, and the Russian handgun thumped on the floor a split second after its owner died. Bolan redirected the stream of Steyr AUG 5.56 mm rounds into the two standing gunman, who were trying to rotate and maneuver their AKs for firing in the crowded jostle. Bolan beat them to the punch, and the rapid-fire rounds kicked them into one another.

The only survivor had been lucky enough to be behind the Makarov owner when the firing started. But his luck wasn't holding out. He scrambled out the door to escape Bolan and began to dance as the Khou villagers used him to test their ability with their new weapons.

The Khou villagers found that their AK-47s were, in fact, relatively easy to fire weapons that killed with startling efficacy.

The boy was standing amid the bodies with a look of silent shock on his face. Bolan felt sorry for him. What he had seen in the past few minutes would haunt him the rest of his life. But at least he was alive.

JIAHUA EMERGED from the bus with the last of the prisoners as Bolan and his army came marching back. The villagers had stripped the dead of all the weapons and spare ammunition they could locate.

"They're all free," Jiahua said. "Now what?"

"These men are free. What about the northwest residential corner and the Lingzheng neighborhood? We were of no help to them," Bolan growled.

"They'll be taken to the prison. Eventually Yan Whan will start up his factories again."

"I say we take care of that problem for them," Bolan said. "Tonight. Ask them if they're in on the deal. And find out which one of them can drive this bus."

CHAPTER THIRTEEN

Life continued in the city of Urumchi as if war hadn't been declared within its boundaries.

The bus drove around the outskirts of the downtown area and headed for the factory called Happy Family.

"Company," Jiahua said as she paced the aisle.

Bolan saw them. It was a city police car, staying within a few lengths of the rear of the bus.

"XSEAs?"

"Can't tell."

"Then we leave them alone."

The driver brought the bus to a halt. The factory was surrounded by a ten-foot-tall chain-link fence, topped with barbed wire. As with all Yan Whan installations, it was surrounded by deserted buildings and empty lots. Bolan spotted four guards stationed at the gate and another two at the front door of the building. How many others were scattered throughout the exterior and interior of Happy Family was a question that was unanswerable until their bodies were counted.

"We're going in," he called above the heads of his army, then uttered a short prayer to the Universe for their safety. They had all witnessed firsthand the viciousness of the XSEAs and had volunteered to strike back.

He pointed at the building. Jiahua didn't need to translate; the driver hit the gas and the bus chugged toward Happy Family.

Bolan watched the reaction of the guards at the gate as they spotted the bus, realized a moment later that it was one of Yan Whan's and realized not long after that it was coming in whether they wanted it to or not.

Bolan pulled at the door mechanism and positioned himself on the steps at the open door with the Steyr AUG assault rifle in hand. He watched out the front window as the bus charged into the chain-link gate and sprang it open with a crash and twang of stressed metal. One of the guards had been running away and was slammed between the gate and the fence with killing force.

The Executioner spotted another guard, farther away, who avoided the flying gate and raised his AK to shoot at the bus. Bolan targeted with difficulty, and a burst of rounds cut the guard down. Another man ducked for cover behind the building before he could be targeted. The bus swung in a wide circle as it braked, bringing Bolan face-to-face with the guards stationed at the front door.

He heard the rattle of AK fire from within the bus and jumped out of the vehicle, circling its front end to lend assistance. By the time he reached the target zone, two more XSEA guards were dead on the ground.

Jiahua was shouting orders, and a front contingent of Khou villagers stormed out of the bus, joining Bolan.

"Tell the others to arm themselves and find the side entrances," Bolan directed her. "What's our police escort up to?"

"Nothing. They're just watching us."

"Fine. As long as they don't get in the way."

Bolan advanced to the front door, and at least fifteen villagers fell in ranks behind him. At his hand signal they spread out along the wall on either side of the front door, and Bolan kicked it in, then fell away. A rattle of automatic fire emerged, drilling into the sides of the bus and pounding at the dirt. Bolan waited for a pause, then ran across the entrance with the Steyr AUG chugging death. He glimpsed a single XSEA guard standing just a few feet inside, his face gleaming with fear and his eyes going wide when he spotted Bolan. The 5.56 mm rounds cut him down before he could react.

Bolan stepped to the fallen man as his fighters spread out, AKs at the ready but hesitant. He couldn't blame them. They weren't experienced fighters.

The big American jogged through a short hallway and into the factory itself. It was a now familiar sight—untold numbers of men, women and children chained to their worktables, to their conveyors and to one another. Unlike his previous probes into Yan Whan's manufacturing facilities, these prisoners weren't crouching in fear. They were watching the Executioner when he entered, with a look in their eyes that he thought might be hope.

There was a young boy near the front entrance who smiled at Bolan and pointed to his left. "There."

Bolan made a quick hunt in the indicated direction, and from an impromptu hiding place behind a steel drum he spotted the movement of two more guards. They were discussing the situation among themselves in rapid-fire Chinese, and didn't seem even to notice Bolan's approach.

Their attention was drawn to a group of armed villagers appearing in the open, vulnerable, but Bolan triggered the Steyr AUG before the guards could make the attempt to fire. The first toppled while the second dived for cover behind a steel cabinet. The villagers fired into the cabinet, creating a racket.

The guard stood suddenly with his hands in the air.

Bolan heard more autofire from within the factory and ran after it while the villagers took care of the prisoner.

He found three more XSEAs trying to hold a side door against the other villagers and Jiahua. He shouted at them, simultaneously ejecting a grenade from the Steyr AUG and stepping behind a steel support column. The three of them screamed as if with a single voice, then the grenade detonated at their feet. The explosion rocked the building.

When Bolan emerged, he found only bloody remainders of the three XSEAs.

"All clear!" he called. A moment later Jiahua stepped through the smoking gap in the wall where the grenade had effectively doubled the door opening.

"Good work!"

"The work is just beginning," the warrior growled.

SEVERAL CARS AND A 4×4 were located on the lot of the Happy Family factory, and rummaging through the pockets of the dead produced the keys for them. More importantly a small cache of AKs and a large store of ammunition were located in the small room that served as the guardroom.

"We've got arms for thirty-seven soldiers," Jiahua reported.

Bolan knew that thirty-seven armed but unskilled men couldn't count for much, but they were all he had. He had surrendered his own extra weapons for the coming battle. The Beretta shotgun was perfect for an unskilled soldier in a tight fight. On the other hand the Ruger sniper's rifle was next to useless in untrained hands.

"He says he knows how to use it—apparently he took some training in the army," Jiahua told him of the man who had taken the weapon.

Bolan handed the young Chinese man, one of the freed Happy Family prisoners, the fifteen extra rounds he had for the Ruger. The young man quickly and efficiently loaded the weapon, without fumbling. He spoke again briefly.

"He said it's a nice weapon," Jiahua translated.

Bolan nodded. "Glad he approves."

The Executioner commandeered the Toyota 4×4. The cars and the bus filled quickly with the growing army. Even unarmed men were insisting on accompanying them, in hopes of coming up with more weapons as their hard probe proceeded.

Bolan didn't like the idea of bringing unarmed men into the battle, but who was he to deny a man an opportunity for revenge on his former captors? Nearly fifty men left the grounds of the Happy Family factory. Those who were left behind were still engaged in the process of freeing themselves from their chains and shackles.

The 4×4 led the entourage out of Urumchi proper and in the direction of the massive prison operated by Yan Whan.

Bolan rummaged in his knapsack one-handed as he drove, coming up with a small brick of plastique and a single radio-controlled detonator, which he had been saving. The Toyota had a full tank of gas, which would add a little muscle to the explosion. He activated the detonator, and a tiny red light glowed. Bolan put the bomb on the dashboard.

He followed the curve in the road, where he had hijacked and freed the first busload of prisoners. A minute later the prison itself swung out from behind a rise in the land.

There were extra guards along the top of the wall. They'd received word of the attacks at Happy Family and in Khou Village. Getting close would be tricky, maybe deadly.

Bolan stripped the knapsack of one of its shoulder straps and tied it to the steering wheel. As he aimed the 4×4 at the front of the prison, he moved into the passenger seat, stretching to keep his foot on the gas, and tied the strap to the seat belt. He thumbed the detonator and accelerated as the prison walls loomed above him and the first rounds of AK fire from the wall hit his vehicle. Bolan adjusted the strap minutely and gave the vehicle an extra burst of gas, shifted into neutral so the truck would coast, then opened the door and flung himself at the rush of ground underneath him.

The ground slammed into him, and Bolan spun crazily on the earth, far too fast at first to attempt to gain control. As he came to a halt, several flashes of pain streaked through his body. He ignored them, watching the Toyota approach the huge steel front entrance. He activated the detonator radio control and pressed the button at the instant the 4×4 made contact with the door.

The 4×4 disappeared in a flash of light. The door sprung open in a bent and twisted mass, and over the explosion's roar Bolan heard the screams of XSEA guards thrown from their stations at the top of the wall.

He had precious seconds before those who remained

on the wall got their wits about them and returned to firing. Now he was a single man, out in the open, a perfect target. He scrambled to his feet only to have his right ankle fail. Bolan used his good leg to drag himself up to his feet and assessed the pain in his leg as he limped to the Steyr AUG, lying in the dirt where he had released it during his frantic roll.

The bone wasn't broken, and he knew he could function well enough with a sprain. Snatching up the assault rifle, he rode out the pain as he sprinted for the wall.

JIAHUA GASPED WITH RELIEF when she spotted her partner hop to his feet for the second time and make for the wall. She thought he'd been shot down.

"I am going to go through! It is going to be close so you had better hold on tightly!" the bus driver yelled, shifting up to highway speeds. He was aiming for the narrow gap between the bent edge of the steel door and the burning hulk that had been the 4×4's rear end.

"Get that mess out of the way so the others can get through!"

"I intend to!"

Jiahua draped her forearm over her eyes and ducked into the stairwell when the bus crashed into the burning vehicle. Fiery debris flew in all directions, and the bus was beyond it without more than a lurch. The driver slammed on the brakes.

Jiahua pushed through the doors and stepped onto the ground in a run. A group of surprised guards was running in her direction, and she opened fire with the MP-5, bowling over all three men in just seconds.

There was a rattle of autofire to her right, and she spun to the rear side of the wall, spotting four armed guards. She triggered the MP-5 in hopes of keeping them down, then sped for the wall. Gunfire rang out, and she heard a scream behind her, turning as she reached the wall to see two of the Khou villagers, just emerging from the bus, collapsing under heavy AK fire. More of the villagers were firing from the bus windows with their own weapons, but Jiahua knew it was highly unlikely they could score on the protected guards.

A figure appeared in the oily black smoke of the explosion, and Jiahua almost fired the MP-5 before she recognized Bolan, approaching with a limp.

"You hurt?"

"I'll live. We've got to get up there." He pointed skyward, then limped to the steel stairs that accessed the top of the wall.

"I'm going up. You be ready to get those people out of that bus when the coast is clear. It's a death trap if they stay in there long enough for the guards to attack."

Bolan started up the stairs, challenged by the screaming of his ankle and the dual needs for speed and relative quiet. His advantage when he reached the top lay in surprise. Despite his best effort the damage to his ankle slowed him. When he was one landing below the top of the wall he heard more fire from the guards close by, directed now at the three secondary vehicles that had accompanied them from the factory. The vehicles had sped inside the prison grounds and were trying to maneuver themselves into a spot where they could get a good shot at the guards on the wall. Instead the guards scored on one of the cars, and it lurched to a halt.

Bolan was as yet undetected. He fed a grenade into the Steyr AUG and raced up the last flight onto the top of the wall, stepping into the open on the steel grate walkway, facing the guards. They turned on him in surprise, the nearest man raising an AK in his direction.

Bolan launched the grenade and triggered the Steyr AUG, cutting into the nearby gunman, who spasmed as he died, firing his rifle skyward.

The Executioner dived back for the stairs and grabbed a steel handrail as the grenade detonated. The three remaining guards sailed screaming down the wall as the walkway twisted like a snake and leaned away from the wall, carried by the mangled walkway to which it was bolted. Bolan felt the grate floor tilt out from under his feet and had no choice but to let go of the Steyr and grab for another handhold. The assault rifle disappeared into the chaos of twisting metal.

Then the movement of the structure stopped with a sickening lurch. Bolan's body flew sideways, his back slamming into a steel projection, his right arm nearly ripping out of the socket while the grate bit into the fingers of his left hand like piranha teeth.

He hung for a moment, racked by pain. Then he lowered himself to the nearest semilevel section of steel and let his body become accustomed to the agony. Some of the pain faded quickly. His back, like his ankle, felt as if it had received more-serious damage.

He began to untangle himself from the twisted ruin and crawl down to ground level.

JETHRO PARL HAD BEEN UP since 4:00 a.m., planning, strategizing, trying to come up with some scheme for getting the CIA agent, or whatever he was, and his woman. He wasn't satisfied with what he and his men had developed. Not one idea was a sure-fire answer to the problem. And a distinct answer was what Don Cariani, and Yan Whan, were demanding.

Some of his stress had been relieved when he returned to his suite to find Yan Whan's German concubine waiting for him in his bed. Birgitte was naked and gave him a glass of wine, and immediately sought to extract some of his pent-up frustrations.

Thirty minutes later Birgitte was asleep and Parl was pacing the suite, becoming agitated all over again.

What the hell was he doing here, anyway, in this Chinese backwater city? Even Chinese people didn't come here. They sent all their cast-offs, the Russians, the Mongols, the Uygurs and all the rest. It was no place for a red-blooded American.

He didn't like the city, and he couldn't function effectively there. He was a failure in China—at least so far—and he had never been a failure in the U.S. He had been an efficient, skilled killer. He had been trusted. The worst consequence of the Urumchi fiasco was that Don Cariani had lost faith in him. To some extent Parl had lost faith in himself.

That all had to change. He had to kill this CIA guy, present his head to Yan Whan on a platter, make the man happy, restore his confidence in the Cariani organization and restore Don Cariani's faith in Jethro Parl.

He had to wipe that agent off the planet. But how? Every scheme he'd come up with was a long shot, which meant he had to wait for the guy to fall into his lap.

And who knew how much more damage to Yan Whan's operation might be perpetrated before that happened.

The phone in Parl's small suite rang, and his mouth went instantly dry. It had to be bad news.

It was.

"Oh, fuck." Parl shook his head and listened for a minute longer. He kicked at the side of the television. "Yeah, I'll meet you out front."

"What is it?" Birgitte asked, blinking.

"The prison," Parl replied, as if that explained it all. He dressed, draped his holster over his arm and stomped out of the suite. He emerged from the low-lying guest houses to the right of the mansion. Yan Whan was coming out of his house at the same moment, stepping down the steps with his eyes locked on Parl.

"I heard what is happening," Whan said. "I hold you personally responsible."

"I don't give a flying fuck."

"You'd better. I want this stopped immediately. I mean now. I don't want to lose any more work staff, and I don't want the safety of my prison compromised. And if I have serious problems with your performance, I'm simply going to change my partners."

"I know. I get the picture."

"Are you going to do anything about it or not?"

"I'm sending my men there now."

"That's not even twenty."

"That's all the men I have!" Parl said, suddenly enraged, his face red. "You want to provide me some fucking backup! You want to take some responsibility for your own mess!"

Whan regarded the American silently, and the silence took some of the steam out of Parl's sails. The enforcer realized suddenly that, for the first time, Whan seemed worried.

"What do you need to get the job done once and for all?" Whan asked.

"I need all the men you've got, so we can go in there, blanket the place and kill everything that moves until we kill the right guy! Give me the house staff!"

"The house staff?" Whan was genuinely alarmed.

"That's all the men that you have left who're not already at the prison."

"You don't think the prison is taken?"

"How should I know? Your guys have been guarding the prison. Do you think it's impregnable?"

Whan scanned the grounds of the mansion. "Leave me at least ten men. Take everyone else. Do as you said you would do. Kill this man and this woman now. Get them out of my hair! And I will guarantee not only to stay with your organization, Mr. Parl, but I will personally give a good report to Don Cariani about your activities here. I will tell him my earlier bad reports were hastily made."

"Good." Parl went to find his trained killers.

"THEY'RE IN THERE! I guess they figure they can hold us off for as long as they want," Jiahua explained. Once Bolan had eradicated the guards on the top of the wall, the Khou villagers and ex-slaves had poured from the bus and other vehicles, driving the surviving guards and staff into the prison building.

Bolan evaluated the building, which jutted from the front of the prison structure and was, essentially, the only egress. The walls were made of concrete brick, as was the prison itself and the walls surrounding the compound. The windows were covered in steel bars. The door was solid steel, likely thick enough to withstand a blast from any weapon in Bolan's arsenal.

The Executioner was trained to assess the weaknesses of such strongholds. It took him seconds to determine the Achilles' heel of the prison.

"I'll get them out," he told Jiahua. "You have the men ready to take them down if they try to fight their way to freedom."

"And exactly where will they exit?"

"The front door. It's the only way."

"No, it's not, Belasko. They'll retreat backward, into the prison itself!"

"They won't."

"Oh, really? And how do you plan to get them to come out the front door into our waiting arms?"

Bolan grimaced. "Don't worry about that." He left Jiahua standing in the yard with a hand on her hip.

He approached from the front, crept along the wall, around the corner, ducking under the two ground-floor windows. He quickly found ladder rungs bolted into the side of the building. The ladder led to the roof, where a guard could be posted.

There had been no sign of a roof-top guard, but Bolan ascended the last few rungs with special care. He was now armed with an AK-47, which he had appropriated from a corpse after finding the Steyr AUG lying in the dirt, too battered from its tumble through the broken stairway to be reliable.

The AK had been well-used, but a quick inspection assured Bolan it was in decent shape.

He pointed the assault rifle and scanned the roof for signs of life. He found a single guard, who had watched the battle and found himself trapped on top of the building. Now he was waiting it out, crouched low to avoid being seen by the enemy, waiting for a chance to get free.

Bolan turned off the AK's safety and flipped the selector switch. He wouldn't need a barrage of autofire to take out this man.

And in fact he would rather avoid using the gun at all. The sound might alert the inhabitants of the building.

He stepped onto the roof and snapped out the AK's folding bayonet, approaching the guard from behind. The man was prone, only his eyes and the muzzle of his assault rifle peeking over the edge.

The roof was covered with pea gravel, and Bolan's foot made the smallest sound when he stepped. He froze, still three paces behind the guard, but the man remained as he was.

Bolan moved two steps forward, and the guard reacted. With a shout he twisted on his back, bringing his AK off the roof. Before the gunner could acquire a target, the Executioner's bayonet pierced his torso and made a grinding noise against the gravel roof.

Bolan extracted the bayonet from the corpse, wiped it clean, folded it, then crept to the air vent.

A gust of hot air wafted from the aluminum opening. He took the knapsack from his shoulder and assessed the contents.

His supply was getting short.

He withdrew an HE grenade from the knapsack, pulled the pin and tossed the bomb down the exhaust vent, then jogged quickly to the front of the building and crouched on the ground near the corpse.

The building shook suddenly. A blast of fire blew the vent ten feet into the air, and when it landed again it was a balled mass of aluminum.

Bolan ran back to the newly widened opening and commenced firing into the black smoke. There were screams and shouts, people running and crashing into the wreckage that now filled the interior. He heard the rattle of AK fire from the front of the building and knew that at least some of the inhabitants were making a break for it. But Bolan was determined to keep them running out the front, not back through the prison. He withdrew another HE grenade, armed it and tossed it into the hole.

This time he headed for the ladder and crouched near the roof edge when the high explosive ripped through the building. It was followed by a slow, grinding crash. The two explosions had compromised the structural integrity of the building, and something was collapsing.

More AK fire told him that more XSEAs were trying to break out the front. He took the ladder descent as rapidly as possible, and by the time he reached the front of the building he found at least twenty men stretched facedown with their hands behind their heads. At least that same number of corpses littered the ground.

"Very cool, Belasko!" Jiahua shouted. "With what we've taken from these guys, we've armed every man we brought with us."

"That's not enough. We've got a prison full of potential soldiers to arm, and we've got to do it quickly. Reinforcements will be here soon."

Bolan ordered a knot of nearby men to accompany him while Jiahua saw to the shackling of the new prisoners. The recently freed factory workers were taking special pleasure in putting the XSEA men in the chains they had worn.

The Executioner and his men picked their way through the rubble of the building's interior. They found no one still alive. All the guards had either fled or died in the dual explosions. Or were buried and as good as dead.

The entrance to the prison was covered, as well. Bolan and the men dragged several chunks of charred wood out of the way before they could get at it. By then Jiahua arrived with several sets of keys and the door was opened.

Bolan was the first inside Yan Whan's prison.

He had been firsthand witness to some of the gravest inhumanities ever perpetrated, but little could compare to the horror of the prison.

The stench was thick and heavy in the air—human waste and unidentifiable rot. The heat was unbearable. There was virtually no light except for a few fluorescent tubes hanging from the corridor ceilings, only half of which were working.

The people who stared out through the bars had the wasted, hollow look of holocaust victims. They were crammed in small cells, sometimes six or eight or more, so that they barely had room to stand. There were no toilets, and it appeared that trenches in the concrete floor were designed to funnel away waste. The walls were dripping with moisture—condensation caused by insufferable heat, cool concrete walls and far too many people crammed into a small space with no air circulation.

One of the freed prisoners from the factory came crawling through the prison door behind Bolan. He said in careful English, "This has been our home."

"But today you all go free," Bolan said.

HE WAS SURPRISED at how able-bodied the prisoners were. Everyone in the long line of prisoners streaming out of the building looked haggard but fit and healthy.

"Those who become weak or crippled, they put them in there," the English-speaking factory worker said. He pointed across the yard to a large pile of disturbed earth, which Bolan had hardly noticed before. "Many are there," the factory worker whispered. "Many."

"But no more," Bolan said. He withdrew the Beretta 93-R as he walked across to the waiting XSEA prisoners, who were standing in their shackles with bowed heads, waiting to be put into the prison they had once guarded. The first prisoner looked up in some surprise when Bolan stepped up to him and placed the gun against his forehead.

"I want to know where the armory is."

"Do no understand."

"Guns! Where is room for guns?"

"We have no room for guns. Just guns we carry."

Bolan pulled the trigger and jerked the 93-R. The prisoner screeched in horror. It took several seconds for him to realize the round flew inches above his head.

The Executioner raised the gun again and carefully placed it against the guard's forehead.

"I will ask one more time. Where is the room for the guns?"

WITH HIS HANDS JERKED painfully behind him, the guard stumbled through the wreckage, pulling Bolan into a spot on the rear wall where it wouldn't have even been clear that a door existed. "In there," the guard said.

Bolan immediately started to direct the clearing of the rubble from in front of the door. It took just minutes to uncover it and to send in men to start passing out weapons.

Just in time.

Yan Whan's men were on the way.

"Our bus driver picked it up on his radio. They've got several Americans and the house staff on the way. That means Yan Whan's personal mansion guard has been recruited to beef up the ranks. We've got him running scared, Belasko!"

"That's what I'm afraid of. How long until they get here?"

"Minutes."

"We've got to get to Yan Whan, right now," Bolan said. "If he's really scared, he'll try to make a break for it."

"We can't let that bastard get away."

"Right. If for no other reason than he's bound to try to set up this same operation elsewhere."

"Then let's go."

"Right."

Bolan found his English-speaker and quickly gave him the details. "You'll have to engage Yan Whan's army without me."

"We handle it. I am ex-army. I will run things."

"Good. Start organizing. They'll be here shortly."

Jiahua had chosen one of the small cars stolen from the factory, and she braked to a rocking halt beside him. As he jumped in the passenger seat, he observed the English-speaker directing troops onto the roof. A good tactical move. He wondered how skilled the man really was, how well he would be able to defend this place against the trained men Yan Whan was sending against him.

A QUICK MANEUVER got them past the approaching army. Jiahua raced away from the prison, then drove the car behind a hill at the first opportunity. Minutes later a column of vans, cars and panel trucks roared by on the road. They waited for another three long minutes before pulling onto the road again and heading for Yan Whan's huge country estate.

Bolan checked his pack. He had the AK-47 and several mags, but no explosives were left.

"How's your leg?" Jiahua asked. "Is it sprained?"

"Yeah, but not bad."

"I warned you about this house, Belasko. It's a fortress."

"Not without most of its staff it's not. Now it's just a big place in the country with a few armed guards."

THEY PARKED OFF-ROAD and approached the estate on foot, passing through copses to stay out of sight as much as possible. They came to the wall unseen.

The barrier was smooth brick, eight feet high and topped with black iron spikes. Bolan jumped, grabbed at two of the spike anchors and hauled himself up. Peering over the edge for a moment showed him no guards were visible. There was nothing but empty lawn stretching between the wall and the distant mansion.

Something made him pause. He hung there on the wall for a minute, attempting to identify a sound he heard, very faint and distant.

Then he knew what it was.

"Come on!" He dragged himself up to the top of the wall, straddling the iron spikes, and reached down to Jiahua. "Hurry. They've got a helicopter."

"Shit! Whan's going to take off."

A moment later they were crouching in the grass, spotting no sign of guards. There was also no easy ingress to the house on that side. Bolan crouched and moved quickly across the lawn.

A figure stepped around the corner and spotted him, going rigid.

"Down!" Bolan shouted, diving to the earth himself and bringing his AK-47 to bear in the same instant. The guard fired at them, and Bolan heard the burning passage of the 7.62 mm rounds not far overhead. He triggered his AK and cut the guard down where he stood.

A quick glance told him Jiahua hadn't taken any hits. "They'll know we're here."

They ran to the corner where the dead guard lay, found the front of the building clear and sprinted forward. Bolan grabbed at the doorknob, found it locked and triggered a single shot at the locking mechanism. The door sprung open, and Bolan rushed inside, sweeping the room.

The massive entryway looked more L.A. modern than rural Chinese. The furnishings were expensive and oversize, the walls white and bare except for small chrome pieces of sculpture.

Another guard popped into view long enough to unleash a volley of autofire, which went into the ceiling. Bolan triggered at the corner and ran forward. The guard stepped into the open and was surprised that the enemy had changed positions. He redirected his aim but too late. The stream of rounds from Bolan's AK struck him down.

Jiahua entered the mansion when Bolan gave the okay, and they made their way through the house, finding it deserted.

Bolan followed the rumble of the chopper, finding himself at a rear entrance to the house, looking out over a well-tended lawn with a sprawling rock garden. The aircraft was down a slope, on a helipad, surrounded by armed guards.

Two more guards were rushing away from the house, with a blond woman and a gaunt, dapper Chinese man between them.

Yan Whan.

Bolan yanked open the sliding glass door and propelled himself onto the ground, triggering the AK on the run.

The guards flanking Whan and his mistress whirled simultaneously, leveling their weapons. One man caught several rounds and fell to the earth. The other jumped in front of Whan and absorbed the stream of 7.62 mm rounds intended for his boss. He toppled backward, driving Whan to the ground, and the woman screamed with a flash of red blossoming on her shoulder.

The other guards were running in Bolan's direction, firing their weapons as he took cover behind a decorative boulder and rode out the barrage of rounds that rained around it.

He waited for a pause, but the guards kept firing a steady torrent. Finally he crept around the side of the boulder. Whan was being helped to his feet by several guards, as was the woman with the shoulder wound. Whan grabbed at the briefcase with his good hand. Bolan triggered his assault rifle, cutting into Whan's hand, but the slaver was inside the helicopter.

Bolan withdrew himself just in time to avoid another lengthy barrage of fire at the boulder. Chips of rock flew around him, and he heard distinctly the rising pitch of the engine and felt the building rotor wash. At the next opportunity he looked over the boulder and saw the chopper rising into the air. The gunman hanging out of its side targeted Bolan again, determined to make a safe escape.

The Executioner launched himself to his feet, ran three paces, then collapsed and rolled, fleeing the autofire that was inches behind him. He came to rest behind a bench and fired his AK-47 over the top, achieving target acquisition on the rotor. One solid hit was all he would need to send the helicopter out of control.

The chopper was at an altitude of twenty-five yards when the AK chugged dry. No time to change the mag. Bolan yanked out the 93-R and stood, chasing after the craft, firing repeatedly until it, too, was emptied, and the helicopter, with Yan Whan in it, was making its escape across the Junggar Basin.

CHAPTER FOURTEEN

Bolan and Jiahua returned to the prison to find well over half of Yan Whan's army wiped out, the rest surrendering. They had been overwhelmed by the sheer numbers and brutal viciousness on the part of the ex-prisoners. Only a few desperate XSEAs had fled into the countryside, along with at least one American. In the barren grasslands of the Junggar Basin, they would be hunted down or forced to surrender eventually.

The Urumchi police were on the scene and were taking responsibility for the prisoners. Bolan approached one of the men, who appeared to be organizing the round-up effort.

"Where's your chief?"

The cop smiled and pointed to a dismal, bent figure with a face blackened by bruises. He was third in a long line of shackled and manacled prisoners.

"He was the third chief this week," the cop said.

"Any XSEAs left in your ranks?"

"No. I am highest ranking who is not XSEA. I am Xi."

"Good to meet you, Chief Xi."

But the loss of life on the prisoners' side was horrendous, and part of Xi's orders were for the collection and identification of the dead. Over the next hour Bolan watched the rows of corpses swell.

He spotted Jiahua standing motionless at the corner of what had become a well-ordered field of death and for a moment he stood beside her.

She looked into his eyes. "Christ, Belasko."

Bolan could have told her about the terrible price that was sometimes required to purchase freedom. He could have explained that he had seen hundreds and thousands of innocent people die fighting for the most basic of human rights. He might have told her that the people of Urumchi were lucky in that they had the opportunity to fight and finally regain the freedom they had lost. How many human beings would live their lives without even having the opportunity to engage in such a battle?

But his words wouldn't have helped to ease her pain.

Hong Kong

"I'VE BEEN ORDERED *not* to debrief you, Ms. Jiahua. Those orders come from the executive level."

She had never met the man but knew he was in charge of CIA operations in China and Hong Kong— very high in the chain of international operations. The idea of him taking orders from anyone outside of the upper echelons of the Langley hierarchy was somewhat amazing, even if those orders come from the executive branch of the government of the United States.

She left the music-marketing company offices that served as a CIA front in Hong Kong and found a pay phone in a hotel lobby, quiet and isolated enough to allow a private conversation. She dialed the number she had used once before to track down Belasko. This time she did so with his permission.

"Hello, Cello." Jiahua recognized the voice of the woman she had spoken with on that night—just days ago, wasn't it?—when she had been running from the Urumchi XSEAs.

"Hi," she said. She didn't know what else to say. She didn't even know this woman's name.

"I'm glad to hear you're okay," the woman said, sounding genuinely compassionate. "You gave me kind of a scare when you called Belasko's contact number."

"Thanks. I'm sorry that I did that."

"No harm done. I understand. Sometimes desperate measures are called for."

"I was nothing if not desperate."

"Of course, if you do that again I will have you hunted down and shot."

"Naturally," Jiahua replied. She liked this woman, whoever she was. "I'm in an unusual situation here in Hong Kong. I've apparently been granted some sort of independent-agent status. Do you know anything about that?"

"Yes. That's our doing. Until we identify Yan Whan's CIA leak, we're keeping you isolated. It got you in trouble once and it could again."

"So what am I supposed to do with myself?"

"There's still Yan Whan. We think he's in Hong Kong now. We've got some information you might be interested in having."

Jiahua's interest was definitely aroused. "Tell me."

On a Flight to Texas

OPENING THE PACK, Bolan found a Toshiba subnotebook computer and a credit card made out to William Butler.

First class was half-empty on the flight, and he had the luxury of an empty seat next to him. As soon as the 747 was airborne, he switched on the subnotebook computer and shoved the credit card into the slot for the telephone mounted at his seat. He placed the receiver in the Toshiba's modem cradle and dialed out.

The number was for an Internet server in Los Angeles. While it connected, Bolan double-clicked the SMF icon, a custom piece of software designed by Stony Man Farm computer expert Aaron Kurtzman, and subtly altered for its each and every use by Stony Man personnel.

The subnotebook logged in, and Kurtzman's software took control. It opened a connection to another server at a university in Kankakee, Illinois, then to a commercial server in Vancouver, British Columbia. The display paused with each new link while it accessed or bypassed log-in procedures, and suddenly the screen opened a Word Wide Web page with a commercial search engine. The search parameters began to configure themselves as if a ghost were typing on Bolan's keyboard. A search under the string "farming" began, coming up with thousands of possible matches. One of the links was selected and the message "URL not found" appeared on the screen.

The software again took control as a highly complex conversation took place between the subnotebook and Kurtzman's computer. It involved the formulation and instantaneous solving of sophisticated algebraic equations. Theoretically the only two machines in the world that could possibly have communicated in this fashion were Kurtzman's and Bolan's, and after the first link was made it would never be retrievable.

A minute after successful log-in, a secure link,

crossing the North American continent several times, was made to the computer system at Stony Man Farm.

Kurtzman wasn't through befuddling potential security leaks yet. The material that began downloading into the subnotebook was useless gibberish until Bolan entered the code phrase he had received from Brognola. The phrase itself was a part of the decryption formula.

The flight attendant brought Bolan a coffee as he got his first look at a crisp black-and-white photograph of Don Carmen Cariani.

He scanned the bio. Cariani was just fifty-two years old. He took over from his father, known in some circles as Cariani the Elder, when the old man died eight years previously. He had fared poorly in some efforts to expand his Houston territory and changed his tack. He began seeking out new, untapped opportunities that the opening global markets afforded a ruthless man. He quickly made friends with various Hong Kong crime figures. Working relationships were formed. Cariani proved himself adept when it came to creating organized-crime business where there had been none. He was a skilled corrupter, good at transforming a legitimate business into a much more profitable—and morally reprehensible—operation.

Slave labor was right up his alley.

Bolan moved on. The next face he saw was a familiar one.

Jethro Parl. An ambitious, high-ranking lieutenant under Cariani the Elder, he became the current Don Cariani's chief enforcer after a few daring and flawless operations carried out during the new regime's early years. He had been noticeably absent during Don Cariani's trips to the Far East, and the supposition was that

Parl was being handed increasing responsibility for the U.S. operations while the Don opened the new frontiers.

But Bolan knew that the face he was looking at was the face he had glimpsed in the attack on the flat where he and Jiahua had been staying in Urumchi. Parl was getting involved in international operations after all.

A dialogue box appeared along the top of the screen.

"Striker? Bear here."

"We secure?" Bolan typed in.

"Sure are. I came up with new encryption algorithm last week. You're using it now. Even if some hacker could get on this line—which I seriously doubt—they'd see nothing but repetitious profanity."

"Price there?" Bolan typed in.

There was a pause. "Here."

"Spotted Parl in Urumchi."

"We knew he left U.S."

"Odd behavior if bio is correct," Bolan suggested.

"Not really. Parl is still the Don's chief enforcer. The Don didn't need international enforcing until you stirred the pot."

Bolan knew that after his quick departure from Urumchi, Jiahua had photographed all the dead non-Chinese and faxed the photos to the Farm. "Parl among dead?" he asked.

He already knew the answer. If Parl was dead, they wouldn't have included his file and picture in the briefcase passed to him by a courier at Los Angeles International Airport.

"Parl not among dead."

Bolan did a quick inventory of the data his computer had downloaded. It included a list of businesses tied to the Cariani Family, a list of all known past and present associates with the Family, a history of the Family and its operations, full criminal records on all its top players, even detailed maps of Houston, Galveston and other areas of the southern tip of the state of Texas, where the Family operated. Highlighted were the locations and shipping schedules of the goods that had been shipped in from Yan Whan's slave-field Urumchi factories. The schedule showed that the latest shipments—and in fact the last shipments that would ever come out of the Urumchi operations—were due to arrive at the dock in Galveston in about thirty hours. The boatload included electronics with a wholesale value of approximately one million dollars. Bolan had no intention of letting Don Cariani become a million dollars richer.

"What's plan in TX?" Price keyed.

Bolan considered the possibilities. "Attrition. Removal of Don Cariani."

"What hardware do you need?"

Bolan's fingers started flying over the keypad.

Texas

BOLAN DROVE SOUTH out of Houston in the rental car. Again Stony Man had come through for him with the hardware he needed. It felt good to know that, when he needed more equipment, it was just a phone call away. He wouldn't run into a situation such as he had faced in the far northwestern corner of China.

What the Stony Man intel had been unable to tell him was if any of the goods from previous shipments remained in Cariani shipyard warehouses. He intended to find out.

He noticed the change in the air before he even reached Galveston, and the moist, warm aroma of the Gulf of Mexico filled the hot summer afternoon air.

Parking the car, he took a stroll down the dock, hands in his pockets. The afternoon sun gleamed off the gulf water. A seagull made an emergency landing on the dock several paces ahead of Bolan, trying to bring a wriggling, rust-colored crab under control. The crab put up a valiant fight, pinching and grabbing for the bird. But the seagull pecked at it mercilessly, stabbing the crustacean again and again. The seagull became alarmed by Bolan's approach and grabbed the crab, taking to the air in a flurry of wings.

Bolan noticed two men lounging around the door of a nearby warehouse, a sign declaring the place to be Wallace Shipping. Two more men waited at the end of the dock, leaning on an oil barrel and engaged in an animated conversation. The four men had been watching him closely from the moment he came into sight and all four wore jackets, despite the heat, to hide their side arms. Another three or four men stood at the open truck-garage entrance into the warehouse. They were back in the darkness and appeared to have been playing cards at a low table, sitting on milk crates, but they eyed Bolan with frank suspicion. They didn't know he'd spotted them, and they didn't know he'd spotted the two shotguns they had propped against the wall in the shadows.

He looked at his watch, looked at the sun, turned and strolled back the way he'd come. But he'd be back. He had found out that the warehouse wasn't empty.

He'd noticed something else that was curious: a cop in an unmarked car was keeping an eye on the warehouse. If law enforcement was on the scene when Bolan made his move, they might very well engage themselves in the action. The Executioner would have to be on the lookout.

He gave the cop a wave. If looks could kill, the glare the cop gave Bolan would have knocked him dead on the spot.

WHO WAS THIS JOKER? Detective Denny Creavalle didn't like the looks of him. Tall, dark, he had an air of quiet strength about him without possessing the gorilla build common among crime tough guys. If he was sporting a piece, he hid it very well. Maybe this guy really was just a pedestrian strolling on the docks. But if he wasn't, he was some type of expert, and that made Creavalle plenty nervous.

The guy gave him a wave. Creavalle's dislike for the guy went up about ten notches. This guy was awfully sure of himself.

He got in a car and drove off. Creavalle watched him go and jotted down the license-plate number. He'd go through some files when he got back to the office, see if he could find any faces to match the one he'd just burned into his brain.

He was obviously not friendly with the Cariani Family. He'd been staking the place out. The Cariani goons had been watching him just as suspiciously as Creavalle had. Maybe he was from a rival Family, checking out what Cariani was up to. Maybe they were trying to figure it out, just like Creavalle was.

Because the truth was, Creavalle hadn't the faintest idea what Cariani was up to yet.

He was mystified. Cariani was running an import business, but as far as Creavalle had been able to ascertain it was legitimate. He brought in cheap electronics from China and sold them to the discount mass-merchandising chains.

Creavalle hadn't believed the operation was legitimate when it started up, and he didn't believe it now. There had to be something crooked going on.

But what that something was had mystified him. He'd stopped three trucks leaving the place. He'd searched the warehouse once himself with dogs, but he'd found absolutely no clue of drugs going in or out.

He had never spotted suspicious-looking shipping activity, no middle-of-the-night transfers of merchandise or discrepancies in shipping bills.

He'd followed and searched the shipments going to local distribution warehouses, followed trucks all the way to Dallas. But he had never found one shred of evidence of drugs.

Wallace Shipping had complained of harassment. Creavalle's boss had agreed and told him to lay off.

"But I know there's something dirty going on there!" Creavalle had protested.

"Of course there is. But prove it before you go searching any more shipments or they're going to bring harassment charges against us—and I tell you, those charges will stick. Then you won't be able to get near the place."

Creavalle saw the old man's point, and he'd been careful ever since. He had watched from a distance and became a fixture on the wharf. He had started identifying the seagulls by their damn markings.

But he had yet to figure out what was going down at Wallace Shipping.

So he was tempted to look at the arrival of the stranger in a positive light. Maybe he would cause some trouble, stir things up. That could only have a positive affect on Creavalle's investigation.

Maybe the stranger was a cop, a Fed. Would the Feds

have sent in somebody without alerting the local law enforcement?

Creavalle snorted and started his car. Of course they would. The Feds—FBI, DEA, didn't matter, since they were all the same—were universally pompous and arrogant. They regarded regional law enforcement as small-time—even city cops like Creavalle. They had no respect for any local officer.

He had spent months on this investigation. There was no way he was letting those sons of bitches take it over from him. He intended to find out who this guy was immediately.

Wallace Shipping wasn't getting taken down without Creavalle involved.

JETHRO PARL CAME DIRECTLY from the airport to meet with Don Cariani.

It wasn't a meeting he was looking forward to.

This entire ordeal, in fact, was leaving a bad taste in his mouth. He'd just spent forty-eight hours kissing Yan Whan's ass, and his ego was sorely bruised. But a lot worse would have happened had he not done so. He had managed, after all, to salvage the working relationship between Whan and the Cariani Family.

Still, the Don was going to be angry when Parl walked in that door, and Parl knew how the Don dealt with people he was really displeased with.

Parl knew, because typically he got the orders to do that dealing.

Still, he was an important man, and he'd performed some tricky negotiating. Maybe the Don wouldn't order him exterminated on the spot.

He had to play this one very carefully.

He walked into the Don's office.

"Jethro." The Don said his name without any emotion whatsoever, which meant Parl was going to get played with. He'd seen the trick a hundred times. The Don would have his meeting with the current screw-up-of-the-month and play his cards so close to the chest the poor sap didn't know whether he was going to get a second chance or concrete work boots. He'd spill his guts to the Don, plead for mercy. Sometimes the poor sap would get it and sometimes he wouldn't—the Don would make a sudden proclamation one way or another, and the meeting was over.

So Parl knew that he was going to have to sit through this meet and wonder the whole time whether he was just making a fool of himself and the Don had already decided to have him dealt with permanently.

"Don Cariani," he said respectfully.

The Don waved to a seat. Parl sank into the leather-upholstered chair.

"What happened over there, Jethro?"

"Well, Don Cariani, our friend Yan Whan didn't give us a clear picture of the situation. We walked into a battlefield. We were outmanned and outgunned. We thought there was only the one American agent and his woman sidekick. But we found out differently. He was just the leader of the pack. He'd started freeing prisoners before we even landed in the city."

That wasn't too much of an exaggeration, and from that perspective it certainly made Parl look better.

"We did our best to get the situation under control, but then this agent and his army staged an attack. We relied on an informant Yan Whan claimed was reliable. It turned out he was in with this American agent. We walked into a trap. We were surrounded and several of our men, as you know, were killed."

"Yan Whan told me there was just the two American agents there, Jethro."

"Yan Whan wasn't there, Don Cariani. I saw the American agents on the scene, but gunfire was coming from everywhere—he must have had a dozen guys with him. It was a deathtrap, and if Yan Whan's intel was good we would never have walked into it. If the situation had been reversed—if Yan Whan had sent guns into our territory—there's no way we wouldn't have known that was a trap."

"And the rest?" the Don asked. "Six more of our boys were killed."

"Yan Whan's men let him get control of one of Yan Whan's factories, and the released prisoners started arming themselves and the whole thing snowballed. They attacked his jail. His men were in chaos. There was no control. We tried to lend a hand, but it was too little, too late. In fact, even before we went over there it was too late, Don. The battle was lost before we got there."

The truth had stretched further and further, and Parl hoped he hadn't overdone it.

Don Cariani remained silent, his expression blank. But Parl knew the Don, had known him since he was a young turk under the wing of his father. He had watched him learn his tricks from the old Don, in fact. When the Don put his hands together, made a steeple with two fingers and tapped them briefly against his lips, Parl knew he had planted some serious doubts in the Don's head.

"Nevertheless," Don Cariani said, "from Yan Whan's point of view, Jethro, you screwed up royally."

"Yes. I know that. I addressed the situation with Yan Whan when I met up with him in Hong Kong. He won't admit it, but I think he knows that I would have had to come to China with an army of cowboys to take care of the situation. So when I got him in private, well, I was able to negotiate a deal.''

That got the Don's attention. ''Oh?''

''The most important aspect of the deal being that he will continue working with us. Our guaranteed status as his sole distributor in North America is secure.

''The second important point is that Yan Whan has teamed up with an organization in Hong Kong called the Lu Ming Family. He said you've heard of them.''

''I have.''

''He says—and I agree with him, Don Cariani—that in order for him to run an operation out of China, he needs a Chinese-based agency for protection. And even as well organized as this Family is, we can't provide it. But Yan Whan has proved he can't take care of himself in this regard. So a third party was required.''

''So Lu Ming is the third party,'' Don Cariani stated.

''Yes, and they're in for a twenty-five percent cut. Yan Whan has confidence in their ability to take on this role. I was in no position to judge. Yan Whan said you would be.''

Don Cariani sat back in his chair and stared into space. ''Yeah, I can make that judgment. The Lu Ming organization can protect Yan Whan as good as anybody in Asia. But Yan Whan, at the moment, has nothing to protect. And we're still his distributor with nothing to distribute.''

Parl felt a slight warming in the Don's voice. He was being won over by Parl's initiative and intelligence.

''He doesn't yet, Don Cariani. But he assures me that with his connections and with the influence of Lu Ming, he can organize at least one more factory within weeks.

He's already targeted a new locale, one he says will offer the advantage of seaport facilities. With that going for us it'll cut several days off of our delivery time. He's also going for a less urban population center where he can disguise his activities better. And we still have a warehouse full of unshipped goods and a full shipment coming in tomorrow. That will hold us over. We'll definitely have a dry spell, but remember how quickly Yan Whan got up and running the first time...."

Don Cariani considered all this carefully, looking at Parl and then at the desk, utterly unreadable.

"And you made this agreement with Yan Whan, did you?"

"No, Don. I did the best impromptu negotiating I could, assuring Yan Whan of our continued interest, and told him I would come to you, where the real decision-making could take place. However, I got the impression that Yan Whan wasn't favorable to further compromise."

"I see."

Don Cariani stood and paced a lap around the office, easily, silent. Parl had seen the move pulled on others in the hot seat. It was a tool to increase their tension. Parl had never dreamed he would someday be in that hot seat, and every time he identified one of these patented Don Cariani tools of manipulation he felt an increasing swell of anger.

But he couldn't place the blame for the anger on Don Cariani. Well, he could partly, and part went to Yan Whan, who had dragged him into this fiasco.

But the bulk of the blame went on the nameless agent who had done this to Parl. Parl had seen his face, briefly, and wouldn't forget it. If he ever ran into that guy again, he was history.

"All right, Jethro." Cariani fell back into his chair again. "You've done your best to clean up this mess, and I appreciate your initiative. But the mess wouldn't exist if you had done your job right from the start. Do you know how much cash we're talking about when we're talking about handing twenty-five percent over to the Lu Mings? A lot more than your salary, I'll tell you that."

Parl was shocked. He'd been convinced he had won Don Cariani to his way of thinking.

"You fucked it up, Jethro. You cost me millions. You hear me? Millions."

Parl could do nothing but look at him.

"Not to mention the fact that you had a bunch of my best guys killed. Now I've got to pay to ship back a bunch of bodies from China. That's not cheap. And I got to throw a bunch of funerals, and I got to let a bunch of mothers and wives yell at me that I had their boys killed. You know what that's like? I hate it."

"I did my best, Don Cariani," Parl sputtered weakly.

"You always have, Jethro, and that's usually been good enough. This time it wasn't. This time you screwed it up big-time. So I've got to bring you down."

"What!"

"I've got to bring you down. I'm going to put you in charge of the Galveston operations."

"Galveston!" Parl gasped the word in disbelief. The Don was demoting him.

"Yeah. You'll run the shipyards there. I got a lot of money coming off the boats. That'll be your new responsibilities."

"Jesus, Don!"

"I don't want to hear it, Jethro! You take it or you leave it. You're getting off lucky with just a demotion after the stunt you pulled. A lot of guys wouldn't be around anymore after a fuckup like that. And the guys aren't going to respect you any more because you killed so many of them. So you've got to take what you can get! Galveston is still a big operation for you—you be satisfied with it!''

Don Cariani dismissed him. Parl wandered out of the office, down the hall and let himself out the front door of the Don's house, stunned.

Galveston! He'd been at that level when he was twenty-five years old, thirteen years ago. What a humiliation. It would take him years to get over it. And he might never start making his way up the ladder again after such an embarrassing demotion.

His career may as well have just ended.

A face flashed through Parl's brain, the face of a dark-haired man who had brought him down.

If Parl ever laid eyes on that guy again...

CHAPTER FIFTEEN

Jimmy DiCarlo stepped on the cigarette. Standing in the truck garage, he looked up and down the dock. This job just plain sucked.

When he was first told by the higher-ups that he was being moved to the Galveston warehouse, he thought he was in for an easy stint. Those guys sat around, smoked cigars, played cards, bullshitted for hours at a time. Relaxing and easygoing, that's what working at the docks was like.

But DiCarlo learned the truth soon enough. The cards and the easygoing hours got longer and longer. There was quite simply not a damn thing to do. The pleasant boredom turned to mind-numbing monotony. Now that he'd been working the docks for a few months, he thought he was going to go out of his mind with boredom.

The dock looked the same as it did every single day. The ocean, the litter, that stupid cop staking out the place from his ugly little car day after day. When was that stupid detective going to get a clue? Creavalle's dogged determination to expose Cariani's Galveston dock works had been amusing at first. Now it was just another chain in the link of irritating sameness.

Shit, if they were smuggling goods into and out of

this building, at least there would be some tension, some suspense, some reason to be here. There was the rub—DiCarlo wasn't even sure he was even needed here. He came to view this job as a low-profile assignment at best.

The more he thought about it, the more he knew he was at a dead-end unless he could get a better gig within the Cariani organization. Of course, he wasn't sure exactly how to go about putting in for a transfer. He'd probably offend somebody if he made the request and do more harm than good to his career.

He turned his back on the ocean, leaning against the wall, watching the union blue-collar guys loading the truck. Small shipment going out. Two truckloads only. There'd been some sort of trouble that had interrupted the supply of goods for the time being. DiCarlo didn't know the details, didn't even know where this stuff came from. China, maybe, or Taiwan. He sure the hell couldn't figure out how the Don made a profit on it.

"Hey, Jimmy," Red Bardi called, walking quickly in his direction.

"Yeah?"

"Big news, man."

"Like what?"

Bardi didn't say more until he had approached, didn't want the blue-collar guys overhearing.

"Carlini's out of here, man," Bardi said. "They moved him up the ladder. He's going to a gig for the Don in Houston."

"Really?" That was news.

"Yeah. But that's not the *real* news. You won't believe who's taking over here."

"Well, tell me."

Bardi grinned. "Parl."

"You're shitting me."

"No."

"Jethro?"

"Yeah, man."

"You got to be shitting me!"

"No, man, it's true. Parl fucked up. I don't know how, but somehow he fucked up really bad. The Don's really pissed at him—was ready to get rid of him, in fact! That's what I heard. But then Jethro talked him out of it."

"Shit! Jethro was the chief man for the old Don—he's a better operator than Cariani is himself!"

"You know that and I know it. But the Don doesn't think so. Not anymore."

"Well, what happened, then?"

"I don't know. Nobody seems to know much. But Parl and a bunch of guys went out of the country on a jet the Don rented for them. They say it went all the way to China. There were problems with the source."

"Our source?"

"Yeah. And there was real trouble when he got there. Like there was about fifteen of the Don's guys killed."

DiCarlo was mystified. The goods that flowed through the Galveston warehouse complex were mundane products. He had assumed they were sourced legitimately. Obviously, if there had been a major battle involved, that wasn't the case. He looked at the pallet of stereos being loaded in one of the two trucks.

"Shit, man! No wonder the Don is pissed! Fifteen guys! Who were they?"

"I don't know. I think Joey Borland was one of them. And Frank Marchetti. I heard some other names I didn't know. But they must think there might be more trouble here 'cause they've ordered double duty for the next eighteen hours. Then tomorrow Parl is supposed to get down here and take over.''

DiCarlo was only starting to get over his shock. "I wonder what kind of a boss he's going to be?"

"Who can tell?" Bardi said with a shrug. "He's been in the high-up post for so long, who knows what he'll do down here with us peons? He's supposed to be as professional as they come. A real hardass.''

"Yeah, but how happy do you think he's going to be, running this dump after fifteen years in the offices in the city, man?''

Bardi shrugged. "Your guess is good as mine. Come on. We're supposed to ride with these loads.''

The trucks were being closed and padlocked. The drivers were starting them up.

"How far?" DiCarlo asked.

"All the way."

"And how far is that?"

Bardi smirked humorlessly. "Tyler. Then we rent a car and drive back.''

"We're going to be gone the whole freakin' night.''

"No shit. And we're leaving now.''

DETECTIVE DENNY CREAVALLE ripped a huge chunk off the crabmeat submarine sandwich and chewed tiredly, feeling defeated and run-down. He'd spent too many weeks sitting on this damn dock without a breakthrough. And this afternoon he had spent three long hours trying to find a match for the face of the man who was wandering around the docks. At one point he found himself sitting in front of a computer monitor, with FBI Wanted photos flashing past, and realized how stupid and pointless the whole exercise was. He'd become absorbed—more like temporarily obsessed—with identifying this man, naively hoping he would turn out to be a chink in the armor that shielded the detective from the true operations taking place at Wallace Shipping.

But at that moment his self-delusion became apparent. He stood and walked away from the computer, leaving it alone to flash its FBI Wanted images to no one.

Now here he was sitting at the dock again, with nothing out of the ordinary to watch. There was Jimmy DiCarlo standing in the garage door, looking as bored as Creavalle felt.

Maybe he'd give up on this site. Whatever was going down here was hidden too well for him to determine without the support of his office, let alone the DEA, who had expressed no interest in the place after Creavalle's initial searches came up empty.

The trucks pulled out. Only two—a light load. They would be going to the retail distributing centers in Tyler or Fort Worth, depending on which of the store chains they were intended for. Creavalle knew because he'd followed them in the past.

He looked for the napkin. It had fallen on the floor, and he reached for it. As he did, one of the trucks pulled past, and Creavalle noticed something strange. He couldn't even tell himself what it was at first. Then the second semi pulled by, and he examined the driver. One of the usual guys, Red Bardi, was sitting next to him—a two-bit hood with no outstanding charges against him.

What was it about the trucks that was odd?

The trucks pulled away and were gone.

Creavalle chewed his sandwich thoughtfully, and all at once he realized what it was. There had never been guards before. They had always made the shipments with just a driver. No guard. Tonight there was a guard in each truck. They had to be expecting trouble.

Or they had to be shipping something other than their usual cheap consumer electronics.

Creavalle dropped the sandwich on the seat next to him and tore out of the parking spot.

THE WORST ASPECT of the situation was that he had been put in a cab with Lenny Andershot. Ingratiating and obnoxious, Andershot was always trying to be friends with everybody. And everybody hated him, which was why he was given truck-driving jobs. It kept him away from everybody else.

"You can tune in whatever radio station you want," Andershot said. He hadn't stopped talking since DiCarlo had jumped into the truck.

DiCarlo grunted and said nothing. It was going to be a long night.

"Would you look at this buttwipe?" Andershot said, then laughed loudly. It sounded like a braying donkey.

The broken-down car had rental plates and was skewed across two lanes of the highway, leaving only a single lane for traffic to steer around. Traffic had slowed to a crawl.

"Why the hell doesn't he push it onto the shoulder?" Andershot asked. A minute later they steered around the car, where a man in a black jacket was leaning under the hood.

Andershot rolled down the window long enough to yell, "Get it off the road, you asshole!" He laughed again and rolled the window back up.

"Asshole," Andershot declared.

DiCarlo glared at the driver and said nothing.

RED BARDI HUNCHED in the corner and folded his arms, relaxed, directly in the flow of the air coming in the open window. The trucks didn't have air-conditioning, but it would cool down soon when the sun disappeared. He'd been smart enough to grab Bosco's truck. Charlie Bosco was an unpleasant jerk, but at least he would keep his mouth shut. DiCarlo was stuck in a cab with Lenny Andershot, the most annoying asshole in the outfit. It would take a bullet to the head to shut up Andershot. And after a couple of hours DiCarlo might just pull out his gun and take care of it.

Bosco grunted and braked. Bardi glanced out the window to see a car stalled in the middle of the road. Bosco slowed to pull around it.

If this was the only delay, they'd reach the interstate in five minutes.

BOLAN DROPPED THE HOOD as the second semi blared its horn, its right wheels crunching on the gravel shoulder as it steered around the stopped rental car. Bolan reached the semi in three quick strides and stepped onto the first cab step, grabbing the door latch and withdrawing the Desert Eagle in the same movement.

"What's going on?" the driver asked.

That was all he had time to say. Bolan slammed him in the temple with the big handgun, flinging him into the passenger. The hardman in the passenger seat shouted in surprise.

Bolan grabbed the steering wheel, pulling himself farther into the window while keeping the semi from careening off the road. The passenger was withdrawing a handgun from under his left armpit. He either had failed to see or was too stupid to react to the Desert

Eagle. Bolan leveled the handgun in the window and triggered it one time.

The hardware thundered in the tiny cab, and the .44 Magnum round slammed into Red Bardi's skull like a sledgehammer wielded by a circus strongman; the results were about the same. Most of the gore flew out the open window, but still, much of the interior became covered with a red gleam flecked with gore and brain.

The truck was chugging to a halt, and Bolan dropped the wheel long enough to shove the unconscious driver into the passenger seat with the corpse and insert himself behind the wheel. He quickly dropped the semi into neutral, allowed the engine to recover and put it back into gear. He yanked the semi onto the pavement and accelerated, closing the distance between himself and the other truck. He loosened his backpack, getting comfortable.

He was going to be driving for a while.

He checked the rearview mirror. There was another car about a mile behind him. In the dusky light the driver hadn't noticed the quick altercation.

The first semi braked for the northbound exit onto Interstate 45. Bolan followed.

CREAVALLE THOUGHT he'd been spotted. The second semi had swerved off the road as it went around the stalled car and almost stopped—he was sure they had seen him in the rearview mirror, and he'd slowed. The truck went on its way again. He'd have to keep the distance between them. He couldn't risk blowing it. He had to get the goods on Wallace Shipping, and this might be his only chance.

He pulled around the stalled car a full minute after

the semi. What asshole would leave a stalled car sitting in the middle of a state highway?

He was a full minute and a half behind but still spotted the semis pulling onto I-45. He grinned. He would never lose them on the interstate.

All these weeks and months of work on Wallace Shipping was going to pay off. Tonight it all came down. Creavalle could feel victory within his grasp.

It felt good.

BOLAN COULD DRIVE all night if he had to. He wasn't about to make his move on a crowded interstate. Later in the night the road would become less populated. Or the other truck would make a john stop. Maybe they wouldn't even stay on the interstate.

They didn't. In fact the trucks' route took them around the city of Houston, then north on State Route 59, which soon shrank from three lanes in each direction to two. The median disappeared, along with the streetlights and paved shoulder. The Houston suburbs were left behind. The night grew dark, and Bolan knew he would have no trouble finding an opportunity to strike.

He heard a groan and the driver, slumped on the seat next to him, raised his head. He found himself lying in the lap of the late Red Bardi, and Bardi's blood and brains covered him head to foot. The driver screamed.

There was no traffic behind Bolan for at least a couple of miles. This was as good a place as any to get rid of them both. Bolan unleathered the Desert Eagle and rapped the driver in the skull again. Then he grabbed the door handle, opened the door and, swerving toward the road, pushed at Bardi's corpse and the driver with his foot. The bodies were carried away into the night as he yanked the truck onto the road again.

There was nothing in front of him for miles except for the other semi. An illuminated ranch house sat a couple miles off to the right, but it would be behind them in minutes. Bolan accelerated.

The truck had been cruising at about seventy-five miles per hour, but Bolan coaxed eighty-five out of the rig and double-clicked his lights, encroaching aggressively on the rear bumper of the truck in front before swerving into the left-hand lane. He pulled alongside the other cab while rummaging in his pack with a free hand.

"Turn on your radio!" he heard the driver shouting over the rush of wind. "I've been trying to raise you for twenty minutes!"

"Okay," he shouted back.

"Hey, where's Red?"

Bolan answered with the mini-Uzi he had stowed in his pack. He leveled it directly at the driver, who was trying to keep his eyes on the road. But the hardman in the passenger seat was leaning forward and somehow made out the shape in the darkness.

"Shit!"

The Executioner triggered the mini-Uzi, and a stream of 9 mm rounds drilled into the driver, pulverizing his jawbone a fraction of a second before they chomped through the lower part of his head.

The rig immediately began to slow. The passenger had to have grabbed for control because the vehicle swerved back and forth on the asphalt without actually leaving it. Bolan slowed, dropping the mini-Uzi on the bench seat and grabbing for one of the grenades stowed in the backpack. He released the explosive out the window.

The device hit the pavement and rolled.

Bolan watched in his rearview mirror, unsure of the accuracy of his timing.

The careening semi reached the spot where the explosive should have been, rolled over it, swerved to the left again, speed still decreasing...

The flash appeared under the rear edge of the trailer and immediately sent razor-sharp fragments of metal ripping through anything that got in its way. The rear left trailer tires were reduced to scrap rubber in an instant, and the trailer lurched to the left. The truck swerved in the wrong direction and lost control, scraping over the pavement, crossing the oncoming traffic lane and grinding onto the gravel shoulder. It lurched over the shoulder, tilted into a culvert and tried to keep its balance for a second. Gravity took over, and the trailer flipped onto its side.

Bolan downshifted and braked, bringing his rig to a crawl. The ground on either side of the highway was too steep for him to execute a U-turn, so he put it in reverse and barreled backward along the lonely stretch of highway. The vehicle backed across all four lanes, over the shoulder and slammed into the other trailer with a crunch.

He jumped out and approached the other rig with his Desert Eagle ready, circling to the front of the downed cab, looking for survivors.

He found none. He put a block of C-4 plastique on the truck's front fender and quickly activated the tiny radio transmitter. Then he moved along the exposed belly of the truck, placing two more blocks and their detonators. Each became activated with a gleam of a tiny red LED. He moved to his own truck trailer, bent and warped from the rear-end impact, planting three packets of plastique along its length after disconnecting the trailer from the cab.

Bolan jumped into the cab and pulled down the road. He found the radio transmitter in the pack and turned it on. The red light glowed a warning. He glanced out the window, judging he was far enough away to ride out the blast safely. Then he pushed the button.

The twin trailers flew open like dropped eggs and filled with blazing fire. The white-hot inferno lasted just a second, then died to a sustainable orange fire. The plastics contained in the trucks added blue-and-green sparks to the conflagration.

Bolan left it to burn itself out. There would be no profits to salvage from that mess.

The Executioner had initiated his war against Don Cariani.

One of them wasn't going to survive it.

CREAVALLE HADN'T SEEN the trucks in almost ten minutes and was speeding up in order to get a glimpse of them again. As long as he did an occasional check on them, he was confident he wouldn't lose them. There was no place for them to go, at least until they reached the small town of Cleveland, Texas.

An empty semi rig raced by, heading into Houston. Seconds later he spotted the fire and headed for it. A crash? A semi truck, maybe? Surely not one of the Cariani semis.

Surely not *two* semis...

"God Almighty," he whispered.

When his car rolled to a stop, he got out and stood next to it, watching the semis burn. There was nothing left identifiable enough to tell him these were the Wallace Shipping trucks, but he knew.

It took him a full minute to come to the realization that the ruin contained two trailers but only one rig.

"Jesus!" he shouted, jumping back in his car. Unbidden, there came to his mind the image of the big guy who had been wandering around the dock that afternoon. That guy had wasted the trucks! That guy was in the rig he'd passed just ten minutes ago!

If he could catch that bastard he'd find out who he was and who was on this case without getting him involved, and then maybe he'd beat the crap out of him.

Nobody was taking down Wallace Shipping without Detective Denny Creavalle!

SIPING TOWER, South Water Avenue. The twenty-story building looked out into the bay on days when a brisk wind swept the pollution off the city of Hong Kong. Most of the time it just stared off into the haze.

At ground level Siping Tower was surrounded at its entrances by doormen who politely ushered in the suits who worked on the first five floors, the international clientele of the hotel occupying the sixth through twelfth floors and the wealthy condo owners dwelling in the upper floors. They kept out the street beggars, the cheap hookers, the assorted trash of the city.

Hong Kong was no different from any city in the world.

But the woman in red was different.

First of all, she was well-dressed. Never mind that her scarlet dress was definitely evening wear and it was only two in the afternoon. It was obviously expensive. It clung to her young body as if it were wet satin. And she wore it well, although it looked like the spaghetti straps holding the top might give way at any moment. She had a sharp, boyish cut to her dark hair that only made her body all the more feminine.

She smiled.

The doorman held the door and didn't say a word.

She gripped her scarlet clutch purse in both hands while standing in front of the elevator. She smiled at the doorman again, who had been joined by several of his co-workers, all trying to stare at her without seeming to.

The woman in red stepped into the elevator.

At the twentieth floor she stepped off. The hallway was decorated with Chinese antiques and fresh flowers. Two men at the end of the hall, at the only door, jumped out of their chairs.

"Hello," she said in Chinese. "I'm here to see Mr. Ming."

"Mr. Ming is not here at the moment."

She frowned. "Will he be back soon?"

"About an hour."

"I was sent to Mr. Ming as a, well, as a surprise for him."

"I see," the guard said.

"A Mr. Yan Whan paid for my services."

The guard looked surprised and exchanged a look with the other guard.

"I understand."

"Would it be possible for me to wait for him here?"

"We'll ask Ms. Werner."

The guards picked up a wall-mounted phone and spoke into it briefly. A moment later the door opened and a blond woman, very non-Oriental, poked her head out. She was wearing a lemon yellow T-shirt dotted with perspiration stains, and her brow was beaded with sweat. Her eyes surveyed the woman in red from head to toe.

"She says Mr. Whan sent her."

"How nice of him," Birgitte Werner said. She stepped back and held the door wide. "What a very nice surprise. Do you speak English?"

"A little," the woman in red said in English.

She entered the penthouse, and the blonde closed the door on the guards.

"Would you like a drink?"

"That would be very nice, thank you."

Birgitte waved at a bar set in the wall. "Help yourself. And make me a whiskey on the rocks, would you? I'll take a quick shower and join you."

The woman in the red evening dress stepped behind the bar and poured two glasses of bourbon. She heard the hiss of a shower in the other room.

She raced across the richly appointed living room and peeked into the bedroom. The blonde's clothes were strewed on a neatly made bed. The room smelled of hot plastic from a stair machine against one wall.

Cello Jiahua stepped into the room and yanked on the drawer of the bedside table, which was empty. She moved to the other side and found it full of earrings and cosmetics. She went to the desk, a large cherry wood piece, and yanked at the file drawer. It was nearly empty. A small attaché caught her attention. It was nestled in the rear of the drawer, an old, battered leather case that had been black once, but was now scraped and worn.

She knew it on sight. It was the case she and Kim Ping used in Urumchi to store evidence they collected against Yan Whan for all those weeks. She had assumed it had been destroyed by Yan Whan.

She grabbed it and unzipped it. Her photography, her handwritten reports, it all seemed to be there.

But for all the trouble she had once gone through to retrieve it, it was now almost useless. The Urumchi operation was closed. What she needed now was evidence pointing to where the new operation was scheduled to start up. And where Yan Whan was.

"Find what you're looking for?"

Jiahua spun and launched the attaché at Birgitte Werner, who stood outside the bathroom door training a Browning Hi-Power on her. She dodged the flying luggage, and the U.S. agent dived at her, slamming into the floor and grabbing for the blonde's ankles. Her hands closed about them and she yanked. Birgitte gave a quick cry and toppled backward, landing on her back with a solid impact. Jiahua scrambled toward her, knocking the gun hand away with a swoop of her forearm and slamming her other hand into the woman's chin, forcing her teeth together with a crack. Jiahua rose to her knees and sent three blows across the blonde's face with the heel of her palm. Birgitte was still.

But not dead. Jiahua grabbed the Browning out of the woman's limp hand and jumped to her feet, snatching a small reading lamp off the bedside table. She quickly tied the woman's hands tight with the electrical cord. She found a hanger of ties in the closet and grabbed two. The first she wadded and stuffed in the unconscious woman's mouth. The second she wrapped around her mouth and head to keep her from expelling the gag.

She dragged the woman into the closet and shut the door, tossing her clothes in after her.

Jiahua wondered how accurate the guards had been when they said Ming would be back in an hour. She scrounged through the files again, seeing nothing of interest. She opened a second drawer and found it barren.

She took the attaché and left the bedroom, searching for an office of some kind. Surely Ming would keep an office here.

She found it—more cherry wood furniture and a cluster of five file cabinets. She began to go through them one after another, and it took ten minutes for her to find what she wanted.

She grabbed the file and stuffed it in the attaché with her old evidence, then shut the file cabinet.

Her last act was to remove a bug from her purse and search for a likely spot. She was probably wasting her time. Lu Ming or Yan Whan would probably have the place searched for bugs after they discovered there had been an intruder. But just maybe...

The office contained a small sitting area next to a bar, with overstuffed chairs and a small coffee table with a smoky glass top. She peeled off the adhesive backing and applied it to the wooden table leg, just out of sight.

Time to get out of there.

She grabbed her purse and her attaché and headed for the door.

She nodded at the guards, who stood as she exited. They gave her leering grins.

"Tore your dress," one of them offered helpfully.

"That will happen," she said with a smile, and entered the elevator.

CHAPTER SIXTEEN

It was the middle of the night, but the patrols at Wallace Shipping were active. There was still inventory to guard.

Bolan parked the rig a half mile down the dock and appropriated a small rowboat tied at a boat house. He rowed quietly through the night, hugging the Galveston dock, more intent on silence than speed. Keeping close to the wharf without banging into the wooden support was a challenge, but he came to a stop in the water just below Wallace Shipping undetected.

He climbed up the ladder far enough to see the building and assess the level of activity within, quickly determining that the news of the attack on the trucks hadn't yet reached them.

He saw a single man in a folding chair, tilted back against the wall. At first Bolan assumed he was asleep, but eventually the man pulled out a pack of cigarettes and lit one.

The garage door was again standing wide open, and a card game was in progress. Four of Cariani's hoods played halfheartedly.

That wouldn't be all of them. Bolan waited. Ten minutes or so later another man strolled around the building. The light streaming through the open garage door revealed the man wore a security-guard uniform and had a .38 holstered around his waist. He ignored the cigarette smoker and disappeared around the corner.

Bolan had expected him. Cariani was attempting to present Wallace Shipping as a legitimate business, and would be required to have the company insured in order to get an import-export license. The insurance would mandate the hired security guard. Bolan would have to consider that factor during every phase of the probe. The guard had to be regarded as an innocent man.

The cardplayers had their jackets off, and their shoulder holsters were visible. Every one of them was armed. They were criminals, killers. He felt no compassion for them and would feel no remorse when they were gone.

The first problem was the guy in the chair. He'd finished his cigarette and flung it out onto the paved dock, as if he could see Bolan watching him and was taunting him with the flick of the butt. He folded his arms behind his head and looked toward the sky. The stars were hidden behind the clouds. A summer storm was forming over the gulf.

The smoker's chair suddenly landed on all four legs, and he got to his feet with a yawn, disappearing inside the building. Bolan saw his opportunity, waiting just a moment longer for a sign that one of the cardplayers would take the watch out front. None did. But the security guard appeared again. He was bunching his walking patrols so he could take a longer break between them.

Bolan watched for a sign of the smoker, but he still hadn't appeared. The Executioner took a gamble, pulling himself onto the wharf. He raced like a fleeting shadow across the wharf, ran to the corner and watched the security guard stroll along the deserted side of the building. Then he glanced back to the garage door. There was a shifting in the shadows that might very well be the smoker returning to his post. Bolan stepped around the corner quickly. He had to take the chance that the security guard wouldn't glance over his shoulder or see something strange with his peripheral vision in the moment he turned the next corner. If he was spotted, Bolan could only flee. He couldn't shoot the man.

The smoker emerged from the front open garage. He pulled the cigarette pack from his shirt pocket and tapped it a few times idly.

The security guard turned and disappeared around the corner. Bolan watched the corner for a long fifteen seconds, but there was no sign of the guard returning.

The Executioner remained unnoticed.

The smoker lit a cigarette, sat in the chair and pushed it back to lean against the side of the building. He'd finished the cigarette and sat still for a long five minutes before Bolan made his attack. It was a dangerous move. But the man simply couldn't be approached in any other way. Creeping along the building, flat, slow, quiet, the Ka-bar fighting knife in his fist, Bolan was trusting that the man was drowsy with boredom. Still, a peripheral glimpse by the smoker at any second would erase Bolan's advantage.

He came to within five paces of the smoker, who sat forward again, the front legs of his chair landing on the ground. Bolan leaped across the empty space, fast and silent like a great black jungle cat striking at prey. The combat knife cut across the smoker's neck, slicing through the carotid artery and windpipe. The smoker looked into the Executioner's eyes, his mute plea was wasted. Bolan only watched the eyes until he was sure the glimmer of life was faded from them.

He maneuvered the body into a relaxed-looking posture and leaned him back against the building as he had been.

In the darkness he looked perfectly natural until one came close enough to see the shining blood that covered his neck and chest, and dripped into a puddle on the ground.

The card game was proceeding as usual. None of the players had their guns out of their holsters. It would take them precious seconds to arm themselves when the shooting started.

Bolan stepped into the open and strode toward the card game with heavy, solid steps, bringing the mini-Uzi to bear at gut level. One of the cardplayers looked up and made a noise that got the attention of the others. They were all jumping to their feet simultaneously, exposing themselves perfectly.

The Executioner triggered the mini-Uzi, sweeping a horizontal figure eight that cut through them mercilessly. There were shouts of surprise and pain, and Bolan released the trigger. He watched the last of the bodies collapse to the ground and approached them, assuring himself there was no business to finish, then strode for the shadowy rear of the loading dock. He wedged himself between two pallet stacks, clicking a fresh clip into the mini-Uzi.

The newcomers betrayed themselves with the sound of their approach. There was a scurrying of feet—Bolan knew one wore hard-soled shoes and the other was barefoot, easily determined by the distinctive slapping of feet on the concrete floor. They stepped into the open, the barefoot man wearing nothing but a pair of beige trousers, and came to a halt several paces from the scene of the massacre.

"Shit! Shit!" the barefoot man cried.

"Who would have done this?" his companion shouted.

"Me," Bolan said, stepping into the light and triggering the mini-Uzi again. The weapon chattered angrily and chomped quickly through the naked chest of the barefoot man, splashing it with red and flinging him onto his back. His companion triggered a panic shot before he came anywhere near attaining his target on Bolan, and was immediately answered with five 9 mm rounds in the chest and face, ending his life abruptly.

Bolan crossed the loading dock, quickly finding the offices for Wallace Shipping behind glass walls. He triggered the mini-Uzi, and the door sprung open. Inside he yanked at file cabinets and started to drag out folders. He recognized import-export forms, which he flung to the floor. He pulled open more drawers, dumping the contents. Finally he found the two files he sought. All he needed was the names that were on them. He extracted a single sheet of paper from each of two files and shoved them in his shirt pocket.

He heard footsteps.

COULTER JACOBS JUMPED to his feet when he heard the distant rattle of automatic gunfire, knocking his legal-case-studies textbook to the floor. He stood still just for a second to catch the sound again. There was no mistake. He ran out of the dingy booth that served as his security station and jogged around the building to the loading dock.

He thought he heard a shout, followed a second later by more automatic fire, then silence. He had withdrawn his gun, a police .38, and felt the heavy piece quivering in his grasp. He'd fired it in target practice three or four times at most. He turned the corner and saw the light spilling feebly out of the open garage door.

Then Jacobs was very confused—there was that guy Dante in his seat, leaning against the wall, casual and relaxed as if nothing was happening. For a fraction of a second Jacobs wondered if he had dozed off while studying and had only dreamed he heard the gunfire.

Then there was more autofire, deeper within the building. At that instant he noticed the thick liquid dripping off the chair and forming a dark puddle under Dante's chair, and the man wasn't moving.

Dante was dead!

When Coulter Jacobs stepped to the edge of the door and looked inside, his heart leaped into his throat—there were dead men everywhere. The loading dock looked like an abattoir. He counted six and knew they were all the guys who worked here—he recognized each and every dead man, which meant their attacker was still alive. And the most recent gunfire meant he was still inside the building.

Trembling with terror, Jacobs entered the loading dock and went in search of the killer.

BOLAN STEPPED TO A WALL, slinging the mini-Uzi over his shoulder and drawing the Desert Eagle. When the security guard ran into the office, hands around a police .38 like he was holding a fresh-caught fish, Bolan stepped up behind him and nudged him with his big handgun.

As the kid whirled with a shout, Bolan drew back, snap-kicking at the guard's gun hand. The .38 flew into a far wall and fell to the ground with a thump.

"What are you doing here, kid?"

"You killed those guys!" The security guard was a tall, powerful-looking black man just out of his teens, and was plainly terrified.

"They're criminals. They're common killers."

"What are you, then?" the kid demanded. Terrified or not, he was outraged.

"I'm not going to justify my actions to you. I'm not obligated, and I don't have the time. But I know you're not one of them."

The guard nodded. "I'm a grad student at Texas State."

"You've got a lot to live for, and you are not going to do it if you hang around here. Get out now."

The kid stared at Bolan wide-eyed.

The Desert Eagle erupted hot thunder, and Coulter Jacobs felt a flash of burning death pass within inches of his ear; a moment later he found himself running through Wallace Shipping, leaping among the nightmarish panoply of death at the loading dock and fleeing into the night.

A car screeched to a halt just feet away from him. Jacobs stopped and retched on his hands and knees.

"What's going on?" someone shouted. "I'm a cop—tell me!"

BOLAN LEFT THE OFFICES and headed for the rear entrance to the warehouse. A single round from the Desert Eagle unlocked the door, and he stepped inside.

The room was black and huge. Half the towering metal racks were stocked with pallets of electronic goods in garishly printed packages, wrapped in clear plastic sheets. A quick glance convinced Bolan he was looking at hundreds of thousands of dollars of products, retail value, profit for Yan Whan and Don Cariani, profit made at the expense of freedom for hundreds of Chinese people.

He intended to see that the profit would never be claimed.

He strode quickly down the rows, placing five blocks of C-4 plastique, preconfigured with tiny radio-activated detonators. He had merely to put them where he thought they would do the most damage and flick a switch. A small red light told him the units were armed.

In three minutes the warehouse was rigged for destruction.

Bolan headed back the way he came, pausing at the loading dock. Nothing moved. He strode among the dead and stepped outside.

"Hold it right there!"

The Executioner stopped and backed into the wall. He saw the car, parked a hundred yards down the dock. It was the detective he had seen staking out the place that afternoon. Now he heard the wail of distant sirens.

The last thing he wanted to deal with was the local police, and he had to get the place blown before any of them entered, or he wouldn't have the opportunity to blow it at all.

He tucked the Desert Eagle into his belt at the small of his back and walked into the open, hands in the air.

"Stop right there!"

Bolan stopped. He could see the detective now, hunched behind his car with a shotgun leveled.

"Let's have the gun! Slow!"

Bolan laid the mini-Uzi on the ground and scooted it across the asphalt in the detective's direction.

"Good—keep those hands up!" The detective walked out from behind the car with his police shotgun in both hands. He approached a few paces and crouched to grab the autoweapon, never taking his eyes off Bolan.

"Who are you, anyway?"

Bolan said nothing. He heard the sirens moving in close. He had to blow that place soon...

"I'm a Fed," he said.

"DEA?"

"Yeah. And I've got ID to prove it."

"Feds don't carry Uzis, my man."

"I've got a badge in my shirt pocket. I'll reach for it slow."

The detective didn't object.

Bolan slowly lowered his hand to his shirt pocket, removed the detonator and depressed the tiny red-glowing button.

Behind him Wallace Shipping cracked as if the gates to hell were opening inside, and a blast of flame and heat exploded out the doors, throwing Bolan forward and knocking the detective on his behind. Bolan felt the asphalt rip at his hands, then pushed himself up again, running toward the edge of the dock.

"Stop, you son of a bitch!"

Bolan ignored the order, flung away the backpack and threw himself into the open blackness of the night. There was nothingness for a moment, then he was engulfed in the pitch-black water.

He grabbed at the Desert Eagle in his belt and transferred it to his shoulder holster as he sank in the cool water. He snapped it in place and heard the curious sound of a shotgun blast churning up the water surface above his head. But he could see nothing.

Although his shoes were lightweight, he made quick work of getting rid of them, then stripped off his black trousers. Despite the holster, his freedom of movement was much improved. He began swimming away from the dock.

He came to the surface when his lungs were bursting, grabbed a quick breath and submerged again. That moment above the surface was enough to show him Wallace Shipping engulfed in fire and belching great clouds of black smoke into the night.

He finally allowed himself to poke his head above water when he was several hundred yards from the dock. The detective was stomping down the dock angrily, yelling at the squad cars rolling in. The shipping warehouse, Bolan was pleased to see, was a complete loss. Better still, the documents he had in his shirt pocket—provided they would be legible once he dried them out—would give the insurance company adequate excuse to deny paying a claim.

It would be a several-million-dollar insult to Don Cariani.

Now to add some injury.

FOR THE SECOND TIME in eighteen hours, Jethro Parl found himself standing in front of Don Cariani in his office. The scenario was the same, but the atmosphere couldn't have been more different.

Parl had heard snatches of rumor. Trouble in Galveston. At the shipping front where they stored goods coming from the Yan Whan operations. Could it be...?

The Don entered through a side door, looking uncharacteristically unshaved and casually dressed. He'd been wakened just an hour earlier to be told the news, and the news just kept getting worse.

"What's going on, Don Cariani?"

"I think your friend followed you home from Urumchi, Jethro."

Parl felt a cold wave pass through him when he heard the words.

"What's going on?"

"Two trucks. They left our Wallace Shipping warehouse in Galveston with two loads of goods from Urumchi, bound for our customers' distribution centers. Left Galveston earlier tonight—nothing out of the ordinary. But we even put an extra guard on them for increased protection. About 2:00 a.m. they're found at the side of Route 59 about an hour outside town—blown up. Not burned—blown up. Trailers destroyed and everything inside them, and all our boys are dead on the scene—like beyond-recognition-dead. And one of the rigs is missing.

"Now, before we even get the news, somebody goes to Galveston, takes out every one of our boys and blows the place up! The only one who made it out alive was the security guard that the insurance company makes us keep."

"Our inventory?"

"Destroyed one hundred percent. We're not going to be able to salvage a single pair of headphones or a pocket calculator from that mess. The only thing that the Galveston fire department was able to save was the paperwork, which has been confiscated while they investigate the cause of the fire!"

"Anything incriminating?" Parl asked.

The Don shrugged. "I don't know, Jethro. Depends on how smart they are. If they're smart enough to figure out what we're doing, then maybe the insurance won't cover us. Then we're out a shitload of cash. If somebody starts cross-referencing some of the import permit numbers, well, maybe they'll figure out our paperwork isn't legit."

Parl nodded. "It could be our man...."

Don Cariani waved his hand in the air, staring at the desk. "The security guard gave a description to cops. He saw the guy face-to-face! Matches the guy you ran into in China pretty close."

Parl nodded. "No reason it couldn't be."

The Don said nothing. Parl was silently thankful that he hadn't yet taken over responsibility for the Galveston operations, which had been scheduled to occur in the morning.

Now there were no operations for him to run.

"What do you want me to do, Don?"

"I want you to go after him. Clean up this mess."

"Sure thing."

"You got a good reason to want this guy?"

"You know I do."

"That's one reason to put you in charge of taking care of it. You'll be most motivated. Take what and who you need. You have my full resources behind you. I'll spread the word. And if you are successful, you'll have your old job back. You'll be my number-two again. We'll forget anything about a demotion, Jethro."

"Yes, Don."

"He's going to go after the incoming shipment. He'll know about it. Protecting it is part of your assignment. That's his next target, I guess. You agree with that?"

Parl considered the possibilities quickly. "Yeah. He doesn't want us to make money off our Urumchi operations. That's his strategy. He wants to make sure everything that we've still got or are getting that's come out of China is destroyed before we can make our money on it."

"I want this problem to go away, Jethro."

"Sure thing, Don."

Parl left the room, feeling invigorated, feeling alive, more so than he had in weeks. Don Cariani was right—Parl was nothing if not motivated.

There was nothing that would make him happier than that American agent's head on a plate.

DETECTIVE DENNY CREAVALLE shouted into the telephone. "No, I don't want to wait for the report. Tell me now!"

He listened.

"Yeah, what else?"

He listened again.

"And what else?"

Short words from the other end of the line.

"No drugs? Are fooling me? There is no trace of drugs at all? Do you guys even know what you're doing down there?"

Creavalle slammed down the phone and stomped to one of the private rooms, where he ripped open the door, grabbed the worried-looking young man and hoisted him against the wall.

"All right, you little prick, I want to know what was going down at that warehouse!"

"Creavalle, what do you think you're doing?" Webb grabbed him by the shoulders and dragged him away from the security guard.

"I'm trying to get some answers!"

Webb shoved Creavalle into the hall and shut the door on the security guard.

"You're going to get this department sued is what you're going to get!" Webb said. "You're not going to learn any more from that kid!"

"He was there! He saw what went down!"

"Just because he worked there, why do you think

Cariani would make him privy to any of his illegal dealings—think, Creavalle, it doesn't make any sense! There's a reason that kid was the only one to get away with his life, and the reason is he wasn't involved in whatever it was that was going down."

"But somebody's got to know something!"

"Creavalle, you're getting out of control here. You're getting irrational. You're taking this thing way too personally."

"Maybe I am taking it personally, but I had the guts to spend time on this case when everybody else, including you, thought it was a waste of time. You thought I was a fool for staking out Wallace!"

"Maybe we did think you were wasting your time, and yes, obviously there was something going on there. You were right, but you had better get a handle on yourself, mister, or I'm going to yank you right off this case."

"You wouldn't."

"I will. I want to see some professional decorum. And some demonstration that you are thinking clearly and rationally. Another outburst like the one I just saw, and I'm putting you on unpaid leave—got it?"

Creavalle nodded. "I get it."

"Good. Now, send that kid home."

ALICIA JONES-LEONARD didn't recognize the tall, powerful-looking man. He wore a well-tailored, athletic-cut suit, carried a new black portfolio and had piercing blue eyes she simply couldn't ignore.

"I'd like to see Mr. Sinclair, please."

"Do you have an appointment?" she asked, although she knew quite well that Mr. Sinclair had no appointments scheduled until after lunch.

"No, I don't."

"I'm afraid Mr. Sinclair is tied up in important meetings this morning, sir. May I make an appointment for you to come in at a later time?"

"I need to see him immediately."

"Sir, I'm sorry, but I simply cannot ask Mr. Sinclair to leave his meetings—"

"Yes, you can. Give him this."

The man withdrew a manila envelope, sealed, so thin it seemed to contain nothing.

"All right, Mr....?"

"Belasko."

The woman took the envelope into the office, where Sinclair was meeting with his vice president of operations and vice president of sales, planning sales strategy for the Christmas season—one of the most important meetings of the year. Jones-Leonard apologized.

"He said you would want to meet with him after you saw this."

She handed her boss the manila envelope.

Sinclair looked as confused as she was. He ripped the envelope and withdrew a single eight-by-ten glossy black-and-white photo. He stared at it for a long moment, his frown becoming deeper, as if he didn't understand what he was seeing.

Then, from behind the photo, he said, "Oh, my God!"

Sinclair looked at his secretary. "Send him in."

ONE DISASTER after another. Jack Selkirk had longed to complain about it to somebody, but of course that was out of the question. No one could know what he had been doing. Not even his wife.

First there had been the problem in China. Cariani

hadn't explained specifically what those problems were, but they had been substantial. The flow of goods out of China would be interrupted. There were production problems. But they would be overcome shortly, and the flow of goods would resume.

That, Selkirk could cover easily enough. His electronics retail buyer was in on the deal with him and could nudge up the number of units he was purchasing from their legitimate source. With some creative bookkeeping no one would ever know the difference.

Well, he would know the difference in his pocketbook. If they had to buy from their legitimate sources, Selkirk wouldn't be able to buy the pleasure boat he'd been eyeing. He couldn't pay cash for it anyway. This bungle would cost him thousands. He told Cariani he wasn't at all happy about it.

Cariani had smoothed Selkirk's ruffled feathers by promising to get him a very good deal on his boat.

Then, the previous night, in the middle of the night, Cariani called and told him there had been fires and their current inventory had been wiped out, including a delivery on the way to the company that very night.

"We've had a small problem. It's being taken care of."

"Small problem! You know how much trouble your small problem is going to cause me, Cariani!" Selkirk tried not to shout. His wife and kids were asleep upstairs. "I'm going to have to do some major number-juggling just to cover my ass!"

He made vague threats to Cariani. Something on the order of, "I'm going to have to rethink this relationship. I can't afford an unreliable vendor, especially when my ass is on the line every time you fuck it up!"

But the truth was that as long as Cariani wanted to

do business, Selkirk was willing to go along with it. The books could always be cooked. Even now, for all the scrambling it would take, he could simply shift his orders over to his legitimate suppliers. To them it would be extra business. They wouldn't look that gift horse in the mouth.

It would all work out.

The desk phone rang.

"Selkirk."

"It's Sinclair. Could you come up for a few minutes?"

"Sure."

Selkirk stared at the phone.

Sinclair was supposed to be meeting with Milne and Granger all morning. Why would he need Selkirk? Could this somehow be connected to Cariani's problems of the previous night? Had somebody spilled the beans?

Selkirk smoothed the front of his suit jacket. No. They were planning the Christmas selling strategy. Probably needed his input on one of the product lines, what kind of sales he anticipated for it.

He reached the president's office, and the secretary gave him a warm smile, as always. Nothing to worry about.

"Go right on in, Mr. Selkirk."

"Thanks, Al."

Milne and Granger were there, with Sinclair, but also a strange man Sinclair didn't know. The stranger was laying out row after row of black-and-white photos.

"Morning, Steve. What's up?" Selkirk said. He didn't like the look of smoldering anger on Milne's face. He liked even less the cold, merciless look in the eyes of the stranger.

Sinclair said nothing, but gestured to the photos, then leaned back in his chair to observe Selkirk's reaction.

Selkirk eyed the others, then bent over the table, trying to make out the photos. They were dark and shadowy, and at first he couldn't determine what in the world he was looking at.

There seemed to be people in chains, Oriental people, gaunt and filthy, in some sort of industrial building. World War II–era photos from some Oriental concentration camp?

Another photo was a close-up of a painfully thin pregnant woman working on an assembly line. It was very plain that she was shrink-wrapping a box. The box held the logo and graphics of a high-end CD player— a CD player that was supposedly made in Germany, and that sold on the shelves of the company's U.S. retail stores coast to coast.

It took a full fifteen seconds more for Selkirk to realize that he was looking at the source of the goods he had been purchasing from the Cariani crime organization.

Sinclair held up a rumpled but legible piece of paper. Some sort of shipment form.

"The jig is up, Jack," Sinclair said.

CHAPTER SEVENTEEN

Freddy Penalver was a pro in every sense of the word. He was dedicated to his craft. He lived and breathed it. He kept up on the latest techniques and technology. He was paid well for what he did, and he liked doing it.

Penalver's job was making things burn.

He free-lanced, but had a friendly working relationship with the Cariani organization. When Don Cariani asked him for a special favor, he was eager to take the job.

Then he heard the details.

"That's pretty crazy," Penalver said to Jethro Parl as they discussed the particulars.

"I know, but you're kind of a crazy guy, Freddy. Everybody says so. And I know if there's anybody who can pull off a job like this, it's Freddy Penalver. I told Don Cariani that this morning."

"I appreciate it, Jet, but the risk involved here is, well, it'd take some careful planning."

"Problem is it needs to be done this morning."

"I don't operate that way, Jet, you know that. I'm in this business for the long term, which means I plan my jobs carefully. I don't fly by the seat of my pants."

"The thing is, Freddy, we need somebody to do this job and do it in the next couple of hours. I know your methods of operating, and I respect them. I respect you. But I also know your capabilities. If there is one man in the business who could pull off a job like this, it is you. You can do it."

"If I don't do it?"

"We'll get somebody else to."

"Like who?"

"I don't know. I'll make some phone calls. There're several guys in the area in your line of work, as you know."

"Most of them are smart enough not to take a job like this. And none of them are as good as me."

"Agreed. But the job has got to be done. If none of the pros agree, then I know of a couple of hotshots among the Don's boys who'd take the job just to make a name for themselves."

"They'll never get away with it."

"Probably not. But the rap won't be too tough, and it'll be well worth it to some of the young guys I'm thinking about. You know, the kind who want to move up the ranks fast."

Penalver shook his head. "They'll never make it."

Parl shrugged. "Thanks anyway, Freddy."

"Wait a second." Penalver was in his early fifties and was thinking about those young men who wanted to make a name for themselves. That had been him once. Maybe a little bit of risk taking would be what he needed to put the life back into the daily grind.

"How much," he said, "is the Don willing to pay for the extra risk involved?"

WEBB SHOOK Creavalle's shoulder.

"Go home, Denny."

Creavalle sat up, blinking, and nodded. Yes, he had to get some sleep.

He loosened his tie with a single finger. There was an older man, graying hair, balding, talking with one of the clerks. The clerk gave a key to an on-duty desk cop, and the old guy left with him.

Creavalle was bothered by it, and he didn't know why. He asked the clerk.

"Shelly, who was that guy?"

"Some lawyer. Needs to photograph some evidence."

That made sense. A defense attorney sometimes needed to photograph evidence for a case and was allowed to enter evidence holding areas with police escort.

It made sense, yes, but it still nagged at Creavalle and he didn't know why.

He was tired. He needed some real sleep. He'd go home for a good four, five hours and come back tonight with a fresh perspective. And ready for whatever tonight might throw at him in terms of the Wallace Shipping mystery.

"PLEASE WAIT HERE, sir," the young policeman said.

"Sure."

The cop walked to the shelves and started scanning the chicken-wire bins and aluminum shelves, stocked with tagged guns, knives, assorted other hardware.

Freddy Penalver was tempted to stick the incendiary device behind the photocopy machine, but the machine might absorb too much of the blast. The fire had to destroy the papers Don Cariani wanted destroyed.

"I can't seem to find it, sir."

"You know, I thought the last name started with an

F but maybe it started with *Ph*.'' Penalver took two steps forward and pointed down the aisle to the *P* section of the evidence holding room.

''I'll check,'' the desk cop said.

Penalver dropped his keys, bent over and glanced at the cop. The guy was scanning the shelves for Penalver's imaginary client.

Penalver slipped the incendiary device out of his pocket and tucked it neatly under the bottom of the nearest shelving unit. He stood back up with his keys.

The cop returned. ''Not there, either.''

''You know, I might have the wrong precinct entirely. I better call my client again. He woke me up early this morning, you know, and I wasn't getting all my facts straight at the time.'' He chuckled.

The cop smiled.

''Sorry for the trouble.''

''Not at all.''

Penalver left the office, walked down two flights of stairs, got in his car and drove away.

He still had ten minutes to spare.

REALIZATION DIDN'T HIT Creavalle until he had stripped down to his boxers and slumped on the bed. Then he remembered the face of the attorney at the police station that morning. It wasn't an attorney at all. It was a twice-convicted arsonist, a pro who did jobs for the Families all over south Texas. ''Penlover'' or something like that. Creavalle punched a number in the phone, but by then the police station was burning.

BOLAN HAD ALLOWED HIMSELF the luxury of five hours' much-needed sleep.

His next self-assigned duty wasn't until that evening anyway.

But his plans changed as soon as he was on the phone with the Farm.

"Cariani diverted the ship," Barbara Price told him. "For some reason he thinks Galveston's become a little too hot. He's sending it to dock in Biloxi."

"ETA?"

"Fourteen hours. What are you planning?"

"A dockside reception. They can't go far enough to escape me."

"That's what I thought you'd say. And I took the liberty of arranging some assistance for you. Our favorite flying friend is going to be landing in Houston in about forty-five minutes."

Bolan grinned despite himself.

"Thanks. That'll be welcome company. What type of transportation will he be coming in on?"

"A Learjet 60."

"That will get us to Biloxi in plenty of time. By the way thanks for getting me those photographs as quick as you did. They were useful."

"Thank Cello. She risked her neck to procure them." Price's voice became almost imperceptibly softer. "You be careful, Mack."

BOLAN WAS at the Houston airport standing on the edge of the tarmac as the twin-engine jet taxied in his direction. The pilot was Jack Grimaldi, the Farm's ace pilot and an able warrior. Grimaldi credited Mack Bolan with almost single-handedly dragging him from the gutter of Mafia life and giving him the opportunity to make himself into a respected member of the Stony Man Farm team. Grimaldi was a man Bolan could, and often did, trust with his life. The man had never betrayed that trust.

The man that appeared in the door of the jet was thin, almost gaunt. His physical aspect had caused him to be underestimated more than once.

"Sarge!"

"Jack." Bolan clasped hands with Grimaldi at the bottom of the short steps.

"Good to see you. I understand I don't have time for a little R&R in one of my favorite cities."

"Sorry, Jack. Things to do."

Grimaldi hadn't even powered down the aircraft, and within minutes Bolan was in the copilot's seat. They received clearance and taxied into a smooth takeoff.

When they were airborne and close to their cruising altitude, Jack said, "Okay, buddy. I heard the official version back home. Now I'd like to get an eyewitness account of what's been going on so I know what I'm dealing with."

Bolan started at the beginning, with a phone call received at Stony Man Farm in the middle of the night.

BARBARA PRICE PATCHED through a satellite feed that had her speaking with the Learjet as if she were waiting in the control tower at Biloxi, watching them home in.

"We've got alternate transportation waiting for you at Biloxi, along with priority clearance. You'll be landing at Runway Three. We've got a chopper on hand for the next stage of the trip. You'll have to hurry. The Coast Guard wants to stop the Cariani ship about fifty miles out."

"We've got to be at a decent distance in order to have time to make this work," Bolan said. "Fifty miles should buy us that much time."

"That's what I figured," Price said. "The Coast Guard is going to be at the meeting point in one hour and forty minutes and is expecting your arrival there. So be on time."

"Tell her we'll be there," Grimaldi said.

THE JET TOUCHED DOWN in Biloxi, Mississippi, and came to a gradual halt a dozen yards from a parked Hughes helicopter. The three-seater chopper had a twenty-five-foot rotor span and a long-range capacity of approximately 250 miles. It flew at a cruising speed of eighty miles per hour. Empty, it would get them out to sea in less than the hour they needed—unless the storm slowed them. The meteorological disturbance brewing in the gulf was centered almost directly south of New Orleans, meaning they would be flying into some serious weather. Grimaldi slid behind the controls and started up the Hughes.

"Let's be on our way, my man," he said with a grin, in his element.

The Biloxi tower gave them clearance the same minute they asked for it. Grimaldi fed fuel to the Lycoming engine, and in seconds they reached an altitude of one hundred feet, rotated ninety degrees and headed out to sea, still ascending.

THE SUMMER BREEZE had turned to light rain that grew less pleasant the farther they moved away from land. Grimaldi played with the controls and rode through the rising winds with an expert hand, making for a smooth ride under the circumstances. Then the wind turned ugly and began thrashing the rain at the Hughes as if trying to spray it out of the sky.

Grimaldi tuned in the radio, then shouted over the

roar of the wind and the rotor, "Weather report. That summer storm coming off the gulf is building up. It could get hairy."

"You comfortable flying in it?"

"You kidding? It's what I live for! Anyway, we'll reach the Coast Guard ship in just a few."

"That ship'll really be bouncing around. How tough is it going to be landing this thing?"

"Tough, but not too tough."

"You sure you want to risk it?"

Grimaldi grinned. "Sure."

Bolan nodded. "I can always abseil down and do this job solo."

"Uh-uh! You're stuck with me on this one, Sarge."

Bolan was glad. There were times when he liked to work alone—maybe even most of the time it was his preferred method of operating. Then there were probes best made with a warrior at your back, someone you trusted and could count on. He was glad Jack Grimaldi would be at his side this night.

The Coast Guard ship appeared like a faded white star shining in the gale, and minutes later the Hughes was descending slowly over its landing pad. The ship was heaving into the air and descending again sickeningly on the agitated Gulf of Mexico. Grimaldi watched it carefully, watched the sea around it, evaluating the pattern and the intensity of the growing storm. He picked his moment: the Coast Guard ship reached a low point and rose again on an ocean swell, and in that instant Grimaldi dropped the rotor revs with deft manipulation of the controls. The Hughes dropped toward the deck; the deck reached its highest point just a few feet under the landing skids, which seemed on a collision course—but the ship peaked and began dropping again and the landing skids cushioned against it as it descended. Grimaldi cut the power. Instantly the Hughes was resting on the ship deck and was riding with it in the storm.

"Nice job," Bolan said.

Grimaldi grinned. "I know."

THE TWENTY-FOUR-YEAR-OLD cargo vessel had gone under three names in the course of its existence. It had hauled fruit from Chile to San Diego. It had hauled lumber from Washington State to Los Angeles. Now it hauled consumer goods from the Guangzhou port in southeastern China, across the Pacific, through the Panama Canal and up into southern United States. The current run had been a long one, but it was nearly done.

Jethro Parl stormed into the bridge of the *China Star.* "Why are we stopping?"

"Coast Guard," the captain stated simply.

"Why're they stopping us?"

"It's what the Coast Guard does."

"What for?"

"To check for drugs and such. It happens all the time, Mr. Parl. They'll come on board, look things over and send us on our way."

"It's a hurricane out there. Why the hell aren't they out saving sailboats?"

The captain didn't answer. He radioed the Coast Guard ship that he was coming to a stop and he would welcome them on board.

"I'd make sure that none of them sees the hardware you're carrying, Mr. Parl."

Parl nodded. "Yeah."

He stomped down the steel steps into the tiny room where his men had been hanging out to escape the storm. They'd only arrived on board a few hours earlier and were already fed up.

"Just the Coast Guard looking for controlled substances. But we've got to hide our hardware while they search the ship."

"We've got to give up our pieces?"

"Relax, Vinny, the Coast Guard isn't going to attack us. But they'll arrest us if they find the hardware, and the Don would be really happy to hear about that, wouldn't he?"

BOLAN LEANED against the rail, holding his face mask in the pelting rain to wet it and to help seal it to his skin. He stretched it over his eyes and nose, then inserted the mouthpiece. He breathed the stale taste of canned air.

Grimaldi adjusted his own face mask.

No words were needed. The plan was set. They were armed and equipped.

The Coast Guard vessel came to a halt. The cabin of the vessel blocked their view of the *China Star,* which had stopped in the gulf for a routine Coast Guard inspection. The Coast Guard captain had been cooperative, although he had been bursting with curiosity. Bolan had pointedly ignored his inappropriate questions. The captain had agreed to make the search as long as possible. He told his men they were looking for small bags of smuggled heroin or opium. They would have to search long and hard.

That would give Bolan and Grimaldi the time they needed.

They launched themselves into the turbulent ocean. The waves tumbled them to and fro until they descended into the blackness. The sound of the storm faded as they descended, and Bolan snapped on his flashlight.

The water was clouded with sediment, and the light traveled only a good twenty feet, but it was bright enough for them to discern the hull of the Coast Guard ship looming before them in the water like the floating bulk of some massive sea creature. They swam toward its rear, around the huge props. The propellers, in their protective steel sheaths, were motionless, but they could feel the hum of the engines. All it would take would be the actuation of a clutch control to engage those props. Anything that got caught in the water flow and dragged into the rotation of the blades was well-minced fish food.

They turned off the light and swam away from the Coast Guard ship, into the great universe of blackness. Grimaldi felt the weight of the ocean around him and the rushing swell of the air escaping his breathing apparatus. He thought he glimpsed a sparkle of light far above him, but then there was nothing. He might as well have been floating in empty space. The only thing that assured him Bolan was still in the vicinity was the tugging on the twenty-foot nylon cord attached to each of their belts.

All in all, he would have been more comfortable back in the chopper.

The texture of the ocean changed almost imperceptibly. Ahead of him Bolan snapped on the flashlight again, and Grimaldi gave a start.

The hulk of the *China Star* sat in the sea just a few feet away, a corroded, blistered, slimy mass, stringy with seaweed. If the Coast Guard ship had been an immense sea beast, this was the sea beast after it had died and lain there floating, corrupting for while. The hull of the vessel had the look of decay. And yet it was massive, covering the sea above their heads as far as the glimmer of the dim light could reach.

They swam under the hull, then started toward the surface again, until Grimaldi spotted a fainted glimmer of light and Bolan snapped off the flashlight.

Their ascent came nearly to a halt when they were just inches below the surface of the sea, and carefully, slowly, they raised their face masks into the open night air.

The unlit side of the *China Star* rose before them like a stark, black wall. There was no movement along the top of that wall, although they heard the sound of voices in the distance.

Bolan watched the ship silently for a long moment. He could almost feel Grimaldi's urgency to get inside the vessel, but Bolan was feeling especially cautious. He couldn't have explained why, even to himself. Maybe he was experiencing the sounding of a psychic warning system that told him imminent danger lay inside. Maybe it was just a warrior's superstition. Whatever it was, he had felt it in the past and he had heeded it. Maybe he was alive today because he had.

JETHRO PARL LEANED against the wall in the bridge with his arms folded and glared at the Coast Guard officers looking over the captain's papers. They were all in order. Parl knew that. So why were they spending so much time poring over them? He didn't understand this search. There had to be a dozen men on board the *China Star*, going through drawers and lockers, closets and storage compartments.

He wasn't worried about the guns. The ship was outfitted with an emergency storage locker, under the floor in the captain's lounge, under the knotted rug. Cariani had arranged for it to be put there when he acquired the ship. The Coast Guard wouldn't find it.

But what worried Parl overall was the attitude of the search. It was too meticulous. What did it have to do with the attacks on the Cariani facilities in Galveston and the shipping trucks? And the CIA agent that had hounded him in China? Could he have somehow ordered this search?

And to what end? Surely that agent knew that the Coast Guard didn't have the expertise to know the import licenses and paperwork were forged. And probably didn't have the authority to act on them if they did. Anyway Parl's reading of the CIA agent told him he wouldn't resort to low-key measures like by-the-book searches.

So what was the deal?

The deal was this was a normal search, conducted by the Coast Guard because they knew that the *China Star* was a Family-owned ship and they wanted to be absolutely sure it wasn't carrying drugs into the U.S.

Parl told himself to relax.

Drugs. That's all these guys were looking for.

Still, he'd feel a lot better once they removed themselves from his ship.

THEY DRIFTED with the swells to the ladder and drew themselves from the tepid, forceful Gulf of Mexico. They hung dripping from the ladder for a long moment before scaling the *China Star* and depositing themselves in the darkness on the deck. They found themselves at the entrance to a service corridor; they entered and peeled off the scuba gear. Bolan switched on the flashlight long enough for them to withdraw their firearms and gear from waterproofed packs, then they stuffed the wet suits behind a small electrical access panel.

The hard probe could begin in earnest.

Bolan led the way across the broad deck, moving among the shadows, which were dark and easy to find in the drizzling, stormy night. When footsteps approached, they retreated into the darkness at the base of a wall and watched one of the Coast Guard officers pass.

There they waited, until they heard the sound of the Coast Guard vessel moving away in the night.

Bolan had used the time to search the dim, shadowy areas for the crew entrance to the cargo hold. He had found it, across the deck on the opposite side of the cargo hatches. He and Grimaldi crept across the steel hatch and entered the door. When the Stony Man pilot closed the door, Bolan stood still for a moment, listening. If there was a guard on duty, the sound of the *China Star*'s engines starting up again drowned out the rhythm of his breathing.

Bolan descended into the darkness, then spotted dim light. He edged down another step and bent into a crouch, looking behind a separating wall that showed him a section of the cargo area.

There was a single guard on duty, sitting in a chair at a small table underneath a bare yellow light bulb stuck in the wall above his head. He had been reading a paper, but sometime in the past minute he had heard a noise that aroused his suspicion. The paper was ignored in his lap. He was looking across the darkness into the stairwell. If he saw Bolan crouched there, he didn't show it.

Then he reached for a small phone on the desk, calling for backup.

Bolan reacted instantly. He had no desire for the probe to go hard—not yet. He leaped up and out, landing at the bottom of the steps with a heavy boom that echoed in the metal, and turned on the guard with the Beretta 93-R. The guard dropped the phone and grabbed underneath the table.

The Executioner loosed a triburst, the rounds stitching their way from the guard's pelvis to his chin. He tried to grab at all the holes simultaneously, his life-blood gushing out, then slumped onto the table and was still.

Grimaldi grunted and stretched his left arm over the railing of the companionway and fired his custom-silenced mini-Uzi into the darkness. Bolan aimed at the spot, but his eyes still saw the ghost of the bare bulb over the table and he didn't see the assailant until he staggered out of the darkness, rapidly losing purchase on a pistol. The man glared at Grimaldi hatefully before he died.

"Thanks," Bolan said.

Grimaldi hadn't taken his eyes off the darkness at the base of the pile of boxes. But by now Bolan could see for himself that there were no more gunmen lying in wait in the darkness. And the closely stacked boxes left no space large enough for a man to hide.

Bolan got down on one knee and began to assemble parts from the waterproof pack. Inside was C-4—a quantity more than sufficient to blast a gaping hole in the hull of the vessel and send her to the bottom of the gulf, taking the products of the Chinese slave camps with it. Don Cariani would lose all the inventory he had coming to him, not to mention the substantial value of the vessel.

The detonator this time wasn't a remote-controlled

unit. A radio-activated device wasn't a good bet inside the hull of a steel ship for the same reasons walkie-talkies couldn't be expected to function. The hull reflected and confused the signal.

Bolan didn't want to take any chances.

He set the timer.

There was a heavy thump, and Grimaldi whirled. Bolan sprang to his feet. Both men were aiming at the noise even as they simultaneously realized what it had been—the gunshot victim on the desk had flopped to the floor as the ship rolled in a swell. The dead man was lying on his back, staring blindly at the ceiling.

Bolan checked the timing mechanism again, then turned it to face the wall so the glowing red display wouldn't be visible.

"What are you giving us, Sarge?"

"Twenty minutes. Think that'll be enough time to get the job done?"

"It'll have to be, won't it?"

ACROSS THE DECK they found the entrance to the forecastle. Bolan withdrew the silenced Beretta 93-R before stepping inside. Grimaldi followed with his mini-Uzi and shut the door behind them.

So far so good. They had penetrated into the belly of the beast without getting spotted.

The stairs were steel, painted gray, rusting in spots. Bolan stepped down them with excruciating care to avoid the highly resonant clang of metal.

They ended up in a dingy passageway with three doors and a single light bulb in a protective cage in the ceiling. Rust-colored water seeped down the wall and collected in a puddle in the corner, ebbing and flowing with the movement of the ship.

They listened at the first door, hearing a television.

Grimaldi twisted the knob and gave the door a shove. Bolan stepped inside, seeking out any sign of a human being to make his target. But there was no one.

"Somebody's coming!" Grimaldi said quietly.

He shut the door quickly. Bolan stood against the wall, the 93-R raised next to his face, and Grimaldi hid inside a nearly empty doorless clothes closet.

Bolan heard voices and pressed his ear against the steel wall. The metal distorted the sound, and all he could make out was a harsh laugh, then the opening and closing of two doors before the door to their room opened.

Two men entered, the first carrying a Glock 17 in a leather holster, the second a bottle of vodka. The guy with the Glock walked directly to the television and placed the piece on top of it, reaching for the volume knob.

Bolan had assumed Don Cariani would have brought local protection in to watch over the cargo of the *China Star*. Now here they were.

He stepped into the open as the door was closing and placed the muzzle of the 93-R against the back of the vodka drinker's head.

"Don't move a muscle."

The hardman didn't listen. He spun on his heel and attempted to use the bottle as a weapon. Bolan pulled back and down to avoid the glass bludgeon and fired up into his assailant's chest. The 93-R spit out a single shot that knocked the hood into his buddy, who was reaching for the Glock. Bolan triggered the 93-R again, but Grimaldi was faster, and his mini-Uzi was already spitting rounds that slammed into the hood's stomach. Before he could double over, Bolan's hit took him in the shoulders. He was dead on his feet and fell sideways into the television. Grimaldi grabbed the limp corpse and lowered it to the floor.

The suppressed gunfire had been the loudest indication of the altercation. Bolan had to hope it hadn't been resounding enough to alert the others.

Hiding places weren't a luxury they possessed. They left the bodies where they had fallen and closed the door behind them.

It was time for some dirty work.

They used the same technique for entering, but this time they were sure the room was occupied. Bolan knew there was a chance that the others he had heard were *China Star* crew members, who might be honest sailors. Thus, he wouldn't fire without making some sort of identification.

Grimaldi swung the door and Bolan stepped inside the tiny compartment, spotting no one at first, and swung to the right where he assumed the head would be. The door was wide open, and an obese man lounged on the toilet with a girlie magazine. He dropped the magazine and grabbed at the Smith & Wesson .45-caliber handgun holstered under his arm with surprising speed. That was positive ID in Bolan's book. He triggered a triburst into the swollen human target, making the fat man jump and twitch in his seat.

The head was so narrow it kept the huge corpse propped up, as if merely sleeping. The Smith & Wesson fell from his limp hand and hit the floor with a thump.

The third room held two men splayed out on their beds, watching a television sitcom, when Bolan barged in. One sprang to his feet immediately in search of his weapon, hanging in its shoulder holster on the corner of the bed. The Executioner fired point-blank into the side of his skull, throwing the man's head into the wall with a thump. The guy didn't feel the impact. He was already dead.

The other hardman was crawling to his feet and sprang out of the bunk at Bolan, just in time to fully absorb the next 9 mm round, which brought him to a halt and dropped him at the warrior's feet.

Bolan and Grimaldi left the staterooms full of death. The battlefield was minus seven fighters.

CHAPTER EIGHTEEN

"Time?"

"Fourteen minutes."

They followed the sound of voices through the dank corridor to a closed door. From underneath came light and conversation. Bolan nodded to Grimaldi, and the pilot put his hand on the knob.

It turned before he could turn it, and the door was pulled open. Bolan wedged himself inside, knocking straight up into the chin of the man and slamming him off his feet, grabbing him as he was falling and driving him bodily into the other occupant.

The young man slammed against the wall and crunched his face in an expression of pain. His companion slumped to the floor and moaned, dazed and shocked.

Both opened their eyes to stare down the barrels of deadly-looking weapons, held by men who knew how to use them very well.

Bolan had immediately determined that they were crew. They had the unshaved, filthy look of ship mechanics who had been on the water for weeks.

"You've got one chance to live," Bolan said to the sitting man, who nodded grimly.

"I don't want to kill you, but I will."

The young man nodded again, convinced.

"How many crew total, including the captain?"

"Eight."

"How many on duty?"

"Four. But there are others...."

"I know all about the others," Bolan said, "and I plan to take care of them. But I'm going to let the crew live. If you get off this ship immediately."

"Get off the ship?" said the victim on the floor.

"Get off this ship right now. If you don't get off right now, I'll kill you. If you try to tell the others, I'll kill you. If you stay here, you'll die anyway. This ship is going to explode and sink in fifteen minutes."

The two of them read sincerity in Bolan's expression. Both were terrified. "Okay," the guy on the floor said. "We'll leave."

"Where's the rest of the crew right now?"

"Two in the engine room, two on the bridge. Two are going to sleep in the quarters across the hall."

Bolan nodded and stepped back, motioning for them to get up. "Get the two across the hall and exit through the back of the forecastle. Go straight to the deck and get on the first escape boat. Get as far away from the ship as you can."

"Some of the men are back there in the stateroom," the guy on the floor said. "What if they try to stop us?"

"They're dead."

The two youths looked at each other, then made quick work of waking their buddies across the hall, who had just bedded down again after the interruption by the Coast Guard. They looked sleepily at Bolan and Grimaldi and quickly came to full alertness. The four young men headed back through the forecastle.

"Time."

"Twelve minutes. How long you think it will take us to reach a safe distance, Sarge?"

"Longer than we've got."

They came to a companionway leading down to the engine room. Another led up to the bridge.

"Tell them to shut the whole thing down and get out of here fast," Bolan ordered.

"You going to try to take out the rest of the Cariani guys on your own?"

"Yeah."

Grimaldi shrugged. "I'll join you in just a sec."

Bolan headed up, holstering the 93-R and bringing his own Uzi out of the pack, his lacking a suppressor. He checked the mag and kicked at the door to the bridge.

He jumped into the open room and assessed the occupants immediately, sweeping the Uzi at two men in the back with automatic weapons slung over their shoulders. The Uzi chattered angrily, and slugs chopped into their bodies. The warrior swung the subgun suddenly to the left and triggered a burst into one of the three men at the control board—the one who was pulling a machine pistol from a hip holster. The 9 mm rounds cored his chest, and he gagged on blood. The other two men raised their hands, one covering his eyes and sobbing.

There was a flash of movement, and Bolan jumped to the floor, microseconds before several rounds from an automatic handgun slammed through the window. He felt the glass raining on his back, heard the gun come up empty and sprang to his feet, achieving target acquisition with the Uzi only to have the target spring out of his field of vision as he loosed a burst. There was a shout of pain, and Bolan knew he had at least winged the target. He opened the door with a body blow and swept the open deck and the empty stairs. There was no sign of the wounded man.

"Are you the captain?" Bolan demanded of the surrendering man, the one who wasn't weeping.

"Yes."

"This ship is rigged to explode in about ten minutes, and there's no way to stop it. Get out of here now."

"I've got to get the rest of my crew!"

"Here!" It was Grimaldi, entering with two dazed-looking, grease-covered mechanics.

"I've sent the four others to a life raft. Now, get off this ship!"

The captain was about to protest.

"Time?" Bolan demanded, not for his own benefit.

"Nine minutes," Grimaldi said loudly.

The captain and his mechanics exchanged looks as they headed out the front of the bridge.

"Who are you?" the captain asked suddenly, coming to a halt.

"You want my life story?" Bolan asked.

"Whoever you are you should know this—the cargo isn't all here."

"What?"

"They came with another ship about nine hours ago. They unloaded all they could into the ship and headed for Gulfport. They rearranged the stacks in the hold so it looked like we still have a full ship."

Bolan stared at the captain for a long second.

"Sarge?" Grimaldi said.

It was a different sound that caught Bolan's attention. There was a sudden thrum that was familiar and alarming. He felt it in the decks of the vessel.

Bolan glanced at Grimaldi, both men knowing what it was.

"Chopper!"

"*They* came in it," the captain said.

"Get out of here!" Bolan ordered, giving the captain a shove in the direction of his crew, who were busily freeing an ancient wooden life raft from its harness on the side of the ship. The captain looked back at him, then ran to join his men.

Bolan landed on the deck with both feet and circled the forecastle in a run as the black sky cracked in two. A white flash of electricity careened through the heavens, and the rain's intensity redoubled in seconds. His feet and Grimaldi's sloshed on the deck with every step.

He ran into the open around the end of the forecastle, and the deck erupted at his feet as a volley of automatic fire hit and bounced inches behind his running pace. Bolan dived for the cover of a ventilation box and crashed to the deck, raising a wall of water. He looked for Grimaldi, saw nothing, then drew behind his cover as another wild series of rounds slammed into the ventilation unit and the steel floor. Bolan rose up, leveled the mini-Uzi and fired, pelting the dark hiding places that surrounded him. There was no target to acquire. At first. Then he spotted a shift in a shadow, a recoil from a close Uzi round. He saw it now, a shape in the darkness. He fired the Uzi at the shape, but the weapon soon cycled dry.

He sank to his knees and heard a volley of fire from his right. Grimaldi was still alive enough to be emptying his mini-Uzi at the shooters. He briefly had thought the ace pilot had been taken out by the autofire that had sent Bolan for cover.

He rummaged in his pack, found a noisemaker, armed it and lobbed it around the ventilation unit. It rolled and bounced across the deck, trailing a line of water to within several feet of the shadowy shooter.

"Grenade!" Bolan called to Grimaldi, then lowered his face behind the ventilation unit. The sky turned white even through his eyelids, and there was a crash of close-range thunder, which seemed to trigger the blast of deafening sound and blinding illumination from the bomb. Bolan stood up even as he was slamming a fresh mag into the Uzi.

The gunner was staggering into the open, blinded and deafened by the grenade, grabbing his eyes and shouting in pain. Bolan leaned into the Uzi and fired a burst. The blind man's stagger brought him screaming into the path of the 9 mm rounds and he danced a jig of death. Then he hit the ground, and the torrent of rain wiped the blood away before it could puddle underneath him.

"Jack!"

"Here!" Grimaldi emerged from behind the forecastle wall. "I almost bought it, Sarge."

"No, you don't. I'm not carrying you back to the Farm."

There was a rise in the pitch of the chopper. It was ready to lift off. They ran back along the length of the ship and spotted it now, on a flat area at the rear of the vessel that served as an impromptu landing pad. The rotors were tilting and the skids were leaving the deck surface.

"Wait for me!" There was another gunman emerging to their left, running in the direction of the chopper.

Bolan stopped and bent into a firm firing stance before triggering the Uzi. The running man caught the rounds in the knees and turned to Bolan in open-mouthed surprise as he plummeted to the deck and squelched up a small tidal wave of water, then lay still.

The chopper was airborne.

The Executioner felt an unpleasant sense of déjà vu as he raised the Uzi and triggered, aiming for the rotors. One bent rotor meant doom for the airship. He emptied the mag in seconds.

He stooped for cover and Grimaldi was beside him, emptying his mini-Uzi at the helicopter.

Bolan grabbed a grenade from his pack and yanked the pin. Grimaldi fell into a crouch at his side and watched his friend mentally count down, then stand and lob the bomb at the chopper. The aircraft had turned sideways, and a barrage of automatic fire cut loose the moment Bolan appeared, driving him back to his knees before he could watch the result of the grenade, but he heard the explosion.

When he looked, the helicopter was spinning and whining, buffeted by the force of the explosion. But the HE round had detonated too far from the aircraft to cause it damage. The pilot was wrestling for control and he gained it. The chopper tilted into the storm and accelerated up and away from the *China Star*. Bolan had slammed another mag into the Uzi and he aimed for the rear rotor, triggering the autoweapon until it was dry again. By then the chopper was out of range, disappearing into the downpour.

Bolan had again lost his prey to the air.

A ragged bolt of static energy crackled from one cloud to another directly above their heads, so close Bolan thought he felt the heat of the blast. It was followed without pause by the explosion of thunder.

"Look!" Grimaldi shouted, grabbing Bolan's shoulder and turning him to the other side of the vessel. Four men lay sprawled on the deck.

"They killed those kids!"

"They know it's going to blow. That's why they ran," Bolan replied. "How much time?"

"A minute. Maybe. Let's get going!"

The dead men had removed the tarpaulin from the weather-beaten life raft, and Grimaldi and Bolan jumped inside, their feet slipping in the inch of water that had already collected. The small boat swung wildly in the wind on its two thin, rusty chains, and far below them Bolan spotted the roiling black gulf. The rear end of the *China Star* rose in a heaving swell.

"Ready to release!" Bolan shouted over the roar of the storm. "One, two, three, now!"

Bolan slammed his hand into the quick release, and the rear end of the boat let loose, but Grimaldi's actuation of the front end had no effect. Bolan suddenly found the boat disappearing from under his feet and he grabbed for a wooden seat, hooking his arm around it and catching his body weight on it so that his arm exploded with pain. Grimaldi grabbed at the rusty length of chain and found virtually no purchase on the rain-soaked metal—he didn't make a sound as he disappeared into the black night. Bolan found the mini-Uzi still in his free hand. He flipped it, grabbing the barrel, and hammered the boat release with the butt of the autorifle. The release gave way, and Bolan and the boat plummeted into the sea.

There was another crack of thunder that wasn't thunder, and the *China Star* gave a sickening lurch as her insides were gutted with fire. The explosion rammed the vessel into the plummeting boat, and Bolan found himself tossed into the falling cataclysm of rain. He slammed into the ocean.

Bolan felt the boat hit the water within a few feet and brought himself to the surface next to it. He dragged himself over the side and flopped inside, finding several inches of water weighing it down.

The *China Star* was shuddering and leaning in his direction in a slow, momentous collapse. Bolan spotted a mass of hair appear several yards away in the heaving sea.

"Jack!"

Grimaldi turned in the water and headed quickly for the life raft. Bolan grabbed his hand and hauled him bodily over the side, and the *China Star* collapsed on its side like a skyscraper falling to earth. It raised a tidal wave that swamped under and over the raft and pushed it away from the dying vessel.

The sky cracked and the sea seemed to be swarming to higher and higher peaks by the second. Grimaldi began scooping out water by the handful as Bolan snatched the radio from his belt. The unit was packed in its own individual watertight pouch and it sprang to life when Bolan activated it.

"Coast Guard, Coast Guard, Belasko here. The job is done and we could use a lift home."

"YOU SURE YOU WANT TO be flying on a night like this?" the mate was shouting to Grimaldi over the storm winds and rain. "It's shit out here, and it's going to get worse before it gets better."

"I'm sure. How's the crew from the *China Star?*"

"Fine. They say there are four more floating around somewhere in another lifeboat!"

Grimaldi shook his head. "Murdered before they could leave the vessel," was all the explanation he had time to give.

The mate looked stunned. Sudden senseless violence wasn't a part of his life scheme.

"Are we ready?" Bolan asked.

"Ready."

"Let's go."

The Coast Guard ship was fighting through the rumbling ocean as the Hughes took off into the sheets of rain and tore into the swarthy sky.

"STONY BASE, this is Stony One."

Barbara Price's voice came over the radio, somehow bringing a touch of warmth into the dank, wet chopper interior. "Stony Base here."

"The *Star* drowned at sea. But there's a snag. The captain told us that part of the cargo was removed prior to our arrival and taken to Gulfport, Louisiana."

"You're on your way there, I assume?"

"Yes. We need to know what our friend Cariani might have in the way of shipping or docking facilities in Gulfport."

"Give me a minute. If they went through regular customs procedures, we'll locate it."

There was a long minute of silence. Ahead of them the clouds were thicker, the sky lower, the night blacker.

"Here it is. Carmine Perinni, a longtime associate of the Cariani family, works mostly out of New Orleans. He owns a small dock at Gulfport, but doesn't use it much, not for legal purposes anyway. It's got paperwork to make it look legit. A ship called *Free Run* docked there several hours ago and was searched by customs. They report no paperwork deviations of note. Import goods. Licenses in order. They let it dock in Gulfport at 10:00 p.m."

"How long would it take them to unload a ship like that?" Grimaldi asked.

"Tough to even guess how much cargo they had, or

what loading facilities the Perinni shipping company has and what they plan on doing with it. They won't leave it sitting there—that's about all we can guess for sure."

"Let me get everything you have on this shipping company of Perinni's," Bolan said to Price.

"That's not much, Stony One. It's been searched a couple of times in the past several years when Perinni was suspected of using it as a drug drop-off. It almost definitely is, but the police couldn't find anything. So we really don't know what goes on there."

Bolan considered that. "We'll know soon, Stony Base."

Gulfport, Louisiana

"THERE IT IS." Grimaldi hovered offshore in the falling rain, watching the only dock facility in Gulfport, Louisiana, that exhibited activity on this miserable night. Bolan watched the workers grow excited, like a farm of ants stirred with a stick, when they spotted the helicopter hovering offshore.

"I bet they think we're cops."

Bolan shook his. "If those are just Cariani's dockworkers, they don't even realize they're doing anything illegal." Then he saw movement behind the warehouse.

Grimaldi squinted into the rain and darkness. "That's the chopper from the *China Star*."

"Looks like they don't want us hanging around."

"I'd like to know what they think they're going to do about it."

The chopper was a Bell JetRanger, bigger than the Hughes, and older, but with a more powerful Allison engine and faster cruising speed. It leveled and barreled through the rain directly at the Hughes.

"I think we're about to find out," Bolan said.

The JetRanger was on a collision course, as if it intended to head-butt the Hughes out of the sky.

"I'm giving you a clear shot!" Grimaldi said, wrenching the Hughes in a forty-five-degree turn. Bolan yanked back the door and availed himself of the extra arms tucked behind his seat. He grabbed an M-16 A-1/M-203 combo and targeted the oncoming helicopter. He triggered a burst at the aircraft, and watched the sparks fly from the rotors. The JetRanger pilot decreased his fuel flow abruptly, and the craft dropped, passing below the Hughes.

THERE WERE CRIES OF ALARM among the dockworkers when they heard the gunfire, and they turned to watch as the JetRanger suddenly swooped in an arc, passing underneath the newly arrived helicopter.

"Come on, let's get these trucks loaded!"

It was as if Parl hadn't spoken. They were all watching the helicopters as if mesmerized. Parl's patience was wearing extremely thin. He dragged out the Browning Hi-Power and fired it into the air, which got their attention.

"I want every box loaded *now!*"

The workers rushed to comply. There were five semi trucks sitting at the dock, engines running, fouling the air with their diesel fumes. It was probably going to be just enough to fit the load from the *China Star*. Parl had strenuously objected to the removal of half the cargo from the vessel when they were still at sea yesterday, but was now glad Don Cariani had overridden him. The cargo that remained on the cargo ship was sitting on the bottom of the Gulf of Mexico. Parl had barely escaped with his life.

He still might very well end up with a bullet in his brain personally from Don Cariani. Might. It all depended on how successfully he was able to get this cargo into the hands of Cariani's retail customers.

The agent, the one who had hounded him in China, was the same one who sank the *China Star* and was in that helicopter now. That was an absolute fact in Parl's mind. He heard another round of gunfire—there would be nothing more satisfying than seeing that helicopter get shot out of the sky right now. He just wished he were up in the JetRanger taking care of the job personally.

THE JETRANGER SWOOPED toward the agitated bay, engine screaming with exertion when it started to ascend again.

The Hughes started to ascend itself, as it turned 180 degrees under Grimaldi's expert control, and Bolan once again had a clear shot at the JetRanger. He aimed down at the whirling optical illusion of the enemy aircraft's rotors. The JetRanger veered sharply away from the gunfire.

"They're right under us!" Bolan shouted over the rising pitch of the engine.

"Not anymore!" Grimaldi dragged on the cyclic pitch control, and the Hughes leaned almost on its side. Bolan gripped the window edge to keep from getting tossed across the cabin, eyes scanning for the JetRanger.

"One-eighty!" he called.

"Gotcha!" Grimaldi said, and the Hughes was already spinning, the JetRanger veering into view.

"Good!" he said, and the Hughes whined in protest

as sudden countertorque from the rear rotors brought it to a standstill in the air. Bolan chambered an HE round into the 40 mm M-203 grenade launcher under the barrel of the M-16 and fired it out the window. The grenade sailed through the vast open chasm that had opened between the two aircraft, and the JetRanger spun to the left as if the pilot had spotted the deadly egg plummeting in his direction. The tiny metal unit dropped stonelike through the open air where the JetRanger had been. It almost plummeted into the sea but instead made impact with a long concrete wharf that stretched more than a hundred yards from the shore. There was a flash of fire and noise, and the concrete disintegrated.

The JetRanger fed all its fuel into putting distance between itself and the hovering Hughes before ascending farther.

"They're going to try to get level with us and take us out," Grimaldi said over the engine roar.

"Don't let them. I can take them out with a 40 mm if I can get over them again."

"I'll see what I can do."

Grimaldi fed fuel into the engine at a tremendous rate, the Hughes thrusting directly up into the air, and for a moment the two choppers were rising at an identical rate so that to Bolan it appeared they were standing still while the world moved away from them. The Hughes started to pull away.

"They've got more horses but more weight," Grimaldi explained.

"Don't let them gain and get closer to them," Bolan said, thumbing another HE into the M-203's breech. He locked it down. Grimaldi was fighting to move the Hughes to a better position over the JetRanger, but the JetRanger pilot wasn't about to let Bolan get into a decent firing position. He veered away while Bolan watched helplessly.

"We'll have to do better than that."

"I'll try to catch up, but it's not going to be easy without losing some height."

Bolan nodded. "Staying above them is our first priority."

"COME ON, COME ON!" Parl shouted as the rear doors to the five trucks were closed in rapid succession and locked.

"Okay, we travel together, got it? I don't want anybody wandering away from the convoy. We got one car up front and two more in the rear. Sammy, you drive the front car. Pete, you take one of the rear cars. I'll be in the last car taking up the rear. I want a gun in each and every truck and two in each car in addition to the driver. I want us to be in constant radio contact. Are there any questions?"

Parl heard another round of gunfire, and his attention was drawn to the sky. The fire was plainly coming from the unfriendly chopper, which was soaring high above the dock and had gotten the JetRanger in his sights. But the JetRanger pitched away from the fire, still fighting for altitude itself.

"Hey!" Parl shouted to the dockworkers, who were craning their necks at the aerial battle. "Get out of here! The job's done, all right? So just get out of here." The men started to move away, and Jethro Parl snapped. He dragged out the Hi-Power and fired at their feet, again and again, and the workmen fled for their lives.

"What are you standing around for!" Parl shouted to his men. "You waiting for me to open the doors for you! Come on, you pussies, let's get this show on the road!''

"I'M GIVING IT all I got!" Grimaldi said.

"Move to your four o'clock and come around thirty degrees," Bolan instructed.

The Hughes twisted instantly, as if it was voice-commanded, and the JetRanger swung into view, still trying to gain altitude while moving away from them. Bolan spotted the trucks on the ground moving out with several cars in a convoy.

Time to get serious.

"Get me closer in a hurry. We've got five hundred yards to work with."

"You got it," Grimaldi said through gritted teeth, and the Hughes swept sideways under his command, dropping rapidly but at a sharp angle in the direction of the JetRanger.

"Keep it up."

"I need distance to pull out of this!"

"Keep going."

The JetRanger spotted their rapid maneuver and pitched away from them like a fleeing deer. Bolan aimed the M-16 A-1/M-203 high and fired. The high explosive grenade flew up and away from the Hughes, arcing through the air and plummeting earthward.

"Is it good?"

"Too close to call."

The 40 mm grenade sped at the JetRanger like a falling rock, and the enemy aircraft gave an extra burst of speed. Bolan knew the 40 mm bomb had missed by inches.

But he was wrong. The grenade slammed into the tip of the JetRanger's rotor and detonated with a fiery roar.

The aircraft's steady roar acquired a chirping quality, and the helicopter slowed its frantic flight.

Grimaldi shouted wordlessly as he wrestled to slow the diving Hughes.

"I scored, but just barely—keep us moving in."

"You're the boss." Grimaldi relaxed his wrestling with the controls and allowed the free fall to continue.

The JetRanger's engines were peaking at incredible rpms, but the craft was slowing fast and was helpless to avoid coming directly into the Executioner's range. It pitched suddenly, a desperate maneuver, and at least two automatic weapons fired up at the Hughes for the two seconds the crippled craft could hold the position. Grimaldi flipped the belly of the Hughes toward the JetRanger, and they listened to a rattle of rounds against the metal underside. Then Grimaldi wrenched the chopper into a hover.

"Clear shot?" he demanded.

"Good." Bolan thumbed another HE into the breech of the M-203, sighted high above the JetRanger and trusted gravity to adjust his aim. The grenade fired with almost no recoil, and Bolan saw the bomb race toward the other chopper, zeroing in on the center of the whirling rotors.

The egg exploded with a flash and a crack of thunder. An instant later the detonation reached the fuel tanks and blasted the JetRanger into a thousand pieces that spun away like fiery comets. Some fell burning to the concrete wharf of Gulfport. Other sizzled and disappeared into the turbulent waters of Bay St. Louis.

CHAPTER NINETEEN

"Did you raise them?"

"It was them that went down, I'm telling you, Jet."

"Keep trying."

The radioman sighed and spoke into the microphone again. "Bird, Bird, come in. This is Ringleader." He waited for several seconds. "Bird, Bird..."

Parl thought about what had been lost that night. A ship. Parl couldn't calculate the value of the *China Star*. The cargo itself. The value to the Cariani Family was maybe more than a million. If they'd lost the helicopter as well... Fuck it. He'd count the losses when a final tally could be made.

He'd spotted the explosion in the air as they were pulling away from the wharf. One of the choppers had gone down. Which one? Or was it both?

Was his nemesis finally dead?

Parl almost hoped not, since he hadn't had the opportunity to bring about that ending personally.

At least it was over for tonight. Or so he assumed. Would the agent be foolish enough to attack this caravan of trucks and cars, every one of them manned with gunmen?

Every single time he had underestimated this agent,

he had been proved wrong. He had astounded Parl with his arrogance, his boldness, his brutality. There was nothing this man wouldn't do. It was as if he had developed some sort of personal vendetta against the Cariani Family, against Parl himself.

He certainly didn't behave like CIA or FBI or DEA. He didn't act like a cop or like a representative of any government agency Parl knew of.

He acted like a madman.

"YOU'VE GOT TWO possible scenarios over the next ten minutes," Barbara Price said over the radio. "They're heading west, which means they're going to have to cross off the Biloxi peninsula eventually. They'll probably turn south to hit the interstate running along the Mississippi Sound. If not, their only other real option is to head north in just a few miles. There's a bridge on Ferry Road that'll take them over a strait between Big Lake and Back Bay."

Bolan nodded. "That's where they'll go."

"How can you be sure?"

"I'm not. But if we wait there for them and they don't show, we'll still have time to pick the trail on one of their routes out of Biloxi."

"Agreed," Price said. "They'll have two ways out of town at that point."

"Pedal to the metal, Jack. We've got make some time getting around this convoy and into their escape route."

"You've got it." Grimaldi fed fuel to the Hughes and increased the rotor angle of attack, and the chopper veered north under Bolan's direction. They were over water again in minutes. This time it was Big Lake, which, joined with the Bay of Biloxi, made a peninsula out of the ten-mile-long strip of land on which sat the town of Biloxi and Keesler Air Force Base.

"There's your bridge. What's the plan?" Grimaldi asked.

"Drop me at the south end of the bridge, then get out of sight. I don't want them discouraged from taking this route." Bolan grabbed his pack and stuffed in plastique, also grabbing several foam-packed grenades.

"You going to blow that bridge, Sarge?"

"As much of it as I have to. As soon as you hear the signal, you can come out and help me clean up."

"Gee thanks, buddy."

Grimaldi swept the Hughes earthward and hovered three feet above the ground. Bolan jumped to the earth with his pack and the M-16 A-1/M-203, then waved Grimaldi off.

"Get out of here—they could be here in minutes!"

The ace pilot had trouble hearing the words but got the gist of the meaning and gunned the engine. Bolan crouched to ride out the tremendous downdraft from the accelerating rotors, and in seconds the chopper was thrusting into the heavens.

Bolan hadn't been exaggerating. The convoy might arrive in minutes or even less. With a quick perusal of the Ferry Road bridge, he developed an on-the-spot strategy and ran toward the center of the bridge.

Then he heard the sound of an automobile coming up behind and turned to see a Mississippi state trooper rolling onto the bridge. Bolan stopped and the trooper started to flash his lights.

Bolan grabbed his walkie-talkie, which was patched through a satellite link to Stony Man.

"Stony Base come in, this is Stony One and I've got a state trooper trying to get in on the action."

"I'm on it, Stony One," Price replied.

The car screeched to a halt, and the driver's door popped open. Bolan heard a burst of static, and the trooper's loudspeaker burst to life.

"Put the gun down and get your hands in the air!"

Bolan peered through the flashing lights, trying to scan the inside of the trooper's vehicle for a partner. He saw no one.

"Get out of here. I'm a Fed," Bolan said.

"Sure you are, buddy! Drop that piece!"

Bolan wasn't about to get rid of the M-16.

"You should be getting orders right now to vacate this bridge," Bolan told him.

"I'm giving you about five more seconds to drop that piece!"

Bolan's internal clock was driving home the need for speed. The last thing he had time for was dealing with a gung-ho state cop. He couldn't blame the trooper for doing his job, of course. On the other hand he might have mere seconds before the Cariani convoy arrived.

"Call in! You'll get your orders!"

"I'm not moving until I have that rifle in my possession."

Bolan flipped the M-16 A-1/M-203 in his hands and achieved target acquisition on the trooper's car. He fired the rifle and sent a burst into the door that was protecting the trooper. The door slammed into the man and sent him staggering. Bolan ran to the car as the trooper fell against it and raised his handgun. The Executioner cracked the muzzle of the M-16 into the man's wrist and sent the gun to the pavement. He nudged it underneath the squad car with his foot and leveled the M-16 at the trooper.

"I suggest you check your radio."

The trooper slid into the front seat and grabbed his radio, which was squawking at him.

"Yeah! Yeah! Okay!" he said into it. "All right, buddy, I'll leave. But I got to have my gun."

"No time. Get out of here now."

"I'm not going anywhere without my gun!" The trooper exited the vehicle.

Bolan had enough. He took his last several pounds of plastique from his carryall, prerigged with a detonator, and set it in the front seat of the squad car. He turned on the detonator and the tiny red light glowed.

The trooper was staring at him.

"That's C-4."

Bolan said nothing, but withdrew the radio activator from his pack.

"You're gonna blow this bridge."

Bolan turned on the radio unit. The sight of the red light coming to life made the trooper jump back.

"Jesus!" the trooper gasped.

"You still here?" Bolan said.

The trooper ran, and Bolan jogged after him to the north end of the bridge. Behind them he heard the distinctive rumble of a semi truck.

"Get out of sight," he said to the trooper, and stepped behind one of the concrete supports at the end of the bridge. He looked around it and watched the convoy approach.

The formation hadn't altered since leaving the dock. One car in front and two in the rear, with five semi trucks in close formation between them, carrying a substantial load of Mafia profit.

Bolan watched them coming, the tiny black plastic radio transmitter getting hot in his hands. His thumb hovered over the switch.

He waited for the perfect moment, when he could inflict maximum damage.

PARL WAS GETTING more nervous with every passing minute. The more he thought about it the less unlikely it seemed that, if he still lived, the agent who had been harassing him since Urumchi would let him get away tonight. Unless his had been the chopper that went down...

That was unlikely. They hadn't been in contact with their chopper since the explosion. It had to have been theirs that went down. That meant the agent was still in pursuit.

Who knew what that madman might attempt.

They had reached the Ferry Road bridge, and fifteen minutes later they would hit the interstate. He'd feel safer then. He dialed up the lead car.

"How's it going up front?" he asked.

"Quiet, Jet. Nobody's out tonight—shit!"

"What?"

"There's a cop car on the side of the road up here. It's all shot up, like there was a firefight."

Parl didn't like the sound of that at all. "Anybody around?"

"Not a soul, Jet."

"Keep a close eye out!"

THE HUGHES HOVERED eight feet above the water a mile away from the Ferry Road bridge, tucked neatly behind an ostentatious pleasure craft anchored a hundred yards from shore. Jack Grimaldi kept a light hand on the controls and an eye on the water.

At any second the water was going to reflect a globe of brilliant light.

Striker's signal.

He noticed movement on the yacht. An older man in a scarlet silk robe was standing on the deck blinking sleepily. He started shouting, and Grimaldi waved back.

THE TROOPER'S CAR was parked at an ideal spot. Bolan's quick structural survey had chosen the position for the blast.

The first car drove by the cop car. He'd deal with them later. One semi drove past it, then another and another. Bolan touched the button.

The car became a blinding nova. The shock wave was a visible force that cracked the bridge, and the road was suddenly collapsing between the powerful concrete supports. In either direction of the explosion two of the semi trucks suddenly found the pavement tilting underneath them, crashing down into the Big Lake strait. The semi trucks collapsed in after it, two becoming engulfed in the explosion as they descended. They slammed into the water and detonated one after another.

"SHIT! STOP THIS CAR!"

The car was already screeching to a halt, and Parl jumped out to watch the road collapse in front of him. Four trucks had vanished as if by magic, and he heard the twin explosions from below. The remainder of the bridge began to tremble under his feet. Another section of the road cracked and tumbled into the nothingness. The car ahead of him suddenly reversed in a panic, slamming into Parl's car, forcing him to dive for cover.

The tremors became worse.

BOLAN JUMPED from behind the concrete post and ran to the front car, which had swerved off the road and come to a halt. Three doors popped open, and the men emerged to watch the destruction taking place behind them.

The driver of the surviving semi truck took an alternate tack. He accelerated, determined to get off the unstable bridge as soon as possible. Bolan wasn't about to be satisfied with an eighty percent success rate. He wanted that semi. He ran into the middle of the road and faced it down, thumbing a high-explosive round into the breech of the M-203.

The driver exercised his only option: he gunned the engine and aimed directly at the warrior. Bolan triggered the HE and drove the 40 mm grenade directly into the grille of the semi from under forty yards. The blast filled the rig's hood, blasted into the cab and melted the driver and his gunman instantly. The truck jackknifed, slamming into the concrete wall of the bridge and blasting through it.

Bolan was already heading toward the surviving automobile. Another HE went into the breech of the M-203, and he fired it over the heads of the gunmen. The HE hit the ground behind them and detonated, slamming one gunner into the automobile beneath a wall of fire. The other two were knocked away from the car by the blast and staggered in the road.

The Executioner chambered a buckshot round into

the M-203, effectively transforming the weapon into a powerful shotgun. He turned it on the two gunmen as they tried to unleather their weapons. They never saw it coming. The blast of lead shot ripped one to pieces and bloodied his partner, who screamed and looked down at the ruin that had been his chest. Bolan triggered a quick burst from the M-16 A-1, and the screaming stopped.

GRIMALDI TILTED the helicopter nearly on its nose and tore across the Back Bay with the waves almost slicing under the skids. He gained altitude and spotted two surviving automobiles maneuvering on the end that was still standing. The first of them was already facing back the way it had come, and a load of white smoke billowed from its tires as it got out of there. The second started forward.

"No, you don't," Grimaldi said. He grabbed a fragmentation grenade with his free hand and yanked the pin with his teeth while sending the Hughes into a radical pitch. He found himself with the automobile directly in his line of fire and he tossed the fragger, then righted the helicopter and fed it thrust. There was a blast behind him, and he found himself doubting he was out of the frag's range. Then the chopper ascended away from the scene, and Grimaldi spotted the auto rolling slowly, filling with fire. The punctured gas tank erupted, and a flailing figure ran from the vehicle, limping and completely ablaze. He stumbled and fell to the asphalt. Grimaldi didn't watch. There was nothing he could do to help the poor sap die more quickly.

He leveled off at about one hundred feet and looked for the fleeing car. By that time there were two police cars moving in the direction of the bridge, and lights were going on throughout the vicinity. He saw no sign of the remaining car. If the driver was smart, he had parked the vehicle nearby and turned everything off, effectively making himself invisible to Grimaldi. In a few more minutes the scene would be crawling with people, and the car could escape in the confusion.

Grimaldi resigned himself to it. Now was the time to grab Bolan and get away while the getting was good.

CHAPTER TWENTY

"I don't see this job as finished."

"I know you don't," Grimaldi said.

"That doesn't mean you have to come in with me. It might be a suicide run."

"Buddy, I'm coming."

"That's not all, Striker," Barbara Price said over the speaker of the hotel-room telephone. "We can give you some extra support if you can hold off a little while. Our friend the Bear says he can get access to a reconnaissance satellite at 11:09 this evening. He'll have access for twenty-three minutes."

"Good. We'll have time to map out strategy."

DENNY CREAVALLE CROUCHED in the seat when the Houston cop cruised by. He waited for the lights to disappear, then sat up again.

Not that he was doing anything illegal. He was just a little bit out of his jurisdiction. He was a Galveston cop and didn't belong in Houston. And he didn't have any business staking out the town house of Don Cariani. Creavalle could almost hear those words as they would come from Webb's mouth when the time came, and the time would come. Because eventually he would get some dirt on Creavalle and would present it to his boss.

He was acting irrationally. He knew it. But he was, well, not obsessed, but driven. He'd been cheated out of the Galveston Wallace Shipping tag. He wanted to get something out of his efforts. He wanted to hurt Cariani somehow.

Tracing some kind of felony activity to the Cariani town house would do the trick.

But how he was going to accomplish this he didn't know. He might sit out here watching the town house for weeks. Eventually he'd get nabbed by Cariani, who would file a harassment complaint, or by the Houston PD. Then he'd have to explain himself to Webb. He had to get something of value before that happened.

It didn't look like it was going to be this night. He checked his watch: 11:03. Not a creature was stirring. Creavalle yawned. Maybe that was enough for tonight.

BOLAN HEARD Barbara Price's voice as if she were whispering in his ear.

"This is Stony Base. We'll have eyes in one minute."

Bolan was ready. He and Grimaldi waited at a streetside door to Don Cariani's town house located in a wealthy uptown district of Houston. The streets were silent and still. A few lights were on in the Cariani home, but he'd spotted no movement in the twenty minutes since they had arrived at the scene.

He knew that meant nothing. Cariani would doubtless have guards on duty around the clock. And with the help of Barbara Price and Aaron Kurtzman's expertise, he would soon have access to a pair of thermal-imaging eyes staring down on the town house from miles in space.

"Here we go," Price said quietly. "Five, four, three, two...I've got it. Stony One and Stony Two, I see you both. You've got a vestibule or small room on the other side of the door, and it's empty at this time." Her voice held the cool confidence that made her a field agent's best friend when the heat started. Bolan set to work on the door with his lock-picking tools.

The lock was the best money could buy. It slowed Bolan for all of a minute, then popped open. He pocketed the tools, and they entered the building quickly, eyes scanning for an alarm-system box. Bolan didn't see one, and knew that meant nothing. Alarms at the guard posts and in the bedrooms might be bringing the building awake at this very moment.

"Stony Base, this is Stony One. We're in. You see any signs of alert?"

"That's a negative. All quiet. The first floor is mostly empty, but there are a couple of warm bodies at the front door. I suggest you take care of them before venturing upstairs."

A look that passed between Bolan and Grimaldi said they agreed with the suggestion. Bolan headed down a hallway. They could hear snoring, and when Bolan glanced through the archway he spotted two guards in their shirt-sleeves, each sporting a shoulder holster. One was reading the entertainment section of a daily newspaper. The other was sleeping in a wooden chair with his head at an uncomfortable angle.

Bolan and Grimaldi stepped into the open with their suppressed handguns drawn.

The guards didn't stand a chance. The guy with the

newspaper regarded them with interest but didn't even realize at first that they weren't supposed to be there. Maybe he assumed they were hired guns he didn't know. Then he had to have realized that none of Cariani's men should be moving around the house with drawn weapons. He scrambled to his feet with an exhaled expletive and grabbed at his holstered weapon.

The 93-R in the hands of the Executioner spoke once, then twice, and two holes appeared in the man's forehead. He crashed to the floor. His sleeping companion was awake now, and becoming alert quickly. He started to rise from his chair, and Grimaldi's 92-F spit out a single 9 mm parabellum round that cored him in the heart. He sat back in the chair and didn't move again.

"Striker here. The thermal images on the ground floor should start getting cooler about now."

"Copy that."

WHEN DON CARIANI WAS really angry, he couldn't sleep. He had never been more angry than he was now. It was eighteen hours since hearing the news, and he still was burning with fury.

Everything had been running smoothly until just a few weeks ago. Now everything was wrong. What was once a well-organized, smooth-running operation had fallen apart. At what moment precisely had his luck run out?

He had suffered setbacks in the past, mishandled drug shipments, big busts. Once five of his guys had gotten themselves all arrested at one time. Those incidents were nothing compared to the disasters that had been strung one right after another over the past several days. They were almost enough to put him out of business, amounting to a severe financial setback. He had invested a lot of capital in that shipment of goods. And the *China Star* had represented a substantial investment. All was lost, little of it insured.

As it was, he would be hard-pressed to make payroll in the next few weeks. He'd planned on having a substantial cash influx coming in from his retail sales in the next few days. That wouldn't be happening. How was he going to come up with enough cash to pay his boys?

This was a serious problem. It was very tough to expect loyalty from men who weren't getting paid. What was worse was that his stature would be diminished. That angered him, too. The best part about being in his position was how everybody looked up to him.

He was going to have to take care of his best man, Jethro Parl. Parl had screwed up every step of the way. He had blown it big-time in China; he'd blown it since coming back to America. Never mind that, even in retrospect, Cariani could hardly think of what Parl could have done to salvage the situations he'd become embroiled in. He had screwed up, plain and simple, and he couldn't *not* be punished as a result of it. If the Don didn't purge himself of Parl, he would be seen as weak and spineless, and that was unthinkable. So Parl, his best enforcer, had to go. That angered him, too.

He rolled onto the edge of the bed and sat with his hands on his knees. He wished he'd opted to spend the night at one of his apartments. He had three girls stashed around downtown Houston. This night would have been a good night to spend with Sheila. Sheila liked to be roughed up. That would have made him feel better.

Maybe he'd spend tomorrow night with her. Right now he'd have to satisfy himself with a good cigar.

"SEVERAL MEN APPEAR to be sleeping on the second floor," Price said. "There are five rooms."

"Third floor?"

"Nobody. But there's one guy on the top floor. He's awake and moving, but he's in no hurry."

"That's Don Cariani," Bolan said. "We'll take care of that issue first."

Grimaldi nodded.

Don Cariani had cooperated with their probe by installing thick, well-padded carpeting on the stairs. They ascended rapidly, Bolan watching above and Grimaldi behind. There was utter silence throughout the huge town house—until they reached the fourth floor and all hell broke loose.

CARIANI WENT to the tiny kitchen he kept for himself in his suite and withdrew the makings for a sandwich from the refrigerator while sucking on a Cuban cigar. The sweet taste of the cool smoke was really the best relaxant there was.

The intruder alarm activated, and he stared at the control panel. There was someone on the stairs. Cariani poked his head out of the kitchenette and saw the two men. They had strange faces, but Cariani knew that they were the men responsible for his losses.

He was almost glad to see them.

Cariani had a piece stashed nearby: a 10 mm Glock 20 automatic pistol. He grabbed the handgun and fired into the hallway, causing one of the intruders to jump for cover in his meeting room and the other to retreat down the stairs. He fired a few more rounds to convince them to stay put, then grabbed for the phone. He didn't hear who it was that answered. He didn't care.

"Get your sorry asses moving. I'm getting attacked up here!"

GRIMALDI RACED down the stairs and jumped into the open, aiming for the first moving figure he saw. The man had just woken up but turned on the ace pilot with a double-barrel shotgun that promised no compromise. Grimaldi squeezed the 92-F's trigger three times, and took the gunner down with at least two of the rounds. Grimaldi continued down the carpeted steps before more men could appear, then crouched just out of sight of whoever might venture into the hall.

"You've sure stirred up the hornet's nest!" Price said.

"I'm on the stairs beneath the second level. Where's Sarge?"

"I'm holed up in the meeting room. Not doing much good at the moment."

Grimaldi heard angry voices in the hallway, one of them shouting orders. He snatched a fragmentation grenade from a pocket of his black sweatshirt and held it ready to lob up into the second floor.

"They're coalescing in the hallway, Stony Two!"

"I'm ready for them."

"There coming at you, Stony Two!"

Grimaldi stood up long enough to lob the fragger, which thumped heavily onto the carpeting at the feet of two of the runners, who were both carrying large-caliber handguns. One of the men shouted and swerved into an open door while the other man sprinted toward the stairs and took them with long strides. Grimaldi brought the 92-F above his head as he sank into a crouch and fired up the stairs. The sound of the second suppressed round was blotted out by the sudden blast of the grenade, which filled the hall with flying shrapnel.

There were screams of anguish, and Grimaldi jumped up and into it, firing at two men who were staggering in his direction, bloodied head to foot. He tagged the first in the skull and brought him down. It took three rounds in the gut to finish off the second wounded man, who finally collapsed and was still. Another man had absorbed the blast of the frag. Judging from the multitude of severe cuts covering his body, he had to have lost most of the blood in his body almost instantly and had been dead before hitting the floor.

"Sarge, there's one coming up after you!"

"He's on the stairs and moving fast," Price added.

BOLAN FLIPPED the selector switch on the Beretta to autofire and searched for his target. The hallway was empty at the moment, but Cariani might start firing again any second, and once Bolan left the meeting room there wasn't much in the way of cover. He watched the stairway for the gunman he had been warned about, but no one materialized. He might have dumped a frag grenade down the steps and solved the problem at once, but that might put Grimaldi at risk. He couldn't chance that.

He had two CS grenades among his stash.

"Watch out, Jack," he said into his microphone. "It's about to get smoky in here."

He rolled a can of CS toward the steps and watched it disappear. A moment later the stairs filled with a cloud of black smoke, and Bolan launched himself into it, thumping down the stairs and swinging solidly at the first body he came to. There was a crack as his fist made contact with the jaw of an enemy gunner. Bolan grabbed him and hauled him up the steps, dumping him on the floor and snatching the handgun from his grip. The dazed man peered through the cloudy air. Bolan recognized him immediately.

And Jethro Parl recognized Mack Bolan.

"You bastard!"

The hall filled with gunfire, and Bolan dived into the meeting room. Cariani was unloading his Glock into the smoke. Parl rolled onto his face and stayed low.

"Don't shoot! It's me, boss!"

"Parl?"

"Yeah!"

Parl rose onto his knees and scrambled for his Smith & Wesson .45-caliber pistol. His hands fell on it, then he jumped to his feet.

"Come out, you son of a bitch! Come out and take what's coming to you!"

Parl stopped at the door of the meeting room. Inside, the smoke was thinner, but the room looked empty.

Then out of nowhere he spotted a flash of steel. As if it was moving in slow motion, he saw an anodized blade, black except for the freshly whetted gleam of its edge, cutting through the air. It was so sharp it entered his stomach almost painlessly.

Bolan's free hand grabbed Parl by the throat, and he walked him backward into the wall. Parl looked at Bolan without malice or bitterness, only a mild kind of surprise.

The Executioner dragged the blade up, cutting

through stomach, liver and muscle tissue, coming to an abrupt, grinding halt against Parl's rib cage.

The enforcer looked at the ceiling, as if seeking deliverance from heaven. He raised the S&W weakly and touched the muzzle against Bolan's temple with a shaky hand.

Bolan gritted his teeth and rotated the Ka-bar, thrusting it in deeper, harder, through any tissues or organs that offered resistance, until his hand was touching Parl's opened flesh.

Parl's S&W dropped to the floor, and his hand fell to his side. His head dropped on his chest, but his eyes were still open and they still held the look of surprise.

"He's down," Bolan said to Price as the remains of Jethro Parl tumbled to the floor.

"Cariani's still moving around up there, however," she said. "And our window's about to close."

"Where is he now?"

"There's a room off the hall right next to the bedroom. Bathroom, maybe. He's inside."

"Got it."

Bolan stepped into the hallway, where the smoke had almost dissipated. He heard gunfire two floors down. He couldn't concern himself with that right now; Grimaldi could take care of himself.

He stepped to the nearest wall and looked into the narrow hallway, which ended in the door to the bedroom. To the right was the bathroom.

"You're within a few feet of each other," Price told him.

"Where is he in the room?"

"Our window's going—damn! I'm sorry, Striker. He

was moving around in there. I can't say for sure where he is now."

"Okay, Stony Base. I'll handle it."

Bolan looked around the corner and saw inside the open door. There was no sign of movement within, but Cariani was there. He could almost feel his presence.

The Executioner took out his second can of CS. Cariani would have to be sharp to recognize it as a nonlethal smoke grenade. Bolan didn't think that would happen.

He pulled the pin and tossed the container through the door, then aimed the Beretta 93-R.

He heard a frantic scrambling of limbs and cry of pure terror, then Don Cariani ran out of the room. His terror grew when he saw the big handgun targeted at his head.

"No!"

As Cariani waved the Glock about, Bolan triggered the Beretta, and a 3-round burst of 9 mm parabellum rounds chopped Cariani's heart. He fell into the wall and slumped to the ground, dead before his body came to rest.

"Stony Base," Bolan said, "it's done."

Bolan descended the stairs until he was just out of the firing window for any gunman on the second floor. He spotted Grimaldi crouched on the stairs. The pilot waved and said into his radio, "Pretty quiet in there."

Bolan nodded and the sound of sirens reached him. "But not out there. If there's anybody left, why don't we leave them for the local law enforcement?"

"Agreed. I'll cover you."

Bolan descended past the second-floor landing while

Grimaldi stood and blanketed the empty hallway with fire. Then they left by the side door they had entered by and locked it behind them.

THE HOUSTON POLICE arrived on the scene three minutes later, and Denny Creavalle burst open the front door as soon as their car came to a halt, knowing they would back him up if he didn't give them a choice.

He found two bodies slumped inside the front door.

There were several more scattered throughout the town house, including those of Don Cariani and his chief enforcer, Jethro Parl.

He didn't know whether to be frustrated or ecstatic.

CHAPTER TWENTY-ONE

Don Emilio LoDuca stepped out of the long black limousine and regarded the facade of the Jubilee Club. He found it a little garish but reasonably tasteful, which was more generous than his opinion of the rest of Hong Kong. The Chinese doorman ushered him into the restaurant with a slight bow. Behind the Don were his shadows, two huge men, one Italian, one Irish. Don LoDuca had rescued them both from poverty and long jail terms, and he knew they would lay down their lives for him if and when the time came.

"Mr. LoDuca, Mr. Lu Ming and Mr. Yan Whan are waiting for you."

LoDuca followed the tiny Chinese maître d' across the restaurant to a booth in the back corner, where Ming and Whan were drinking vodka and discussing some topic earnestly. The restaurant was virtually empty—there was a man who looked like an English professor sipping broth and reading from a big, ancient book, and in another booth was a couple holding hands across the table.

"Mr. LoDuca!" Yan Whan said, rising to greet the men.

"Mr. Whan. Good to see you again. It has been a long time."

"Let me introduce you to Mr. Lu Ming. Mr. Ming is one of the top men in Hong Kong. This is his restaurant, in fact."

LoDuca shook the man's hand and sat himself in the booth. He knew that Whan had more or less prompted him to compliment the restaurant, thus Lu Ming. He ignored the prompt.

His Irish bodyguard moved to a table on the left, the Italian to a booth on the right. Neither picked up menus.

"Scotch," LoDuca said.

The waiter brought the drink in what seemed like seconds.

"Did you read the proposal I faxed to you?" Whan asked.

"About a dozen times on the flight, and I have several questions I'd like answered."

Yan Whan nodded benevolently. "Go ahead."

"First of all—no offense Mr. Ming—but how do I know you can provide Mr. Whan with the support he needs to sustain operations? After all, his operation in Urumchi was seen as being virtually impregnable. I remember my good friend Don Cariani telling me all about it not two months ago, and now look at what has happened. Everything fell apart. I'll be attending Mr. Cariani's funeral as soon as I get back into the U.S."

"A reasonable question, of course," Lu Ming stated. "Let me tell you about my operation and its capabilities."

THE IRISHMAN ATTEMPTED to listen to the suits in the booth talking about men and weaponry and states of preparedness, but his mind quickly wandered. He tried to find something of interest in the restaurant. The guy in the glasses sipped a spoonful of soup and turned the page of his big book. The Chinese girl kissed her boyfriend quickly but passionately, then looked around the restaurant to see if they were being watched. She looked at the Irishman and giggled like a little girl.

If that petite hunk of woman was his, he could show her a thing or two, show her what a real man was capable of, although her boyfriend didn't look like any slouch. He was a big guy, European or American, and his eyes seemed to have a blazing intensity that was unmistakable even halfway across a dark restaurant.

In fact, now that he thought about it, something about that guy disturbed the Irish bodyguard.

He tried to look away, but his instincts told him not to.

Movement caught his eye. It was the professor. All he was doing was rubbing his neck. The Irish bodyguard berated himself for being so easily spooked. It had something to do with being in a foreign country. He didn't like it.

The boyfriend got to his feet, helping his girlfriend up.

The professor got up, looked at his check and placed some money on the table.

The woman reached for her purse. Her boyfriend looked at the check and reached for his wallet. The Irishman tried to make himself relax. When the woman moved away from the booth she was holding a submachine gun. Her boyfriend whipped out a big handgun and aimed it at the bodyguard.

BOLAN SAW THE BODYGUARD spring to his feet and grab at his holster and he triggered the Desert Eagle, sending a .44 Magnum round slamming into his chest cavity and knocking him back into the booth. Jiahua wedged the Heckler & Koch MP-5 into the crook of her arm and triggered a burst into the second bodyguard, who tumbled forward and hit the floor spasming, then he was still.

Grimaldi spun in the direction of the kitchen, where the tiny maître d' appeared with a Kalashnikov. The ace pilot fired his mini-Uzi and knocked the maître d' into a flowering plant, and both of them fell to the floor in a dirty heap.

Bolan walked toward the booth, where the three crime lords watched in shock.

"I have my rights!" Yan Whan said suddenly, trying to get to his feet. "I demand to be arrested!"

"I was in Urumchi," Bolan said simply. "I saw what you did to those people. Where were their rights, Whan?"

Whan's amazement silenced him.

Don LoDuca had had enough. Under the table he raised his leg to his hand and unstrapped his hideout automatic. He stood and raised the weapon to take care of this righteous American bastard.

Bolan squeezed the trigger and achieved his target on LoDuca at the same instant. The Magnum round slammed into his face and crushed the front of his skull to putty, crashing bone fragments into his brain. It stopped functioning before the Don even heard the sound of the shot.

Whan shouted wordlessly.

The Executioner turned the Desert Eagle on Lu Ming,

firing once, watching as a massive bloody crater appeared in his chest.

Ming slumped onto the table, tipping over his vodka, the Makarov pistol he had been preparing to fire clattering to the floor at his feet.

Whan was weeping. "Arrest me! Arrest me! You can't kill me! You can't."

Whan looked at the young Chinese woman. Surely she would hear his pleading words. "Don't let him kill me, please!"

Then he looked in her eyes and saw a cold mercilessness that matched the icy death he saw in the eyes of the American.

Whan knew then that his life was forfeit.

Cello Jiahua fired a burst from her MP-5, blasting Yan Whan's skull from his neck.

It was over.

**The Stony Man commandos deliver hard justice
to a dispenser of death**

STONY MAN™ 33

PUNITIVE MEASURES

The Eliminator—a cheaply made yet effective handgun
that's being mass-produced and distributed underground—
is turning up in the hands of street gangs and criminals
throughout the world. As the grisly death toll rises, the
Stony Man teams mount an international dragnet against a
mastermind who knows that death is cheap. Now he's
about to discover that Stony Man gives retribution
away—free.

Available in February 1998 at your favorite retail outlet.

Take
4 explosive books
plus a
mystery bonus
FREE

Mail to: Gold Eagle Reader Service
3010 Walden Ave.
P.O. Box 1394
Buffalo, NY 14240-1394

YEAH! Rush me 4 FREE Gold Eagle novels and my FREE mystery gift.
Then send me 4 brand-new novels every other month as they come off
the presses. Bill me at the low price of just $16.80* for each shipment—
a saving of 15% off the cover prices for all four books! There is NO extra
charge for postage and handling! There is no minimum number of books I
must buy. I can always cancel at any time simply by returning a shipment
at your cost or by returning any shipping statement marked "cancel." Even if I
never buy another book from Gold Eagle, the 4 free books and surprise gift
are mine to keep forever.   164 AEN CF22

_____
Name   (PLEASE PRINT)

_____
Address   Apt. No.

_____
City   State   Zip

_____
Signature (if under 18, parent or guardian must sign)

* Terms and prices subject to change without notice. Sales tax applicable in
  N.Y. This offer is limited to one order per household and not valid to
  present subscribers. Offer not available in Canada.   AC-96

Don't miss out on the action in these titles featuring THE EXECUTIONER®, STONY MAN™ and SUPERBOLAN®!

The American Trilogy

#64222	PATRIOT GAMBIT	$3.75 U.S.	☐
		$4.25 CAN.	☐
#64223	HOUR OF CONFLICT	$3.75 U.S.	☐
		$4.25 CAN.	☐
#64224	CALL TO ARMS	$3.75 U.S.	☐
		$4.25 CAN.	☐

Stony Man™

#61910	FLASHBACK	$5.50 U.S.	☐
		$6.50 CAN.	☐
#61911	ASIAN STORM	$5.50 U.S.	☐
		$6.50 CAN.	☐
#61912	BLOOD STAR	$5.50 U.S.	☐
		$6.50 CAN.	☐

SuperBolan®

#61452	DAY OF THE VULTURE	$5.50 U.S.	☐
		$6.50 CAN.	☐
#61453	FLAMES OF WRATH	$5.50 U.S.	☐
		$6.50 CAN.	☐
#61454	HIGH AGGRESSION	$5.50 U.S.	☐
		$6.50 CAN.	☐

(limited quantities available on certain titles)

TOTAL AMOUNT	$
POSTAGE & HANDLING	$
($1.00 for one book, 50¢ for each additional)	
APPLICABLE TAXES*	$ _____
TOTAL PAYABLE	$ _____
(check or money order—please do not send cash)	

To order, complete this form and send it, along with a check or money order for the total above, payable to Gold Eagle Books, to: **In the U.S.:** 3010 Walden Avenue, P.O. Box 9077, Buffalo, NY 14269-9077; **In Canada:** P.O. Box 636, Fort Erie, Ontario, L2A 5X3.

Name: _____

Address: _____ City: _____

State/Prov.: _____ Zip/Postal Code: _____

*New York residents remit applicable sales taxes.
 Canadian residents remit applicable GST and provincial taxes.

GOLD
EAGLE®

GEBACK19

James Axler

OUTLANDERS™

OMEGA PATH

A dark and unfathomable power governs post-nuclear America. As a former warrior of the secretive regime, Kane races to expose the blueprint of a power that's immeasurably evil, with the aid of fellow outcasts Brigid Baptiste and Grant. In a pre-apocalyptic New York City, hope lies in their ability to reach one young man who can perhaps alter the future....

Nothing is as it seems. Not even the invincible past....